"Evil stalks the streets of Rome. A serial killer searches for his next victim amidst the ancient ruins and modern wonders. A smart, resilient, resourceful young woman crosses his path. How smart? How resilient and resourceful? Find out in *The Sculptor*, a page-turning, spine-tingling heart-stopper that will keep you up all night. And when dawn comes and you turn the last page, you will agree that Gina Fava is one of the rising young stars of the thriller genre."

— **William Martin, New York Times bestselling author of *Back Bay* and *The Lincoln Letter***

"After thrilling us with her action-packed debut novel, *The Race*, Gina Fava takes a slightly lateral move to an intimate, suspenseful, at times creepy but always gripping, mystery tale in *The Sculptor*. Just when I thought that I figured out the bad guy, Fava threw me a curve, and then another, until I reached the shocking, satisfying conclusion."

— **J.H. Bográn, author of *Firefall* and *Treasure Hunt***

"Nonstop action, with vivid settings, sympathetic characters, and a serial killer to die for. Highly recommended."

— **Douglas Preston, #1 New York Times bestselling author of *The Monster of Florence***

"Another fast-paced thriller; kept me guessing right up until the hold-your-breath climax. An excellent read!"

— **Steve Ulfelder, Edgar-nominated author of *Wolverine Bros. Freight & Storage***

PRAISE FOR
THE RACE: A HELL RANGER THRILLER

"A high-octane thriller, rich with action, imagination, and intriguing suspense."
— **August McLaughlin, author of *In Her Shadow*, an Indies Excellence Awards finalist**

"This is what you want to read when you think of a great thriller. The action sequences are really exciting and…You LOVE the characters. Tough one to put down for sure!"
— **J. Korman, Amazon reviewer**

"All the thriller essences of Dan Brown, and the cheeky humor of Harlan Coben."
— **C. Florio, Amazon reviewer**

"[I] found myself drawn into the story…and falling in love with the characters. It is exciting to me that this book is just the first in a series of HELL Ranger Thrillers."
— **Amy Marbach, of *Bad Groove* car racing blog**

"Thrilling action and intrigue at its best!"
— **Steven M. Moore, author of *Survivors of Chaos* and *The Midas Bomb***

THE SCULPTOR

GINA FAVA

STEEPO PRESS

NEW YORK ROME BOSTON TORONTO SYDNEY

THE SCULPTOR
By Gina Fava

Copyright © 2014 Gina Fava

Cover design by Bruce Skinner, copyright © 2014 by Gina Fava
Cover art by Ed Latawiec, limited copyright licensed © 2014 by
Gina Fava
Author photo by Bruce Skinner, copyright © 2014 by Gina Fava
Layout design © 2014 by Cheryl Perez

Excerpt from *The Race* copyright © 2013 by Gina Fava
Excerpt from *Raging Waters* copyright © 2014 by Gina Fava

First Steepo Press trade paperback edition May 2014

ISBN: 978-0-9893587-5-0   (Print edition)
ISBN: 978-0-9893587-6-7   (Smashwords edition)
ISBN: 978-0-9893587-7-4   (eBook edition)

Printed in the United States of America

This book contains an excerpt from the forthcoming book *Raging
Waters* by Gina Fava, coming soon, and an excerpt from *The Race* by
Gina Fava, now in paperback and eBook. These excerpts have been
set for this edition only and may not reflect the final content of the
editions.

www.GinaFava.com

For Mom and Dad,
my very first fans.

Crossing the ocean has proven a blessing
for all of us.

PART I:

GYPSUM INTO PLASTER

**"A sculptor wields the chisel,
and the stricken marble grows to beauty."**

—William C. Bryant,
American poet and journalist

Chapter 1

SIX YEARS AGO...

Halfway down the Harlach Trail, Abigail stopped to adjust the buckle on her ski boot, grateful that she'd left behind her grad school classmates in Rome to tackle the Alpine double-diamonds on her own. Her friends just would've slowed her down. Abigail embraced the solitude of the mountain, which was devoid of skiers likely too skittish of ice patches from last night's rain. A wind gust swirled white powder across the mountain and sped past her as quickly as it had come. She shivered and adjusted her goggles against the sun's glare. Knees bent, she jammed her poles into the groomed snow, ready to thrust forward to the next pine grove. But before she could, what could only be a rogue skier lashed the back of her thighs so hard that her legs buckled.

Hot, searing pain shot up her spine. She bellowed a cry and nearly went down, but she snowplowed to maintain her balance. She gripped her backside with both hands in misery and swung around at the waist to confront whatever jackass thought that whipping her thighs might be fun.

Five meters back stood a man on Rossignols, maybe six feet tall, covered from head to toe in a black snowsuit, gloves, and a ski mask. He clasped two ski poles together between both hands and swayed side to side, like a tennis pro gearing up for the next shot.

Through his goggles, the man's dark, deep-set eyes pierced hers. She gasped, and her chest tightened beneath her snow bib. He had rape-murder-plunder-type of eyes that instantly made her fear for her life. Time to haul ass.

Again, she thrust her poles into the packed powder, but this time, with a leap, she bounded downhill. Crouched low into a racing stance with knees bent, poles pulled in close to her sides, chin tucked and eyes forward, she bulleted toward the pine grove. She planned to weave through the trees once she got there and shake him off, just like the game that she, her father, and her younger sister had played on a ski trip to Colorado before grad school.

Abigail stole a glance back to gauge how much distance she'd put between them. Her adrenaline surged when she found him mere strides behind.

Ahead and to the left, an ice patch glistened like a small pond. She aimed for it and deftly cut across it with all the precision and grace that she, a three-time junior national champion, possessed.

She heard a heavy grunt and smirked. He must have hit the ice and smashed his face.

She glanced back. He'd not only managed to traverse the sheet of ice, but now he was gaining on her.

She clenched her body tighter, smaller. Like a racer. The back of her thighs still burned from the smack she'd withstood, and the muscles in her legs throbbed from exertion. But she pushed faster.

She flicked her eyes left to right to seek other means of escape. Nothing but rocky cliffs on both sides.

She shouted for help, but there was no one around to aid her. Solitude was overrated. She'd never ski alone again.

Even if she reached the bottom of the Harlach Trail, the ski lift operator was a rail-thin girl who'd never survive the hulking assailant with the sadistic eyes. Abigail's only hope was to serpentine through the grove of trees. Almost there.

The shadow that her pursuer cast upon the snow drew closer still. Until, seconds later, he was beside her, keeping her pace.

She was breathing so fast now, she worried whether she'd hyperventilate. He was only a couple feet away. What if he reached out and grabbed her? Or knocked her down, only to…

He did not edge closer. Instead, he maintained his distance. He stretched his arm back behind his head, and unzipped the top of his backpack. His eyes bore through her as he slowly withdrew something that gleamed like steel from the bag. It was long and thin, like a poker. Or a lance. Or a spear.

She gasped and barely missed careening into a tree. He sidestepped it with ease. She pushed faster and drew ahead of him. Rivulets of sweat trickled down her back, cold like fingers. Even if she made it to the grove, the chances of evading him might not stack as high as she once thought. And if their paths collided, she wanted no part of that weapon in his pack.

His shadow again loomed closer. He was no longer skiing parallel to her, but rather bearing down on her from behind like a speed train. His skis skimmed over the backs of hers. She wobbled, flailed her arms, then regained control. Too close. If she went down, she was done. She clenched her teeth and pushed harder to get away.

After a few seconds, she managed to put some real estate between them. Waves of anxiety constricted her throat. Her heart pumped faster. *Why is this man chasing me? And, how the hell do I lose him?*

Then she remembered how. Earlier, on the gondola ride up the mountain, a ski patrolman hoping to get lucky had revealed to Abigail the location of a hidden chalet that sat about halfway down—

There. Like a flashbulb, the sun had glinted off of a window. Abigail never would have seen it had she not known about it. Up ahead and beyond the grove, tucked away from view by a massive clump of brush, it had to be the chalet. This was her chance to lose her pursuer. But, she'd need to get there quickly, before she passed it, and without him following her.

She maintained her lightning pace for a few seconds longer. Timing was critical. If she missed this opportunity, she cringed at the thought of what he would surely do to her when he ultimately took her down. The skewer, or whatever it was, would slice through her like butter.

A gust of freezing wind blasted up the slope, thwarting their momentum. The wind whipped her exposed cheeks and pushed against her body with incredible force. Seconds later, the violent vortex whirled away.

She heard him dig in his poles to regain his speed. With a grunt, he shot forward. But when he coasted in beside her, she seized her only chance. She jammed the edges of her skis into the snow and halted to a full stop.

He flew past her, cursing as he did. Nearly thirty feet downhill, he braked, but he lost control and sprinted forward even further to avoid colliding with a spruce.

She immediately scooted behind a cluster of bushes and, out of his line of sight, she skied laterally toward the eastern section of the grove nearest the cabin. He'd clearly overshot her position and his speed had carried him way too far down the slope to back-track. No one could walk or ski all the way back up such a steep incline. She had officially dropped him like a bad habit.

Abigail traversed to the front of the cabin, longing for the chalet's warmth and security. She stopped at the entrance and exhaled deeply to release the knots in her back and stomach. Only then did she absorb the full weight of what had happened.

Someone had attacked her, chased her down a mountain, and likely would've finished her off if he'd caught her. But why?

Perspiration trickled down her back, and she shivered. She'd eventually have to ski down the rest of the slope. When she did, would he be there waiting for her? She needed a plan. But, first, she needed to warm up and recharge.

She poked her pole into her binding to release it. The binding popped open, at the same time that the door to the chalet swung wide.

He'd found her.

Steam emanated from his body. Snot dribbled down his ski mask from his mouth and nose. His nostrils flared, and he panted like a gorilla in heat. His dark eyes gleamed, not with desire or victory, but with unbridled malice. Without a word, he charged her.

She screamed, teetered back, but caught herself. She butted his nose with the thick handle of her pole. She heard his nose crack. His hands flew to his face, and in that moment, she snapped her boot back into its binding and lunged away from him.

He reached for her and seized her arm. But she yanked hard, pulled him forward, and jammed her pole right into his groin.

He growled and bent forward in obvious anguish, but still he gripped her arm like a vise. She poked his scrotum again, harder this time, and then again, until finally he released her.

She burst forward, and skied around the cabin and back onto the trail. Controlling her breathing, she crouched into a slalom stance and headed for the spruce grove.

With a backward glance, she spotted him, upright on his skis and covered in snow as if he'd fallen. Again, he was barreling down the mountainside right for her.

In seconds, he was nearly on her. So close, even the aroma of pine wasn't enough to mask the stench of his sweat. It reeked of murderous intent.

He grumbled through every twist and turn. The sound of his primal grunts pushed her faster.

Real fear enveloped her now. She sideswiped a thick spruce, hoping he might become tangled in its low-hanging boughs. She glanced back to check, but still he gained.

She faced forward, and thrust in her poles to surge faster.

And smashed headlong into a tree.

***

Abigail awoke in a haze, with a vague awareness that her body lay in a crumpled heap, slumped over to one side on cold ground. After some time, she saw light through the haze. Speckled light. Nothing more.

She heard short, shallow breathing—her own. A shudder of pain coursed through her and subsided into cold shivers. Her skull seemed to throb against itself. Every heartbeat seemed to worsen the pressure inside her head.

She opened her eyes to slits. Sunlight felt like tiny daggers slicing through her temples, even through her goggles. She discerned tree boughs through the speckled light, low hanging limbs of a thin, twenty-foot sapling that reached toward the sky. Then, she realized that she'd smashed into that godforsaken tree, and she wished she would've at least taken it down with her.

She shifted her torso, screamed in pain, but continued to shift, needing desperately to edge her weight off of her legs that were bent beneath her. She unfolded her right leg, but when she tried to unbend the left, she howled. It was broken.

She needed her mother right now. Not that her mother would care. Her father would, her little sister maybe. Not her mother. Still, she was desperate for comfort.

Her hands trembled in the snow, and her eyes stung. Blood had seeped into her Oakley's, and she knew she must have one massive gash for there to be so much blood. But, she was alive, and she was grateful.

Then, she remembered the man with the evil eyes.

She wrenched her head up to look around for her pursuer, and the light that inundated her wide eyes threatened her consciousness. She bit her lip, took a deep breath, and felt coherent again.

That's when her predator announced his presence, by clubbing her again with his ski pole. Again, and again.

Abigail covered her head with both arms and writhed against the blunt, forceful lashing of her backside. "Stop! Please, stop," she cried.

She heard a rib crack, and her body convulsed to one side. She thrashed, and still he lashed.

She clenched her chattering teeth, blinked away the blood from her eyes, and forced herself to think. Her only chance for survival was to rob him of his weapon in between lashings.

He hauled back again, ready to strike. When he did, she raised her head, thrust out her arm, and lunged for it.

No good. She was too slow, and he'd seen it coming.

He stepped forward, and stomped her arm with his ski boot, pinning it to the ground.

"Wait!" she cried.

He stopped.

Her eyes sought his goggled face, his blazing eyes. His sweat, mixed with funky tobacco odor, made her retch, but she held his gaze and clung to the notion that she might reason with him.

"Why are you doing this? I'll do anything if you stop." Trembling, Abigail pushed her goggles back, hoping that the sight of her pleading face might appeal to whatever humanity he might possess.

Through his goggles, she watched the wrinkles around his terrifying eyes shift. He appeared to be…smiling.

"Who are you?" She choked back sobs. "Please, what do you want from me?" He threw down the ski pole.

She exhaled. Sweet relief swept through her. Now, if only he'd remove his hundred-ton ski boot from her forearm.

Instead, he thrust his hand over his shoulder as if to pull an arrow from a quiver. He rummaged in his backpack again, and from it, he unsheathed the long, metallic, pointed skewer. No, not a skewer.

A chisel.

"Oh, God, please, no," she whimpered.

He removed the ski mask from his face.

Abigail gasped. "You?"

He raised the chisel high above his head and smiled broadly. "None other."

Chapter 2

SIX WEEKS AGO...

Mom's going to love this woman, he thought, and then wondered why he cared, because Mom never did.

I adore her.

The woman asleep on the bed beside him bore a slight resemblance to Angelina Jolie, only less severe. More like Ava Gardner. He stroked the dark brown hair from her closed eyes and listened to the soft purring of her breath. She slept on her back, one arm raised above her head. Her other arm was slung across her bare abdomen, allowing him to see the grapevine tattoo that trailed across her pelvis and around to her back. Her full lips curled up, as if hiding a secret.

I covet her.

He'd spent an entire semester secretly desiring the vocalist, a twenty-two-year-old opera student at Rome University. He skimmed his gloved finger over her vocal cords. He kissed her throat. She did not stir.

On Friday evening, he'd spoken to her for the first time. The student body had abandoned the campus for end-of-semester parties before holiday break, and she had stayed behind to tape her "Vissi d'Arte" aria demo for the spring *Tosca* auditions. In the campus parking lot, he'd asked her if she'd join him for a drink. She'd spent the rest of the weekend holed up in his apartment, proving to him that she'd been secretly coveting him, too.

I desire her.

He sniffed her hair (berry shampoo), her full lips (faint traces of coconut lip balm), and her neck (subtle jasmine), and wished he could feel her soft, musky skin beneath his fingertips. He'd explained that, on account of a recent brush with poison oak, his lambskin gloves were the closest touch either of them would share. She'd slipped a lambskin condom on him and told him it didn't matter, and that she'd waited far too long to let poison oak get in the way of their fun. His fully shaved body and head had thrilled her. A sheen of sweat now glistened on his bare chest.

I love her.

Ample conversation, wine, and prosciutto filled the breaks in their marathon lovemaking. They'd shared things that two vulnerable lovers exchange—family photographs, favorite movies, and hidden scars.

I miss her.

The Big Ben alarm clock on the bureau ticked off the remaining time that they would share. Tomorrow, she planned to board a plane to return to Australia, away for a month. It was Sunday afternoon; they had tonight. He'd sworn to make it memorable for both of them.

I need her.

He rose to relieve himself, and, when he returned, he placed a pitcher of milk and a large bowl of flakes on their bedside table. He sliced a loaf of bread and placed it there too. As she slept, he sprinkled some powder on her cheeks and caressed the contours of her jaw line. He felt her body radiate beneath his gloves. Tears trickled down his face at the notion that, no matter the ambitious plans they'd concocted for their long-distance relationship, he'd never feel her warmth again.

I want her.

They had such little time left together. He brushed soft kisses on her eyes and mouth to rouse her from her slumber. He poured the milk into the flakes and mixed. "Wake up, *amore*," he crooned softly.

Her eyes fluttered and opened. She stretched her naked, taut body and smiled at him before settling back into the comforter.

"Hungry?" he asked.

"Hungry for you," she murmured. She danced her fingers down his back. She spied the cereal bowl and the sliced bread on the bedside table, and she licked her lips. "Matter of fact, I could eat a horse about now." The Aussie propped up her lustrous head with her bent elbow, and pulled up the comforter for warmth. "Hand over a slice, will ya love?"

He tucked the blanket just beneath her chin, kissed her nose, and reached toward the bedside table, happy to oblige.

I want to keep her. Forever.

He clutched the bread knife, turned, and winked. She grinned wide. Then he slashed her throat from ear to ear, severing the chords of her operatic instrument.

Her eyes and mouth flew wide. Her hands flailed, reaching for her gaping flesh, only to come away dripping with blood. He pressed the comforter to her throat, minimizing the arterial spray.

She gasped for air, for answers. Her brow furled, likely in desperate contemplation of her short life. Her delicate face, contorted in anguish, matched the misery he'd felt at the idea of their separation.

He reached for the large, heavy bowl of paste—the mixture of gypsum flakes and milk—and cast the batter against her visage of silent, grotesque torment.

She swiped and clawed at the thick, clumpy, hardening mask, to no avail. She bucked and kicked for many minutes. But her asphyxiated brain ebbed her strength, and her struggles diminished, until her body stilled. She convulsed once more, and finally collapsed against the bed.

With a trowel, he smoothed the surface over the contours of her face, and then he left the plaster cast to set. He washed her hands, clipped her nails, and rubbed her hands smooth with lotion, before he affixed a ribbon of fuchsia silk around her middle finger.

She is mine.

After a few hours of bleaching and vacuuming her studio apartment, it was time to carefully cut away the plaster impression from her head. He cracked the mold using a hammer and his most prized chisel.

He must ensure the sanctity of the mold, because her anguished face was what had defined his dying flower. He must replicate her beauty exactly as it had been in life, just as all sculptors strive to do. After all, imitation is the sincerest form of flattery.

After precise manipulation, the sculptor finally rendered the mold away from the flesh with his scalpel.

He exhaled in relief. He'd captured this beautiful subject's essence, forever. The mold was perfect.

Just like all the others in his collection.

Chapter 3

Mara Silvestri crammed her dad into the overhead compartment of a Rome-bound flight at JFK. Amid the bump and grind of the other boarding passengers in the aisle, Mara wedged the hard-case, plaid duffel, that bore her father's ashes, between a beat-up, gray backpack and a pin-striped vinyl number with wheels. She smiled. Her dad would've laughed at the idea. Her mother would have rolled her eyes and sauntered off to the first-class section.

Mara exchanged her high-heeled leather boots for her UGG slippers, taking her from five feet nine down to five feet seven, and jammed each of her boots into the spaces around her suitcase. One of the boots resisted, caught on a pocket zipper of the gray backpack. She shoved harder and prodded the boot behind the zipper. But the heel caught, and the pocket unzipped, unleashing a hailstorm of jellybeans.

"Oh, shhhhhh...ugar!" Mara planted one foot on her seat and hoisted herself up, eye-level with the deluge. She yanked at the zipper that now refused to budge. She tried to reposition the backpack but couldn't heave the weight. Apparently it belonged to a jellybean smuggling kingpin.

She felt the eyes of hundreds of travelers in the capacity-filled cabin boring a hole into the back of her head. She could take one for the team—just open her mouth wide and catch the sugar torrent that rained down on them. Damn, how many jellybeans did this person need?

"Allow me." Someone behind her thrust a wide-brimmed hat, *à la* Indiana Jones, into her hands. She snatched it and trapped the downpour in the overturned crown. As she did, the hat's owner stepped up beside her. She couldn't see the man's upturned face in the confined space, but his musky scent beguiled her.

He yanked the luggage zipper back and forth a few times, the tendons in his muscular forearms pulled taut like guitar strings, until finally it shimmied shut. He scooped the bean-laden hat from her grasp and jumped down.

"I can't thank you enough..." She stepped down to the floor and turned toward him, but he was already headed into the tail section.

"Thanks cowboy," she shouted to the hat-covered ponytail that bobbed away through the chaos of settling passengers.

He tipped the brim of his bush hat to salute her before continuing on. She'd never once glimpsed his face.

"I would've helped, but my seat belt was jammed. Lucky that hot guy with the hat passed by." The girl in the next seat offered up a cocktail cup overflowing with jellybeans. "Caught these. Want to share?"

Mara laughed. "Sure. Any pink ones?" She plunked down into the seat beside Kristen James, a friendly philosophy doctoral candidate that Mara had met that evening in the security line.

Mara's cell phone signaled an incoming text.

A young flight attendant with a plastered smile appeared between Mara's seat and the empty one across the aisle. "*Signorina*, you will need to click off your mobile in preparation for take-off, please," she said with an accent.

Mara quickly checked her message. It read that Stella Luna, Rome University's housing complex, had assigned her a new roommate. She groaned.

This was her first semester with the Rome program, and Mara had appreciated the school's initial match—an opera student with a schedule that complemented Mara's laborious study habits. The text also relayed that a new roommate would be designated upon arrival. She'd suffered bad experiences with overbearing roommates at Oxford during undergrad. With what sort of student would she be paired this time?

Mara powered down her cell phone just as the plane lurched into taxi mode. She rested her head back and glanced over at the discarded tabloid newspaper on the next aisle seat.

The headline, "Rome's 'Sculptor' Carves Life From Sixth Victim," chilled her. But, she chose not to read the story. She'd kept up with the murders as she'd planned her trip for the past year or so, but she'd convinced herself that fear would not keep her from living her life. Eventually, the police would find him and put him away. Worrying about it in the interim was fruitless; it would just take too much energy away from her studies.

Chatter about Rome's serial killer had run rampant through the international terminal that evening, especially among the dozens of American graduate students that had converged at JFK, bound for the Rome work-study program.

The plane, already burdened by snowstorm conditions, would have to endure eight hours of this smarmy lot, now packed into the jet's mid-section. Some students were reconnecting after the holidays. Others were meeting for the first time. Many of them laughed or shook hands, or exchanged numbers and air kisses. A few bit their nails or gripped their armrests with eyes closed. One couple had already run to the restroom to join the mile-high club, while still on the ground. The whole bunch represented her peer group for the coming semester, and they appeared about as dysfunctional as she and her family.

No matter. She didn't have time for smarmy this semester. Her purpose for the trip was to shed her dysfunctional baggage and begin building a professional life that left little room for personal drama.

"Want one of these?" Kristen waived two Snickers bars. Mara declined, and Kristen bit into one of them. Although Mara had only just met the Ohioan, the two had become instant friends after chatting about school. They both stood about five foot and a half, but where Mara possessed an athletic physique, Kristen appeared waif-like and almost gaunt. So much so that Mara had begun to feel somewhat protective of her.

"I eat when I'm nervous," Kristen said in between bites. "Aside from the idea that a serial killer's roaming around town, I'm also not a fan of this whole take-off and landing thing." She blushed. "Plus, this is my first time away from home. Commuted all during undergrad, and..." she trailed off and took another bite.

"I'm here for you." Mara patted her arm. "The school's taking every precaution with our safety." Mara spied the drink cart rolling out of first class. A little rum would dampen Kristen's anxiety. "And, you're going to do just fine this semester. I've been to Rome a few times, and getting around is easy, I promise. No worries, okay?"

Kristen nodded. Her scrunched shoulders relaxed somewhat, and she lightly twirled the ends of her shoulder-length brown hair between her fingers. Kristen gestured to the stowaway bin. "So, what's in that suitcase that you've been guarding so closely? You didn't even check it at the airport."

Mara sighed. "My dad's in there. His urn anyway. I'm finally spreading his ashes in Italy. He died my freshman year at Oxford. I'd always meant to give him a proper ceremony, but I never got around." Mara's throat constricted. She glimpsed the receding lights of the New York skyscrapers through the cabin window.

"Was he born there?"

Mara nodded. "He's a native Tuscan. We used to travel back and forth a bunch of times. Traveled all over actually."

"Army brat?" Kristen said.

"No, Dad was a freelance photojournalist. Mom's a tennis player, and—"

"Silvestri. Oh, wow, Kat Silvestri's your mom? She was the number-one seeded women's singles champion for years."

Mara nodded. Her hands clenched. Even her toes clenched. "While she played the circuit, my dad and I joined her. I was tutored on the road until Oxford—that was the first time I'd ever been away from my dad." Mara's throat tightened again, and she turned away toward the aisle.

"Is that the drink cart already?" Kristen said. "I really have to pee. Order me some kind of wine spritzer, will ya?" Kristen climbed over Mara's seat and disappeared into the tail section.

Mara wished that her dad had been alive to see her graduate Oxford magna cum laude. Her mother hadn't even made her graduation due to an Australian finals match. Mara's nose crinkled, and her toes clenched again.

The drink cart slammed her armrest. She ordered two Chianti/Sprite spritzers, sipped one, and mellowed into the aroma of lasagna wafting through the plane.

The seatbelt sign turned off with a "ding," and a young blond woman poked her head around her seat. "Hey there. If you don't mind my asking, was your daddy Arturo Silvestri?" she asked with a touch of Southern twang.

Mara's stomach tensed. "How did you know my father?"

The woman shrugged her rounded shoulders, and her apple cheeks plumped big with a smile. She slid a tattered *National Geographic* magazine into Mara's lap and pointed to the cover story about Paris runway models. "He took the most amazing pictures. I swear, after he shot this article…well, he's the reason I decided to go into fashion merchandising. This layout was so sensational that I carry it with me. You should be very proud of your daddy."

Mara brushed back her brown curls and felt the strange knot in her stomach loosen. "Thank you so much for saying so." It was true. No matter the subject, Arturo Silvestri's photographs always told a story, and they always made her proud.

Now, after years apart, she and her father were finally headed back to Italy together. Returning to Rome on a work-study program with Ferrari, Mara knew in her heart that her father would have been proud of her too.

***

Kristen returned to her seat just ahead of the plastic dinner trays. Mara introduced her to Lana Tinello, the blond student behind them, and Lana shifted to the empty seat across the aisle. To take their minds off of the undercurrent of serial killer discourse and the vile in-flight meal (sauce-less eggplant lasagna made with 100 percent durum cardboard), the three wiled away the hours of the long flight sampling the onboard rum.

"So you were born and raised in Hawaii?" Mara said.

Lana's dimpled apple cheeks bobbed up and down.

"So, why do you speak with a Southern drawl?" Kristen asked.

"Not sure. Maybe because my daddy watched a lot of those spaghetti westerns."

"My dad loved those too," Mara said. Her dad, and Clint Eastwood, both rocked.

"I heard you've got your daddy's remains on the plane with us, I'm so sorry." Lana grabbed her hand and squeezed.

Mara smiled at the kind gesture. She'd always been someone who kept to herself, and sharing like this, with perfect strangers, was outside her comfort zone. She worried that if she became too friendly, she'd lose her competitive edge. After all, she was goal-oriented, not driven by petty emotion. Yeah, that was it.

When it came down to it, Mara really knew that she refused most personal relationships simply because she was frightened. Terrified that they might die.

She squeezed Lana's hand in return, grateful for the token of friendship. The more she talked to these two, the more she enjoyed their company. She'd be spending the next few months with them, as well as all the other RU grad students. Maybe she could open the door to developing personal relationships. Just a little bit.

"How did he die?" Lana conveyed heartfelt concern, yet still managed to wink at a tall, lanky American with bloodshot eyes likely on his way to the bathroom. He flicked his eyebrows and nodded at her, kept going.

"My dad's swamp boat capsized on a photo expedition in the Everglades," Mara said. There, she'd confided the tragedy aloud, and she hadn't exploded from the force of it. Mara had never shared this story with anyone before. Why was she doing it now? What if she got too close and something terrible happened?

"Your family must have been devastated," Kristen said.

Mara sipped her rum and Coke and braved her way through it. "I was devastated, yes. But, my mother just kept tramping on from country-to-country, upholding her status as a stellar player, both on and off the court. Now, she and I make fleeting attempts at holiday greetings, and we catch up a few minutes by cell phone a couple times a year."

"So, it's just you and your mom now? Or, do you have other family you're close with?" Lana asked.

Mara gulped her cocktail and continued. "Six years ago, my older sister died in a skiing accident, and—"

"Your sister died too?" Kristen leaned forward and put her hand on Mara's arm.

Mara shrugged, what she always did when Abby was mentioned. "Ours was…a disconnected relationship. Even when we were together, for holidays or family trips, we weren't on the same page. There was never animosity, we just didn't gel. I'm sad she's gone, but I don't feel that she left as big of a void in my life, like the one my dad left when he died."

"Big age difference?" Lana said.

"Only five years, but we just…held different ideals, I guess." Mara shrugged again. "She attended RU for undergrad, and then a year of grad school, before she died. But she spent most of it skiing and boffing her professors—"

"Six years ago she went to RU? Then, she must have slept with some of the current profs. Did she mention any?" Kristen leaned back in her seat. "Oh, I'm so sorry. This isn't a tabloid story, this is your sister. I didn't mean—"

"It's okay; I really didn't take any offense. My family's drama does play out a bit like reality TV doesn't it?" Mara laughed. "But, somehow, I'm okay with that."

As long as Mara didn't get too close to anyone, then they wouldn't die. She'd surmised this truth from the regular pattern of her life. Start figuring out your older sister, she dies in a freak accident. Take refuge as Daddy's sole little angel, and he dies. Bottom line: Stay detached, and no one gets hurt.

Mara scanned the sea of other graduate students again. She'd likely study and work alongside many of them, and she worried for them.

The mantra flapped its wings through her mind again: Stay dedicated to school and career, stay detached, and no one gets hurt.

***

A couple hours after the three of them had fallen asleep, Mara woke to the smell of breakfast coffee permeating the cabin. Her dry mouth watered, and the pain behind her eyeballs heralded the onset of a wicked hangover. The overhead lights illuminated, and the groans of neighboring passengers signaled their similar fate.

While Kristen and Lana continued to sleep, Mara switched on the onboard satellite TV screen in front of her, tuning it to the international morning news. The weather forecast showed light snow in Rome, with a storm on the way. The anchor then took a serious turn in news coverage.

Splashed across the screen was graphic footage of the latest hand-crafted victim of Italy's vicious serial killer, dubbed "The Sculptor." Mara's initial reaction was to shut her eyes and block the lurid images. Too late. She knew that what she'd seen could never be erased.

She opened her eyes to gather more information from the closed captioning on the screen. Chick Sticht, the sixth female victim, had been a Rome University student. All the other victims had been graduate students, too, from the three main colleges in Rome. Butchered remains and plastered body parts had been left behind in a gruesome tableau at every scene. Rome police and school officials were working in close cooperation. Still no leads.

A shiver ran through her. She crossed her arms to retain warmth and inhaled deeply. The images had depicted a deliberate display, almost as if this so-called sculptor had left behind a gallery exposition of his artwork.

Mara curled up her legs onto her seat for more warmth. The newsreel had left her feeling breathless and drained. For some reason the victim's name sounded familiar to her, but she couldn't place it. She didn't know anyone in Rome.

Her cell phone slipped from her back pocket and clunked to the floor. She picked it up and powered it back on, prepping for landing. Another text might—

Then she remembered. Chick Sticht. From the news broadcast. An opera student at Rome University, slain in her own apartment. In Mara's apartment. The serial killer's latest victim was to have been Mara's roommate this semester.

Fear and dread gripped her. Her would-be roommate had been murdered. Would lightning strike twice in the same spot?

She took a deep breath and forced the panic away. The horrific murder had been tragic, but the police and school officials surely must have leads. They were probably unwilling to share these leads with the public, simply to prevent jeopardizing any advancements on the case. Otherwise, the university would have canceled the semester.

Besides, she had big plans. There was no turning back now. She would scatter her dad's ashes and work on her professional life. Stay focused, and no one gets hurt, she reiterated to herself.

Mara continued to justify the trip in her mind, even as the plane began its descent into the dangerous epicenter of the serial killer's proving grounds.

She wondered what her dad would have thought about the criminal element that had seeped into her semester plans. She hoped that whatever his actions would have entailed, she might closely emulate them.

Imitation was the sincerest form of flattery.

Chapter 4

Mara's plane landed at a snow-covered Leonardo Da Vinci airport, where a handful of Rome University faculty welcomed their hundred or so students. The assistant dean dispelled rumors of canceling the semester and lectured them all on personal safety. A private bus shuttled them to the Stella Luna apartment complex.

There, the groggy collective awaited their roommate pairing in the spacious lobby of the complex. Mara sank down onto the carpeted floor, slumped against her luggage, and relented to the hangover/jet lag that stampeded over her.

Lana kneeled beside Mara on the floor. "There are some hot guys in this study program, don't you think?"

Mara yawned. She dragged her eyes over some of their faces. A hot Samoan with dark hair and tattooed arms that she'd met on the plane now dozed on the steps of the atrium's central staircase. Next to him, a blond, turtle-neck-type with a pompous sneer on his face scrutinized the student handbook. Alone by the entrance, a skinny guy with hair down most of his face like a New Wave front man kept striking a lighter that wouldn't light. A beefy jock dressed in green from his cap to his running shoes sipped from a juice carton by the reception desk.

Mara nodded. "Not too bad. Good international assortment. But, I prefer some of the faculty we met at Da Vinci. Some of those profs look like they could do some delicious damage." She winked.

Kristen giggled. She sat cross-legged beside Lana and had taken to twisting the ends of her hair again. This time, she bore tiny cuticle scissors, which she used to clip millimeters of split ends off of the tip of one twist before moving on to another. It seemed a soothing habit, and Mara chose to leave that baggage alone.

Mara returned to sizing up the travelers, and she settled her gaze on that good-looking, budding film director with the leather jacket and nice teeth who'd helped her lug her massive, black and red striped suitcase up the suicide hill to their complex. He stood by reception chatting with his buddy, who looked like an '80s rock star has-been.

The rock star sported a jet-black mullet that hung low into his thick fur-lined denim jacket. A gold earring dangled from his left ear, and so much stubble coated his chin that his face looked dirty. He laughed at something the budding director said, and the rock star's dimples performed a lethal drive-by.

Mara sat up straight. Why did this guy find it necessary to hide those adorable dimples beneath that scruff? And really, an earring? Plus, that stupid denim jacket...it couldn't help but bring out those blue eyes, so why the mullet? All that thick, black hair...shit, she could spend hours running her hands through those locks, and he thinks a mullet is the way to go? What was this guy thinking? She licked her lips.

The rock star suddenly caught her gaze, grinned, and waved in her direction. Mara couldn't register the greeting as friendly or creepy, so she turned away. Her cheeks burned and she removed her jacket. And straightened her hair.

"Thank God my roommate bowed out, and I'm flying solo this semester," Lana said. "A lot of these weirdoes look like they're serial killer material."

Mara flashed back to the graphic news footage. Would she be paired with serial killer material? She briefly clued in Kristen and Lana to the plight of Chick Sticht, her slain would-be roommate. Speechless, the three merely exchanged horrified expressions of fear and grief.

Kristen nudged Mara. "Your name's been called. Go to the desk. Get your roommate and key."

"I wonder if they've changed my room since the murder," Mara muttered. She inched her away across the atrium, stumbling through travel-weary twenty-somethings and their suitcases, until arriving at the main reception desk. Seated was a man with black, sunken eyes, a shaved head, and gaunt cheeks who greeted her with a whisper of a smile. A spindly arm poked from his t-shirt, and he handed her the key to room twelve.

"*Ciao, Signorina.* You are Jesse?" he said with a strong Italian accent.

"No, my name is Mara Silvestri." She rubbed the sleep from her eyes and tried to focus.

"*Va bene.* Jesse Tonno is your roommate. Please find her, and give her the other keycard to room twelve, okay? But, first, sign here."

Mara bent to sign the paperwork, and a deep, sexy male voice behind her said, "I'm Jesse."

Mara looked up to see the rock star smiling at her.

"Hey beautiful," he said, "looks like we're roommates."

***

Mara pushed her chocolate brown tendrils aside to gaze into a pair of ocean blue eyes. She dove in, and for a second, she found herself drowning.

"So, what do you think, roomie? Who are we to question Fate, right?" Jesse asked. He ran his hand through his black hair which hung longer in front and kept creeping low over one eye. Adorable, until she spied that mullet.

"*Scusi, Signorina,*" the desk manager said. "Please, there are many other students who need rooms. This Jesse is okay, for a roommate?"

Jesse's grotto-blue eyes bore into her, as if pleading for her assent. He smelled like woodchips and pine needles. And she happened to love the outdoors.

Well, why not? He's probably a nice guy…

Raucous laughter bellowed behind her. The film student in the leather jacket patted Jesse on the shoulder, while another student, a real poser with high cheekbones and a brush-cut, sauntered over to them, a cigarette dangling between his pursed lips. The poser offered his hand. "Stan Kiever."

Somehow Lana had finagled her way into the mix, ninja-like in her stealth, and grabbed his outstretched hand. "Kiever, like the famous movie actress?" Lana said.

A solemn look passed over Kiever's face like the shadow of a cloud blowing over the ocean. "The same," he said and lowered his gaze.

The film student elbowed in between them. "My boy here is also the son of a U.S. Senator, my dear." He gave Kiever a pat on the back, and Kiever perked up with a smile.

Something had rattled Kiever, about his mother or his father. Mara recalled reading about a recent FBI investigation of a U.S. Senator, something about embezzlement charges turning up squat, but Kiever hadn't been the politician's name; it was Sugar-something. She couldn't place it.

Kiever took a long puff from his butt, and, as smoke slithered from his nostrils, he kissed Lana's hand. "You can call me Stanky, like my boys, over here." Stan Kiever had obviously regained his cocky composure, and Mara realized that she no longer cared about his background.

"Ooh, Stanky, a worldly, manly man," Lana cooed. "I saw you pass by me on the plane last night. You get around."

"Yeaaah, I'll say we do. Weekend before Christmas break, Amsterdam kicked ass, didn't it, boys?" Stanky Kiever said. "Think we need a trip back next week too, Utica?" Stanky elbowed the film student, who rolled his eyes and blushed. Utica was the one who'd carried her suitcase.

Stanky turned to some of the other guys and addressed them in a raspy, low whine. "Jesse and Utica and me turned that Red Light District upside down, man. Ain't that right, boys?"

Jesse flashed a strained smile, and blushed too. Utica shrugged, and while most of the other men hooted and hollered, Jesse and Utica cast their eyes to the floor and shifted on both feet. "Yeah, we sure did," Jesse mumbled.

Mara was not impressed with the Red Light posse.

The desk clerk cleared his throat loudly. "Miss Silvestri. Please, is this Jesse okay for a roommate?"

Mara took a step back from Jesse, dried herself off from her momentary lapse in her grotto of insanity. These party boys might be right up Lana's alley, but Mara needed none of that hanging around her apartment while devoting herself to her studies.

"*No, grazie,*" she replied to the man behind the counter. She turned to Kristen who'd remained speechless in a drowsy stupor throughout the meeting, and took hold of her arm. "This is my roommate, please?"

Kristen nodded and smiled at Mara's request. They both signed the paperwork, and the clerk handed Kristen the papers and the entry swipe-card. Mara picked up her plaid, hard-case duffel and took a last look at the lothario with the captivating eyes.

Jesse appeared crestfallen. She figured he'd get over it. He tried to speak, but she cut him off.

"Thanks for the offer," Mara said. "But, I'm sure Fate will provide you someone else to shack up with this semester." She strode off across the lobby, with every intention of ignoring the louse for the duration of her work-study program.

***

The Sculptor felt anxious about the new students, like he did every new semester. A fresh batch, so eager to learn. He couldn't wait to choose one of them, maybe a handful of them. To join him. In contributing to Rome's culture, and becoming a part of its thriving art scene.

Chapter 5

Mara and Kristen spent Friday and Saturday moving into their apartment, registering for classes, and experimenting with pasta. She and Kristen set up a fifteen-gallon fish tank with a handful of African Cichlids, and they brushed up on Italian phrases. Lana joined the two women on jaunts throughout the city, where Mara familiarized them with Rome's transportation system and shopping district, as well as the tourist sites and eateries that she'd often visited with her dad.

Sunday morning, Mara, Kristen, and Lana marveled at the decorative transformation that Stella Luna's atrium had undergone in preparation for that night's Orientation Festa, a party thrown by Rome University on the eve of every new semester. The three women spent the better part of the day getting manicures and buying shoes for the event.

After two hours of chatting up the night's festivities with the proprietors of Mino and Mary's on Via Condotti near the

Spanish Steps, the three sloshed through the slushy piazza for the nearest bus stop, arms laden with packages.

Kristen twirled a strand of hair poking from her woolen hat while she read the schedule on a bus stop stand. Mara stomped her frozen feet and wondered aloud about whether there would be music at the gala. A small, dark-skinned, wiry little boy of about eight sauntered between them, reading a newspaper.

"I just don't know how they're going to squeeze all the students and faculty into that atrium, let alone food and a DJ," Kristen said.

Mara nodded to Kristen and glanced at the boy. A pink *La Stampa* shook in the boy's widespread hands, and his eyes darted back and forth across the newspaper. Mara couldn't imagine how the boy could read with such long hair in his eyes. He glanced up at them through his sheepdog bangs, and Mara winked at him. He turned away and leaned against the bus stop pole. After a minute, the young boy folded the newspaper and draped the long pages over his arm like a trench coat.

"There's a big ol' conference room at the end of the atrium hall," Lana said, shifting her four bags of shoes. "They take down a temporary wall, and the atrium doubles in size. I saw a catering crew setting up when I did my laundry this—"

Before she could finish, Lana crashed to the pavement on all fours at Mara's feet.

"Oh!" Kristen cried.

"What the hell…" Lana drawled, struggling to regain her footing amid the avalanche of parcels.

"Are you alright?" Mara reached to help her.

So did the boy. He scuttled between Mara and Lana, and impeded Mara's assistance with his newspaper-curtained arm. He pulled Lana to her feet and then kissed her hand. His face reddened, and he bolted down the street toward a subway entrance.

Lana shook her head and rubbed her knees. "I thought the little brat pushed me down, but then he was so sweet to help me up." She nodded toward the fleeing child. "Looks like he thinks the subway's a better option than the bus."

Kristen helped Lana rearrange her packages. Mara stared after the boy, baffled by the incident.

A sickening thought struck. Mara checked her wrist; her watch was gone. So was her sling pocketbook, containing her driver's license, school ID, credit card, photos, keycard, and some Euros.

Mara glimpsed the boy, almost fifty yards away from them now, heading down the steps of the subway entrance. That little shit. She tore off after him without a word, leaving behind her two friends, helpless to assist in their high-heeled boots.

Wearing the cross-trainers with which she jogged the five-mile radius of her neighborhood every morning since her arrival, Mara quickly closed the gap between her and the young boy. She nearly caught up with him, but a horde of subway riders exited the stairwell and cut him off from her view.

She darted back and forth through the crowd and down the packed stairwell. When Mara reached the bottom, she glimpsed the black-haired brat sliding down the metal banister of the long, slow escalator that plunged into the depths of the subway station. She descended the escalator steps by twos, but the flow of people widened the distance between her and the child still further. She lost track of him.

At the bottom of the deepest subterranean level, screeching trains echoed through the maze of tiled tunnels that sprawled in every direction. The air was warm and steamy, making her feel clammy all over. Dark-skinned vendors sold purses, scarves, and belts on blankets that patch-worked the floor. Old women hunched over their parcels with rosaries dangling between their fingers. A gray-haired man wearing an undershirt, tattered corduroys, and old-man shoes sold bottles of water, rolls of bread, and toiletries.

A throng of commuters waited at the turnstiles to punch their tickets and enter the platform area dedicated to the Termini train station, Rome's main transportation hub. The wily kid must have ducked beneath the turnstile to elude her, knowing that she'd be barred from entrance without a wallet to purchase a ticket. She kicked the turnstile. "Damn it," she muttered.

Suddenly, she glimpsed a pink newspaper, attached to a little arm, just outside the turnstile. The boy darted around a bend, past a yellow sign that designated an abandoned subway line. She, too, sped around the bend and into a corridor.

Empty.

Aside from a homeless woman curled up asleep beneath a bench, the entire platform area was deserted.

"Damn it!" Mara said again. More than the inconvenience of losing her cheap watch, credit cards, and about 100 Euros, she was sad that she'd lost her favorite picture of her and her dad. She was also pissed that she'd been duped by a kid.

He was a *zingaro*, a gypsy child, she realized now. In Rome, *zingari* usually traveled in small packs. The pick-pocketing women and children were harmless and easily identifiable to a prepared traveler, and thus easily avoided. Mara felt like kicking herself that the oldest trick in the book, the newspaper over the arm, had bested her.

A mangy dog sauntered past her, sniffing at garbage along the way. He stopped to urinate on the sleeping homeless woman.

"Hey, get outta there!" Mara scooted the dog away before it was able to relieve itself, but the elderly woman awoke, stretched and rolled out from the bench. Mara signaled that she had no money to give, and the old woman scraped her thumbnail against her front teeth, an obvious gesture of disdain, before ambling around the corner.

The corridor, devoid of travelers, suddenly seemed ominous. Mara rubbed her shoulders, trying to chase away the creepy feeling that enveloped her. She struggled to take a breath; her lungs couldn't seem to get enough air. She could swear that whispers emanated from the dingy, tiled walls.

What had she been thinking, darting down here into an abandoned subway tunnel by herself? She hearkened back to the faculty warnings upon her arrival and realized that she'd acted way too impulsively. The threat of an assault should have been a higher priority than recovering her wallet out of principle.

Aside from the menacing whispers, heavy panting suddenly echoed out of the darkness at one end of the tunnel. She darted her eyes around, until she finally spotted it, emerging from the gloom.

The grungy canine.

Mara exhaled a sigh of relief as he trotted past her, scooted under the bench, and disappeared from sight. She bent to examine the underside of the long, narrow seat.

A large opening stood where the wall had once been. She heard voices issue from the cavity; likely those responsible for the eerie whispers murmured in the corridor. She peeked inside and adjusted her vision to the darkness, but she leaned too far forward and tumbled headlong into the crevice.

She rolled into a crouched position and found herself in a torch-lit cave about the size of a two-car garage. Small groups of single-mothers and breast-feeding babies huddled along the walls. *Zingari.* They were likely refugees, war widows, or battered families, all waiting for their older children to return with whatever means of support they could steal.

Mara spotted the young boy who'd stolen her wallet. Apparently, he was the man of the house. He stood, arms folded and legs spread apart with an insolent expression on his face, protecting an elderly, one-armed woman resting on a heap of newspaper.

Mara approached him and knelt on one knee. Whispering in Italian to the child she said, "Keep the money. I just want back my identification and my picture, please."

Though the boy's defiant scowl never left his face, Mara thought she caught his lower lip tremble. He reached into a cardboard box and thrust Mara's wallet and watch toward her. The photo and her ID cards stared up at her. She smiled at the boy, nodded at the others, and then crawled out of the dark, poor underworld.

Once back at the busy Termini platform, she unzipped her change purse and found that the boy had never removed the 100 Euros.

Mara was bumped from behind by a large backpack.

"*Scusi,*" she said.

"*Non c'e niente. A lei mi scusi, Signorina.*" The traveler turned to further express his apology, and she recognized him instantly.

It was Michael Utica, the handsome, dark-haired film student that had hauled her overfilled suitcase up the hill to their apartment a few days ago. The same guy who haunted bars in the Red Light District of Amsterdam with his buddies.

One of the other lotharios stood beside him. Stan Kiever.

Kiever reached out his hand to shake hers, and he pulled a short cigar from his thin, pursed lips with the other. He squinted through the smoke he blew between them. "Hey, hey, nice to see you. Good to see you again. Remember me? Stanky."

Kiever ruffled his fingers through his brown, quarter-inch brush-cut that she could tell he was still getting used to. The hair matched the freckles sprinkled across the bridge of his nose. He gestured back to the Termini subway tunnel. "We just got back from another slick trip. Paris this time, baby. Ever been? You should come next time. Lots of smooth jazz and soft beignets, baby, in the Latin Quarter, ya know?"

She nodded and smiled, and wondered how a bright, educated son of a Washington diplomat and an illustrious movie actress could have acquired such a strong skate-boarder speech pattern.

Utica interjected, "Hey, you headed to the Festa tonight? Jesse'll be there." Utica had a long, aquiline nose akin to Adrian Brody and a kind smile that exuded a polite, trustworthy, lovable vibe.

"Jesse will be there? And that's significant because?" Mara asked.

"He's gotta thing for you. Really." Utica nodded his head up and down like a child convincing his mom to give him one more cookie. His eyes grew wide as if to prove he hid nothing behind them. "He noticed you first thing, soon as they started handing out room assignments." His Long Island accent endeared him to her the more he spoke. "Jesse nudged me like he does, pointed over to you, and he told me, 'I'm gonna marry that girl someday.'"

"Yeah, he said that," Kiever said. "But I thought he was talking about Kristen, the hottie standing next to you. She's hot, ya know, like all those sweet Parisian girls we scored this weekend. Yeaaah!" Kiever turned to high-five Utica, but Utica shook his head and just left him hanging.

Utica turned his back to Kiever and faced her. "So, maybe go to the party, and get to know him a little better. He's a stand-up guy. A real gentleman."

"A gentleman? So, he didn't go to Paris with you two?" Mara asked, wondering why she cared.

"*Certo, baby*," Kiever spoke skate-boarder Italian too. "He most certainly joined our rabble-rousing; nothing like Paris in the wintertime, ya know? He's not here now because he taxied over to a friend's house from Termini, before heading to our flat. Probably a little more rabble-rousing...am I right?"

"You guys have a flat? You don't live at the apartment complex with the rest of us?" Mara said.

"My dad bought me a flat in Trastevere, by the Vatican," Kiever said. "Been staying there since undergrad. Utica, Jesse and I, and some other dude have been rooming since our first Amsterdam trip five or six years ago." Kiever paused to take a deep hit of his thin stogie.

Utica rested his elbow on her shoulder. "It's too bad you gave Jesse the heave-ho at Stella Luna. He's been moping ever since."

"If the three of you share a flat in Trastevere, then why did you all show up for roommate pairing at Stella Luna?" Mara said. "And, how was Jesse assigned as my roommate?"

"Early bird gets the worm, baby," Kiever said. "We pay off the clerks to pair us with the newbie chicks every semester, feign a mix-up and lickety-split, we got dates with no strings, long before the jamokes at school even lay eyes on them."

Mara shook her head and smiled, bowled over by their clever boldness. Nonetheless, she stepped out from Utica's snaking appendage. "I look forward to seeing you guys at the Festa. First drinks are on me, boys." She winked and walked away amidst their goodbyes, laughing to herself when their comments to each other proved that they had no idea the party would feature an open bar.

She looked back down at the wallet still in her hand, and the 100 Euros still folded safely within the change purse.

Ten minutes later, Mara returned to the underground cave in the abandoned tunnel. She crept inside and found the group of *zingari* just as she'd left them. She set down four plastic bags, overflowing with rolls and water bottles that she'd purchased with the 100 Euros, and left without a word.

Chapter 6

"Where the hell have you been?"

Before Mara had a chance to explain the outcome of her gypsy mugging, Kristen pulled her into their apartment and thrust her toward the bathroom. A roller fell from Kristen's wound up nest of hair. "Go get cleaned up."

"And, use some of my kiwi shampoo," Lana said. "I can smell you from here." Lana sat at the bedroom mirror applying mascara.

In the small narrow bathroom, Mara stood beneath the hot shower. She could hear her friends in the main living area of the thin-walled apartment talking about meeting the resident students—not the ones that had flown in last week with them from America for a semester abroad, but those natives that considered Rome University their home for undergrad and graduate studies.

The landline rang in the bedroom, where she and Kristen slept in two twin beds. She heard Kristen tell Oslo, the spindly reception attendant, that she'd bring down their apartment's nineteen-inch black and white television to the front desk, for use as an extra surveillance monitor during the party. Consideration of Rome's serial killer was a top priority at the school, and the dean was obviously beefing up security for the gala.

An hour later, Mara's hair glistened with as much shine as her freshly glossed lips. Her short, aubergine, lace dress revealed enough cleavage to score, but it hid enough to be taken seriously as a professor's teaching assistant.

Her Oxford credentials had secured her a top marketing position with Ferrari, upon the two-year completion of an internship, a Master's thesis, and teaching experience alongside an international business professor at Rome University. She and the professor, an American whom the students referred to as "Signore Jack," had corresponded via email thus far, but tonight would be their first face-to-face meeting.

Mara sprinkled some flakes into the Cichlid tank, and then rubbed her fingers across the cherry wood box that held her father's ashes atop the living room credenza. In the nearly five years she'd held onto them, waiting for the right time to release his ashes back into the poppy-laden fields of his Tuscan homeland, she always patted the urn for a little luck.

Mara, Lana, and Kristen sashayed into the foyer, and Lana slipped a silk Hermes pashmina around Mara's waist. "I think this suits you."

"Let's have some fun tonight, girls!" Kristen slapped their asses, and the three headed out for a night none of them would forget.

Chapter 7

Meanwhile, on the other side of town, Jesse Tonno rapped his knuckles in sequence against the wooden entrance built into the ancient stonewall that surrounded Roma Centro. Sheltered from view beneath the canopy of an ancient dogwood, he fidgeted with his mullet, yanked up his Levi's and pounded out the sequence again. He darted glances from side to side, ensuring that he hadn't been followed.

Jesse heard footsteps pull up short behind the door. One gray eyeball among a web of wrinkles appeared in the bronze peephole. A number of locks cranked open, and the door creaked back a few inches.

Jesse pushed open the door, scanned the deserted area a final time, and slipped inside.

Inside the wall now, in a small abode, he spotted the man, Enzo, standing behind a mahogany chair to the side of the door. The smell of cabbage in the air nauseated him; Jesse spotted a steaming pot bubbling like a cauldron on the eight-burner stove in the next room.

Enzo beckoned to him. One hand bore a cigarette. In the other, a pair of glistening shears.

Jesse swallowed hard. He hadn't come prepared, and Enzo was apparently very ready. Jesse clenched his paws into thick fists. Fight or flight?

Enzo was no amateur; Jesse knew that. Even though the man was closing in on seventy, the short, fit, wily man could still take him.

"Let's do this if we're gonna do this. Now or never, kid," Enzo taunted him in Roman dialect. Jesse scanned the man's wrinkled, yet still handsome face. Enzo's salt and pepper locks were thick and full. He caught a glimmer in the old man's smiling gray eyes. That sonofabitch was enjoying this!

Jesse glanced at his surroundings. Nearly every surface gleamed in marble and stainless steel. Every piece of furniture, a work of art. Immaculately clean, the only feminine touch appeared to be the lace dresser scarves that covered many of the pristine surfaces. All of them embroidered by Enzo's childhood sweetheart and wife, Matilda, who had died years earlier. A number of doors surrounded the main dining and living room. All of them stood closed. Jesse wondered if he should bolt for one of them while he still had time.

"You're a pussy, little boy. Forget about it, and just go home!" Enzo lowered the shears and stomped out his cigarette.

"No!" Jesse shouted. "Let's do this thing." Furious now, Jesse squeezed both fists, and rushed the man while the shears were down.

But, Enzo was too fast. He raised the sheers high and sliced through the air, catching Jesse off guard.

Jesse slumped to the floor. "It took me five long years, and you just…"

Enzo held the black ponytail high above his head. "It was time, son. Now, get in the chair, so I can finish you."

***

Feeling lighter now that his unruly mullet had been severed from his head, Jesse kicked the soccer ball back and forth with Enzo on the bed of soggy pine needles just outside the dining room slider. Beneath a hand-crafted wooden pergola over which snaked thick, brown Sangiovese grapevines, Enzo deftly skirted the ball away from the younger man and shot it into a shoveled snow pile beside the trees surrounding the small courtyard.

"Bravo, *Zio!*" Jesse encouraged his uncle in affectionate praise.

Jesse retrieved the ball from the mound of snow and winced at the pain in his left ankle. February's cold dampness always wreaked havoc with the metal pins that had held his ankle together since the age of nineteen. The former captain of Roma Sud's football team was now relegated to pick-up games on a Sunday afternoon. He swallowed back the bitter taste of melancholy and resumed sparring with Enzo. It more than made up for the damn haircut he'd just endured.

"Your mother told me you're getting married?" Enzo halted play by bouncing the ball up and down on his knee.

"Word travels fast. I only met my future bride a few days ago." Jesse whipped a snowball at the soccer ball, knocked it from his uncle's knee, and resumed dribbling. "She's a grad student. Beautiful. Opinionated. Packs heavy baggage. But, I plan to marry her. She just doesn't know it yet."

"Good thing I gave you the haircut then; that should help things along." Enzo went inside to tend to his cabbage rolls. He'd been cutting Jesse's hair, except for the ponytailed mullet, once a month, every month for the past eight years or so. It all started when his mother had suggested to her brother that Jesse was spending too much time with the wrong crowd. *Zio* Enzo and his *Zia* Matilda, welcomed him, guided him, and tried to keep a watchful eye on him.

Enzo returned with sparkling water and homemade anise cookies. The two sat on an immense, hollow log that Enzo had spent ten hours carving into a bench on the night Matilda died. Lopsided and weather-worn, his uncle and the bench both bore their burdens with dignified grace.

"Bring her by for cabbage rolls tonight. I'll make you some sausage and beans, too," Enzo said, pouring drinks. Before Jesse could reply, the door buzzed, and Enzo excused himself.

Jesse downed a full glass of water and wiped the sweat that dripped from his brow. He leaned his back against one of the beams of the towering pergola and marveled at his uncle's generosity. Even through Jesse's numerous entanglements with the wrong side of the law, Enzo had never given up on him. That meant a lot.

Years ago, Enzo had even arranged for a professor at Rome University to mentor him. The same carpenter who'd crafted Enzo's pergola also taught business courses at the school, and somehow Enzo had known that Jesse would reap the benefits of his tutelage.

It had been years since Jesse had had a run-in with the police. Publicly, anyway. Jesse preferred to keep his extra-curricular activities under wraps these days.

His uncle returned, and behind him stood a tall, skinny, uniformed cop, about Jesse's age. They stepped onto the patio and the police officer extended his hand to Jesse. The man had one ear.

A shudder ran through Jesse, but he gripped the man's hand, shook it, and smiled.

Enzo patted Jesse's shoulder. "Forgive me, nephew, I must attend to some important business. But, here, take the cookies home with you."

"No need for apologies," Jesse said. "I have to get to a school event anyway."

"She'll be there?"

Jesse felt his cheeks warm. He shook his head as if it would ward off the blush, but he couldn't help smiling. He flicked his eyebrows at his uncle, gave both men a wave, and jogged through the house to the front door before the heat in his cheeks made him sweat more.

Former football star, turned law-breaker, turned grad student. Even at twenty-five years old, Jesse still blushed over girls. Especially in front of his uncle.

Enzo just had that gift of coaxing sheepish guilt out of anyone.

Which was why Enzo was the top-ranking police inspector in Rome's Homicide Department.

***

The Sculptor had been out playing today. He'd found a piece that he really wanted to make his own, and he'd sweated himself into a frenzy.

He'd spent the rest of the afternoon chiseling and molding. And, then finally, perfection. Another fresh work of art, interpreted by his own imagination.

Tonight, he would attend the bi-annual gala that the university held for its students. The Festa always pleased him, as any pageant would. Young bodies on display, like an animated museum. He couldn't wait to introduce himself to all of them.

Chapter 8

"Have you ever seen more glorious busts in one room?" Dean Arella asked Mara, only a half hour into the kick-off gala.

Mara suppressed an urge to laugh by sipping her Pinot Grigio spritzer.

She'd approached Rome University's Dean of Students, Benedetto Arella, fifteen minutes earlier to formally introduce herself. Continuing the flow of conversation proved difficult. Since then, they'd simply surveyed the atrium of the Residence Stella Luna, decorated like a glitzy Academy Awards after-party. It brimmed with RU students, professors, alumni, and the wait staff.

Not sure how to respond to his query on busts, she shoved a cracker into her mouth and ignored it. She discreetly inspected Dean Arella while he guzzled a warm can of Diet Coke. Head of the student body for the past fifteen years, fifty-something, pasty-skinned, and capped off with a bad weave, Arella swayed back and forth on the lifts inserted into his shiny brown Bruno

Maglis. He deposited the empty can on a passing tray and wiped his hands with his aubergine pocket square. The urge to laugh overcame her again, so she turned back to the atrium.

Champagne bubbled from a fountain in the middle of the room. Lights speckled the ceiling like stars. Rich fabric draped the central stairwell. Hundreds of balloons rendered the worn indoor-outdoor carpeting nearly invisible. The DJ softly played Bocelli amid the sweet, oaky aroma of wine barrels filled with rose petals that lined the walls between the ground-level apartment doors. Students and professors co-mingled with dozens of far more prominent guests: authentic, life-size, marble statues. And glorious busts.

Composed now, Mara responded to Dean Arella with a smile. "Professor, I'm certain that there must be more authentic busts here than in all of Hollywood. Simply breathtaking. Cheers," she saluted the dean with her glass.

Mara slipped past the dean's son, Fritz Arella, who serpentined wearily through the other guests, glass in hand, eyes to the floor, a suicidal look playing out over his handsome features. Rumor had it that the senior undergrad student had been involved with Chick Sticht, the most recent victim of the Sculptor, the same beautiful young woman that the flight news feed had shown butchered. Whatever their relationship, the fact remained that the younger Arella had spent much of the fall semester in the woman's company. And now, Mara had overheard that this openly despondent young man was Rome police's only suspect in the case.

She elbowed past Ryan Volker, RU's Art in Rome professor, a tall, lanky Englishman in his mid-thirties with short black hair and a pair of bright blue eyes hidden behind wire-rimmed spectacles. He mingled with the art instructors of Rome's two other leading educational institutions—Trinity College and the Liberal Arts College of Rome, known as "Libby" to most.

Mara snagged a shrimp canapé from a passing waiter and overheard Professor Volker explaining to a group that Stan Kiever's father, an RU board member, had lent the statues, pieces of his own collection, for the gala. Mara wasn't sure if the look was more Uffizi Gallery or Madame Tussauds, but shortly after Dean Arella's lecture at the start of the night about personal safety in light of the serial killer, the statues had since infused a sense of the macabre.

A gust of cold air swept through the room, and a sixty-something, gray-haired man entered Stella Luna. He stomped snow from his galoshes and nodded to Dean Arella. Dressed in a wool coat over a dark suit with a loose tie, a crumpled collar, and winter galoshes, the new arrival was a dead ringer for Columbo, only slightly edgier. He sauntered to the middle of the room and addressed the group of staff and students in a raised voice. "*Signori*," the Italian Columbo said in accented English, "forgive the intrusion; I am Rome's Chief Inspector Enzo Tranchille."

The music halted, and chatter ebbed. "Over the coming days, I'd like to speak with each of the three colleges' art professors about the Sculptor case we're working on. In hopes you might provide expert opinion on evidence our forensics unit has collected…sculpting tools, chips of plaster, articles of that ilk."

Enzo stood for a minute, allowing a pregnant pause to fester, likely using those moments to scrutinize the reactions of all three instructors. "Of course, if anyone else has any piece of pertinent information about the murders to contribute, do not hesitate to let me know." A veil of palpable gloom settled over the entire crowd. He opened his mouth to continue.

Until, Signore Jackson Sugardale took over the DJ's microphone.

He tapped the mike. "Uh, is this thing on? Testing…"

The inspector submitted to the interruption with a knowing smile.

Mara recognized Professor Sugardale's face from the university's website. He resembled a younger Jeff Bridges, with slicked back blondish-brown hair that was long on top and buzzed in the back. His build told the story of a former soldier who'd sought to forget the days of war with beer. His relaxed, slate blue eyes and apple red cheeks softened his face.

She recalled Sugardale's Texan drawl from their two telephone conversations weeks earlier, regarding her responsibilities as teaching assistant to his International Business class. From their talks, as well as various email correspondence, she anticipated that this soft-spoken, former U.S. Army Ranger would likely issue a serious, professional speech.

Instead, Sugardale said, "Lovely ladies and hog-tied gentlemen, allow me to introduce myself. Professor of International Business, Jackson Sugardale, at your service. 'Signore Jack' will suffice. Let me assure you that this champagne fountain to my left is not the only thing going tonight. I'll be whipping up some pommie-grenade martinis and single-malt shooters within the hour."

A whoop of cheers bellowed from the crowd.

"I can guarantee that all of us here at RU will be working our asses off all semester, so tonight, I expect some heavy-drinking…"

A louder cheer resounded throughout the hall.

"…Some heavy-petting,"

Boisterous catcalls emanated from the corner in which Kiever, Tonno and Utica stood.

"…And some hard-core line-dancing!"

The entire atrium burst into applause and cheers. At that, the police inspector entirely relinquished his brief hold on the spotlight with a nod to the professor and disappeared through a side door.

"And, I expect that each and every one of you students, by the end of this lovely evening, will have skinny-dipped in that champagne fountain." He raised his glass to toast the crowd. "*La dolce vita*, my friends."

"*La dolce vita*," they all shouted.

Sugardale pointed to the DJ, who nodded, and then blared the Italian mega-band Zucchero loud enough to vibrate every bust in the room.

**

After a late buffet service of the finest seafood, roast beef, exotic fruit, cheeses, breads, and wines, Mara found herself sampling the champagne fountain. She used a lovely piece of crystal, while Lana and Kristen took turns dipping their faces right into the arched streams.

Kristen ran back to the room, and returned minutes later with her hair in a ponytail and three pairs of UGGs in hand. Mara tossed her five-inch spikes under a table, and the three women squished their toes into their fleece boots.

Kristen grabbed her arm. "C'mon, I love this song!" Lady GaGa had everyone jumping and gyrating on the dance floor.

"You two, go. I'll be there in ten minutes." While Kristen and Lana bounced around amid the sea of red, white, and green balloons, Mara decided to take a minute to introduce herself to her boss, Signore Jackson Sugardale, before the champagne began to slur her speech.

The professor sat puffing a Macanudo on the central staircase that was sheathed in red velvet. A small posse of students hung on his every word. Mara approached from the side and listened in with the others. In his rich, thick Southern drawl, Jackson told one student, "Thanks, darlin'. I will make a note of that." A gaggle of laughter broke free.

"Professor, you were the biggest and the baddest!" said an Asian-American student from Seattle. Though he wore a tuxedo, the gangly kid, who went by Boots, sported long hair, sunglasses, and a bandana, an Asian version of Axl Rose.

"Well, now, I suppose I was somewhat successful, which is why Dean Arella was kind enough to allow me to teach here, and—"

"Somewhat? Wall Street calls you the 'king of trade shows.' You're a goddamn guru, world-fucking-renowned!" Boots said.

"I appreciate the support, I do. But, I see that one of my teaching assistants is now present, and I'd prefer that we keep the kudos to a minimum." Signore Jack promptly stood, swigged his Pabst, crushed the cigar stub into the empty can, and exited the crowd. To Mara's astonishment, he swung an arm around her shoulder and shuffled her toward the bartender.

"Ms. Silvestri, my sincerest gratitude for saving me. I'm not one for compliments, and the heat was a bit hot in the kitchen over there. Time to cool off with another cold one. May I offer you a beverage, little lady?"

In just those few exchanges that Mara had witnessed, she realized just how much Signore Jackson reminded her of her father—fun-loving and animated, yet kind and generous. She liked him instantly.

Mara held up her half-full champagne glass to decline another beverage. "How did you know I was one of your TAs?"

"Former Army Ranger. Intel comes out of my pores. It was easy to find creds and photos of both my TAs. I know a lot about you. Like the fact that you're a very accomplished young woman. Oxford background. Magna cum laude. You're also a brown belt; you can take care of yourself. In these times of vicious serial killers, that's a good thing. But don't worry, my intel left out a few things—like, your shoe size."

"Don't ask," she said, and smiled.

"Bet you don't know much about my other TA, though. Quite accomplished. Brilliant with numbers. Very personable. Have the two of you met yet?" Jackson asked.

Mara shook her head. She hoped that whomever it was would prove just as driven as she.

Behind her, a voice chimed in that made her cringe. "My shoe size is a whopping twelve and a half, Professor." Obviously not the voice of one as driven as she was. "And, you know what big feet means?" It was Jesse's voice.

"Big shoes." Both Jesse and Sugardale broke into a fit of laughter. The professor extended his hand behind her to shake Jesse's. "Perfect timing, son," the professor said. "Mara, allow me to introduce my other teaching assistant, Jesse Tonno."

Mara steeled herself to bear the brunt of her disgust with Jesse the slacker.

As she turned to face him, Signore Jack raised his can of cold Pabst for a toast. "The three of us folks will work very closely as a team to provide a sound education to my biz majors."

Through the sudden onslaught of a champagne haze, Mara raised her glass too.

"To well-oiled machinery!" Jackson said.

It was then that Mara finally settled her gaze on Jesse Tonno, the man who was now her semester-long partner, and realized…he'd chopped off his mullet.

She gasped. And then she belched. Loudly, from the depths of her belly.

Her eyes widened, and her hand flew to her mouth. "Professor, excuse me. I must have had a little too much to drink." Her face burned with embarrassment.

"Don't be silly, darlin'. That's just your body lettin' in a little room for more. Please excuse me while I help the bartender mix up some more of my famous 'armored tanks.' They'll make you forget everything." Jack saluted them and sauntered behind the bar.

Jesse offered her his arm. "Maybe a little fresh air? Might help us get off to a fresh start, what do you think?" He stood before her with his head cocked to one side like a puppy dog. His jet-black hair had been cut short in back, and the longer front was freshly quiffed and gelled. His blue grotto eyes beamed from his freshly shaven face and penetrated her so deeply, she thought she might need a cigarette. His lothario grin had been replaced with a sweet smile that beckoned her to join him. So she did.

She took hold of his arm, impressed by the sheer bulk of his python-like biceps. The fabric of his black sport coat rubbed against her bare shoulder; it gave her an itch too lascivious to scratch. He smelled like freshly mown grass, and baby lotion, and chalk, things that for some reason made her feel like a dirty little schoolgirl.

She gazed up at his face. He was watching her. Gone was the rock star wannabe. Here was the sweet, rugged, intelligent man from all of her fantasies. They walked out the door into the cold, snowy, February night, and she realized that she was in serious trouble of falling for him.

Until Utica and Kiever joined them.

Stan Kiever swooped in and captured Jesse in a headlock.

Mara's grip on Jesse released.

"Hey, Mara, I see you found Jesse," Utica said. "He cleans up pretty good, huh?"

"That rascal was just plain dirty in Paris, though, am I right, Utica?" Stanky said with a cigarillo pursed between his lips. "Good times, my man!"

Suddenly, Jesse broke free from Kiever's grip, whipped Kiever's arm around, and pinned it to his back. Jesse thrust Kiever to the wall, wobbling a nearby bust of Medusa. "You headlock me again, I will break your arm off. Got it?"

Kiever reached up with his free hand and slipped the cigarillo from his mouth. He slowly exhaled a long puff of smoke. "Oh, hey man, I got it. No worries. I was just playing, ya know?" He drew from the cigarillo. "Hey, it's all good, man."

Jesse untwisted Stanky's arm and punched him in the shoulder.

Mara shook her head. She had ambitions. No time for a babysitting job. She'd just get through the semester working with

Jesse, and then grab the brass ring with Ferrari at the end of it all. She turned to head back inside.

Jesse grabbed her hand and gazed at her with that puppy dog look.

Not gonna work this time. Too bad. He'd lost his bone.

She edged away from his grasp. "I look forward to working with you, first thing tomorrow morning. Don't be late." Mara scuttled off toward the bar in her UGG boots. She needed a dance floor to pound.

***

At 1:30 am, after hours of relentless dancing, Mara finally realized that the two vodka-rum-tequila "army tank" concoctions she'd tossed back had left her feeling sluggish, to say the least. She hugged Kristen goodnight and told her she'd meet her back at the apartment. Lana had left an hour earlier, glued to the lips of Miguelito, a student from Samoa whose hulking features reminded her of Frankenstein's monster.

The party had thinned considerably, and the few students that remained lazed sleepily on the stairwell, on couches, and on each other as slow songs kept them going. A native Italian couple, namely the tall, brooding Massimo "Mimi" Torta and his lithe, lovely Katerina Fila, six-year veterans of RU, serenaded each other beneath the stairwell. Mara said goodnight to the bartender and picked up a bottle of water that she swigged on the way back to her apartment.

A piercing scream reverberated through the atrium, and she choked on the drink. She glanced in the direction it came from— the apartment next door to hers, belonging to Jason, a fellow business student, and his life partner, Lance, an International Law major. No one else in the atrium seemed to have noticed the scream right out of *Psycho*.

She ditched the plastic container and picked up a glass beer bottle, poised to use it as a weapon. She bolted to the propped open door to determine if someone inside had been hurt. Before she reached the entrance, more screams and shouts.

From a group of football fans.

A giant, flat-screen TV on the wall showed the Buffalo Bills beating the pants off the Dallas Cowboys in the third quarter. Of course, she'd forgotten. Super Bowl Sunday. The live showing that started around midnight in Italy. And, holy crap, her favorite team was winning.

She twisted open the bottle she was prepared to wield at an unsuspecting thug, and drank long. Lance called her over to the other side of the apartment, and he offered her a seat with a great view of the television. She hugged him, curled up in the comfy IKEA cushions, and settled in for the big game.

Beside her was another matching chair. In it, sat Jesse Tonno.

Jesse snuggled a bag of ridged chips in one arm. He took one out, gnawed it with his front teeth like a beaver cutting wood. "Now that's a chip!"

Still in his sport jacket, he'd since unbuttoned the top few on his shirt and his once-gelled quiff now hung low over one eye. He grabbed one chip after another, gnawed them, all the while grinning so that the edges of his mouth curled up, like a Cheshire cat. She hated cats.

"How about a chip?" Jesse offered one up. She declined. He set the bag aside, sipped a beer. "Who're you rooting for?"

"I'm a Bills fan," Mara said.

"Hmm. Me too."

"Really? Why? No one's a Bills fan," Mara said.

"I like their coach. In his interviews, he seems like a good guy. Real family man. Good to his players."

Valuable assets in any man. She was sure Jesse lacked all of them.

"Why are you a Bills fan? You like their team colors?" Jesse's grin widened.

She felt her nostrils flare. "I don't choose teams based on colors. They've got a top-rated quarterback, the best defense in the league, and my cousin is their field goal kicker."

"Nickelsby? Get the hell out."

"You get the hell out. I'm comfortable." She nestled deeper into the pumpkin-colored cushions and placed a throw pillow on her lap. She set down her beer on the end table beside her, curled her legs up under her cocktail dress, and adjusted the strap that threatened to reveal more cleavage than Jesse Tonno was worthy.

"No, I won't get the hell out," he said. "I like it right here. I'm glad you're comfortable. You're also beautiful."

Mara blinked, speechless.

Twenty or so other students leapt from their seats and cheered, "Touchdown!" Jesse grabbed her by the hand and jumped up. "Bills score!" A dozen or so others threw foam koozies at the screen.

They watched the replay, and she freed her hand. She grabbed the beer she'd set down, wondered whether it was the right one, shrugged, and tipped back.

When they sat again, he firmly parked his forearm on the arm of her chair.

"Excuse me, but mine was there first," she said.

"And then you moved it."

"Unfair. You're the one who moved my arm."

"Okay, you can have it back." He moved his elbow, and snatched her hand in his.

Her breath caught in her chest. His hand so warm, and ridiculously soft and gentle, placed hers back onto the armrest. He caressed her fingers with his.

"Is this the way you plan to get to know all the students at RU?" Mara's voice had come out husky and ragged.

Cheers roared around them as the Bills ran back an interception for another touchdown. He never took his eyes off her.

"I just plan to get to know you, beautiful." Jesse's fingers were now firmly entangled with hers. "By the way, I think the Bills scored."

"As long as you realize that they're the only ones who'll score tonight."

He smiled. "Mara, in case you haven't noticed, my heart is pounding, and I can't seem to catch my breath." Somehow, their faces had edged closer since the score. The tuft of hair that crept over his eye tickled her nose.

Her heart was ready to burst through the front of her silk dress it was beating so hard. She heard the apartment's phone ring, and she heard Lance answer it, but it seemed like miles away.

She could smell Jesse's neck. His scent was even better up close.

"I think you ought to know how I really feel," Jesse said. "I've known it since I first saw you."

A faint commotion in the room. Probably another score. So what.

She just wanted to feel Jesse close to her. She wanted him even closer. Her dress strap fell again. She left it.

Her eyelids fluttered. His wet, full lips were so dangerously close to hers. She just wanted to suck one of them into her mouth and see what it tasted like. Just one.

Jesse whispered, "You should know that I…"

"Yes?" she said.

"I'm really a Dallas fan."

Her lips parted, and she inhaled deeply.

She felt his eyelashes on her cheek when he blinked.

His lips met hers.

The room's power went out, and they were pitched into full dark.

"*Bomba! Bomba!*" Oslo, the apartment manager, shouted the bomb warning from the door. "*Bomba! Bomba!* Go, now!"

Chapter 9

Ensconced in utter, suffocating darkness, Mara felt like a trapped Chilean miner.

The idea of a ticking bomb somewhere on the premises momentarily paralyzed her in the confines of her IKEA chair. She had to get out, through the darkness, without getting trampled. She steadied her rapid breathing while recalling the layout of the room.

All around her, a cacophony of voices grappled with the anxiety of a possible explosion, in a place that had just started to feel like home.

"Bomb threat!" Boots shouted. "Lemme the fuck out!"

A girl she didn't recognize said, "I can't see. I can't see. Hey! Who the hell's pawing me? Get your damn hands off me, perv!"

A loud slap, followed by the unmistakable giggle of Stanky Kiever.

Jesse spoke up beside her, in a firm, authoritative voice. "Everyone, stay calm. Walk; don't run. Feel your way to the atrium. Oslo will lead you outside from there."

Then scurrying footsteps, the sound of furniture as it was bumped and shoved out of the way, the crash of a lamp.

"Easy, guys!" Lance said. "You're breaking my stuff. If this is a hoax, I'm taking inventory after this. If anything's missing, I'm coming after each and every—"

Lance gasped and grunted, as somehow the wind was knocked out of him. People were shouting louder now, panicking in the darkness.

Other residents were likely flooding the atrium from their own apartments by now, and corking the group in Lance's room that rampaged the door like shoppers on Black Friday.

Mara knew she had to take action, but whatever she'd drunk that evening had slowed her reaction time. If there was indeed a bomb, she needed to flee the building without getting trampled. Her best bet was to crawl out of one of the windows in Lance's ground floor apartment. But, she'd lost her bearings in the darkness.

Soft, comforting words arose in her head, "I'm here, Mara. You're going to be alright." The soft, encouraging voice sounded like her dad's, but it was actually Jesse's tender, deep murmur that reassured her now. "It's been about three minutes. The generator should kick in at any moment. We'll make our way to the windows and get out safely." Minutes earlier Jesse had used his fingers to flirt, now he enmeshed them with hers and clutched tightly. "Stay with me, Mara, and you'll be safe."

She gripped his hand, and together they stumbled away from the mob crushing through the door jamb and felt their way through the main living area of the 400 square foot, studio apartment.

She knew that this dorm resembled hers and the other apartments in the complex: one small bathroom nearest the door to the atrium, a galley kitchen opposite the bath and along the back wall, followed by the living/dining room with two mullion windows, and finally the small bedroom alcove.

Mara rubbed her knuckles along the closed accordion door that shut away two twin beds. When the faux door ended, she stepped sideways toward the mullions and jammed her foot into a table leg, grateful her UGGs had cushioned the blow. Finally, she brushed the cold windowpane with her bare shoulder. Escape.

"Don't open it yet," Jesse said to her. "Once you do, everyone will rush this way. And we'll only have a few seconds to get out before they crush us in panic."

She squeezed his hand.

"Put this on," Jesse said. "Or, you'll freeze in that dress." Scratchy, heavy material draped around her shoulders, his sport jacket. It smelled like him, and she swore if she lived through this that she'd never give it back.

She heard him prop one of Lance's folding chairs beneath the window, step on it, and test its strength. Then, he pulled her up beside him. Inches apart, she felt his breath on her face again. She reached for his face with her free hand and felt stubble on his cheek.

Then, she kissed him. Quick, but deliciously satisfying.

She reached for the window handle, slid it up and pulled it toward them, opening it all the way. It creaked to a foot wide, enough to scoot through. Thick, wet snow that had blanketed the window sloshed to the floor.

A cold blast of air hit her in the face. Ice pellets seemed to nick her skin like razor blades. Red and blue lights flashed outside, police responding to a bomb threat call. Mara could see the faint outline of the trees in the field that ran along the back of the complex.

Jesse boosted her up and out, and she plunked into a snow bank. She stood and shook off clinging clumps of snow. Chills shook her body, and she gathered Jesse's sport coat around her.

Whump! Jesse landed beside her in the snowdrift. "You okay?" He jumped up and brushed himself off.

"Freezing, but otherwise fine." Her teeth chattered. She wobbled and found that the cold had slowed her movements. Jesse rubbed his hands up and down her arms, warming her. "We've got to move."

Mara nodded.

He gripped her hand, and they ran away from the edifice, distancing them from possible explosion. They circled the perimeter until they arrived near the main entrance of the complex. The building's generator had still not kicked in, but the headlights and flashers of a half-dozen police cars lit the night from a safe distance. Dozens of students, some still dressed in their finest and some in night clothes, loitered around the *carabinieri* cruisers.

Onlookers approached. Professors that had since left the gathering returned in their cars. The few faculty that had stayed to party filled them in on truths and rumors.

Mara and Jesse approached Signore Jack, who stood with Stanky, Utica and Boots. Mimi enveloped Kate in his arms, and they huddled with Lance and his partner. Ms. Thompson, a school secretary with tattoos on her neck, was explaining that a bomb threat had been phoned into Oslo at the main reception around 2:00 am. Oslo then called the police and placed a round-robin call to the entire complex. It wasn't until he started banging on doors that residents took him seriously. Now, it was close to 3:00, and the building still had not been emptied or secured.

Dean Arella stood hunched beneath a winter coat with his arms crossed, telling an explosives officer that this had to be the work of the serial killer. "It's the Sculptor. He's decided to take out the entire building, in one fell swoop."

Mara overheard the cop tell Arella that the police had not yet determined the veracity of the threat, or the identity of the caller, and that he shouldn't waste time worrying until they had. Nevertheless, Mara still agonized over the people left inside. Where were Kristen and Lana?

Stanky lit a joint and said that his father would be rippin' if he lost his priceless statues and busts.

Art Professor Volker slapped himself on the forehead. "*O'Dio*, we have to save the sculptures!" A *carabiniero* gripped Volker's elbow and told him in Italian to stay put or spend the night locked up.

Mara spied Kristen exit the building, and she released Jesse's hand to run to her through the heavy, falling snow. She hugged her roommate, dressed in a heavy robe and UGGs, and realized at that moment how much Mara valued their friendship. "So glad you're okay. Have you seen Lana?"

"She went out clubbing hours ago with Miguelito." Kristen swigged orange juice out of a plastic half gallon and twirled the ends of her hair with the other. "I got the bomb call; lights went out; felt your bed, was still made up. Grabbed the juice; went in the hall; got tangled up in all the people." Her eyes barely open, Kristen continued to guzzle juice. "Want some?"

Mara's stomach lurched, and her head spun for a moment. "No, thanks. I need to sit a minute." She stumbled back against one of the police vehicles and crouched with her head between her legs. She shook her head to shake off the dizziness.

Suddenly, the lights in the building powered up. They blazed through the snow so bright, it looked like it had burst into flames—a bit of a jolt during a bomb threat evacuation.

A police van arrived. Officers dressed in bomb removal garb jumped out, conferred for a moment with Dean Arella and the senior crime scene officer, and then trudged inside. Kristen wandered closer to the van.

Though her body was freezing, Mara placed her head against the cold steel of the police car to rid herself of a sudden pounding headache. After a few minutes, it subsided. She stumbled away from the crowd of onlookers, toward a clump of trees near the road that led into the complex, knowing full well what was coming next.

She hurled. Hurled some more.

Her stomach felt much better. But, her head still felt...dazed. She didn't think that she'd had *that* much to drink. A couple "army tanks," some champagne, a couple beers...then again, maybe she had exceeded her limit.

A weird thought permeated her fog. She questioned that last beer and recalled wondering at the party whether or not it had been hers. It occurred to her now that it had tasted slightly off.

No chance to consider it for very long, though. A gaggle of four or five police officers in black uniforms sporting AK47s strapped across their chests that had been talking earlier near their cruiser now approached her.

Oh God, she did not want company right now. Please no interrogations, no statements, no idle chitchat. She was cold, sick, and exhausted. And the only place where she could sleep it off might explode at any minute.

The smoking, gun-toting, twenty-something bunch of *carabinieri* sauntered closer through the sleeting snow, smiling at her, ogling her.

Mara looked toward the complex, and realized then just how far she'd wandered away from the crowd. Amid the chaos, and through the storm, it was likely that no one would hear or see her if anything happened to her.

One of the cops reached out and touched her shoulder. "*Ciao, bella,*" he purred. Like hyenas drawn to a feast, the rest of the group circled around her. A few whistled, while others agreed with their comrade's appreciation of her physical assets.

Mara slapped away the hand on her shoulder. "*Buona notte, polizia,*" she said, bidding good evening to the officers and attempting to slink away from their circle.

Another officer had snuck up behind her, and he ran his fingers over her snow-wet hair. "Oh, but, you are so beautiful. Please stay and talk awhile." Others concurred or threw kisses in the air.

Mara struggled to arrange her limbs into her brown-belt defense stance in case things got too ugly, but her damn head kept spinning, and her stomach lurched again. She scooped up some snow and rubbed it on her cheeks.

The five swarmed in closer, too close for comfort, and she swung out blindly at them, her head swirling too fast for her fist to connect.

Snow whirled. Lights spun. Thoughts flashed through her mind: the bomb, the serial killer, Jesse, her career, her dad.

She took a step back and lost her footing, and fell backward through the blinding snow into a tall drift.

One of them laughed. Another's radio requested assistance, but the five men continued to stand over her, taunting her with their indifference.

A scuffle ensued to which her consciousness was not entirely privy, and one of the cops hit the ground.

She heard a muffled voice through the haze, shouting at all of them, but she could not make out the words, nor could she discern a face through the storm.

She crawled away from the brouhaha, and back toward the red and blue lights surrounding Stella Luna.

Still on her hands and knees, she encountered some rocks, switched direction in the dark, overcompensated, and ran out of real estate. She lost her balance and pitched forward, tumbling in the darkness, and then splashed into a ditch of freezing cold water.

She must have landed in the ravine by the road. Water soaked through the sport coat, and she knew she had to get out quickly or risk exposure and hypothermia.

Her weakened body would not obey the direct orders of her brain. She felt sluggish and clumsy, and could not climb free of the mangled branches in the snow-filled gully. She lay still for a moment and gathered her strength.

The faint sound of tiny ice pellets slowly building a coffin around her limp body frightened her. But, her legs were so cold they had become immobile. Her feet felt like heavy blocks of ice, her bare hands like slabs of frozen meat.

The smell of Jesse wafted to her brain from the wet coat around her body, and she wished she'd had the chance to know him better.

The cold, along with that off-kilter beer that she'd imbibed, finally overtook her. She could not break through the haze, nor did she want to. She had no fight left. She just wanted to sleep.

At that moment, she felt herself being lifted. Strong arms embraced her, enfolded her against a mercifully warm body.

Then, the two, as one, were running.

Mara's last thought before finally losing consciousness: Rescuer or captor?

Chapter 10

Parched. So thirsty. Mara's tongue felt like a line-dried towel.

She licked her lips. They were dry and cracked. Her toes and fingers ached. She stretched her legs and cracked both ankles. She felt warm beneath the covers and didn't want to get up. But, she needed to drink some water.

The last thing Mara usually ever did when she woke up was open her eyes. As if in denial, she always put it off until the very last second. Now, through her crusty eyelids (she must have forgotten to wash off the eye makeup last night), the natural light of a gloomy morning filtered in through the windows of her apartment. She pulled the pillow over her head and rolled over. And kept rolling. Across the wide expanse of a comfy, double-sized mattress.

Except, she didn't have a double bed. The Stella Luna complex provided lumpy singles. Where the hell was she?

She cracked open one eyelid and peered out at the room through her lashes. Not her room.

Her vision adjusted to the dim light, and she opened her other eye.

The mattress lay without a frame in the middle of a 100 square foot room, atop a glossy wood floor, surrounded by chipped and peeling plastered walls. She pulled the sheet and wool blanket up to her chin and slid up to a sitting position. There was a single closed door, two slightly ajar bi-fold closets, and a closed windowpane with partially open wooden shutters. Other than a desk and chair, the room was bereft of furniture.

She was alone, and yet she suddenly felt consumed with paranoia. Her hands trembled so much that they fluttered the blue polka-dot sheets. Terror gripped her, and she felt like her chest would explode.

She felt eyes upon her as if they were all around her. Looking out from every direction, they indeed glared at her.

Life-size, plaster statues lined the walls. Nearly a dozen of them; most of them whole, and some of them missing limbs. She felt like a patient in a teaching hospital, where an entire group of interns had assembled around to observe the removal of her spleen.

What the hell kind of place was this? A museum? A shrine? A church? What kind of sick freak collects armless, faceless statues of men and women and—

Suddenly it dawned on her. The Sculptor. She'd awoken inside the chambers of the serial killer.

She clawed the covers from her chest and looked down. Her cocktail dress. It all came back to her now. She'd been buttonholed by the police officers while evacuating RU's Festa at Stella Luna, and then she'd fallen into the ravine. The serial killer must have taken down the cops and then captured her. She remembered passing out in someone's arms during the storm, cloaked in a drugged stupor (perhaps he'd surreptitiously slipped something in her drink at the party). The monster must have shuffled her off to...where the hell was she? The boudoir of his slaughterhouse?

She silently scrambled off of the mattress and tugged on her UGGs. Grateful the sick bastard had not removed her dress, she wrapped the wool blanket around her shoulders and ran to the window. She peeked through the slats of the shutter and saw a snow-splotched tin roof outside. She surmised from the position of the sun that it had to be about 6:30 am. Classes were to start at 9:00 am, and she wondered how long it would take the university to learn that she would soon become the Sculptor's next serial victim.

The window overlooked a small courtyard, almost three stories up. She opened the window a crack and scooped in some snow. She put it in her mouth, relishing the moisture, but did so slowly, careful not to upset her stomach. She was desperate to quench her thirst and rebuild her strength.

The slope of the roof looked steep enough to break both legs if she tried to escape. The surrounding apartment buildings were too far away to draw the attention of anyone who might be looking in her direction. She slurped down more fresh snow and turned back to the room, hoping to seek out a weapon. She'd have to fight the bastard and flee through the door, or die trying.

The closet behind the bi-folds held a few pairs of jeans, a furry denim jacket, a worn, brown sport jacket, t-shirts, soccer cleats, and a couple pairs of running shoes. She searched for a wire hanger to poke out the killer's eyes, but they were all plastic.

Mara glanced at the statues, wishing they'd stop eyeballing her. She remembered the graphic newsreel about the killer plastering his victims' body parts. Some, he left behind at the crime scene, to show off his flair for technique, and others, he collected as trophies. Did any of these statutes boast an actual head or someone's appendages? And which parts of Mara's anatomy was he planning to use to further complement his décor?

She ran to the window and sucked in more cold air to ward off a panic attack. There was no way she'd let him take her.

Then, a noise from the other side of the room sounded. At the room's entrance, the porcelain doorknob turned slowly. He was coming for her.

She quickly scanned the room again for some sort of weapon. Nothing.

Wait...

She dove for the mattress and slid her hands beneath the fitted sheet and yanked two fabric buttons from the pillow top. Three-inch-long, metal corkscrew tips jutted from each fastener like thick wine bottle openers. She nestled them in both hands between her fisted fingers and decided to corkscrew the sonofabitch.

The doorknob twisted hard and came away from the jamb.

Mara jumped to her feet and shrugged off the wool blanket.

The door creaked open an inch.

Then, it slowly inched forward until a foot-wide gap appeared.

Should she pounce on him from across the room like a wild banshee? What if he had a gun? He'd shoot her dead before she'd have a chance to impale him with her corkscrews. She wished she'd had time to sneak behind the door and jump him from behind.

Too late. He was coming in.

Mara grasped both metal mattress hooks, maintained a proper karate stance, and waited to meet the whites of his eyes, ready to take down the biggest menace to society since Jack the Ripper.

Chapter 11

In he came.

It was a man, holding a tray, laden with breakfast fare and grinning wide.

"Wow. You are not a morning person," he said. "More like Medusa meets Captain Hook meets Karate Kid. Bet you could use this espresso."

Jesse Tonno greeted her with all the boyish charm she loved to despise, and she never adored him more than at that precise moment.

Mara lowered her weapons and eased out of her attack position. "I didn't know where I was when I woke up." She gestured at the statues that comprised most of her surroundings. "I thought I'd been abducted by the Sculptor."

She glanced at the steel coffee pot as he lowered the tray to the desk. Her reflection showed snake-like coils of hair that seemed to stand on end atop her head, and black mascara that shadowed beneath her eyes like a raccoon—Medusa would have been an improvement.

Feeling sheepish, she pulled back her hair and wound it into a bun atop her head, tucking back the tendrils that fell onto her face. She smiled as he poured her a double espresso. "I thought you were the serial killer," she said.

"How do you know I'm not?" Jesse said. He winked at her and offered a plate of cookies.

She bit into an almond cookie, and then wolfed it down. She took two more and ate them, licked the orange icing from her fingertips. How did she know Jesse Tonno wasn't the serial killer? Maybe he was just fattening her up so that he could plaster her into some authentic Renaissance sculpture?

"I love a woman who's not afraid to eat, and you can really pack it in. Go freshen up, and I'll make you some eggs." Jesse led her into a common area with a table and chairs, and pointed out the bathroom off to the side.

After showering, she'd squeezed back into her silk dress for the impending walk of shame, and sniffed her way into a narrow galley kitchen where she found him cooking bacon. The only other man who'd ever cooked for her was her dad. Serial killer or not, she could get used this.

While they feasted over scrambled eggs, Jesse explained that, according to Signore Jack, the bomb threat had been a prank, and that after four hours, all the residents of Stella Luna had been allowed back inside.

"When we separated after escaping through the window, I tracked a trail of UGG boots down to the ravine by the road. I found you there, nearly unconscious. Scared me out of my mind."

She smiled. "I'm sorry I scared you. I felt so woozy. I think I drank a doctored beer, not sure if it was meant for me or not."

"Well, I took down one of those lousy cops who left you there. A sergeant came and reprimanded the rest of them." Jesse further explained that he'd whisked her from Stella Luna to his own apartment so that she could recover far away from the chaos.

Satisfied with his interpretation of the night, Mara opened the conversation to discussing their school apprenticeship. Jesse showed her his plans for imparting the finance and economics aspect of the international business curriculum, and she shed light on her agenda for the marketing side.

"I'm impressed," Jesse said, pushing back his plate and sipping his hot tea. "I knew you had solid credentials, but I never expected such a well-planned classroom strategy. You've constructed great deductive reasoning lessons, Miss Marple."

She felt herself blushing. She normally dismissed accolades, not that most people were as forthright with them as Jesse was. She always felt that her dad was proud of her, but he was never one to gush. Jesse's praise threw her off her guard, and she escaped by carrying her dish to the kitchen sink.

He edged in behind her in the narrow walkway of the prep area. "I'm sorry if I embarrassed you. Just wanted to let you know I respect our teaching partnership."

She rinsed her dish and felt him brush past her back. He reached to put the syrup bottle back into the cupboard above her, and she flicked her wet fingers over her shoulder, spritzing his face with cold water.

He cupped a handful of tap water and splashed her face. She stood wide-eyed, incredulous that he'd be so bold as to douse her in a cocktail dress.

She turned and threatened to dump a mug of water over his head. But, he jumped back, grabbed her wrist, and pulled her toward him.

Their lips just inches apart, he tugged her body closer, pressing her into his broad chest.

Then, before she knew what was happening, he angled the faucet sprayer right in front of her eyes.

She ducked and averted the stream that jetted through the kitchen, and dashed into the common area, out of reach of the spray. The wall clock struck the top of the hour and she realized just how little time she had before class. Her career always took precedence over fun. Time to go.

She went back to the bedroom for her boots, passing a TV room with three other bedrooms off the back. She thought that they probably belonged to Jesse's roommates—Utica and Kiever. And someone else.

In Jesse's bedroom, she screwed the two metal plugs back into his mattress. She pulled on her UGGS while he lingered in the door jamb. "What's with all the creepy statues?" she asked.

"They belong to Stanky's dad," Jesse said. "His father, the Senator, is on RU's board, and he inundates the school with originals and replicas to enhance the art appreciation of students. As if there aren't enough statues to visit on every street corner of Rome, right?

"He bought this flat for Stanky to live in during undergrad and grad school. Utica and I have been here about five or six years. And, Professor Volker, RU's art prof lives here too.

"This flat represents the statue surplus zone. He rotates displays every few months. Volker loves the Botticelli displays. Utica doesn't care. Stanky keeps Michelangelo's *Rape of the Sabine Women* in his room. I like to keep all the Caesars," Jesse said.

"Is Stanky an art major?" She rubbed her hand along the bust of Marcus Agrippa.

"Stanky doesn't really have a major. He dabbles while Daddy pays for it. Mostly, he swims."

"Swims?" Mara said.

"He swims for RU, Trinity, and Libby—all three teams. That's his passion."

Jesse gave her a hooded sweatshirt to wear for the cold trip back to Stella Luna. It bore his scent, the same one that lingered on the sport coat that she'd worn during the evacuation. She recalled his outdoorsy smell and the feel of his stubble against her neck when he'd slipped the jacket on her at the party the night before.

Easy girl. He's your colleague.

Then, he reached under the table for something on a chair. He showed her a hat, a wide-brimmed bush hat. She gasped. He placed it on her head, and the enormous crown bobbled atop her mane. She removed it, and sniffed the inside of the crown. Smelled like jellybeans.

"You were the one who helped me catch the falling beans on the plane?"

He blushed and flashed a smile. Her own face flushed with heat.

She handed him the Indiana Jones hat. "Thanks, but I like it much better on you." Together, they walked to the exit, and lingered at the threshold.

"Thank you for helping me with the jellybeans. And, I never did thank you for saving me from those policemen and plucking me out of the ravine last night," Mara said. "Not sure I like the work ethic of Italian cops."

"Mmm. I've run into my fair share of lousy cops," he said. A dark look crept over his face that she wasn't sure how to interpret, but something told her that Jesse's implied run-ins with the law would not improve her opinion of him, so she didn't press the matter further. What she didn't know wouldn't hurt her.

"Thank you," she said. "For whisking me to safety during the bomb threat. For saving me from those brutes. For the warm bed, and for breakfast." She kissed him on the cheek. "I'm really looking forward to working with you this—"

The door to the flat burst open, and laughter ushered in Kiever and Utica. Behind them followed four thirty-something, bodacious women dressed in not much more than tight mini-skirts and creamy blue eye-shadow.

The six seated themselves, wasting no time in pouring a bottle of vodka into clinking glasses that seemed to surface out of thin air.

"C'mon you two. Sit and drink with us," Kiever said. "A little breakfast before class." He drew a long puff from a cigarette. "Jesse, I brought two redheads back to the flat, baby. Just for you. They're the spitting image of my actress mom. Only these bitches don't spit, you know what I mean?"

"Neither did your mother." Utica laughed hysterically in Stanky's face. Stanky slapped his knee and laughed with him.

As if on cue, the two redheads with bright painted cheeks and short fur jackets snaked their limbs around Jesse's neck and chest, purring Italian obscenities into his ears.

In that single moment, the scene in front of her solidified in her mind that the only relationship that she'd ever share with Jesse Tonno was a purely professional one. Jesse was smart, fun, and personable. Way too personable with the ladies to ever measure up to her standards.

Mara threw a wave at the group and walked through the door. She'd spend the next few months with a clear focus: bury her father and springboard her career, all the while safeguarding her personal safety against a killer at large.

"Mara, wait!" Jesse shouted to her, just as the door slammed shut.

Downstairs, she stormed through an arched atrium and out of the building without looking back.

***

An unexpected treat lay sprawled across the mattress in the morning light, a redhead who resembled the glorious silver screen beauty Maureen O'Hara, both in her appearance and her fierce passion.

He'd prepared the pasty white plaster in the wee hours of the night for another work he'd hoped to sculpt that morning, but time and circumstances had gotten away from him.

Instead of wasting it, he used the batter to encase the perfect set of breasts that this lavish siren presented him, nipples up. With gloved hands, he spread the creamy paste over her soft, porcelain swells.

She stared at him with large, expressive eyes. The Sculptor knew she would have responded to these soft caresses just as she had when they'd made love, had he not pumped her veins full of antifreeze first.

There. Time to set and dry. He'd chainsaw her perfect tits in the next couple of days and adhere them to one of his Botticelli pieces by the end of the week.

He cleaned up and left, and hurried to catch his subway train.

He did not want to be late for his first day of class.

Chapter 12

Ten o'clock Monday morning, Chief Inspector Enzo Tranchille entered *la Questura di Roma* on Via San Vitale, Rome's central police precinct. He took the stairs two at a time to the Homicide Division on the third floor, and strolled into his small office at the end of the hall.

The Sculptor file lay in the center of his cherry wood desk, a relic from the Byzantine era that had been passed down for generations through his late wife's family. When Matilda had died five years earlier, he had the desk moved to his office, his home away from home. Her favorite lavender-perfumed stationery remained undisturbed in the middle side-drawer, and every morning he opened it to allow her favorite scent to permeate the otherwise dank room.

Right now, the lavender mingled with the aroma of the coffee that he set to brew on the hot plate in the corner. Everyone, including Matilda, hated his coffee. Everyone but his boss, Police Chief Dante Asciugamano, whom everyone affectionately referred to as *Capo* Sciug. Enzo occasionally enjoyed a fine espresso, but he and Sciug loved their weak, American coffee, with lots of cream and sugar in oversized mugs.

Enzo carried two cups of the steaming brew into the police captain's office and shut the door. Sciug nodded his thanks, and Enzo sat himself in the leather chair that faced the desk.

Without looking up from a file he was reading, Sciug addressed him in the same Tuscan dialect in which he and Enzo had been raised. "Give me the latest, Enzo."

Enzo had carried in the Sculptor file beneath his arm. It sat on his lap for reference, but he knew the details of the file by rote. He'd typed in the most recent updates around four that morning, after the Stella Luna bomb evacuation, and then caught a couple of hours of sleep before reporting to work. He rubbed his eyes and proceeded.

"First off, as you know, the Stella Luna bomb threat proved a hoax. An incident arose during the evacuation. A handful of rookie officers just transferred from the Civitavecchia precinct have been suspended without pay, pending investigation."

Sciug looked up from his file, shaking his head. His dark hair had thinned over the years, but he'd stopped the comb-overs last May after a fluke skydiving accident almost scalped him. Physically fit for a police captain and as genial as a corner pub bartender, Sciug earned his position after years of solving high-profile drug trafficking investigations.

He and Enzo had graduated the police academy after their required military service, and even when Enzo had gravitated toward Homicide, the two maintained their weekly *Scopa* and *Briscola* card tournaments. Now, they sipped their coffees slowly, savoring the flavor of Enzo's special Kona/Colombian blend.

Enzo continued, "Prior to handling the Stella Luna evac, I attended their RU gala, mingled with the students and professors. Nothing formal, just making my presence known among the handful of Sculptor suspects."

Sciug touched his forefinger to his thumb as if counting off. "There's our primary suspect, Fritz Arella. He's the latest victim's boyfriend, and son of the dean, right?"

"Stepson. Fritz attends Trinity U, but they're on trimester, and his father must have urged him to attend, as the three colleges participate in a lot of functions and activities together. He looked like hell, suicidal even. It could be just a good show while he stalks other victims? I've got a man on him wherever he goes."

Sciug counted off the second suspect with his middle finger. "There's that Kiever kid. Lifelong student of RU. Son of the American Senator who collects all those sculptures, right? Is the kid an art collector, too? Or, is he taunting us, publicizing the statues like trophies? He's gotta couple close buddies we should keep our eye on too, but this kid has means, motive, and opportunity."

Enzo nodded. "So many of them do. That's the problem. The three other suspects are the art profs of the universities that the killer seems to target. All had access to the sculpting tools and plaster residue we found at many of the crime scenes. But, so did their art students, who we're also tracking."

Enzo then pondered the relationship between Jesse and his other American roommate, Michael Utica. The two appeared to share a solid friendship, but for some reason Utica always acted nervous whenever Jesse brought him around. Better to explore that avenue further before divulging premature notions to the police captain.

"Go on," Sciug urged.

"There's also an American professor who's been teaching international business at RU for a few years, Jackson Sugardale. Kids call him 'Signore Jack.' Ex-Army Ranger, and former CEO of a huge trade show company. Settled on Italian soil for about twenty years now, tight with the RU board of directors. Signore Jack likes sexy relationships with young female students—so, lots of opportunity.

"All in all, it's a good size net, so far," Enzo said. "But, we have a few things to hang our hat on, a few leads we're heavily pursuing."

Enzo tipped his head back and emptied his cup. "The six victims, the ones that we've uncovered anyway, all resemble classic American movie starlets. Our killer has a penchant for courting and then...preserving, I guess, dead ringers for beauties like Rita Hayworth, Lana Turner, Jean Harlow, Sofia Loren. Perp's probably acting on latent mother issues."

Sciug leaned back in his leather chair.

Enzo smiled. He knew Sciug respected him for dipping into perpetrators' psyches, but his boss only wanted to hear the facts.

"Each crime scene is unique," Enzo continued, "but one common thread is just that—a fuchsia-colored silk ribbon or string that the killer somehow weaves into the victim's remains. Sometimes it's hard to find, stuffed deep into an orifice, or sewn into the skin. Other times it's simply wound around a finger, or tied into the victim's hair.

"The lab's been banging their heads because the thread's origin is so far indeterminable. The material's composition is unique. Can't trace it to any manufacturer, anywhere in the world. We've widened our research, and have gotten in touch with Europol and INTERPOL for assistance."

"And?" Sciug asked.

"So far nothing." Enzo stood. "Wish the lab had more to work on, but the bastard hasn't left an iota of his own DNA. Only assorted sculpting tools, clean except for the dried plaster, and the thread, as his signature. Sonofabitch is crafty."

Enzo rubbed his head behind his right ear, an action that relaxed him. Matilda would do it when she'd find him up late working. "This case reminds me of the one from twenty years ago. The serial killer who murdered all those canoodling couples in the Florence countryside."

"I remember it. A journalist at *La Nazione* had dubbed him *il Mostro di Firenze*, The Monster of Florence," Sciug said. "Cold case now. Perp might be in his fifties or sixties, or even be dead by now." Sciug looked up at Enzo. "Weren't you on that case?"

Enzo nodded. "I was a rookie cop; I wasn't allowed in on it, but I followed along, unofficially at least. Case was completely bungled by everyone involved, right on down to the prosecutors.

"The journalist who named the Monster seemed to work out the truer details, and the prosecution tried to pin it on him. Before he disappeared from the public eye, the reporter had told me about a silk sash found tied around the Monster's victims' necks or private parts. Coincidence or not, might be worth putting some men on tracking down the old forensics reports from the Florence *Questura*, see if they tie in." Enzo stood.

"Consider it done."

Enzo patted the file. "That's it so far."

Sciug came around the desk and shook Enzo's hand. "Keep up the good work, *paisano.*"

"I'm headed over to the three colleges today. I'll try to nose around campus life. I'll be in touch," Enzo said.

"When you get to RU," Sciug said, "give my regards to your nephew."

Chapter 13

Jesse scrambled into International Business class late that first morning. Even so, dashing in at 10:10 he was one of the first to arrive.

Aside from Signore Jack. He sat behind his desk, feet up and his hands crossed behind his head, waiting for the rest of the stragglers.

"I don't know why the school has a shindig the night before school begins, but it is what it is," Jack told Jesse, seated in the front row. "When I get to fifty percent attendance, I'll just start slapping my jaws together and see if anyone pays attention."

Jesse popped two Excedrin, and Mara walked in. He bolted upright in his chair. So did the professor.

Jesse recalled her bedraggled appearance earlier that morning and was shocked by her transformation. She strode into the classroom dressed in business casual, with a briefcase over her shoulder, and her hair pinned perfectly atop her head. He thought she was as delectable as a hot fudge sundae.

He loved hot fudge sundaes.

Mara murmured apologies to the professor and removed her scarf. She sidled into the empty seat beside Jesse, smiled curtly at him, and faced the front board. Severe freezer burn.

Jack approached the two of them, his carefree demeanor replaced by professionalism. The three spent five minutes comparing notes, five more handing out syllabi to the now nearly full class of sixteen, and thirty seconds were spent posting their office hours. Then, *il Maestro* took center stage.

Jack explained that Monday mornings would entail review and the delivery of brand new IntBiz material. Tuesday and Wednesday evening classes would encompass lecture, research, and lab work. Thursday morning involved a quiz and more new material. Of course, for Mara and Jesse, additional hours of homework and preparation were necessary to fulfill the internship requirement, but most weekends were free for travel or an occasional field trip.

The most revered tradition of the spring semester was the Venice/Alps field trip. All three major colleges were invited, involving undergrads and grads of all disciplines and majors. The two-day trip to the floating city on the Adriatic featured visits to museums, prestigious corporate headquarters, athletic facilities, wineries, and ancient libraries. It culminated with two days skiing in the nearby Swiss Alps.

Jesse had two full weeks to convince Mara to hang with him on this trip of a lifetime. He looked over at her swept up hair, lined lips, shined shoes, and accordion file of papers. Ice princess.

She met his eyes, winked, and rose to hand out a class forecast, and he swore she'd brushed against his arm deliberately. Full of promise, anxious for the challenge, he prayed that the ice had begun to melt.

***

Tuesday evening's class was arduous. Jesse returned straight home to his empty flat to grade a statistics exercise and then write the introduction to his Vespa project, followed by some other work that he'd put off for too long.

All three roommates were out. Volker had stayed to haunt the school library. Utica and Kiever had headed to The Pit, a hangout near the university created by three American undergrads two years back. The Pit featured Budweiser on tap, Springsteen and U2 on the speakers, and bar stools and couches in a dimly lit underground cavern, beneath a street-level Italian coffee bar, called American Bar. At first, it catered to homesick undergrads, but word spread and the little pub took off with all three major colleges. It was a great place to grab a quick beer after class or to stay and dance the night away on the subterranean dance floor.

By midnight, Jesse had finally completed his work. Time for a run. He went to the closet to fetch a pair of running shoes. His hand skimmed past the pair of soccer cleats in his closet, but then he reached back to them. Should he head to Enzo's for a quick scrimmage? The man rarely slept and Jesse was sure that they could both use the company. He slipped on the left one and laced it. For a split second, the smell of the grassy mud that stuck between the cleats transported him to the last professional futbol game he'd ever played.

In a championship game between Roma Sud and Lazio, he'd scored two goals in a row to tie the game. He knew he had it in him to score the final one and claim victory for a team that had had a stellar season. With minutes to go, he'd tangled with Lazio's best player, Randolfo Fettini, stolen the ball, and scored the winning goal, which earned seventeen-year-old Jesse Tonno a place in Roma Sud history as the youngest Most Valuable Player in a perfect season.

Unfortunately, that same goal had ended his career. Before the ball had sailed cleanly into the net, Jesse's battle with Fettini for control of it had also resulted in a torn ankle ligament. The moment he'd heard his ankle snap, Jesse knew that his short career as a professional ball player was over.

In his room now, Jesse threw the cleats back into the closet. He flexed the pins that held his left ankle in place. The ones that ached during rainstorms, and after too much sport. He plopped himself onto the floor mattress, rolled off of a loose button that jabbed into his side, and threw a pillow over his head. That night, in his dreams, he replayed his best, and worst, sports memory ever.

***

The next night's class was just as tough as the first. Signore Jack was a superb teacher who kept everyone rapt with attention. After forty-five minutes, he interrupted his lecture for the usual fifteen-minute break. Students milled around him with questions.

Jesse glanced at Mara. For the first time since he'd known her, she appeared flustered.

After two classes, gone was Mara's business-casual attire which was replaced by a pink Buffalo Bills hoodie and tight gray sweatpants. She turned to face him, swinging her ponytail. "He covers so damn much," she whispered, peering at him with those long eyelashes and rosy apple cheeks. "And he does it at lightning pace. My head's spinning."

Jesse wanted to reach out and touch her small button nose with the tip of his finger. Instead, he grabbed her hand. "I've got an idea. Come with me?"

She smiled and nodded. "Where to?"

"Trust me." Jesse led her through the throng of students by Jack's desk and out the IntBiz door. They ran through the short corridor, past Ryan Volker's Art in Rome lecture room and six other classrooms on that floor.

Jesse halted at the exit to the stairwell to sidestep a man hunched over the drinking fountain. *Zio* Enzo. His uncle, the chief inspector, had to be checking up on potential suspects in the serial killer case. Time to go. Jesse was in no mood to listen to any updates. Not here. Not now. He tugged Mara's hand before Enzo spotted him and busted through the door to the narrow stairwell.

He entangled his fingers with Mara's, and together they tore down two flights of stairs, until they reached the ground floor. Out of breath, they both raced through the small university lobby and out the front double doors into the mid-February night air.

"Holy crap, it's freezing out here," Mara said. The falling snow took seconds to cover her flowing brown hair.

This time, he did it. He reached out with one finger and flicked snowflakes from the tip of her button nose. He couldn't help himself.

Still grasping her hand, he tugged her down the small side street and into the inviting warmth of the American Bar café. They dashed to the counter and Jesse held up two fingers to the barista. "*Due cappucini, per favore. Con doppio espresso. E, un po di ghiaccio.*"

She looked at him with wide eyes and a brilliant smile that he felt in his groin. "Oh, boy, cappuccinos with a double shot of espresso. I might not sleep tonight," she said.

The coffees and a glass of ice water arrived. Still holding her hand, he dumped two scoops of sugar in each, and then tossed three ice cubes in each one. He reached for her, brushed his lips against hers. Then, he raised his demitasse cup to salute her. She raised hers and they clinked. Together, they threw their heads back and downed both cappuccinos in seconds flat.

She looked over at him with a wide grin. "Aaaah. That was delicious."

"Oh, my God," he said.

"What is it?" Mara said, a look of alarm spreading across her face.

"You have a foam mustache. You've never looked so damn cute."

She laughed at him. Then, she tugged at the hand he was holding and yanked him out of the bar. He'd just had enough time to throw a few Euros on the wood when she pulled him out the door and tore back across the street. They slipped on the ice, but remained upright.

"Easy girl," he said, grinning while she pulled him toward the door.

The espresso carried them back up the steps, two at a time until they reached the second floor. They arrived at the door to the classroom just as Signore Jack was taking the podium. Jack nodded as they slipped into their seats, and then he turned to the blackboard.

Mara turned to Jesse, her face flushed. "That was so exhilarating!" she whispered.

He squeezed her hand before letting go to take up his pen. "Next class, another run?"

She nodded and giggled. "Next, time, we make it a beer run."

That's when Jesse knew for sure.

With Mara, he'd reached the point of no return.

Chapter 14

As class wound to its end that evening, butterflies still frolicked in Mara's stomach from their run to the pub. Damn it, she'd let her guard down. She'd sworn to keep this relationship with Jesse professional, but the things he said, the way he looked at her, his carefree manner, always seemed to push her over the edge. She would just have to keep reminding herself to rein it in. Stay on course. Career first.

She slipped out into the hallway, where dozens of other students mingled. She edged over to the tiny office that belonged to Signore Jack, where she and Jesse held office hours while Jack taught his undergrad classes. Jesse and Jack were already inside discussing tomorrow morning's lecture.

"Come on in, darlin'," Jack said. "I spoke with the rep over at Ferrari today. He was extremely impressed with your semester outline and proposal. He's looking forward to meeting you in Venice next week."

Mara smiled. "Me too."

"Before you go, here's your copy of tomorrow's plan," Jack said.

"Please excuse me," a voice said from behind her. "Is it possible to have a few brief words with the two gentlemen?"

Mara turned and faced the short Columbo-esque detective that she'd seen at the cocktail party, the one in charge of the serial killer case.

"Please allow me to introduce myself," he said to Mara. "I am Chief Inspector Enzo Tranchille. It is my pleasure to make your acquaintance."

He was short, sweet, and enchanting. And, he smelled nice. Kind of like Old Spice aftershave. She wasn't sure if they wore that in Italy, but he smelled just like her dad used to. She shook his hand. "Mara Silvestri."

"Forgive the intrusion," Enzo said. "I happened to be on campus when class ended and thought I'd stop by to ask these fine gentlemen some quick questions."

Mara shook her head. "Not a problem, Signore Tranchille—"

"Please, *cara*, call me Enzo, I insist."

"Alright, Enzo. I'm finished here for the evening. They're all yours." She thanked Jack for the lesson plan, waved to Jesse, and left.

Suddenly, she felt the hairs on her neck stand up. Was it because she felt the three men watching her as she walked down the hall before stepping inside the stairwell? Or was it because Rome's chief detective on the serial killer case had questions for her boss and colleague, two men whom she was just beginning to feel like she could trust?

***

Mara put her hood up and zippered her fuchsia ski parka to keep out the cold. She trudged through the crunchy, frozen slush to the corner of Via Salustio, took a right and headed down Via Veneto, the main thoroughfare that would lead her to her subway entrance.

She cradled her folders and notebooks to her chest, cursing the fact that she should have taken the time to put them in her oversized black Prada shoulder bag. Her hands were freezing. She shuffled the papers with one hand in an effort to keep her fingers moving and as she did, she noticed that she had the wrong folder. She'd taken Jesse's Vespa notes from Jack, instead of her Ferrari notes. Coincidence?

She turned and jogged all the way back to their shared office space at school. Inside, Signore Jack leaned against the desk, chomping an apple and reading a report.

Jesse and Enzo had already left.

"Hello again, darlin'! To what to do I owe this pleasure?" Jack said.

She explained her mix-up and swapped folders.

"Seems like a happy accident to me. I was just about to head over to Trilussa for a beer. Care to join me, little lady?"

"Trilussa? Where's that?" Mara asked, suddenly feeling like she could slug back a couple Peronis.

"The old Jewish ghetto. Trastevere. Near the Vatican. I know it's a bit far from Stella Luna apartments, but I have my car and I could drop you after."

She nodded. She could use a beer, and a few tips from the Great Trade Show Promoter.

He locked up and the two walked down the corridor toward the stairwell. They passed a few students preparing to leave for the night. In the small lounge at the end of the hall, she spied a group of five lingering on the worn couches and chairs, smoking and laughing.

"Mara!" Kristen called to her from the arm of one chair. Beside her was Lana, sitting on Miguelito's lap. From behind a wooden pillar, Jesse spun around to face her. His eyes lit up when he saw her, and he grinned. Then, he spotted Jack, and Mara watched Jesse's face grow dark.

"*Professore* and I are going to a bar called Trilussa. Want to come?" she said to the lot of them.

Suddenly, Michael Utica appeared from behind the other wooden pillar. "Trilussa! Big ol' boots of beer, baby! I'm in." Utica grabbed Kristen and Lana both by the waists, and they and Jesse ambled toward the exit.

Twenty minutes later, they'd all arrived in Trastevere via bus #492, which dropped them off in front of Santa Maria Church. They walked the few blocks to Trilussa and found students from RU, Trinity, and Libby College gathered there.

An hour after she'd emptied a full 60oz. glass cowboy boot of Peroni, Mara felt a bit more carefree. They'd spent the time discussing Jack's decade of trade show experience, but now she was ready for more juicy tidbits of his personal life. "So, how did you end up settling in Rome? Why RU?"

Jack smiled, and took a long sip of his third bootful of Heineken. His face red and his eyes droopy, he slurred his Texas drawl down to a snail's pace. "I'm here because of a woman."

Juicy stuff. She sipped and nodded. The rest of the group had gone off to mingle, but Jesse remained glued to her side. He, too, listened in rapt attention.

"As an Army Ranger, I'd found myself on a mission in Naples many, many years ago." He sipped. "When I finished, I made my way up to Rome for a little R&R and met Manuela. She was a curator at Villa Borghese, and she taught me...how to appreciate art." He rolled his eyes up to the ceiling. "I also learned to appreciate that she had a body like Venus."

Jesse groaned. Mara shot him a furtive glance. "Go on," she said.

"That's it. She and I got engaged. It didn't work out. I still stuck around Rome. My brother got me a job at RU, and I've been here ever since."

"So, what happened with 'Venus di Manuela?'" she said, winking at him.

"She's dead now." Without another word, Jack rose, excused himself, and headed for the men's room.

Mara turned to Jesse. "He's a strange man. Brilliant, but with a tortured soul. And, a true Southern gent—"

"He's a pig," Jesse said. He gulped from the boot that he'd barely touched, and then he took her hand. "I want you to promise me that you won't ever put yourself in a situation where you're alone with him."

"What? Oh, Jesse, he's not like that. He's—"

"There's more to him than meets the eye. I can tell these things. And, I don't like the idea of any woman alone with him. Most of all, you. Promise me?"

"Well, Jesse, I'm his TA. He's my boss. I can't just—"

"I'm his TA, too. Let's keep this a team effort, and everyone will be happy. Anytime you find yourself in a situation where—"

"You're jealous."

His face blazed red. "No, that's not—"

"You're jealous." She smiled and finished her beer.

"Mara, we don't know enough about him. And, I'm just saying, you should keep your guard up until—"

She put her forefinger to his lips and slurred, "Me thinks thou doth protest too much." She winked at him, and felt his breath on her finger. "Here he comes now. Keep it together, will ya?"

Jack returned to the table, and slammed into it with his thigh. "You ready for me to take you, darlin'? Home, that is?" He hiccupped and laughed, and got really up inside her space.

Mara felt her face redden, and she took a step back. "Jesse has offered to drive us both home, Signore."

"Huh?" both men asked in unison.

Jesse caught on and swiped the professor's keys off the table. "C'mon, Signore. The lady needs her beauty sleep." He smirked at her, and she gave him the finger.

A half hour after dropping Jack at his flat, Jesse dropped Mara off at Stella Luna. She waved and headed into the apartment complex. She opened her door to the steady rhythm of Kristen's snores.

By 1:00 am, she'd removed her makeup, drunk down a cold glass of water and some headache medicine, and then closed the long accordion shutter door that separated her and Kristen's beds from the rest of the apartment.

She slipped between the covers and stretched. She smiled at the fun she'd had that evening, on the cappuccino run with Jesse and at Trilussa with her friends. So much for her mantra of staying detached. She pulled the blankets over her head and rolled onto her side. Almost asleep, she reached her hand up from under her pillow and rubbed her eyes. When she placed it back, her knuckles smacked against cold steel.

While Kristen snored in the twin bed a few feet away, Mara closed her hand around the mysterious object and turned on the lamp beside her bed. She took her hand out from under her pillow and examined what she had just found.

A sculpting chisel. Caked with dried plaster.

Chapter 15

Sitting straight up in bed at 1:00 in the morning, Mara looked at the gleaming chisel in her hand. Was it meant to be a real threat, evidence of a crime, or a prank?

Her well-being and the safety of her roommate were of utmost importance in her mind, and she was too dog-tired for someone to be messing around with her.

She grabbed the can of mace which she kept hidden in her bedside bureau. Quietly, she extracted herself from her bed sheets and picked up a pointy, five-pound, dolphin-shaped glass paperweight that Kristen kept on her bed table. She held them both at shoulder level, prepped to strike, and padded through the small apartment.

She checked in every closet and nook, and behind all the furniture for any signs of a crazed killer, but found none. She noticed that the lid on her father's cherry wood urn appeared slightly off kilter. She righted it.

Kristen muffled something into her pillow, and then went back to snoring.

Mara checked the windows and doors. Locked up tight. Fatigue caught up with her, and she decided to deal coherently with the situation in the morning.

Mara hooked the bedroom wall shutter and dragged her slippered feet back to bed, put the mace in the drawer, slipped the sculpting tool into her gym bag beneath the bed, and left the dolphin on the floor within reach. She scooted under the covers, set her alarm for Thursday morning's IntBiz class and tumbled off to sleep.

***

The front door crashed open, jarring Mara instantly from sleep. Her adrenaline surged, and her wide eyes scanned the room where she and Kristen slept.

Someone must have jimmied the lock and barged in.

She glimpsed Kristen in the shadows cast by the early morning sun in her bed a few feet away. She'd already swung her feet to the floor. "Mara, someone's in the apartment."

"Call the police," Mara said. She felt around the floor for the heavy glass dolphin and picked it up, ready to strong-arm it at the intruder. Through the bends in the shutter door, she saw someone pass from the small foyer and into the living room. Her heart thumped faster in her chest.

Kristen fumbled for her phone on the bedside table, and the alarm clock tumbled to the floor, showing 6:00 am. Kristen looked up at her, panic-stricken. "My phone is out of a charge," she whimpered.

Mara felt around the cluttered bedside bureau for her own phone. Shit, her phone was on the living room table, out there. There was always the sculpting tool in her gym bag. She reached for it, but froze when wheels scraped and squealed, and stopped right at the door handle of the partition. Someone yanked and pulled at the cheap latch; it seemed likely to snap at any moment. Then, it stopped.

She and Kristen stared at one another, both poised to strike; Mara with her dolphin paperweight and Kristen with her cuticle scissors from hell.

Suddenly, from the other side of the partition, two older women began shouting at each other in what sounded like Armenian. They seemed to break off in opposite directions; one headed for the kitchen, the other the bathroom. And both were wheeling squeaky buckets.

Maids.

Suddenly recognition dawned and Mara set down the dolphin weight. The adrenaline began to subside from her body, leaving her groggy and very relieved.

Every Thursday, the apartments were entitled to a scrub-down by the Stella Luna maid service. Closest to reception, theirs must be first in line for cleaning. But, at six in the freaking morning?

For the next fifteen minutes, the two maids lobbed vehement barbs in Armenian-spiced Italian at one another while they cleaned. Then, one of the crazed Lysol-sniffing heathens rapped on the slider that separated them from the bedroom.

Mara looked at Kristen, who shrugged silently. Both remained quiet, feigning sleep. The two maids shouted what must have been curses, wheeled their lopsided buckets out of the apartment, and slammed the door. A jangle of keys sounded, the women locked the door, and they were gone.

She and Kristen burst out laughing. Tears rolled down their cheeks as they mimicked the foul-mouthed women who'd crashed through their apartment like a tornado. Minutes later, Kristen was snoring again. But Mara couldn't go back to sleep.

She headed for the shower and turned it on full blast. As she stepped in she let the steaming hot water stream over her and focused her mind on the previous night's events.

The sculpting tool. Who'd planted it beneath her pillow— the serial killer, or a prankster? Was it a warning, or a joke?

She thought about her options. Report it to the police, and if it turns out to be a hoax, she's the idiot of the year. Disregard it, and if it turns out a viable threat, then she risks her life as well as Kristen's.

How did the person plant the chisel beneath her pillow and go undetected? There were no signs of forced entry during her inspection last night. So it must have been someone who had access to the room while they were out. Or, had she or Kristen perhaps left the door unlocked while they ran to a neighbor's?

When Mara came out of the bathroom, Kristen was awake, sipping coffee, and reading a book on Sartre. Mara fed the fish, and sat down at the table.

"We've had an intruder," Mara said.

Kristen snorted with a smirk on her face. "I know, right? What was up with those maids? Could they be any louder?"

"You're right. But, that's not what I meant. Last night, I came home to find this under my pillow." Mara pulled the six-inch, steel chisel from her gym bag and held it up. "Any idea who might've put it there?"

Kristen's eyes flew wide. All hints of sarcasm disappeared. "You don't think…"

"The Sculptor? Maybe. I don't know. Or, it might just be someone messing around."

"You have to tell that cop from the party," Kristen said.

"Enzo. I like him. He could take a look at it, maybe give us some answers." Mara dropped the tool inside her shoulder bag. "Either way, if it's just some idiot acting stupid, or if it's the psycho, promise me you'll watch your ass?"

"I will. And you should, too. I mean, if someone could sneak in and leave a chisel in the bed, he could just as easily stab one of us in the heart with it. Right?"

Mara nodded, and shivered. Had the Sculptor's most recent victim shared the same conversation with her own roommate before she'd been murdered?

School administrators had brushed over the details, conveying to the current student body that the dean himself had found Chick Sticht's remains and notified her family.

Rumor had it that a torso, no head or appendages, had been propped in the corner of the piano elevator of the music department where the victim had studied opera. Chick's former roommate had already transferred to the Florence program at the end of the semester, and Mara and Kristen now shared their former abode, as replacements in the eyes of RU staff.

Without a word, Mara stepped forward and hugged Kristen, resolving to stay on guard, and refusing to let either of them step into the shoes of the Sculptor's next potential victims.

***

Later that afternoon, after finishing her first full week of classes, Mara visited *la Questura*. She asked the desk sergeant for Chief Inspector Tranchille, and he gestured upstairs. Sidestepping two handcuffed hookers and a middle-aged man holding a yellow bucket of broken glass, she found the stairwell. She jogged up two flights of worn wooden steps to the Homicide Department. Rounding the corner, her search ended quickly as she ran directly into Enzo.

The inspector warmly shook her hand, led her to his office, and seated her at the most beautiful desk she'd ever seen. He offered her a cup of American coffee, which she gladly accepted.

After a few minutes of describing how she'd found the chisel, she produced it from her bag and set it atop his blotter. "Signore Tranchille—"

"Enzo, dear."

She smiled. "Enzo, I have to apologize. It's covered with plenty of my fingerprints, as well as those of my roommate."

"*Non c'e problema, cara.* Not a problem for forensics. The lab will dust it and later match any prints to yours and Kristen's. Hopefully, we will glean others that will give us more information.

"You were right to bring it in," Enzo said. "Whether this is a joke or a serious threat, neither should go unchecked. Nor unpunished. Not if I can help it."

They spoke a few minutes about personal safeguards. She refused police protection; she could take care of herself.

Before he could further persuade her to accept his offer, she changed the subject. "I love this desk." She stroked the dark cherry surface. "It's so ornate, very lovely."

"It belonged to my late wife, also ornate and very lovely," Enzo said. "This one was a family heirloom. Matilda and I also used to shop for antiques. I remember the trips we took to find each one."

"Such masterful scrollwork on the legs," Mara said.

Enzo nodded. "She loved scrollwork. A few years back, we had a lovely wooden pergola built over the patio of our courtyard. It had the same grapevine pattern as the desk."

Mara ran her hand along the desk's fine detail. "The pergola's construction must have taken a long time."

"All three months of the summer. The carpenter's handy with a chisel and hammer, quite a perfectionist. You know him; he's a professor at RU. Signore Jack."

Mara gazed up at him, curious about the professor's alter-ego.

Before she could question him, the door flew open. A man walked in, his head buried in a sheaf of papers.

Enzo cleared his throat.

The man looked up, saw Mara, and his eyes went wide.

"Jesse?" she said.

"Mara. I'm just...I'm...hey, what are you doing here?" Jesse said. Concern nestled in with the surprise and contorted his features. "Are you alright?"

She recounted last night's discovery, and spent the next couple of minutes deflecting his demands for her twenty-four-hour police protection.

"Thank you, but no thanks. I'm going home to catch up on some sleep," she said. "Tell me, how is it that you just barged into Signore Tranchille's office like that?"

Jesse looked at Enzo. Enzo looked down at the desk. Jesse looked at the sheaf of papers in his hands and then offered them to Enzo.

Jesse turned to Mara. "Enzo is my uncle, on my father's side. He was instrumental in hooking me up with my business internship, through Signore Jack and Vespa." He turned to Enzo.

"I've come to show you my presentation, for next week's Venice trip, *Zio*. I'd love your feedback."

Mara stood. "I was just on my way out. Don't let me interrupt. *Zio* Enzo, I hope you enjoy reading the Vespa proposal as much as I did. Jesse's brilliant with numbers."

Enzo immediately stood and shook her hand. "*Cara*, please do not hesitate to contact me anytime. I wonder, do you have friends or family nearby you might stay with?"

She shook her head. "No one aside from Jesse and his crew," she said. "Everyone else I know in Italy lives in Stella Luna. We're all there for each other.

"But, as far as family goes...not so much. My mom...travels for work. My older sister...she...died tragically a few years ago...skiing accident. My dad would have stayed with me," she continued. "But he passed a few years back. I plan to spread his ashes in Tuscany in the coming months." Mara rubbed the fine grain of the desk and squeezed back tears.

Enzo patted her shoulder. "I'm sure even now your father is watching over you. But, so will I. If there's anything out of the ordinary—"

Mara smiled. "I promise to let you know."

"Don't worry, *Zio*," Jesse said. "I plan to keep an eye on her, whether she likes the idea or not."

Mara said goodbye and left police headquarters. She realized that she indeed liked the idea very much.

***

"So, this is the woman you feel destined to marry?" Enzo shut the door and resumed his seat behind the desk. "She's a bright girl with a warm heart. I could tell right off, both from the Stella Luna party, and from this meeting. I can see why you're so fond of her, Jesse."

"Is it that obvious how much I like her?"

Enzo leafed through the papers Jesse had handed him, and nodded with approval. "Excellent work, son."

"Thank you."

"If she feels the same way, then you want it to be obvious." Enzo walked to his tabletop copier and duplicated the documents. He handed the originals back to Jesse. "And, from the way she looks at you, I believe she does."

***

When Jesse left his office, Enzo reviewed the latest forensics report for what seemed the sixty-sixth time.

Trace amounts of chlorine and nicotine at the crime scene interested him, though both were easily explicable.

Forensics had analyzed the fuchsia thread, stitched into the latest victim's navel. They'd compared it to that found on all the Sculptor victims; the material was a match in every case. A silk spun from a rare arachnid found in the Amazon region in the '50s. The *Avicularia fuchsia* later became extinct, and its silk was indeed a rare commodity. Enzo's team was tracking fabrics into which the silk might have been spun, but so far nothing.

Enzo recalled his discussion with Sciug, that the use of a silk string in the Roman Sculptor case resembled that of the sash in the Monster of Florence case. The similarities stopped there, but it still intrigued him, and he hoped to hear back from *la Questura di Firenze* soon.

The lab had also compared the sculpting tools and plaster residue left behind at the crime scenes. They were all tools belonging to all three art professors—Ryan Volker of RU, Angelo Forte of Trinity, and Filipo Truri of Libby College. Was one of them the perp, or was the killer actually using the professors to confuse the police and throw them off his trail?

Enzo considered the shortlist of suspects again, and wished with all of his heart that some of them did not have to be there.

He also wondered if, after the upcoming field trip that mixed up all three victims' schools like a martini, whether the serial killer might indeed settle to the bottom.

Chapter 16

On Friday, when Mara stumbled out of the bedroom, the bright noon sun had filled the living room with comfortable warmth. She cracked a window by the fish tank and found that an early spring had crept into town.

Entering their small kitchen space, Mara found that Kristen had left a note on the kitchen table that read:

```
Frankie Bergamo's in town for two days!
Maybe you could clear out for tonight?
Love and light, Kristen
```

Bergamo was Kristen's hometown boyfriend who was studying in Florence. Apparently he was parking himself at their apartment for the better part of the weekend.

Thanks for the advance heads-up, Kristen. Mara tried to think of a place to stay, but put off the decision until later. Coffee, first.

By one o'clock, Mara was lazing on a park bench in Villa Borghese, sipping a cappuccino and grading Thursday's quizzes. The lions roared in the park's zoo. Birds praised the weather from the treetops. Purple crocuses broke through the slushy mud. Her wool sweater and fleece-lined boots were enough to keep her toasty on this mid-February afternoon.

An hour later, she polished the Ferrari presentation that she would give to the senior executives in Venice next week, and her growling stomach rivaled the roars of the caged lions. She packed up and strode across the park toward Via Pinciana, a main thoroughfare that ran alongside the Gardens, just near the museum, and stopped at a fountain to fill her water bottle. On the other side of the massive marble geyser, she spied Signore Jack, leaning against the wide rim of the structure puffing a long cigar.

She waved and called to him, but the waterfall blocked the communication, and he didn't notice her presence. Mara capped her bottle and slid it into her backpack. Papers fluttered out the side, and she stooped to pick them up.

When she stood up again, she noticed that Fritz Arella, the boyfriend of the latest slain victim, had appeared, standing inches from Signore Jack. And shouting into the professor's face.

Her interest piqued, Mara decided to linger and observe the confrontation from afar. Jack appeared to ignore Arella. He leaned against the fountain and puffed his stogie, a smirk tugging up the corners of his mouth. Arella's face soon grew redder and his shouting rose louder.

After a couple more minutes, Mara became uncomfortable watching the exchange. Time to go. Whether it was a disagreement over a grade or a girl, Mara didn't want to be privy to anything that might jeopardize her assistant position. But, before she turned to head for the main street, Arella let fly a right hook.

She gasped.

Jack flicked the cigar onto the sidewalk and stood ramrod straight. Even in light of the assault, he didn't make a move toward Arella.

Arella continued to shout at him, but Jack stood his ground. Then, it was over.

Arella stormed south toward Piazza del Popolo. Jack lit a cigarette and shook his head. He dabbed at his cheekbone with a red bandana, replaced it in his back pocket, and sauntered west toward the zoo.

Mara shouldered her backpack and headed east again, toward the main street. What had transpired between her IntBiz prof and the ex-boyfriend of a murder victim?

She just remembered that Arella attended Trinity, not RU, so the issue likely didn't involve school. Unless, Signore Jack was somehow in trouble with Arella's father, the dean of RU. That wouldn't bode well for her and Jesse's TA positions.

On the other hand, perhaps their skirmish had to do with Arella's deceased ex-girlfriend, Chick Sticht? Had Arella discovered something more than just a student/teacher relationship between his on-and-off girlfriend and the professor?

Just then, Mara spotted Jesse stepping off a bus onto Via Pinciana. She waved, and he saw her. His broad smile affected her like a shot of adrenaline, and her pulse raced.

"I'm headed to my favorite pizza rustica joint," he said. "Grab some with me?"

***

Minutes later, Mara was faced with a complicated decision, in the form of a glass case stacked with long, rectangular trays of pizza. No cheese and pepperoni on cardboard to waste her time. Instead, flatbread focaccia swathed in mozzarella with only the most interesting toppings to entice her: cherry red tomatoes and garlic; sliced potatoes and rosemary; eggplant and basil; artichoke and lemon slices; chicken and spinach, and so many more.

She ordered a can of Coke and two square pieces of potato/rosemary. The aroma of her freshly baked slices, each wrapped in crisp parchment paper, made her salivate like a hound.

Jesse ordered sausage/basil and an orange drink, and together they strolled back into the park, where she divulged the details of the bizarre confrontation between Fritz Arella and Signore Jack.

They feasted, leaning back to back on a marble bench outside the Borghese Gallery. Pigeons came and left in a huff, barely scoring any crumbs. In between bites, Jesse peppered her with questions about what she'd witnessed. He nodded, and seemed to tuck away the answers for further consideration.

"Told you the professor's smarmy," Jesse surmised.

"Smarmy?" She laughed. "You mean like a pirate, smarmy?"

"You just be wary of that guy. He's smarmy."

"You're smarmy," she said.

He grunted, casting aside her aspersion; both of them were too content from their feast for further banter. The sun disappeared behind a cloud. She closed her eyes to savor the quiet moment. And then the rains came.

She and Jesse scurried to the double doors of the Gallery entrance and into the pristine interior of the renowned museum. Mara recalled a visit when she was little, but she had no recollection of what treasures were inside.

She and Jesse bought tickets and found themselves amid fifty or so art majors from RU, Trinity, and Libby College. Jesse's roommate, also RU's Art in Rome professor, Ryan Volker, led the group.

They turned into the sculpture hall, where they approached a long, rectangular glass case of instruments. Inside were sculpting tools once used by such Renaissance Masters as Botticelli, Michelangelo, Raphael, and Bernini, during the sixteenth and seventeenth centuries.

Volker lectured, "Even as time has progressed, the basic tools of sculpting, in their myriad shapes and sizes, remain similar to those used in the trade today." He pointed to various instruments. "Flat and claw tools, chisels and mallets, rasps, rifflers, and brushes. The elongated and short saws, scissors, clamps, wire wool, and calipers…" On and on he continued.

Mara pointed to a particular chisel and nudged Jesse. "That looks like the one I found on my pillow," she murmured to him.

"You sure? They all look the same to me."

She pointed to the glass. "Length is the same. Width of the steel tip. Girth of the handle. The rings that provide the grip. The slightly curved handle, also steel not wood."

"You'd make a damn good investigator," Jesse said.

She turned and smiled at him. "Thanks. I've always secretly wanted to be an investigative journalist."

"What happened?" he said.

"For years, my dad drilled into my head that journalists only report what big business wants people to know anyway. So, I went into international business to market big ideas to the masses."

"Because Daddy thought it would be a good idea?" Jesse said.

"No, that's not it at all." She crinkled her nose and forehead. "Well, I mean maybe he had a hand in…he guided me…he, okay, I let my dad live vicariously through my IntBiz major. Big deal. He's dead now, anyway."

"Exactly. Maybe you shouldn't let the memory of your dad continue to dictate your future?" Jesse said.

Mara ruminated over Jesse's blunt suggestion while Volker guided the group to various masterpieces, including Bernini's version of *David*, as well as *Apollo and Daphne*. Volker described techniques the Masters used for sculpting, cutting, polishing, and even coloring their marble works. When he broached molding and casting, Mara shifted her gaze from the provocative statue, *Rape of Proserpina*, back to Ryan Volker.

She became acutely aware of his abundant expertise in the sculpting field. Was this the type of person that puts his expertise into practice on human victims? Does someone so enthralled with this form of artistic expression use it to torture and preserve the mutilated bodies of young college women? He seemed an obvious suspect due to his profession, but was Ryan Volker a serial killer? She wondered how well Jesse really knew his roommate.

She whispered to Jesse, "Rain or no rain, what do you say we head back out into the land of the living?"

"I couldn't agree more," Jesse said. They exited the museum into a light drizzle. "I should head home," he said. "I still have to grade my stats quizzes. Want to come?"

Mara hesitated. She liked him, but didn't want to send the wrong message. She enjoyed his friendship, but didn't have room for anything more.

"Purely professional," he said, as if reading her thoughts. "We'll pitch proposals to one another 'til we get them down pat."

He was good. Egging her on with winsome thoughts of career advancement sealed her decision.

Twenty minutes later, Jesse and Mara sat sipping a bottle of Santa Margherita Pinot Grigio on his balcony, due west of the Vatican, while two stray black kittens sampled bits of prosciutto from off their fingers. The rain had disappeared, and the sun was now setting over Brunelleschi's dome in Saint Peter's Piazza. A Harry Connick, Jr. CD played softly from the living room, and she and Jesse dazzled each other with spreadsheets and summations.

An afternoon of pure tranquility.

Until Jesse's roommates showed up.

Chapter 17

Jesse always thought that his friend and roommate, Michael Utica, had a way of making a grand entrance. Today was no different.

Utica busted into the apartment carrying an overstuffed pack on his back. He plunked it on the living room floor and greeted them on the terrace.

"Goddang *scioppero della ferrovia*! Had to kiss Paris goodbye for this weekend, kids." Utica helped himself to a glass of Pinot Grigio and flopped into a wicker chair. "Damn train strikes! They happen about as often as Stanky gets laid."

Utica's entrance was upstaged by Stanky's. Stan Kiever slammed through the front door, attached to the lips of his on-again-off-again, Penelope Fraise. With short, mousy brown hair, pale skin, and cankles beneath her short skirt, the art major was nothing to write home about. But, she liked to swim and suck cock, two things Stanky most enjoyed.

Jesse had first met Penelope a year ago, when he strolled into his apartment one afternoon, and found her painting naked in front of an easel in the middle of his living room. Covered in paint splatter, she'd asked if he'd like to fuck. He told her to go fuck herself, and their relationship had maintained the same cold, indifferent status ever since.

Pen and Stanky now shed their clothes as they finagled their bodies through the kitchen and into Stanky's room. The door slammed behind them.

Utica shook his head. "See what I mean? Train strike—Stanky gets laid! Reminds me of a movie…"

"Woody Allen?" Jesse said.

"You know the one I'm thinking of. Came out last year?"

"With Kate Hudson? Big flop?" Jesse said.

"That's the one." Utica propped a fresh cigar between his teeth, and offered a stogie to both of them. Jesse took one. Mara shook her head and poured more wine.

On their short journey from Borghese Gardens to the apartment, Jesse had shared some insights into his roommate and close friend, Michael Utica.

The native New Yorker had been raised on the mean streets…of East Hampton. The son of one of the largest dry cleaners on Long Island, and the youngest of seven other brothers and sisters, Utica's love of films began at an early age, when his mother's childhood friends, Marty Scorsese, Al Pacino, and Ann-Margret had come to stay for a weekend. Many pitchers of mint juleps later, the all-star bunch had regaled the family with movie history. By the end of the weekend, Marty taught Utica to appreciate fine cinematography.

On their Roman balcony, Utica wowed Jesse and Mara with his knowledge of film.

"Okay, I have one," Mara said. "'Sometimes…dead…is better.'"

"*Pet Sematary*," Utica said. "C'mon, give me a tough one."

"'I'll have what *she's* having.'"

"*When Harry Met Sally…*" Utica rolled his eyes.

"'Bring out your dead.'"

"*Monty Python and the Holy Grail.*"

Mara smiled. "'Pink is my signature color,'" she said with the sexiest Southern drawl that Jesse had ever heard.

"C'mon, give me some tough ones." Utica puffed his cigar and rolled his eyes at Jesse, who shrugged. Utica said, "Uh, that would be Julia Roberts in—"

"*Steel Magnolias.*" Ryan Volker strolled onto the terrace with a lit cigarette between his fingers and a portfolio under his arm. He tossed his beret onto the couch in the living room. "Love that movie."

"Me too." Mara smiled, thoroughly enjoying the company of Jesse's roommates for once.

Shortly after the sun set over Rome, the harsh winter cold settled back in, and Ryan, Utica, Mara, and Jesse moved themselves from the balcony into the living room. Each took a chair and a long fleece blanket.

Throughout the night, Jesse opened a few more bottles of wine, and the group took turns crooning a medley of favorites, including a drunken rendition of "Sittin' On the Dock of the Bay." The four eventually dozed off, long after the moaning in Stanky's room turned to snores.

***

Mara's legs twitched, signaling that she was on the cusp of sleep. She loitered in her sleepy, pre-dream state, and she giggled softly into her fleece. Utica's lightning quick recall of famous one-liners impressed her. But that couldn't even compare with his uncanny familiarity with all of the silver screen sirens.

How Utica had regaled her and the group with actresses' names, first husbands, bra sizes, and co-stars tickled at her consciousness. Moments later, Mara drifted off to sleep. She dreamed of gondola rides—the type that glided over meandering seawater canals, and those that bused up steep ski slopes.

Any kernel of concern over the fact that Utica shared the same affinity for gorgeous old-time movie actresses as Rome's serial killer never had a chance to propagate.

***

A high-pitched movie scream riled the four of them from their slumber. It was coming from Stanky's bedroom.

"Stop! Please, God, no! Stop!"

"It's Pen," Mara said in alarm. "She's in there with Stanky."

In the grayish sunlight barely penetrating the living room shutters, Mara watched Jesse and Utica leap to their feet. Jesse reached for the baseball bat just inside the balcony door. Volker yanked a desk drawer open, and whipped out a pointed sculpting riffler that he held up over his head.

Another scream pierced the morning.

Utica busted open Stanky's bedroom door, and he, Jesse, and Volker crowded into the room, ready to strike.

With phone in hand, ready to call the police, Mara looked in over their burly shoulders, and found Pen, naked and face up, tied to the bedposts.

Stanky stood over her, feather in hand. Penelope was giggling hysterically. Between breaths, she issued another blood-curdling scream, then, "You're killing me, Stanky!"

The three men stood motionless in the doorway.

"What the fuck, Stanky. We thought you were tearing her apart." Utica stormed out of the room.

"He did that this morning, baby," Pen purred salaciously.

Jesse grunted and headed for the bathroom.

Stanky faced Mara, his muscular body fully naked, a cigarette hanging from his pursed lips. The peach fuzz formerly atop his head that he'd likely sprouted over Christmas break had been shaved. She drank in the fact that the competitive swimmer had also removed every other bit of hair from the rest his body. Stubble in certain parts must be a bitch. For him, and Pen.

"Penelope, are you alright?" Mara asked.

"I'm so fiiii—" Another scream of hysterical laughter. "Oh, baby, I couldn't be better. You all need to try this. C'mon in. The more, the merr—"

Another scream at seven in the morning.

Mara closed the door, waded through empty wine bottles to the kitchen, and brewed some coffee...industrial strength.

Chapter 18

The Sculptor exited his home that morning to the tolling of church bells. He walked to the Vatican, lit a votive, and said a prayer for his mother. His father didn't deserve any.

The artist stopped for an espresso and two crème-filled *cornetti*. He ate one and saved the other in a cardboard bakery box.

When he arrived at his mother's, he stamped out his cigarette, like always. In her room, his mother sat alone in a rocking chair by the window, staring out at a grassy courtyard. Dressed in a pale pink embroidered dress, she did not speak, nor did she look in his direction when he placed the *cornetto* on her bedside table. His mother still looked like the ravishing movie actress that she'd once been, even though time had stolen from her the memories of her roles.

He sat beside her on a plastic bucket chair and held her hand. He told his mother about school and the upcoming trip to Venice and the Alps.

He braided a silk sash along the neckline of her embroidered frock with gentle hands, and with precision, tied it into a bow at the base of her throat. It was the same sash spun of the rare *Avicularia fuchsia* silk, from the exotic spider of the same name, gifted to her from a Saudi sheik in the late '70s, at the height of her stardom, before the accident.

He kissed her on the cheek and told her he'd be back soon.

When he closed the door, he noticed that a tuft of the exotic silk ribbon clung to his corduroy pants. He snatched it up, sniffed it, and stuffed the strands into his pocket.

He'd find a use for them later.

***

For the Sculptor, the following week sailed by. He'd busied himself, maintaining his gallery before his jaunt up north.

Hidden in plain sight, the location of his personal gallery resembled a typical flat. Inside, he maintained living quarters that he kept up for appearances. A secret room tunneled through the bedroom closet, and it led to his homemade museum on the other side. The museum consisted of three main rooms: a workstation, a storage facility, and his personal showroom.

As the curator, he was proudly responsible for selecting, and interpreting every one of his works. He was also diligent about proper organization, labeling, and cataloguing of all of his pieces.

As an artist, he cleaned and polished every one of his tools and stacked them in their respective drawers. Today, he ensured that his containers of mixed plaster maintained the proper temperature, and that all of his unmixed materials, including clay, Vaseline, detergent, starch, and gypsum, were sealed airtight. He encased his plaster and resin casts in sealed drawers, at the proper temperature, so that they would be ready for use when he returned from his trip.

And, as the custodian, he knew some might consider him a clean freak. He wiped his counters and sink free of debris until they shone. He regularly cleaned the showroom, keeping his artwork free of dust, mildew, and grime. He changed bulbs to ensure optimum lighting, and he adjusted pedestals for stability as needed.

Today, he double-checked the temperature of the refrigerated storage bin, feeling secure in the knowledge that his backup generator would conserve his stored pieces in case of power outage. Lastly, he re-tightened the seals on the jars of formaldehyde, all of which contained specimens and keepsakes.

With everything in order, the Sculptor returned to the showroom for a last look around at his priceless masterpieces. He turned off the overhead lights so only the soft, recessed fixtures were illuminated, highlighting his work.

With a soft chamois, he polished the rounded breasts he'd solidly attached to an armature a few days earlier. Once dried, the piece had required quite a bit of sanding, but now Lana Turner's tits appeared as authentic as those belonging to the actress herself.

He turned to the empty pedestal beside hers. There, he hoped to bestow a new addition to his collection, perhaps after his trip.

He'd bring her back whole, and alive, so that she might fully appreciate the extent of his workmanship. There, the acquisition and the creation stages would meld into one, right under the roof of his gallery.

He'd affix her to the standing armature and plaster her torso, fully awake; this was to ensure she would comprehend the extent of his flattery.

Finally, he'd inject her with formaldehyde until her last breath left her. Then he would plaster her face to capture her final expression of human emotion, forever imitating her essence.

Imitation. Flattery. Immense artistic gratification.

It was the least he could do for his beloved subject.

Chapter 19

It was hard to believe that only an hour earlier, all sixteen second-class train compartments had been teeming with nearly a hundred partying students, from all three of Rome's major universities. But, Mara had a pounding migraine to prove it.

Around one in the morning, she'd escaped her six-seated compartment for one of the long, empty corridors that ran along the train, leaving behind the drunken card-players, touchy-feely flirts, and tooting saxophone players, all headed to Venice.

Alone now, except for the occasional straggler that would pinball between adjoining, smoke-filled rooms, Mara pressed her head against one of the cold windowpanes that overlooked the passing countryside. The moon cast a blueish-silver glow over the sea of snow-covered vineyards, where an occasional stone castle tower bobbed up from the surf like a buoy.

When the sounds of a live steel drum band emanated from one of the compartments, she wondered for a second how those instruments might have been toted aboard, but then her mind wandered to the people she'd met over the last few weeks.

Some of the relationships forged were sure to become future lifelong friends and colleagues, like Mimi and Kate, and her next-door neighbors Lance and Jason, and even Jesse's oddball roommates. She'd also grown to enjoy Professor Jack's insightful business acumen and jolly companionship (which Jesse ensured was never out of his radar range). She'd developed close friendships with Lana and Kristen, and a fondness for Jesse's *Zio* Enzo. And she'd come to rely on her relationship with Jesse, whatever the hell *that* was built upon.

The rhythmic clatter of the wheels against the rails soothed her, and her headache finally eased. She felt a tap on her shoulder.

Jesse.

He offered her a steaming Styrofoam cup. "Tea," he said. "Looks like you could use it." The gesture meant the world to her.

The two spent the next four hours comparing notes on a variety of things: favorite movies, from *Edward Scissorhands* to *Casablanca*; sports teams, of course basketball's best front-court ever had belonged to the Boston Celtics in the late '80s, who didn't know that; and music, in which Jesse refused to acknowledge that Bon Jovi was a "classic rock" band. Their mutual unbridled enthusiasm for casual conversation, the type that two people sling when forging a new relationship, made her feel giddy, scared, and excited.

The sun was just beginning to rise when the train arrived in Venezia Santa Lucia station. Mara thanked Jesse for the tea and the company, and she wound her way back to her compartment, to find Lana's current boy-toy Miguelito asleep on her backpack.

The students disembarked and boarded ferries outside the station that transported them over the choppy, winding Grand Canal to Hotel Monte Carlo, situated around the corner from Piazza San Marco.

When she was fully settled in her room, Mara watched the bells tolling in St. Mark's Campanile from her hotel room window. With Kristen, Lana, and three other female roommates sleeping off their stupors in their bunks, Mara bundled up against the frigid north winds and stole out into the maze of narrow alleys that comprise the city. She downed a double espresso at a corner bar, and trekked her way over myriad bridges to the produce market behind the Rialto Bridge. The air smelled crisp and salty, her apple cheeks bitten by the cold. She watched the boats line up along the canal and unload crates of wares, while a fruit vendor packed her some ripe, brown pears. She bought a wedge of Asiago and a bottle of water from an *alimentari* and set out to explore the archipelago.

Rows of shops lined every street. Masks stared back at her, more so than usual, as it was *Carnevale* season. She reached for a hand-painted, black and silver glittered porcelain mask sporting a long, crooked nose. But it was already attached to a face.

Mara shrieked.

Until, the man behind the mask revealed himself.

She put her hands on her hips and glared at him. "You scared the hell out of me!"

Jesse settled the mask back onto its plaster mannequin, laughing. "I'm sorry, I couldn't help it. Walk with me? I'm on a hunt for a cookie wheel."

***

By noon, Mara and Jesse were gazing at mosaics inside Doge's Palace, and sneaking nibbles from their cookie wheels, the ice cream laden cookie sandwiches they'd hidden inside their jackets. They'd joined Trinity's Angelo Forte and Libby College's Filipo Truri for an Art in Venice lecture, along with half of RU's students who'd finally roused themselves.

The two art professors, Forte and Truri, tag-teamed the two-hour class, one of them highlighting mosaics, the other briefing on the paintings in the palace, and both spewing knowledge about the various sculptures.

Mara had met both men at the beginning of the train ride and, though originally drawn in by their good looks and abundant arts savvy, she grew bored by their persistent competition with one another.

Now, as the group meandered through the various floors of the immense palace, the instructors seemed to have learned to play nice, and shared an affinity for teaching their respective lessons.

"They really know their stuff," Mara said. She licked the vanilla ice cream dripping down the back of her hand.

"They're bright," Jesse said. "Volker has them over the apartment now and then. The three are trying to put together a gallery in Rome featuring their works, as well as those of their students. Mostly paintings and sculptures."

"Sculptures?" Mara said. Though sick and twisted, a public gallery might be an ideal cover for a serial killer. There was something to be said about the idea of hiding in plain sight.

At that moment, Mimi posed a question to both Truri and Forte, about Venetian plaster. While one of them fielded the answer, Mara was struck by a thought.

What if the serial killer was not one art aficionado, but was actually multiple murderers?

***

Before Mara had had time to consider her theory, the group had moved on. One by one, the students trekked over the famous Ponte dei Sospiri that connected the centuries-old Doge's Palace, where prisoners were sentenced to life imprisonment, and then sent over the bridge to the dank prisons in which they'd been cast.

Jesse gripped her hand and sighed, as they traversed the Bridge of Sighs. She squeezed his hand, looked through the barred windows overlooking the canal, and mimicked his sigh. Both of them started giggling as they headed straight into the dungeon.

Once inside the prison, Mara glimpsed the tall, slender Professor Forte staring back at her surreptitiously. He smiled, and then quickly turned back to the group to finish a short lesson on the architecture of the bridge.

Had the art professor been flirting with her? Or sizing up his next victim? Mara shivered at the thought.

The group traipsed out of the palace doors and into the piazza, where the lecture continued.

"Thanks for keeping me company today," Jesse said. "Besides the art class, we must have trekked through every inch of the mainland. I can't think of anyone else I'd want to hunt down cookie wheels with."

She smiled. "How about your lackey roommates? I haven't run into them at all."

"Stayed back in Rome. Utica met a girl with a motorcycle. Stanky had a swim meet. Volker hung back at RU while the other profs played hooky with us. Guess he has the least seniority."

The two professors addressed the bell tower's architecture. While Truri lectured about the golden weathervane in the form of the archangel Gabriel, Forte cut through the crowd toward the Campanile's entrance. As he brushed past her, his hand slid across her back, and lingered for a moment, before he continued on. He turned back, eyed her up and down like a panther sizing up its prey, winked, and trotted to the door, whereupon he took up the lesson on the pyramidal spire.

She shook her head, shocked by his boldness.

Jesse grabbed her hand and whispered in her ear. "What do you say we blow off the rest of the class and go steal a gondola?"

"You're nuts," Mara said.

"Not nuts, dead serious." Jesse nodded in the direction of an unmanned gondola, bobbing in the lagoon like a little lost toy boat. "You game? A little Venetian joy ride?"

She felt tingly, alive. She nodded yes.

They strolled away from the group as if they'd never been a part of it, over to the edge of the lagoon. They teetered on the smooth marble precipice of the Grand Canal, while small waves licked her Wellie boots.

Jesse gripped her hand tightly while they glanced around for any sign of the boatman that steered the beckoning black gondola. Not many tourists haggling for gondola rides in winter, so pickings were slim to begin with. The gondolier probably snuck away for a hot espresso, anticipating meager demand.

Jesse stared at her. Not the panther-like stare of Forte, but rather a "don't worry, I've got your back" kind of look. It reassured her, and enticed her at the same time.

She winked back her assent. In seconds, she'd slipped into the boat.

Holding tightly to both sides, she was careful to distribute her weight evenly in the long, narrow, flat-bottomed craft. Then, Jesse expertly stepped onto the carpeted deck and took hold of the gondolier's pole, as if he'd done this before.

He eased them quickly and quietly through the green-gray water, past the marble walkway, and into the churning water of the Grand Canal. They were off, and no one bounded toward them screaming Italian obscenities. Yet.

Mara's head bobbed in time with the waves. She relaxed her now-white knuckles and settled back into the velvet-lined chair. She closed her eyes, and enjoyed feeling the wind rush over her face and through her hair. Oh boy, what the hell was she doing?

Jesse deftly angled the boat into the Rio di Palazzo. The area was mostly deserted, and the few street vendors that braved the cold never took notice of them as they headed right for the Bridge of Sighs.

"Are you okay?" Jesse asked.

She nodded.

"You ready for this?" he said.

She nodded a second time, her knuckles white again. Never before had the exterior of the bridge looked so clean and white. Some of the marble visages carved into the structure smiled at her eerily, and the lion's face at the center bared its teeth as if warning her. Right before the gondola's bow glided beneath it, she noticed human hands reaching out from the barred windows, those of waving tourists that resembled the desperate prisoners of long ago.

Directly below the center of the Bridge of Sighs, Jesse and Mara sighed deeply, giggling at their drama. Their laughter reverberated loudly beneath the bridge.

Not louder than the screeching blare of the whistle.

A police boat puttered quickly behind them, and the *carabiniero* hailed them down.

Gripped with panic, Mara turned back to Jesse. Should they bolt, and possibly capsize? Or stay, and be arrested?

She simply could not be arrested. School. Career. Future. What would her dad have thought if she threw it all away over a boat ride with a man she barely knew?

A few hundred feet ahead, there was a caravan of six boats congregating at the pier of a small church. People dressed in tuxedos and dresses were heading inside—a wedding party.

Mara looked at Jesse and knew he was thinking the same thing. The only way to evade the law was to become wedding crashers.

Behind them, the officer must have spotted the wedding because he ceased his whistling out of respect for the ceremony. Still, he continued to gain on her and Jesse. At any minute, he'd slap cuffs on them and her future would sink to the bottom of the lagoon.

Before she knew what was happening, Jesse grabbed her wrist. He'd sidled the gondola next to the pier in between two gondolas which were currently unloading bridesmaids and parents. He yanked her from the boat, scooted past some of the guests and dashed into the church.

As the door shut slowly behind them, they heard more shouts and whistles from the lagoon. The officer had likely called in backup.

Jesse pushed her into a small room built around a baptismal font. "Take off your clothes!"

"What?" Mara asked incredulously, only to then guess his strategy. Quickly, they stuffed their jackets and thick sweaters under a wheeled, cloth-covered table, threw on white lectern robes, and together pushed the cart down a side aisle amid chattering guests awaiting the sacred rite. No one noticed. Not even the four policemen who swarmed into the front of the church while Jesse and Mara scooted out the back.

In a small piazza filled with children kicking soccer balls, she and Jesse ditched their robes, ducked into a café and then scooted out its back door. There they hailed a water taxi and took off. Minutes later, the taxi deposited them back onto Saint Mark's Square, where their art class was still assembled.

Once they'd solidly mingled among their fellow students, Mara finally felt safe enough to confront Jesse Tonno. She turned to him, and planted a sloppy wet kiss on his succulent lips.

"I cannot remember the last time I had so much fun!" Mara said, catching her breath.

"Apparently we're still friends, then?" Jesse said. "Any other girl would have killed me for that stunt."

"I almost want to do that again," Mara said. Her blood raced, like she'd just won a marathon. "You were amazing. I cannot believe we got away with—"

The screech of a police whistle suddenly echoed through the rectangular piazza, drowning out everything, even the dueling orchestras whose music was heard from competing restaurants.

"Oh shit, how the hell did they find us in this crowd?" Mara said.

"Hold on. I don't think they're coming for us," Jesse said.

He pointed toward the Campanile, where Professors Forte and Truri, both dripping wet, argued back and forth with two policemen that Mara didn't recognize from their gondola chase.

A woman with long black hair and legs as long as stilts was gesturing wildly with her hands. Her chunky jewelry rapped against her abundant chest as she lobbed Italian curses at both professors. She accused them of groping her, the reason she'd shoved them both into the lagoon.

The officers hauled the drenched instructors away in the police boat, and it hit her how close she'd come to being arrested. Mara yawned, attributed her perpetration of grand-theft marina to severe sleep-deprivation, and decided to finally go and sleep it off.

***

That evening, Mara and Jesse met again, this time with friends under a huge tent in a small piazza behind the naval museum. All of the professors and students on the field trip, as well as dozens of locals and foreigners, had gathered to celebrate *Carnevale*, the Italian festival celebrated just prior to Lent, akin to Mardi Gras. Most wore masks, and all of them spent the evening drinking and eating way beyond capacity.

Mara danced with Kristen and Lana, who'd slept through the afternoon, missing the antics of the two professors. Mara filled them in.

"Miguelito said the woman who tossed them is a Brazilian actress," Lana said.

"Anyone hear what happened to the two profs?" Mara said, tipping back a bottle of beer.

"They've both been kicked out of Venice." Signore Jack scooted in among the three, shaking his hips and arms to the music like he was teetering off balance. "Truri and Forte are headed back to Rome as we speak," Jack said. "I would've thought it'd be easier just to court a woman, instead of accosting her in public, ya know?"

Mara nodded. "We haven't seen you this whole trip, Signore."

"I took a speed train in this afternoon, just for the party. I'll accompany you and Jesse to the presentations tomorrow morning." Jack raised one knee, twisted, and then raised the other, his hands in the air. Some people shouldn't dance.

Jesse joined them. He too seemed to march in time to a different song. "Are you headed to Flumserberg tomorrow night, Professor?"

"Switzerland is not on my agenda, son." Jack took a swig of his Pabst. "I've never found the idea of drinking beer and attaching skis to my feet a very responsible thing to do. So, early on, I chose beer. Suits me better."

The music slowed suddenly. Lana and Kristen slipped away, leaving Mara alone on the dance floor, with Barry White, Signore Jack, and Jesse. The sudden change in pace, and in her company, signaled it was time to go.

Mara donned her mask and ducked out of the tent. She dashed the few alleyways back to the hotel, hung up her mask, washed her face, and set her alarm.

Tomorrow was the presentation that she hoped would guarantee her professional future as an esteemed international businesswoman. A goal that she'd always aspired to reach. She drifted off, wondering if it still was.

Chapter 20

A couple days later, Mara donned two downhill rental skis and deftly tackled the magnificent eastern peaks of Switzerland's Flumserberg ski resort, high above the southern shore of the Walensee.

The sun was high and warm, the snow was powder fresh, and her ski buddy was…downright adorable in the navy blue snowsuit he'd borrowed from an elderly Vatican priest. Mara pulled over by a clump of trees, careful to avoid a klutzy snowboarder surfing by in a hockey helmet, and turned to Jesse Tonno.

"Did you really just take a phone call?" she said.

Jesse laughed. He slipped the phone into the chest pocket of his suit and zipped it shut. "Four bars. Best reception I ever had." His five o'clock shadow had surfaced around noon, and his mouth looked delicious when he flashed his toothy smile.

"Sorry I had to take it. Uncle Enzo." Jesse slipped his poles over his wrists, and reset his goggles. "Wanted to hear how the Vespa presentation went."

"Did you tell him you nailed it?" Mara said. "And that you were brilliant?"

His cheeks reddened, and his goggles fogged up. "No, but I told him that *you* kicked ass and took names with Ferrari, and looked smokin' hot doing it."

She stuck out her tongue.

"I mean it. You were amazing. You've got that internship all wrapped up."

She crossed her fingers that he was right, and changed the subject, embarrassed by his adulation. "Any word from Enzo about the Sculptor?" Mara said.

"Prelim forensics report came back on the chisel under your pillow. No prints, besides yours and Kristen's."

"Damn." Mara wondered how many other details Jesse was privy to, but before she could ask him, Jesse pointed through the thicket, to the mogul hill on the opposite side.

"Some serious moguls over there," he said. "You in?"

"Not sure it's a marked trail," she said.

"Thought you told Ferrari you're a trailblazer?" Jesse said. He knew exactly how to provoke her.

She evaluated the enticing mogul hill in the distance. The fact that her sister, Abby, had died on impact with a thick spruce while skiing an Alpine mogul trail, did not dampen her adventurous spirit. Abby would've told her to go for it.

And Jesse was encouraging her with that drop dead smile.

Mara winked at him, thrust her poles into the packed powder, and hurled herself forward on her skis, gaining ground in seconds. Jesse swished along in tandem, only fifteen feet to her north. Together they expertly maneuvered through the dense spruces, swishing side by side toward the mogul run.

In spite of her daily jogging regimen, her hamstrings started burning. She'd need a breather before taking the plunge downhill.

She glanced uphill to let him know of her plan to rest, but she'd lost track of him. No matter, she continued on. They were headed to the same clearing up ahead, or else they'd meet up at the bottom.

She trudged forward at a good clip. Her lungs burned; perspiration dripped down her back. Only a few more feet until the thicket ended. Then, she'd plant her poles and catch her breath.

Closer still. Almost to the edge of the trees.

She glanced up ahead. The moguls didn't appear as lofty as they did from further away. Now they looked icy and dense, and less convex.

She exited the dim light of the thicket, and the bright sun blinded her for a second. She squinted through her tinted goggles but couldn't focus. Her depth perception must be off. Because, now, it looked like the moguls on the downhill run had disappeared, and that the trail was flat. Almost as if the moguls had…sunk?

She tried to slow, but hit an ice patch. She jammed the edges of both skis into the snow and wrenched her body sideways to stop her forward momentum, but the expansive ice patch carried her closer to the edge of the mountain.

Running out of ground, she dug in and pushed harder against her skis. She braked so hard that she jettisoned ice shavings all around her like a snow cone maker.

Finally, her body halted. Mere inches from a straight plummet into a massive, fifty-foot wide sinkhole, fallen away from the rest of the mogul run.

Using her poles for balance, Mara edged gingerly away from the precipice. Nausea overtook her, and a brief bout of vertigo sent the world spinning.

Her feet held steady, and she forced her searing, rubber band legs to slide her forward, inch by inch, away from the frigid void. She took long, even breaths, and soon her nausea abated somewhat, her eyes refocused. She couldn't imagine her mother bearing the burden of yet another daughter lost to a tragic ski accident.

Almost ten feet away from the edge now, it struck her that she needed to warn Jesse of the dangerous cliff, before it was too late. "Jesse!" His name echoed all around her, unanswered. She looked up and down the mountain but failed to spot his navy blue jumpsuit amid the dense thicket.

She opened her mouth to shout his name again, but before she could, thick, heavy hands of a strong man shoved her from behind. Shoved her again. Hard.

She tried to whip her body around, to determine the source. But he pushed her again, and she stumbled forward. Her ski boots kept her upright.

She hadn't heard or seen anyone approach. Somehow, someone had skirted in between her and the precipice, and he was pissing her off shoving her around like that.

She gripped a pole in each hand like a club, tried to propel around like a helicopter to thwart another assault. But, he cuffed her against the side of the head. For a second she saw stars. Now she was afraid.

She crouched down low to avoid further attack, but that's when he gripped her sides with both of his hands, lifted her into the air, and spun them both in a semi-circle, facing the opposite direction.

Now, back on the path she'd just traversed, again facing the seemingly bottomless chasm before her, she doubled her efforts to ward him off. Squirming and wriggling, she tried to thrust her body to either side in order to break free of his grip.

He held tight.

She snowplowed her skis into a V-shape and forked her poles into the thick snow. She hoped it would stop their forward momentum. But he thrust her onward, back to the edge.

The man behind her dug his gloved hands into her parka. Who was this bastard, and why wouldn't he leave her alone? She spotted his black ski boots and rental skis beside hers, and his blue and black zebra-striped Gore-Tex gloves on either side of her rib cage, the only features she could even identify given that he refused to let up.

He gripped her sides harder, like ice picks gripping a block of ice. He grunted and hoisted her body. Her skis left the path. He hurled her body through the air.

She flew outward, and then down. She screamed.

She was falling. Into the snowy abyss. Her terrified screams echoed all around her.

She clawed and grabbed for a tree limb but missed. Her head banged against the side of the crater. Arms and legs flailed. Her leg hit the chasm's icy wall, and her ski snapped off from its binding.

Mara thought of her sister, and she called out for her dad.

Then, she landed. Hard, and on her back. On a mountain, all alone.

She did not move. The wind had been knocked out of her, and she lay prone, sucking in air until the elephant climbed off of her chest and she resumed normal breathing. Sudden, jarring, stabbing pains in her arms and legs brought her tremendous relief, in that she could feel them at all. Her muscles felt like week-old Jell-O, but miraculously, no bones appeared to be broken.

She sat up, only to slump back down. After a few minutes, she willed her body to sit up again, and she remained upright. Both skis must have popped their bindings in the fall. And hell if she knew where they'd landed.

She glanced uphill, at the thicket of trees through which she and Jesse had traversed. She wondered if Jesse had fallen from the cliff and into the crater too, and her heart beat faster. She called out his name. No answer.

She scanned the horizon. No more moguls at the top of the run. Just a concave orifice where the snow must have given way. Poking out of a plateau, less than midway up the immense cavern, was one of her skis. But, no sign of Jesse. Or her other ski.

She could probably use some of the protruding tree limbs as hand and foot holds to grab her ski and climb back up the crater to the original trail. But she might risk another sinkhole or even a major avalanche. And the bastard who'd attacked her might still be up there waiting for her.

On the other hand, the crater's leveled bottom appeared to open on one side and ease into a steep but manageable slope. She could grab her single ski from the plateau and then maneuver on that ski down the crater's unmarked, ungroomed trail toward an unknown wilderness.

Both options sucked. But either one was better than freezing to death all alone on a Swiss Alp. She shouted for Jesse again and scanned the area, to no avail. A cloud blocked the sun, and it began to snow. Time to move.

She crawled her sore body to where the spruce saplings protruded from the crater wall, and she proceeded upward. The powder here was fresh and light, and in some places where she'd attempt to secure a foothold, the white bank would swallow her leg whole, right up to her pelvis. This quicksand effect terrified her, but she resisted the urge to scream for fear of avalanche.

She clung to the crater wall with every bit of her strength, and she used each tree bough as a rung to pull herself up, struggling not to slide back down as the powder sometimes gave way or else fluffed into the back of her jacket like ice cold cotton puffs. Oxygen depletion didn't help her cause. With twenty or thirty percent reduced intake up here due to the altitude, her lungs and aching muscles screamed for more substantial air. Short breaths. Inch by inch. Slow, but sure.

Where was Jesse? Had he met with a similar fate? Had he too plummeted into the chasm, and to what end? If not, had her vicious attacker also confronted Jesse on the main trail and unleashed his rage on him? Her eyes threatened tears that would likely freeze to her cheeks, but she swallowed hard and fought them back.

Time for tears was later. Time to act was now.

Grip by grip. She edged past a concave indentation, staying as far away from it as possible and clinging tightly to the trees so as not loosen more snow.

Every muscle threatened to give out. But, her ski was her beacon, and she could almost reach it now. Just a few more feet.

That's when she heard it. A voice. It was beckoning her through the flurry of snow. Jesse? Or her attacker?

She could see someone, a man by his shape, up near the point where she'd exited the thicket. He called down to her again. In Swiss. In Italian. Then, in English. He waved both arms, encouraged her forward.

It couldn't be Jesse. Mara didn't think he spoke Swiss, and Jesse's snowsuit didn't bear red stripes like this man's.

Was it her attempted murderer, coming back to finish the job? She'd never had the opportunity to glimpse his snow pants or jacket. But, no zebra-striped gloves on this guy. And this skier wore red boots, not black.

Now she could see, he had a snowmobile. The setting sun gleamed off its side mirrors through the dense trees from where she'd come.

Standing back from the edge, he lowered a looped rope and snagged her ski by the binding. He put it inside the snowmobile, and started up the machine. In a fit of panic, she thought, *Oh, God, he's stealing my ski, my only way out of here!* Her stomach clenched with fear as the snowmobile zipped away from view. Gone.

She began to tremble. Slowly, carefully, she made her way back down the chasm walls to the ground below. Her body shook with desperation and fear. She was alone now, with no means down the mountain.

Then, minutes later, she heard it. The snowmobile had come back. It sped up to her from the vast wilderness below, bearing the same driver with the red-striped jacket and her ski. She could see her rescuer clearly now. Tan, with big sunglasses. His parka read Flumserberg Ski Patrol. He was a ranger. And she was saved.

But, where was Jesse?

***

Inside the cozy, one-room, ski patrol chalet, Mara rested her icy cold feet on some logs beside a wood-burning stove. The logs inside of it hissed and crackled with spectacular heat. Wrapped in a wool blanket, she sipped hot chocolate with tiny pink marshmallows. She thought the brew could use some Baileys, but otherwise, it was comforting and delicious.

Franz, the ranger who'd saved her from the ravages of nature and raced her to the cabin on his snowmobile, now chatted on a landline to the main lodge, inquiring as to Jesse's whereabouts.

When he'd plucked her from the mountain, her well-being had been his main concern. But, upon their return, she'd endured a well-deserved lecture.

Franz had told her of the countless times in the last thirty-five years he'd rescued skiers from unmarked trails, and about those that weren't found in time, "frozen angels," he called them. The tall ranger in the red-striped ski parka had smiled from under his fur-lined hood. When he'd pushed it back, he revealed a kind, tan face with full, wavy hair, all of it gray from worry, he'd said.

She'd then blurted out her story of her attack on the mountain, and the etched worry lines on his face seemed to deepen. He told her she'd have to repeat her story in order to file a full report later, but for now, they pushed the search for Jesse to the top of the list.

Mara's hands ached as they regained circulation, gripped tightly about her warm mug with anticipation as her rescuer sought answers from the lodge. She wondered whether Franz had been the one to find her sister after the accident years earlier.

A few minutes later, Franz hung up the telephone.

Mara sat up. "Anything about my friend?"

He sauntered next to her and sat down at a granite table. "The other ranger found him out there, roaming about the trail on his skis in the navy snowsuit, unhurt. Still looking for you. Calling out your name. Crazy kid."

She exhaled deeply, and realized she'd been holding her breath since Franz hung up. Jesse was safe, thank God. He must have been sick with worry over losing her on the mountain. She felt all warm inside. She felt bad, but she couldn't help smiling.

Franz stood and poured two more cups of hot chocolate. "He's alright though. A little shaken is all. He and the other ranger should be here any minute." Franz shook his head. "Not many people try to make it through that thicket to Devil's Plunge, the mogul hill. Most turn back. You're the first two to try it in a few years."

Mara stood, swayed a moment before settling on both feet. Her head ached, and she massaged a solid goose-egg on her forehead that she'd gained from her fall, while she paced around the hut. The blood circulated freely now through her thawed body, and her hands and feet tingled and burned painfully.

While Franz typed up some paperwork, she gazed around the room at the posters plastered along the cabin walls. Every wall had its own label, typed out neatly on a piece of paper near the ceiling.

On the wall labeled "Missing," photos and descriptions wallpapered the thirty feet of space, donated by the loved ones of the skiers, hikers, snowboarders, and snowmobilers that had never returned from their expeditions along the endless miles of the Swiss Alp terrain. Those "Missing" flyers on the wall ranged in date as far back as the early 1940s and as recent as last week.

Another section boasted thank-you notes, letters of praise, wedding photos, and baby pictures, likely mailed in by those whose lives had been saved. This wall, labeled "Found," sadly took up a third of the space as the previous.

Mara finished her cocoa just as she made her way to the final wall. This one was posted with official, local police declarations that bore names and dates of those bodies that had been found dead, buried deep in the snow. It consisted of those individuals whom Franz had solemnly referred to as "frozen angels."

Most of these details focused on the exact mountain and town in which the body had been found in the vast Alpine region, the victim's description, and the likely cause of death, including traumatic fall, collision, lost in wilderness, heart attack, or avalanche.

Mara scanned the wall and pinpointed the name she was looking for chronologically, "Abigail Teresa Silvestri." Her sister.

She read Abby's report. It described the injuries that she'd sustained from smashing into a tree on the Harlach Trail—a broken leg; bruising to her head, chest, and back; cracked ribs; and…Mara paused a second. If her sister had smashed head-on into a tree, then why the bruises on her back? Perhaps another fall, or something else?

The finality of her sister's tragedy weighed on Mara now. Tears stung her eyes, but through them she noticed something else. She finished the remainder of the report, and her heart seemed to catch in her throat. She wiped her eyes and read it again.

Mara's empty porcelain mug slipped from her hand, hit the granite table, and shattered into pieces.

The document on the wall did not ascribe the impact with the spruce as her sister's fatal injury. Instead, the official cause of death named an injury which she either sustained prior to or subsequent to the collision.

The reason for Abby's death was the sculpting chisel driven deep into the back of her skull.

***

The door to the rescue cabin banged open. Cold air blew in, as did swirls of snow. Jesse lumbered inside, followed by his rescue ranger. Thick, heavy, wet snow covered them like blankets.

A red-haired ranger nodded to Mara and slammed the door, shutting out the chill.

Jesse stomped the snow from his boots and smiled at her. He removed his goggles, and she could see that he was unharmed. She rushed to him and threw her arms around him. Despite his wet, snowman appearance, she pulled him close.

Jesse squeezed her body in return. "Hey, beautiful, it's okay. I'm not hurt. Why are you trembling?" He released her and pulled back, and his smile transformed into a look of concern. "You're not hurt, are you?"

She shook her head and forced a smile. "No, I'm okay. I was just so worried. I thought you might have…no, I don't want to think about…"

"Wow, I feel like you might care about me a little bit." Jesse tapped her nose with his gloved finger and winked.

Mara took a deep breath. "What happened? Where were you out there?"

"I got lost. We must have separated near the pine grove. And with the snow coming down so hard, I couldn't find you. I kept calling for you, wandering around and calling, and then, I got lost." He turned away, and rubbed his eyes with his snow-covered gloves. "I was going crazy, because I had no idea where you were."

He raised his head and gestured to Franz's cohort, who now sat at a computer on the other side of the room. "Liam zipped by on his ranger snowmobile from out of nowhere. Told me he'd take me to the lodge, but I…wasn't ready to go yet."

Liam turned from his computer, and in accented English said, "He would not leave the peak. Kept asking if I'd found a girl on the mountain. 'Has Mara been found dead or alive?' he said to me. I wanted to knock him out and drag him back, but lucky for your friend, Franz had just radioed to say that you were safe."

Jesse lowered his flushed face.

She was unable to funnel her thoughts into words. Her brain was overloaded, and her emotions were scattered. She was thrilled that Jesse was alive and well, and that he'd cared so much about finding her. But, she still felt stricken by the truth of her sister's death.

Franz thrust a steaming cup into Jesse's snow-covered gloves and ambled to the corner of the chalet to hover over Liam's computer.

Jesse gulped the warmth. Some of it trickled down the side of his mouth, forming a rivulet through the snow on his stubble.

At that moment, she wanted to engulf herself in his arms and stay there. She wanted him to tell her that everything would be alright.

She wanted to tell him what she'd just learned, that her only sister had not died by accidentally slamming into a spruce on the Harlach Trail in the Swiss Alps as she had been told, but rather that she'd been brutally murdered. Worse yet, from what she'd gathered from the report, Abby's killer had used the weapon of choice most favored by the Sculptor.

Jesse plunked his empty cup on a desk, pulled out the plastic bucket chair, and collapsed into it. He thrust his legs out and tipped his head back, clearly exhausted.

She gave Jesse a minute to regain his strength and walked back to Abby's report to sort through her swirling thoughts. It occurred to her that perhaps the same man that had run her off the mountain earlier had not been just some random perpetrator, but rather someone who'd somehow targeted her. She wondered how much of this attack was tied to her sister's demise.

She needed to question the Flums police and Franz's ski patrol about just how much they knew about her sister's incident. And, whether they'd made any kind of connection between this murder on the slopes and what had been happening with Rome's serial killer.

She turned to Jesse. The time had come for her to divulge the story of her attacker to him and Franz, though she knew Jesse would likely never let her out of his sight again. But then, she, Jesse, the rangers, and the police could put their heads together to possibly find her assailant, and discern whether there was any connection to her sister or even to the Sculptor murders.

She could handle all of it on her own, but, she hated to admit it, Mara Silvestri actually needed someone to lean on right now. As if reading her thoughts, Jesse smiled, hoisted his body from the chair, and clunked toward her in his black ski boots like Frankenstein's monster, reaching for her with open arms.

He still wore his hat and gloves. The snow on them had finally melted off, and she could see that they were soaked through to the bone.

That's when her heart sank. She gasped, consumed by Jesse's outstretched hands. She choked back a scream, too afraid to divulge what she hoped to God wasn't true, for fear of what might happen if he realized she knew.

The gloves on Jesse's hands bore the same blue and black zebra-stripes as her attacker.

Chapter 21

Most of her life, Mara had come to rely on herself alone to settle any challenges. This time was no different. Especially since she feared the repercussions if Jesse learned that she suspected him as her attacker.

While she had no conclusive evidence pointing to Jesse's guilt, she still felt wary of him. After all, his only alibi was that he'd been wandering around looking for her; he would have had plenty of time to throw her from the mountain and still feign concern for her whereabouts.

She figured she'd keep her suspicions in her back pocket, to sort out later when she had more to go on. For now, she'd keep Jesse, and her friends and faculty, in the dark until she could sort through this mess with the proper authorities.

She planned to head straight to Inspector Enzo upon her return to Rome to dump in his lap the details of her attack, what she'd learned about her sister's incident, and about possibly adding Jesse to the top of the Sculptor suspect list.

In the meantime, she'd bid goodbye to Jesse and her friends at the Flumserberg main lodge, and while the rest of the students and faculty from the three universities traveled back to Rome on a night train, she opted to check into a hotel near the station for a chance to catch her breath before a scheduled meeting with Franz the following day.

***

Just before she and Jesse had boarded the sky gondola for the main lodge the day before, Mara had pulled Franz aside and requested a private meeting, feigning she was writing a story about the heroic ski patrol. He'd accepted, and the two had met in the lodge's main office before her departure for Rome that morning.

Mara again extended her gratitude for his rescue. Then, she produced the official document that she'd surreptitiously pocketed from the "frozen angels" wall of the rescue chalet. She asked Franz point blank about why she and her family had never been informed that her sister had been a victim of a murder, not a skiing accident.

The fifty-five-year-old man laid both palms open on the table. He looked straight into her green eyes, and said in his heavy Swiss accent, "It was a cover-up, clear and simple."

Her mouth dropped open.

Franz continued. "I've been head of security in the Flumserberg region for decades. Your sister's murder six years ago was the first that ever happened on that mountain. I was the one that found her." He shook his head. "I've seen my share of crashes, all of them gruesome and unfortunate. But, when I found that steel pick protruding from the back of her head, I knew I'd never forget it."

"It was a sculpting chisel," Mara said. She recalled the ski patrol's photograph of her deceased sister's body—her face mangled from the crash, her leg bent backward, and the long-handled stainless steel chisel that impaled her brain. The coroner's report had declared the stab wound the official cause of death, not the collision with the tree that followed. Mara cringed—her sister must have suffered unimaginable anguish.

She choked back tears and continued. "So, why didn't you call the police? Why wasn't there an investigation? Why wasn't my family informed?"

"Ms. Silvestri, trust me when I tell you, my intentions were honorable. When I found your sister, I contacted the Flums police," Franz said. "Notification of the family, a subsequent investigation, and an official press release were all scheduled.

"Then, a day later, I received a call demanding my silence." Franz clenched his fists. "Swiss Intelligence ordered me to cover up the incident, and refused to allow me to speak to anyone about it, including my rescue squad, the Swiss, American, and Italian authorities, and of course, your family."

Incredulous, Mara forced herself to take a deep breath. "But, how could they? They have no right. The circumstances surrounding my sister's death might be linked to a serial murder case in Rome," Mara said. "Evidence in the investigation might shed enough light to stop a madman from killing others." Jesse popped into her head, and her voice caught in her throat. Fritz Arella, Jackson Sugardale, Michael Utica, Stanky Kiever and all three art professors formed a police lineup beside Jesse in her mind, all with varying degrees of potential guilt. She shuddered.

"I sympathize with you, Ms. Silvestri, as I do all victims' families," Franz sighed. "I acquiesced to the demands of Swiss Intelligence because I had two sons at the time, and I worried what might happen to them if I didn't."

"Then, you can understand how my mother was destroyed," Mara said. "Also, my father died believing circumstances that were entirely different from what he'd been told. If we'd known my sister was murdered, our lives might have turned out differently." Different paths, different life choices? "You should have told our family."

"You're right. I had a moral obligation to inform the family, regardless of direct orders by Swiss Intelligence to sweep it under the table." Franz stood, walked to a desk, unlocked the bottom drawer, removed a brown paper bag, and carried it to the table.

"I actually did file an official report with my boss." Franz sat down, gripped the edge of the table. "A day later, a city refuse vehicle ran down my boss. On the same day, one of my sons was killed in a car crash."

Mara gasped.

"I retrieved the only copy from my boss's files, to protect my other son's life," Franz said, his face ashen white. "I hid it, among the hundreds of others tacked to my memorial wall. You're the only other one to ever find it, read it."

"Why didn't you just destroy it?"

"Again, moral duty. That wall of 'frozen angels' is a tribute, to those for whom I wish I could have done more." He pulled out his wallet, and showed her a picture of three little blond girls. "My other tribute. My granddaughters. Born of the remaining son whom I swore to protect. Forgive me, Ms. Silvestri, but in my heart and mind, I feel justified in my decision not to pursue the matter."

Stunned by the implication that Swiss Intelligence had been responsible for his son's death, and humbled by Franz's innocent, young grandchildren, Mara realized that she'd collided with her own fatal obstacle on the issue. Franz had taken her into his confidence, and she now bore the burden of protecting this man's family.

She put her hand over his on the table. Neither spoke, but she felt certain he understood she meant to uphold his need for silence.

After a few minutes had passed, Mara felt it was time to enlighten Franz to the incident she'd endured on the mountain the day before. She recounted the details of her attack, sat back, and waited for his response.

He took a deep breath. "This is the second incident on this mountain to involve foul play, or the attempt at it. Both incidents involve two women that are related to one another. Perhaps the assailants are one and the same, maybe not. But, I'm rather certain we should not expose this incident either, based on the same reality I confronted when covering up your sister's attack. I believe the personal welfare of your family and mine depend on it. Do you share this opinion, Ms. Silvestri?" Franz tossed the ball in her court and awaited her response.

Mara thought of her mother, and Franz's grandchildren and remaining son, and made her decision. She nodded. "I won't contact the authorities, but I reserve the right to do so later if it could potentially save the lives of further victims."

Franz nodded. He opened the brown paper bag on the table before him. "Your sister's effects. I was ordered to discard them, and I worried they'd find out if I returned them to your family. But I just didn't feel right throwing her belongings in the rubbish."

Mara emptied the contents. A hair clip, a wallet, a packet of Turkish tobacco, and rolling papers. And a long, silver necklace, bearing a dark blue sapphire pendant.

She couldn't remember a time when her sister had not worn the piece. Mara slipped it over her head, determined to always wear it close to her heart. As a tribute.

Mara was now convinced that her own assault was not just a random act of violence, but rather another incident in a long line of foul play, including her sister's murder, by a single, ruthless perpetrator—the Sculptor. This not only frightened her, it angered her.

She gripped the pendant in her hand, extracted whatever life force her sister had transferred to it. Then Mara transformed that life force into solid determination.

She cast aside any need for self-preservation, and committed herself to seeking justice, for her family, and all those lives affected by the serial killer.

Chapter 22

"Two reasons why I got a Ducati?" Taka panted, huffing and puffing her side of the conversation in perfect English, lilted with her native Norwegian accent.

"Mostly speed. I like to move fast," she said.

(huff, huff)

"Funny…how we didn't hook up faster…"

(huff, huff)

"…this semester."

Her accent didn't bother the Sculptor as much as he thought it would. So, he let her talk while she rode him on her living room sofa.

Taka picked up the pace of her strokes, and he knew it wouldn't be long. "Second reason…"

(huff, huff)

"I love…"

(huff, huff)

"…the vibrations…"

(huff, huff)

"…between my legs."

Wearing a pair of zebra-striped winter gloves, he gripped her ass tighter with his leather-padded fingers, pumped her up and down while her hair flew wildly in every direction.

"I'm almost there," he told her. He gritted his teeth, restraining himself. "Put on the helmet. Ride me harder."

"Ooh…"

(huff, huff)

"…you kinky thing," she cooed. She reached for the motorcycle helmet on the floor, slid it over her head. The dark visor hid her face. She slammed him harder, started to moan.

He gripped the sides of the couch cushions. "Do you want to live forever?" he asked.

She raked her nails down the front of his hairless chest, moaned again.

"Do you want to live forever?" he prodded.

"I want to feel…"

(huff, huff)

"…like this…"

(huff, huff)

"…forever; oooh, so ready…"

"Open the visor," he said. "I need to look at your face. Open it now."

She arched her back, and flicked open the visor on her helmet. Her face was awash in ecstasy—wet mouth open, nose crinkled, eyes closed. She was perfect.

The Sculptor pulled the molding riffler with the double-edged blade from beneath a couch cushion. He slammed it through her chest and straight into her heart.

Her eyes, so alive, flew open. She tried to scream, but he shoved his shirt into her mouth, choking it off. Her hands grasped the riffler and pulled. Another stifled scream.

She kicked and clawed, tried to thrust herself up and off his throbbing shaft, but he gripped her there with his zebra-striped, leather-clad hands. Her blood pumped from her wound, spurted his face.

She thrashed so much, her face beneath the helmet began to turn blue, and he pulled his shirt from her mouth, not wanting to taint the goods with an ugly hue.

Her legs trembled. Her arms fell to her sides. Her convulsions slowed. Life ebbed from her, and she fell atop him with a dull moan.

He detected her pulse from deep inside of her, and when it stopped, it was too much for him to bear. He climaxed, just as her life force ended.

He pushed her aside onto the floor, exhaled deeply, and then rallied himself for his strict, routine clean-up. He washed himself and then scrubbed the bath. After clipping her fingernails, he pocketed them along with the used condom. He bagged his gloves and his shirt. He'd burn the evidence later.

He strapped on the HAZMAT suit from his overnight duffel, and then he rummaged through his tool bag. He sawed through her flesh and spinal cord, until he finally rendered her head in his hands. He packed it, still encased in the helmet, in his oversized cooler with dry ice.

Famished, he rewarded his hard work with a quick dinner. He pulled a five dollar foot-long from the Piazza di Spagna sub shop out of his duffel bag, and he finished off the meatball sub and Gatorade in minutes. He stripped from his coveralls and gloves, and put those into his bag with most of the other sculpting paraphernalia. He pulled up the handle of the wheeled cooler and attached his bag with a bungee cord, then headed for the door.

He turned back for a moment and eyed the remains of the Norwegian on the floor, beside the couch. The intact torso and appendages lay sprawled, as if inviting another good lay. But he'd rather no one else invade the space that had once belonged to him.

He re-gloved and concocted a small mixture of plaster. Then he stuffed her like a Thanksgiving turkey, until he was sure that no one else could mess with his bird.

Just before parting, the Sculptor performed one last act. He inserted a fuchsia silk thread into the plaster.

Looked almost like a meat thermometer. And this bird was done.

Chapter 23

After her meeting with Franz to discuss her sister's murder in the Alps, Mara boarded a hopper train from Flums to Zurich around noon, but later missed the 3:00 Milan connection to Rome. She grabbed an early dinner at a café, and then caught the 5:00 Rome-bound train.

Five hours later, Mara peered out at the landscape that signaled the approach of Rome's Termini station, and realized she'd spent the entire ride pondering the serial killer case. She'd considered the most probable suspects, all those with motive, means, and opportunity. The art professors surged to the forefront. So, did Jesse and his roommates, as well as the dean's son.

She figured that she should investigate those students and professors whose tenure overlapped with her sister's at RU six years ago. Utica, Kiever, Jesse, and Arella had all attended undergrad studies then. Professors Sugardale, Volker, Forte, and Truri had all been employed then as well. This list would suffice for now, but she planed to accrue much more information on the case from Jesse's uncle, Police Inspector Enzo. The trespass and subsequent plant of the sculpting tool beneath her pillow linked her to the Sculptor investigation, and she felt that she had every right to pursue details, even though the Rome PD might not share that sentiment.

The late February sun had long been supplanted by nightfall when she disembarked at 8:30. But, she felt as if she had just breathed new life. She felt pumped, energized, and purposeful. She felt ready to kick ass.

***

In the station, Mara noticed posters signaling a general train strike for the next twenty-four hours, beginning at 9 pm. She'd made it back to Rome just in time. Maybe luck was on her side.

She swung her bag over one shoulder and bought a Coke from a vending machine. Tonight, she planned to pour over the yearbooks she'd once spied in the Stella Luna lobby. Then, with classes canceled tomorrow due to some saint's feast day, she'd track down the police inspector for some intel.

Undeterred by the still throbbing goose-egg from her plunge into the snow crater, Mara sprang out into the cold winter night to board a city bus bound for Stella Luna's neighborhood. The buses stood dark, nearly all of them lined up with no drivers.

Damn, general strikes include the bus and metro system, too.

She readjusted her backpack, ready to hoof it and locate a taxi along the way.

That's when she spotted Utica and Jesse, also hunkered down with backpacks, exiting the terminal, headed straight for her.

As they approached, she spotted Jesse's blue and black zebra-striped gloves and cringed. When he tried to high-five her, she left him hanging.

"We were headed up to a concert in Bologna," Utica said. "But the damn train strike starts at 9:00."

"Sorry, boys," Mara said, nonplussed.

"How was skiing?" Utica asked.

She glared at Jesse. "Eventful."

"Jesse mentioned you went ass over end, almost got killed. You okay?"

"Still kicking," she said.

Utica gestured west of Termini. "Our place is close by. Come grab some beers, and you can tell us about it."

She shrugged her acceptance, and the three hiked off toward Trastevere. Would she find answers, or was she walking straight into the lion's den?

***

Mara, Jesse, and Utica pit-stopped at a bar named Babylonia off Piazza Barberini. It was hopping with people stranded by the strike, yet the three finagled a corner table in the back.

After their Kronenbourgs showed up, Mara dove into her story about plummeting from the Alpine cliff, leaving out the key fact that a madman had put her there. Jesse shifted in his seat and avoided eye contact through most of it.

Annoyed by his agitation, she asked him, "So, I never did get your whole story. What really happened to you in the wilderness?" She dared him to cave, reveal that he was her assailant with the zebra-striped gloves.

But, he didn't. "I told you, I got lost looking for you." Jesse stood and finished his bottle. "Ski patrol brought me back to their cabin. You were there, safe and sound. Not much to it." He strode toward the bar and leaned against it, waiting for the bartender to serve him.

"What's his problem?" she asked. Utica shrugged.

She was convinced Jesse knew she suspected him, and was glad Utica was there in case Jesse snapped. Though she'd resolved with Franz to keep the matter of her own attack from the authorities, she now felt compelled to privately meet with Inspector Enzo the next morning to share the details, and raise the possibility of Jesse's involvement in the matter. She'd never forgive herself if she withheld pertinent facts to an investigation out of fear, only to find that it had given the perpetrator the edge he needed to kill another innocent victim.

"Jesse told me your sister died a few years back, skiing over the same cliff? Difficult then, but scary as hell now, to think you almost took the same leap," Utica said.

Mara nodded, gulped her Kroni. "Yes, Abby was on the same RU ski trip six years earlier, but she…died from crashing into a tree." She dignified her sister's memory by leaving out the chisel planted in her brain.

"Wait a minute, your sister was Silvestri—Abigail was *your* sister?" Recognition clouded Utica's face. "Jesus, I'm so sorry." He set down his glass, and his eyes glazed over. "I remember…she looked like a movie star." He gulped down the rest of his beer.

There was that thing again that Utica had about movie star comparisons. "You knew my sister?" Mara said.

"Kiever introduced us. They'd had a…physical thing, for a little while, but then he met someone else, and he thought I might help him, take her off his hands, I guess. He was crazy to leave her. She was lovely." Utica swigged his second Kronenbourg, and then continued. "I was a freshman; she was a first year grad. We got close, fast, just after school started, until…" Utica looked up at her. "Until, the ski trip."

Stunned speechless, Mara just blinked at him.

Utica had an odd, melancholy look on his face that made her feel strangely uncomfortable.

"How 'close,' may I ask?" Mara shifted in her seat.

"I asked her out my second week there. She was incredibly beautiful, a dead ringer for Kathleen Turner in her *Romancing the Stone* days. She told me in no uncertain terms that she'd hang with me, but that she was seeing a few other guys, and did I have a problem with it? No guy turns down the body of Jessica Rabbit."

Mara smiled. Men did adore her sister.

"So, I agreed, and we…hung out. We had an amazing time for a solid month. Then we did the school's Venice/Alps trip, and she broke up with me out of the blue, no explanation. I had no idea what I did wrong. I mean, it's not like I wasn't okay with her playing the field, no worries. And it wasn't like she figured it was time to settle down with one guy she'd fallen for, because I saw her hook up with a professor and another student on that same trip." He pulled on his Kronenbourg and looked off into the distance. "I remember, we were riding the ski lift up Harlach Trail, and she broke it off for good, don't ask me why. Then she took off by herself, left me as open-mouthed as a fresh water bass."

Mara opened her own mouth to speak, then shut it. She scratched her neck, massaged her goose egg, and cracked her knuckles. Then, she spoke. "Are you telling me that you dated my sister, then you both went to the ski trip, and she broke it off right there on the Alps? Right on the trail where she died. So, you were probably—"

"I was the last person to see your sister alive," he said, looking off blankly toward the dance floor. He turned back to Mara, his face crimson. Had he just realized the gravity of what he'd just admitted?

"I'm sorry, Mara, about your sister," Utica said. He set down his half-empty beer and strolled toward the restroom.

"How sorry?" Mara muttered aloud to no one in particular.

She shuddered. Utica just moved up a few pegs on her suspect list. He and her sister had been on the same mountain, after she'd ended their relationship, just minutes before her murder. He'd had the means, motive, and opportunity. Then, and now.

***

Jesse and Utica returned to their table together with a tray of assorted beers. Jesse had a couple. Mara had a couple. Utica had a few. Boots and Arella dropped by, played darts, and took a couple. During that time, Utica regaled them with the story of his past weekend's adventure, spent motoring through the Tuscan hills, with a girl who owned a silver Ducati 6000.

Around midnight, the three heaved on their travel backpacks and stumbled out of the bar. The full moon lit the snow-covered *Tritone* Fountain like a beacon. They ambled west toward the *Trevi* Fountain, and then over to the Pantheon, before angling south onto Via Arenula. This long, broad avenue led to the Garibaldi Bridge where the roommates' commuter bus typically crossed over the Tiber and into Trastevere.

Tonight, the street was lit by the moon and little else. Vandals had smashed many of the streetlights months ago on New Year's Eve, and the city had never bothered to replace them. The three of them, hunkered over by their backpacks, walked side-by-side down the middle of the vacant avenue. Mara felt like they were tramping through a ghost town.

The air was frigid. Her hands and feet were freezing. Her nose was cold to the touch. She'd had way too much to drink, and she was dehydrated. Mara wished she were asleep in her bed. She eyed a snow bank and meandered toward it, thinking it might be a nice place to sleep. Hypothermia, be damned.

A vehicle approached from a nearby street, the wheels crunching through the snow. No engine sounded; it was like it was rolling, or being pushed. She turned. A white, unmarked van was creeping toward them, about two hundred feet behind. Its lights were off.

Jesse must have already spied it, because he grabbed her hand and angled them from the median and onto the shoulder of the road. Utica crossed to the other side, allowing the van to pass.

Another few seconds went by, but the van had still not passed. Jesse and Utica glanced at one another, nodded.

Jesse gripped her hand tighter now and sought access through the high snow banks to the sidewalk, but found none. He spotted a driveway about ten feet up, and quickened his pace.

Before they could reach it and skirt the snow bank, an icicle whizzed past her head and a stinging sensation seared there that she felt through her whole body. She looked up. No tree bough, no overhanging wires or rooftops.

She reached up with her hand at the stinging pain, and it came away smeared with her blood. Jesse stared at her, speechless. That was when she knew. It was not an icicle that had grazed her, but a bullet.

The lights of the van flashed on. Tires screeched. The van accelerated right toward them. Jesse yanked her toward the cleared driveway apron, and screamed a warning to Utica over his shoulder, "Run!"

She heard the pop of a gun with a silencer attached, but the damage it caused—a blown out car window, a smashed tree trunk, then a busted red mailbox—prompted her to run faster.

Jesse yanked her toward the other side of the street. "Serpentine!"

Together, she and Jesse ran for their lives. As more bullets sliced through the freezing night air, she pumped her legs faster than any 10K she'd ever run. Pain stabbed her chest as the freezing air chilled her lungs. She wanted to stop. She *needed* to stop and breathe.

But, Jesse relentlessly pulled her along. They snaked back and forth across the wide avenue, dodging bullets.

Jesse broke his hold. She ran alone.

"Keep your head down," Jesse yelled from across the street.

She heard the loud, sharp crack of four more shots echo through the air, this time likely fired from a handgun with no silencer. Was there someone else shooting now?

Jesse grumbled and cursed. Joining her again, he grasped her hand. The massive stained glass window of a church shattered a few feet away from them. Still, they outran the van.

Jesse continued to lead them back and forth across the street. Mara focused on finding an alleyway clear of plowed snow, or some small doorway through which they might escape. She found none.

The van's headlights drew closer, gaining on them. At any moment, one of the bullets would slice through them, or they'd be run down.

She spotted a long, two-lane street tunnel, lit by lights, up ahead. Jesse led them there. No way, they'd be sitting ducks. She tried to tug away, but Jesse wouldn't release his grip.

As they ran, she glanced around for Utica. She caught sight of him, across the wide avenue. He abruptly dropped to the ground. Mara gasped. Utica must have been shot.

But wait. She saw him cross his arms and roll beneath an SUV parked in the street. Had he been injured, or was he evading gunfire?

Suddenly, the van slowed, crept past the SUV, its side door sliding open. A tall, muscular, blond gunman with shoulder-length hair emerged, sporting a semi-automatic machine gun. He sprayed the SUV with a barrage of bullets so intense that car alarms went off up and down the avenue.

A bullet must have ripped through the SUV's gas tank, because a second later, Utica's cover exploded into a massive ball of fire.

Mara screamed.

Utica was surely dead.

The blond gunman looked up ahead, toward her and Jesse. He scowled and hauled the machine gun around, and aimed at them. But a second explosion from the SUV caused the van driver to swerve, and the blond shooter coiled himself back inside. The van gunned it, and surged past the burning SUV, directly toward them.

She and Jesse arrived at the mouth of the tunnel. Jesse yanked her hard left toward a fence running beside it, nearly popping her shoulder out of its socket. They slammed into the fence. She dug her hands and feet into the holes of the chain link fence, and started climbing the twelve-foot barricade. Bullets still pierced the air.

"No, wait. Through here," Jesse said. She spied the opening torn into part of the fence, jumped down, and pushed through the gaping hole.

Her parka got caught on the fence. She tugged it as hard as she could, until it tore free. Her hair caught in the wire mesh, and pain tore through her grazed scalp wound. She pulled it free with her fingers just as Jesse stumbled through.

He grabbed her hand and they bolted through a lot, and then along the outside of the tunnel. Bullets continued to fly, until fewer and fewer peppered the air around them. She stole a glance backward; no one had pursued them through the fence.

It was only when they heard the vehicle roar away that they finally stopped running.

"Need…to breathe." Mara bent over at her waist and sucked in air. Her adrenaline had burned off much of the alcohol she'd consumed, and now that she had a free second to think, she felt ready to throw up.

She stumbled, still doubled over, her hands shaking and her mind reeling. Someone had actually shot at her. With a freakin' machine gun. Her head was grazed. By a bullet. She'd been shot at, right there in the streets of Rome. What the hell was going on?

A couple minutes later the nausea passed, but her hands did not stop shaking.

Jesse gripped her hand again, gently this time. "Here, let me take your backpack." Jesse had already resumed normal breathing. She shook off her pack and let him carry the burden.

"Who the hell was that?" Mara said, still panting. "And why the hell were they shooting at us?" She shook her head. "And thank you for...getting us the hell away from them before they..."

Jesse pulled her to face him and locked eyes with her. "I don't know who it was, or why they tried to kill us. But, you can always count on me to keep you safe."

She began to speak, but sputtered badly, and decided to shut her mouth. She nodded instead.

With his left hand, he stroked the hair back from her head to examine her wound. "We should get you to a hospital."

She brushed it back. "No hospital. Just grazed. I'll live." She inhaled sharply, struck by the realization that Utica likely had not lived through their ordeal. Her throat constricted, and Jesse's face became a blur through her tears.

He pulled her into his arms. "It's okay. I know Utica," he said, as if having read her mind. "If anyone could've found a way out of that bind, it's him."

"But, there's no way...you really think he's still..." She couldn't finish the words. Jesse must be in shock over the loss of his close friend, and denial was his coping tactic. Still, they had to be practical. She wiped her eyes free of tears. "We need to call the police, or call Enzo. Yes, you should talk to your uncle right now," she said.

He waved her off when she mentioned Enzo, and that's when Mara saw it.

Jesse's right hand was wrapped in his bloody scarf.

"You've been shot!" she said.

Jesse held up his hand, wiggled his fingers. "Just grazed. I'll live." He winked. "And, we'll call the police after we get you safely back to the apartment."

She nodded.

Jesse chuckled. "You've got a bleeding scalp, your jacket's all ripped up, and your hair's sticking out all over. But, you couldn't be more beautiful."

She had no idea how to respond. They'd just been shot at. Their friend was probably dead. She was still suspicious of Jesse based on the zebra-striped gloves he wore on the day of her Alpine attack. And now, Jesse appeared almost drunk with shock over the whole shooting incident, enough to try to make her feel better. She couldn't have felt more confused. Every time she was convinced that Jesse Tonno was either a good guy or a bad guy, he did something to make her believe otherwise.

But then she reminded herself, that was how conmen worked.

***

Lost in their own thoughts, Mara and Jesse wound themselves through the maze of old cobblestone streets, until finally arriving at his door on Via Della Lungara. She and Jesse stumbled through the central courtyard, and dragged themselves up the four flights to the penthouse apartment.

Jesse unlocked the door, and the two stepped into the entry that opened into the kitchen. Standing at the sink was Utica, sipping from a brandy snifter.

"You're alive!" She ran to him and embraced him, splashing brandy from his glass. "You rolled under the SUV. It exploded. How are you here right now?"

Jesse patted his back, splashing more brandy onto the floor. "You made it."

Utica stuck out his lower lip. "Aww, thanks for giving a shit, guys." He kissed Mara's cheek and walked to the cabinet. He pulled out two more glasses, and poured them all enough brandy to ease their strained hamstrings and soothe their nerves.

She and Jesse stared at him. Jesse leaned against the counter, arms crossed, tapping his foot. She roamed her eyes up and down Utica's frame, amazed that he'd suffered only minor abrasions. "Well, what's your story?"

"Stop, drop, and roll," Utica said. "Slipped out the other side of the SUV before it blew, low-crawled it into the bushes, and high-tailed it when the blond Terminator drove on. Not a scratch on me." He handed them tall drinking glasses filled to the brim with Remy Martin. "You two on the other hand look like hell. Drink these and I'll cart you over to the hospital."

"Grazed. No hospital," she and Jesse said in unison.

Utica took a step back and put up his hand as if to shield himself. "I'll get the bandages then."

They wrapped their injuries, and the three spent the next hour patching holes in each other's versions of the incident, until Mara finally stood. "I feel like the walking dead. The police are going to want us to rehash this whole thing again, but I'm not going to be able to hold my head up. Before you dial Enzo, just let me grab a quick shower." She scrounged for her sweats in the backpack she'd dumped beside the door.

Her hand came away covered in thick, foamy white "Lady Legs" shave cream. "Ugh, what the hell?"

She rummaged some more, pulled out the shave cream can, and gasped. She held it up to Jesse and Utica.

The formerly pressurized can bore the jagged gash of a bullet hole.

"I'd stuck this can into my toiletry bag," Mara said. "The bag sits inside my backpack, behind the base of my skull. Whoever shot at us was a professional."

Utica locked eyes with Jesse. "Dial Enzo, now."

***

Mara had finished dressing just as Stan Kiever returned home from his weekend swim competition. Jesse and Utica recounted the highlights of their shoot-out while they awaited Enzo's arrival.

Chain-smoking something that smelled like ass, Stanky managed to lighten her mood some. Through a perpetual cloud of smoke, he recapped his feats of aquatic athleticism to them through pursed lips and squinted eyes while sprawled on his back on the carpet. Mara felt that her well-being was never at issue, because they all anticipated Enzo's arrival at any moment. So, she relaxed, enjoyed a few laughs, yet remained alert to any clues that the three suspects might unknowingly drop in her lap.

Ryan Volker soon returned home. He strode into the living room, arm-in-arm, with Fritz Arella. Formerly suicidal in appearance, Arella seemed downright jovial tonight. Crazy drunk and falling over laughing, he and Volker poured brandies, flounced into Volker's room, and slammed the door. The apartment was apparently the venue for a prime suspect convention.

"What the fuck was that about?" Stanky said.

Jesse shot Mara a curious look, as if something just occurred to him.

Before she could ask, someone pounded on the door.

"Who the fuck is here now?" Stanky whined. He drew a puff from his septic cigarillo, withdrew from his prone position, and crawled on his hands and knees to the door.

"Couldn't be Enzo already. He's coming from the other side of the city," Jesse said.

More loud knocking.

"Hold your horses, already! Who the fuck is it anyway?" Stanky said, reaching up for the latch.

No one answered. The heavy fist continued pounding.

"This better be some hot bitch in heat," he said as he slid the chain. "Or else I'm gonna be pissed." He turned the knob and jimmied the door open a crack.

The cigarillo dropped from Stan Kiever's pursed lips. The door was pushed wide open, and he was thrown from his knees and onto his back.

Filling up most of the doorframe was seven and a half feet of muscle, capped off with blond, shoulder-length hair.

Mara began to shake. She pointed to him with a trembling hand and shouted, "It's him! Oh, hurry, shut the door, Stanky!"

The monster from the van had arrived. The same man who'd machine-gunned the SUV and blown it up like a nuked potato, and who'd tried to poke holes through her and Jesse with a silenced handgun. The big-boned skyscraper stood in the doorway staring at the huddled group in the living room with a glare that could only be interpreted as pissed off.

"Shut the fucking door!" Utica shouted. From the living room, he hoisted a twelve-pound piece of Roman cobblestone they used as a paperweight and hurled it at the man's chest.

The rock bounced off the man's wide, pectoral expanse and clunked Kiever in the head, knocking him out.

Jesse jumped up, brandished one of the wrought iron table lamps, and barreled toward the intruder.

But before he could slam into him, a short, wiry Italian man with spectacles sneaked out from behind the blond man and stood squarely in front of him. Jesse halted.

The five-foot beanpole in the suit held up his credentials. *"Agenzia Informazioni e Sicurezza Esterna."*

"Excuse me?" Mara said.

"Italian Secret Service," Jesse translated.

***

Utica entered the kitchen, and stood behind Jesse.

Jesse set the lamp that he'd been brandishing back to its spot on the table, and offered the man a seat with a look of confusion on his face. The three of them sat, while the blond hulk stood guard on the threshold.

"What's going on here?" Mara said to Utica. "That blond gargantuan, along with some other guys in a van, shot at us. Why are you two kowtowing to his skinny little sidekick?" Mara turned to Jesse. "Shouldn't we call the Embassy?"

"Enzo will arrive any minute," Jesse said to her. Then he turned to the wiry little man. "My uncle, Inspector Enzo

Tranchille, has contacts at the Embassy, and we'll straighten this whole thing out."

Stanky stirred, pulled himself up into a kitchen chair, and rubbed his head. He waggled his finger at the blond hulk and his companion. "I'm telling my dad on you. He's a United States Senator. He'll have both your heads on a fucking silver platter." He eyed them while he lit another foul cigarillo. Taking a long drag, he held it in, and then exhaled.

Mara looked around the table. "Kiever's right. Shouldn't we inform our government that these Italians are bullying Americans? Why the hell were they shooting at us anyway?"

She looked to Utica, then to Jesse. Both remained silent. And both appeared guilty as hell. "What the hell is wrong with you two?" She plucked the credentials off the table and examined them. "How do we even know these are real? That this 'Milan Station Chief Michele Ponte' is really who he says is?"

The man pulled out an envelope from inside his jacket. He unfolded three sheets and placed them in front of Utica, Jesse, and Mara. Then, he spoke to them in perfect English. "Please sign these. We regret that you three were mistaken for terrorists that fit your description. When we saw you with backpacks, we assumed malevolent intentions, and we acted to disarm you."

"Disarm us! You blew up an SUV!" Mara exclaimed. Her temples pulsed, and the muscles in her neck tightened.

Station Chief Ponte ignored her outburst, and she huffed at his disregard.

"These affidavits will release the AISE from any wrongdoing in the matter and will render the matter closed," Ponte said. "Copies will be forwarded to Switzerland's Information Service—"

"Switzerland? Wait, what the hell are you talking about?" Mara said.

The wiry man explained. "A possible terrorist situation was called in to both the Swiss and Italian intelligence bureaus. As of yesterday, Ms. Silvestri, you were believed to be a person of interest. We waited until you arrived in Rome to ascertain whether you had accomplices. We naturally assumed these two gentlemen—"

"Assumed?" All of a sudden something had clicked for her. "The secret police of Italy and Switzerland sure make a lot of assumptions." She was sure now that the "terrorist situation" was somehow linked to her conversation with Franz the day before. The shooting must have been Intel's way of ensuring that she stay quiet about her sister's murder. "I understand the full ramifications of your presence here," she said to Ponte, "and I assure you that none of this was necessary."

The suited man nodded. "As long as we share a mutual understanding."

Mara nodded in return. She planned to cooperate long enough to find her sister's murderer, and ultimately stop the Sculptor from ever killing again.

She glanced at Jesse and Utica, both silently evaluating the situation. She again wondered if their silence stemmed from guilt, and she shuddered.

"What the fuck is wrong with you two jamokes?" Stanky shouted at Jesse and Utica. Spittle flew from his lips. "Cat got your fucking tongues, or what? Now she's gonna sign their little silence agreement? I strongly suggest you two rethink this!"

Stanky stood and put his hands on his hips, waved his Zippo lighter in the blond hulk's face. "I've got fire, and I'll use it if I have to! I'll burn you, motherfucker!"

Blondie pulled a long silver Luger from the back of his pants, and placed it against Stanky's temple.

Kiever stopped flicking the lighter. And wet his pants.

Utica and Jesse jumped to their feet, moved toward the blond, fists clenched, ready to take him down before he could shoot out Stanky's brains.

That's when Inspector Enzo Tranchille finally walked through the unlocked door. "Stop this now," he said.

A mixture of relief and confusion played with Jesse's features.

Then, a woman's voice, loud but sophisticated in timber, resounded from the hallway, directly behind Enzo. "What kind of mess have you created this time, you overgrown piece of meat?"

A tall, leggy blond of about fifty sashayed into the room in an aubergine silk robe, high-heeled slippers, and a Prada handbag. She plucked the Luger from Blondie's thick mitt. "Stop playing with guns and get the hell out. Both of you," she said to the blond and to Station Chief Ponte.

Blondie turned to leave, and she smacked the hulking policeman against the side of the head. His massive shoulders slumped, and he shuffled out the door. Ponte collected his documents and followed him into the corridor.

The woman turned to Enzo. "My sincere apologies. The children overreacted. As head of AISE, I promise it won't happen again." She sauntered to the door, and then looked back at Enzo with piercing eyes. Her robe had fallen from her shoulder, revealing a leopard-skin negligee. "I certainly hope that you'll allow me to make this up to you." She winked at him, and then she was gone, her silk robe fluttering behind her.

Mara stared at Enzo. "What the hell is going on? And, with all due respect, sir, what the hell took you so long?"

Enzo placed a hand on her shoulder. "I received the call from Jesse about the shooting, and I'm happy to see that you're alright, Mara. My apologies for not arriving sooner. Police matters detained me."

She nodded and took a step back. "A lot's happened; I'm sorry if I came across a little strong." Her face stung with heat.

The inspector waved it off. "*Non ti preoccupare, cara.* You've been through a great deal."

She smiled. Enzo turned to Jesse and glared at him, shaking his head, likely wondering if his nephew was falling back on his old ways of getting into trouble. Utica thrust out his hand, and Enzo grasped it and shook it. Stanky went into the bathroom to clean himself. Volker and Arella had never even poked their heads out.

Enzo turned back to Mara. "I'm not sure I understand everything that's happened tonight; it was a short call. But, I hope you know that Jesse will always look out for your best interests."

Mara nodded. "Thank you, Enzo, for putting a stop to the chaos with the secret police before things had gotten any worse." So much had happened, and all she could think of was sleep. She knew that she, Jesse, and Utica still needed to give a statement to Enzo about the night's events, but she just needed to rest her eyes a moment. She lay her head into her arms at the kitchen table, completely drained.

Utica touched her elbow. "I'll get you a blanket and pillow. Be right back." He slipped into his room and shut the door. Mara yawned. She hadn't even considered the rest of the evening, a long lapse of time when the police chief would be leaving her and the prime suspects to their own devices. She yawned again, rubbed her eyes. Her fatigue far outweighed her personal safety now; hell, she'd flog herself for irresponsibility after a few hours of shut-eye, providing she was still alive to do so.

"*Zio* Enzo, is there any way we could finish this tomorrow?" Jesse asked.

Mara raised her head, eyes open just enough to glimpse Inspector Enzo relent with a much welcome nod. The two men shook hands goodnight. Enzo obviously entrusted her protection to his nephew for the rest of the night; she prayed it was well-founded.

"'Night, Enzo." Mara got to her feet and yawned. She stretched both arms over her head, cracked her knuckles, and nudged Jesse's shoulder with her own. "Thanks, Jesse, for the roller-coaster ride tonight," she said. "I had fun."

He kissed her cheek, and as she headed for the couch, his scent made her salivate. She smiled, and wondered if fun was the word for it. In her sleepy, vulnerable state of mind, she flirted with the idea of detouring toward Jesse's bed and taking it over.

Or, maybe even sharing it with him.

A moment later, the woman who was the head of Italy's secret police reappeared in the doorway. She gestured to Enzo like someone used to getting what they want. "By the way, I'll need a report on my desk by tomorrow, Inspector Tranchille."

Enzo nodded.

The woman then turned to Jesse. "You, too, Inspector." She waved and slammed the door behind her.

***

Mara froze. She looked at Jesse. Jesse returned the stare. Both stood wide-eyed and unable to move, like deer in headlights.

She took a deep breath. "You're a cop?" Mara muttered. She clenched her fists, and felt her face burn with anger.

Jesse lowered his eyes and nodded.

Memories flashed through her mind—beer runs, the Super Bowl party, rehearsing business presentations, the all-night heart-to-heart on the ride to Venice, his kiss.

All of it had been meant to disarm her, cajole her, con her, use her. All of it was meant to play-act the role of a fellow grad student to solve a case.

None of what they'd shared had meant anything to him beyond his job as an undercover cop. None of it had been real.

She exhaled slowly, as if deflating. Her body slumped into a kitchen chair. Her mouth felt dry, and the goose egg on her forehead began to throb again.

She'd spent most of her life detaching herself from personal complications, because anytime she'd ever allowed herself to grow close to someone, she'd lose them. She thought of her father, and her sister. And, the handful of men who'd tried to penetrate her emotional barrier but had given up on the effort as futile.

Jesse had been the only one she'd let in, even just a little. And in the end, she'd lost him, too.

"You lied to me," she said in a voice that came out just above a whisper.

Enzo slipped out into the hallway.

Jesse opened his mouth to speak, but she held up her hand to stop him.

"You just made it all up as you went along—our studies, the laughs, the dancing, the kissing—all of it was part of your cover." She looked away, licked her lips. "*I* was your cover."

"Hey," Jesse grabbed the tips of her fingers and held them loosely. "I always had your back, no matter what. I still do," he said.

She looked back at his face, and reached out for his stubbled face. Then, she backhanded him, hard.

He released her fingers.

She allowed a smile to creep across her face, and Jesse took a step back. "It's funny," she said. "All this time I thought Jesse Tonno was…a little bit dangerous, yeah, a bit of a wild card. At times, even a potential serial killer."

Jesse stared at her, his eyebrows knitted into a puzzled expression.

She chuckled. "Yep, you made it onto my personal suspect list after I spotted your zebra-striped gloves, ones that matched my attacker's gloves in the Alps."

"You never told me you were attacked. What happened?" Jesse said.

"Oh, please wipe that pathetic look of concern off your face. You don't need that disguise anymore, Inspector."

Jesse shook his head. "I meant everything I ever said to you."

"Through it all, and for no reason I can name, I always gave you the benefit of the doubt. But, please, allow me a shred of dignity, would you? Do not stand there and continue the charade that I ever meant anything to you beyond the job."

"I will never forget the time we shared together," Jesse said.

"And I will never forget wasting my time with someone who *pretended* he cared."

***

Enzo cleared his throat from the hallway, and after a few moments, he stepped back inside the apartment, looking sheepish.

At the same time, a toilet flushed, and a moment later, Utica stepped from the door to his bedroom into the living room. "I forgot I was supposed to get you these." Utica rubbed his eyes and handed Mara a pillow and blanket. "Can't believe you're all still talking. Did I miss something?"

"I was just leaving," Enzo said.

Utica shrugged. "'Kay. 'Night, Inspector." He shut the door, and the creak of his bed signaled he must have gone to sleep.

Enzo extended his hand to Mara. She hesitated, and then took it, and he covered it with his other. He held her gaze, too, as if seeking forgiveness.

Mara took a deep breath. "I meant to discuss another matter with you alone at your office in the morning, Inspector. But, under the circumstances," she aimed a barrage of disdain in Jesse's general direction, "I think it wise to share it with the police now." She poured herself a glass of ice water and spent the next few minutes recounting the details of her assault on the mountain, her revelation about her sister's death, and her pointed discussion with Franz.

Through it all Enzo sat quietly, taking notes. Jesse paced, wringing his hands and running them through his bedraggled hair.

"I thought the police should know all of this," Mara said, "in case any connections arise between my sister's murder, my attack, and the Sculptor case. But, in light of the length to which certain intelligence agencies will go in the name of discretion, certain information might be best kept close to the vest, for the well-being of others." She sighed, recalling Franz's despair when he spoke of his son's murder. She reminded herself that she too had literally dodged bullets only hours earlier.

"Thank you, Mara. You have my word that we will handle the matter delicately. Also, you have my deepest sympathies over the loss of your sister," Enzo said.

Jesse caught her gaze, nodded. "I'll do whatever to it takes to catch the bastard that killed her, and hurt you." He reached to touch the bruise on her forehead, but she recoiled, and he turned away.

Enzo sighed. "My dear, as you aware, this is an ongoing investigation. Any pertinent information relative to this case must remain confidential.

"Including my nephew's status as an undercover police officer. We'd like to maintain his cover as a fellow student, so as not to disrupt the progress we've made in our search for the serial killer." The Chief Inspector released her hand and stepped back, awaiting her response.

"Enzo, my thoughts are with the victims' families." She swallowed hard. Ever since the discovery of her sister's murder, she'd considered herself "the victim's family."

"I promise to keep quiet the identity of—" she spoke her next words with slow precision, "Inspector Jesse Tonno? That's probably not your real name, is it?"

Jesse shook his head. "Last name's Autunno. Jesse's short for Giuseppe."

Mara nodded. "I promise not to blow Inspector Autunno's cover. I also plan to fulfill my duties as a co-teaching assistant with Jesse to Signore Jack in the graduate business department. And I'll fully cooperate with the police in capturing the killer. Please let me know if there's anything I can contribute," Mara said.

"I knew I could count on you, my dear," Enzo said. "It's more important than ever that we're all onboard, especially in light of new developments in the case."

Mara and Jesse both looked to the Chief Inspector and hoped he wouldn't say what she knew full well he would. But, he did.

"We just found another body. The Sculptor has murdered his seventh victim."

***

In his studio around the time the sun was just beginning to rise, the Sculptor stood before the empty pedestal draped in velvet fabric. He grasped the decapitated head by its tendrils, and impaled it onto the iron armature, upon which he'd also later impart plastered body parts. When he found the right ones.

He prodded open one of the eyelids and pined for their vitality. He rubbed the strands of her black hair between the both hands, coiled one of the long curls around his middle finger. He nudged the cheeks with his knuckle, lamenting that the bloom in them had faded.

She did not hold for him that look that he sought to recreate as his masterpiece.

But he knew there was someone out there that would.

He wouldn't stop until he got her.

PART II:

SKELETAL ARMATURE

"The Sculptor produces the beautiful statue by chipping away such parts of the marble block as are not needed—it is a process of elimination."

—Elbert Green Hubbard,
an American writer, publisher, artist, and philosopher, and founder of the Roycroft artisan community in East Aurora, NY

Chapter 24

The sun rose over the Aventine Hill. Shadows lingered over the Trinity College duplex rented by Norwegian film student, Taka Fergen, who also happened to be the latest victim of the Sculptor.

Inspector Giuseppe "Jesse" Autunno sat on the apartment's third step, leaning against the metal railing of the entry. He tipped his head back, shut his eyes to the rising sun, and rolled a few antacid tablets into his mouth.

Four to six of the tablets hit his tongue. He chomped them to bits and swallowed the thick paste of saliva and calcium carbonate slowly, in a vain attempt to soothe his raging heartburn. While he waited to inspect the crime scene with the Chief Inspector, he replayed the previous evening's debacle in his mind.

Jesse had been responsible for a civilian's protection many times before. But, he'd never developed feelings for a protectee.

He had never fallen so hard for *anyone*, ever. That is, until Mara Silvestri came along.

He'd meant to tell her, plenty of times, that he was an undercover detective planted years earlier at RU to hunt down the Sculptor.

Since the first murder of a Brazilian woman at RU five years ago, the killer had begun a spree of sporadic killings at all three of Rome's main universities. Captain Sciug had determined early on that infiltrating one of the colleges that worked so closely with the two others, would be the best course of action to shake out the perpetrator.

Jesse never even had the chance to tell Mara that he was a cop, or that he had fallen in love with her.

Chief Inspector Tranchille cleared his throat as he climbed the steps. "Helluva night, my boy. Nothing we can't learn from, and then move on. How's the hand?"

Jesse pulled his bandaged hand from his jacket pocket, the same hand that had been wounded the previous evening by the secret police who had tried to run them down.

"Last two fingers grazed, broken, and taped." Jesse shrugged. "I've had worse."

"Patrolman found your gun where you said you'd been tagged, minus the four rounds you'd spent at the scene. Evidence, now."

Jesse had considered himself lucky when he'd managed to conceal his weapon from Mara while returning gunfire during the van incident. A firearm would have certainly diminished the blanket of trust he'd worked so hard to weave around the two of them. The same one that he'd then shredded to bits shortly afterward.

"Thanks, I was issued a new one this morning," Jesse said. He hated breaking in a new gun. He downed two more antacids. "Ready to go in?"

"Lead the way," Enzo said.

They ascended the exterior steps, donned latex shoes and gloves, and walked in.

"No forced entry?" Jesse asked.

"Never is," Enzo said. "Just like the others, victim invited him in, consented to sex, then he turns on her."

Already inside were crime scene investigators, wrapping up the task they'd begun the evening before. At the archway to the living room, Jesse paused for an overview of the CS before proceeding further.

The carpeted, 200 square foot room, outfitted with a sofa, two chairs, a coffee table, and a television bore a minimalist, neutral, earth-tone décor. The killer had since redecorated in various shades of blood red, sanguine maroon, and plaster-of-Paris white. From the archway, Jesse spotted something that the Sculptor must have missed. White flakes, resembling corn flakes but snow white, powdered the interior of the nearest coffee-table legs.

The victim's body lay on the floor beside the sofa, arms and legs sprawled outward. Each appendage, as well as the internal cavity of the female victim, had been cast in plaster to varying degrees of dryness, and marked with a small wisp of reddish-purple thread in between her legs. The first rays of morning sun shone in through the shutters and highlighted what the CSIs had also surely noted with their lamps—more flecks of white powder along her inner thighs.

"Her head?" Jesse asked.

"Removed with some sort of saw, we think; no weapons at the scene," Enzo said. "He took the head with him."

"A fucking trophy," Jesse muttered.

"Just met with Chief Sciug," Enzo said. "Victim's been positively ID'd: Ms. Taka Fergen, Oslo, Norway. Confirmed via a Mickey Mouse tattoo on the victim's pelvis, large birthmark on top of the left foot. Parents notified; fourth year undergrad at Trinity College. She appears to have been a friend of a friend of one of your roommates, a Ms. Penelope Fraise from the States."

Jesse nodded. "Penelope is Kiever's fu—um, buddy."

Enzo peered over at him, and then back to the bloody scene before him. "I'd like you to phone Penelope in the next day or two. We tried to contact her, but she'd already caught an early flight back to her parents in the States. See what she knows."

Jesse nodded. "Any leads from forensics so far?"

"Various art tools are at the lab."

"I would've liked the chance to walk through myself first thing, sir," Jesse said. "I'm not certain why last night I wasn't—"

"The girl's parents had just arrived for a surprise visit and found her like this. Scene was taped off by a responding officer, and then reopened for CSI." Enzo looked up at Jesse. "Otherwise, you and I are the first to walk through, Detective."

Jesse nodded. "I just don't want to miss anything, or muddle any evidence. This case has surpassed ugly. When we find this guy, I want him to pay."

"He will," Enzo said. "In the meantime, get to school. Time for you to face the music."

***

Jesse popped four more antacids, and stepped through the door of the IntBiz classroom. It was abuzz with talk of the latest murder and Mara was noticeably absent. Jesse took his seat in front of Signore Jack's desk. He waited for the professor, and Hurricane Mara, to arrive.

When she finally entered the classroom and took her seat next to him, he expected her to unleash the full fury of hell. Instead, she opened her notebook, sipped from a steaming to-go cup, and waited silently for the professor to arrive.

This was bad. Hellfire he could deal with. Polite silence was foreign to him, and he had no idea what to do or say next.

Signore Jack sauntered into the room, and the class proceeded as usual. Minutes after it ended, Mara stood and left the room, without a word.

Jesse shrugged and made his way to the professor's tiny office, where he spent the next three of his designated office hours alone. No students or professors stopped by so he diligently worked the Sculptor case file all morning.

Around midday, Mara appeared at the door. Jesse braced himself.

She pulled a bulging manila folder from her bag and slid a sheet of lined paper across the desk. Seven names were listed alphabetically: Arella, Forte, Kiever, Sugardale, Truri, Utica, and Volker. She'd named the top suspects in the Sculptor case. He looked up at her and waited for an explanation.

"I'd promised Enzo that I wouldn't out your professional status in this investigation, and I meant it," Mara said. "However, this case affects me directly. I believe that the Sculptor killed my sister, with the same sort of weapon used to murder some of the other women. And I think there is a reason why the sculpting tool was planted beneath my pillow. Also, the Italian and Swiss secret police shot to kill us last night, to keep quiet my knowledge of their bungled investigation into my sister's death. I have a personal stake in this case, and want to solve it as much as you do."

Mara's eyes blazed with determination. Her adorable nostrils flared.

"Now, I don't know if anything you ever said to me was the truth," she said, stabbing him through the heart with her statement, "but if I ever meant anything at all to you, Jesse, you have to tell me what you know. I cannot sit idly by while some deranged—"

"No way," Jesse said. He sympathized with her desire to contribute, but he'd never live with himself if anything happened to her.

Mara's eyes flew wide.

"I cannot risk your personal safety," he said.

She stood from her chair. "As long as this bastard roams the city, my personal safety, and that of hundreds of other female university students, remains at risk. You need my help. You—"

"Stay out of police business, that's how you can help. Otherwise, too dangerous."

"I can take care of myself," she said. "And, if you don't work with me on this, I'll just proceed on my own."

Jesse stood, slammed his hand on the desk. "Don't you give me an ultimatum!" He stepped around the desk and came within inches of her face. "I'll haul your fine ass in and lock it up, and make damn sure nothing happens to you."

Mara slammed her fist on the desk. The blood rushed to her face, and Jesse felt his blood rush south. "How dare you threaten me?" she said, waving her hands in the air. "I'm offering you my cooperation, my assistance, and any—"

He took hold of her wild hands. "I know you're smart, and you're tough. And, that you're angry and scared."

She furled her eyebrows. "I am *not* afraid of that sonofabitch."

"That's *exactly* why I cannot let you go chasing after the psychopath," Jesse said.

Mara tried to yank her hands away, to no avail. He was not letting her go.

"You thickhead, Mara, don't you understand?" Jesse said. "I would die if anything happened to you."

Mara stopped tugging away, and relaxed her arms. She stared at him.

"I'm a cop," he said. "It's what I know. I've never met anyone like you, and now I'm completely messed up over it."

She pulled out of his grasp. "I'm sorry that I messed up your life." She shrugged, turned away. "Get over it."

"I don't want to get over it," he said. "I meant everything I said to you."

"You played me." She walked toward the office window. "I poured out my heart to you. On the way to Venice. In your apartment. In the park. You pretended to confide in return."

"No. I did no such—"

"Don't deny it," she said. "This entire pretense was a scam, a lie, a part you played to infiltrate the student body and do your job. I get it. I don't like it. But, it's done. I'm over it." She faced him. "I just want to know what you know, so that I can do my part. To end all of this. I want to find the guy who murdered my sister."

"I'm an undercover cop; catching this killer is my job. But, none of what I felt about you was a lie." He took a step forward. She took a step back. He turned away.

He looked down at the desk, rapped his knuckles against the wood, shifted the blotter, and tossed a few things over in his mind. Their combined efforts would likely prove more productive than Rome's police force so far. There was no point in coddling this woman, and working together might be the only way to keep her out of trouble.

"If I share *some* of my information, I have to know that you won't divulge any of it," Jesse said.

She turned to face him. "Of course, you—"

"Hold on. There's more," he added. Mara looked so...hopeful. He wanted to kiss her so badly. "I need to know that you won't go after the sick bastard yourself."

She shook her head. "I'll be careful, I promise. Now, tell me what you've got, and I'll tell you what I've got." Her eyes sparkled with mischief.

He grinned and offered his hand. "Friends again?"

"Not on your life," she said. "You're a conman, through and through, Inspector. Not falling for that smile of yours ever again." She grasped his hand and shook it. "But, you've got information I need, and I plan to use you like a two-bit whore."

***

"So, what you think about my suspect list?" Mara sat behind Signore Jack's desk now, hands folded, straight in her chair. All business.

"They're all viable," he said. "All seven had the means, motive, and opportunity. I've been roommates with three of them for the past six years, and they all stand on equal footing. The two art profs and the ex-boyfriend are on the list for obvious reasons. But, why do you put Jack on the list?"

"He's been around RU as far back as my sister, and he doesn't have an alibi for any of the victims," she said. "Though, the fact that he's friends with Enzo seems to diminish—"

"He's not."

"What?" Mara said.

Jesse shook his head. "After retiring from the Army, Jack was a general contractor. Enzo hired him years ago, even before the case was open, to build his backyard pergola. Just so happened he was hired at RU around the same time."

Mara jotted a few notes. "What can you tell me about the latest victim?"

"She was…" Jesse trailed off. He knew that Mara had no right to the details of the investigation, and divulging this information made him worry.

"Just come clean, so I don't have to dirty my own hands, would ya?" she said.

Jesse had spent his life breaking the rules, getting into trouble. When he got hurt, stopped playing pro ball, he broke more rules. That is until Enzo set him straight and provided him a new life, dictated by making sure others played by the rules. Control was what Jesse had needed, and now this beautiful woman was asking him to relinquish.

"The victim was a Trinity film student. A friend of Kiever's girl," Jesse said.

"I'd heard from Lana that Penelope returned to the States, but she didn't know why," Mara said. "Poor Pen."

He nodded. He opened his mouth to speak, but hesitated.

She raised her eyebrows. "Go on, give me whatever you've got. You should know by now that I can take it." She smirked.

"Fine. The victim was decapitated, butchered, and plastered." He looked up to gauge her reaction.

"What else?"

"There were sculpting tools left behind, as is his MO," he said. "But, this time, the Trinity College insignia was engraved on the wooden handles of some of them."

"The same types of tools left behind at all the other crime scenes?"

He nodded.

"Akin to the same size and type left on my pillow?"

He nodded again.

"Of course, it easily points to Trinity's art department, but the killer could have planted them to lay blame elsewhere," she said.

"Or the killer's getting careless."

"Or wants to get caught," she said. She flipped through the rest of her file, and then looked up at him. "Think about it, any one of these suspects had the opportunity to commit the murder yesterday, and then show their face at your apartment, as if nothing was amiss. What's this guy's goal? Amass as many bodies as he can before getting caught? Populate a museum? Public notoriety? Revenge?" She picked up the suspect list. "Similarly, what makes these guys tick?"

"Utica, Kiever, and Volker have been living with me for years. I already know them like the back of my hand."

Mara nodded. "But it's also true that some married people learn decades later that their spouse has been living a double life."

"True. But we need to learn more about the others. The other night, Volker had Arella over. Volker never has anyone over, ever. But, they sure seemed like good buddies. I'll ask them out for beers, see what they know."

Mara nodded. "Volker's tight with the other art profs too, from all of their field trips together over the years. I'm sure you can ask him more about their backgrounds, too."

Jesse nodded.

"And, I can work on Jack," Mara said. "I'm his TA for God's sake. I'll just hound him like a groupie."

"No, I don't want you close to that guy by yourself. I don't trust him. We play him as a team."

"It's not like I'm offering him any of *my* T&A," she smirked.

Jesse looked up sharply. "Don't even joke. He's a scoundrel with women, especially students."

"Let's not forget that I am a student, Detective. And that he may be a legitimate professor. This may be your cover; but my Master's degree is on the line here."

A commotion arose on the other side of the door, and they both hurriedly packed away their Sculptor notes. Jesse heard a woman laugh, and then something slumped against the door jamb.

Mara rose and opened the door. Signore Jack stumbled back into the room, attached to the lips of a graduate student who was known to solicit high grades any way she could. Jack regained his footing, shook the young woman's hand awkwardly, and shut the door on her. He sauntered further into the room, beet-faced. "Pardon my indiscretion. I plumb forgot you two held office hours today."

Jack turned and shut the door, and Jesse shot Mara a told-you-so glance. "I was just telling Mara that I'd been feeling left out of the juicy discussions you two have about IntBiz class," Jesse said, and stuck out his tongue at Mara, just before the professor turned to face them. "From now on, I'd like to uphold my duties as fellow teaching assistant and join in on the party."

"Of course, we'd love to include you, my man. You're a big part of this IntBiz team, and we'd love to have you engage in a bit of intercourse right along with us. I mean, it's not like Ms. Silvestri and I are planning on running out to some bar and getting completely plastered while we grade papers." Jack hung his long suede coat on the coat rack in the corner. "Son, I promise never to get this woman plastered without your help."

Chapter 25

The following day, Mara sat across from Enzo in his office. Jesse sat beside her. While Enzo poured them steaming mugs of American coffee, Mara marveled at how much the dynamic between all three of them had changed.

She thought about the first time she'd sat in this office, after reporting the chisel beneath her pillow to Chief Investigator Enzo weeks earlier, while the flirtatious Jesse kept secret his and his uncle's working relationship. She'd been a passive observer then, reacting to the people and events around her. In effect, she'd drifted off course from her usual proactive, headstrong self.

But when Jesse's cover had been blown two nights ago, she regrouped. She shored up her vulnerability to Jesse's wily nature and reset her course. From now on, she would actively pursue her career goals, move ahead with disseminating her father's remains back to Italian soil, and take the reins on vindicating her sister's murder. This meant working in tandem with Jesse and the police, exchanging information and chasing down leads on equal footing.

Yesterday, she'd convinced Jesse of her determination, and for over an hour this morning, after some shouting and violent hand gestures, she'd managed to sway Enzo as well. Now, the three sat at Enzo's desk with hot coffee and all the cards on the table. Including her own.

Quid pro quo, she rehashed, officially this time, every detail of her encounter with the attacker on the Swiss mountain, as well as her follow-up discussion with Franz, the ski patrol ranger, whose identity they swore to conceal, for the time being.

Enzo's phone rang. He answered, listened briefly, and hung up.

"Forensics lifted prints from the tools left at yesterday's crime scene. They ran a comparative analysis to our prime suspects and hit pay dirt."

Jesse leaned forward. "What have you got?"

"The tools may have belonged to Trinity College," Enzo said, "but only one set of prints were found on all of them. They belong to an RU professor."

"Who is it?" Mara said with raised eyebrows.

Enzo took a deep breath and met her eyes. "Ryan Volker."

***

"There's an Art in Rome class at the Vatican in two hours. Volker will be at our apartment preparing for it." Jesse stood.

"I'll head him off there, make sure he hangs around long enough for a uniform to show up and bring him in."

"There's more," Enzo said. "Those flakes you found on the coffee table, and on the victim's inner thighs—more gypsum flakes. Similar to the other crime scenes."

"Gypsum flakes, used to make drywall?" Mara said.

"Drywall, and also the same kind found in plaster of Paris—an artist's brew for plastering and sculpting," Enzo said.

Jesse's eyes widened. "Volker's always working on some kind of pasty art project in our kitchen. Let's see if we can match up some of his plaster to CSI's plaster." Without another word, Jesse pushed aside the chair and bolted from the room.

Mara met Enzo's gaze. "So that's 'Jesse the cop.'"

"Jesse the cop is the same as Jesse the man. Still mortal. What worries me about my nephew is I'm not sure he knows that."

"Whomever he is, he's also an incorrigible liar."

"He's in love with you."

Mara stood and gathered her jacket and bag. "I can't love someone who lies."

"He lied to protect you. Why do you keep lying about being in love with him?"

"Sir, how can you presume such a thing?" Mara said.

Enzo waved away her denial. "It's quite clear to me that you love him." Enzo stood and opened the door for her. "I understand that you're hurt. But, Jesse is a good man." He touched her shoulder tenderly, like her dad used to. "You may want to spend a little time investigating that too, my dear."

***

Mara stepped out of the police station and into the gray March day. She boarded the bus that would return her to Stella Luna, and found Kristen and Lana waving from the back. She wove through other passengers to take a seat across from her friends.

"We lost track of you after Venice," Lana said. "Both of us went shopping in Milan—"

Kristen interrupted. "Mmm, then I ran into Bergamo who was backpacking in Milan and I stayed a few days 'til this morning."

"Sounds like love?" Mara said,

"You never know…" Kristen blushed.

"Heard you and Jesse took off to ski by yourselves. You two hook up?" Lana drawled in her Southern accent.

"We're just colleagues." Mara changed the subject. "I spent the past weekend studying mostly. Only a week and a half until midterms, then spring break. You two planning any trips?"

"Bergamo and I talked about going to Pompeii, with a lot of other RU kids for Hedonism Week," Kristen said.

"Stan Kiever just cornered me after class today and asked me to go to Paris with him," Lana said. "Enjoy our own bit of hedonism, with no strings attached, just the way I like it." She licked her finger and buffed the tip of her brown leather boot.

"You and Kiever?" Mara said.

"Mmmm, Senator's son, Mr. Kiever is yummy, and wealthy," Lana said.

Mara considered her friend's safety, and the possibility of her hooking up with a man that might be the Sculptor. The police were arresting Professor Volker within the hour, so maybe there'd be nothing to worry about. She kept her concerns to herself for the time being.

"But, what happened with you and Miguelito?" Kristen said.

"Just a boy-toy," Lana said. "Besides, no worries, y'all. I'm not looking for commitment. Just some hot lovin' by someone with the means to spoil me in good fashion." Kristen laughed, but Mara's worries deepened, and apparently it showed on her face.

Lana put her hand on Mara's shoulder. "Don't worry, so far I've been a good girl. Last night, Stanky and I went out clubbing. He asked to come over, but I am not the type of girl to fool around on the first date, moneybags or not, no sir."

Mara relaxed her shoulders and exhaled.

"I'll screw him on the second date, maybe, but certainly not the first."

Mara cringed and shook her head.

"Wouldn't mind Stanky calling me tonight, cross fingers," Lana said. "If he's busy with Pen, I can always try Miguelito, him and that sexy saxophone of his—"

"You didn't hear? Pen's gone home. Her Trinity classmate was murdered," Mara said.

Kristen opened her mouth and released a small squeal. She hooked a finger through her curls and turned to look out the bus window.

"Another victim of the Sculptor," Mara muttered.

"Oh, God, that's awful," Lana said.

The bus neared their apartment and when Kristen turned back to face them, she seemed composed, until she murmured to them, "She was murdered during the Ides of March."

The bus dropped them at Stella Luna. As the three shuffled into the apartment, Mara wondered if the Ides of March held more in store for them.

The person seated at her kitchen table provided the answer.

Chapter 26

"Place looks like a fucking bomb went off."

Arms crossed, a cigarette hanging from his lower lip, Kiever surveyed his ruined apartment from the kitchen archway. He whined to Jesse who sat at the table, "Books and stuff on the floor, cupboards open, drawers dumped out—we must have been robbed."

Jesse stood and patted his friend on the back. Stanky had arrived minutes earlier, but shock had knocked the speech out of him until now. He continued to pan the living room, and looked like a little boy who just saw his dog get run over by a garbage truck.

"Shit, they messed with my porn collection," Stanky said. He gestured to the dozens of DVDs collapsed like an avalanche in the corner of the room. "Took me forever to alphabetize all those."

Jesse bent to pick up his bush hat, disgusted with the slipshod way that his police colleagues had executed their search warrant earlier. The police had swept through like a tornado, apprehended their roommate Ryan Volker, and left minutes before Stanky ambled through the door to the scene. Jesse tossed the hat onto his bed from the doorway and glanced at Volker's closed bedroom door. "Stanky, you should know...Volker's gone."

"They stole the professor? What the fu—"

"Nope, we weren't robbed. While I was studying, the cops came and took Volker in for questioning and then they searched the place. Because, the guy who killed Pen's friend left evidence behind, and Volker's fingerprints are all over them."

The butt dropped from Kiever's lip, landed on one of his folded arms. "Volker smoked her? What the fuck?"

"That's the word on the street." Jesse reached into the fridge for a beer, then offered one to Kiever who took it. Jesse popped open the Moretti and took a long swig.

"They left with his computer, some school stuff and the sculpting supplies he keeps in his room." Jesse gestured to Volker's door. "One of them walked out with a cardboard box, overflowing with plaster body parts."

Kiever shook his head in obvious disbelief, knocking the lit cigarette butt from his lips, off his elbow, and to the floor. "Ah, burned a hole in my fuckin' arm." He stomped the butt, and left a burn hole on the fake Oriental rug. "Body parts? What the fu—
"

"Plastered hands, feet, a full set of plaster teeth, fingers, a sixteen-inch plaster cock..." Jesse said.

Kiever eyes went wide. He grabbed his stomach and fell to his knees, and rolled side to side on the floor, laughing in loud, gasping bursts of raucous amusement.

Jesse gulped his beer, waited for Kiever to stop. He'd wanted to evaluate what would happen if Kiever's feathers were ruffled. Typical Stan Kiever response. This suspect offered nothing new, for or against his own case. In Jesse's mind, even though Volker was in the tank, Kiever was still on the shortlist.

Red-faced and panting, Kiever finally composed himself and stood. He swung his rucksack over his shoulder and headed toward his room. "I never would have suspected that laid back dude was a fucking axe murderer, man." Kiever swigged a few gulps of beer, belched, and shrugged. "Guess you never can tell," he said and slammed the door.

*****

On his mattress, Jesse leaned his head against the bedroom wall. He'd just dialed Enzo at headquarters but was put on hold. While he waited, he eyed the marble statues in his room, and thought about the time Mara had awakened there. He wished it had been with his arms wrapped around her warm body. He wished that was the case now.

"Sorry to keep you waiting," Enzo said. "Sciug just came in for a rundown. We just processed Volker. We plan to hold him a couple days. So far, he's not talking."

"Let me have a crack at him. I'll get him to spill." Jesse opened the window in his room to let in fresh air. Dark clouds piled together like sacks of coal.

"Not just yet," Enzo said. "We want to maintain your cover, in case he's not our man. We'll break him, don't worry."

"What did Captain Sciug have to offer?" Jesse said.

"The two other college art professors, Forte and Truri, have both been cleared in the latest slaying of the Norwegian girl. Both have solid alibis and negative polygraphs. We're connecting the dots on the other cases, and each man had at least one alibi for the other victims, so Sciug wants us to strengthen our focus on Volker, polygraph him in the morning," Enzo said.

"Forensics?" Jesse said.

"They're still sifting through the plaster body parts and the computer files. Way too early to tell," Enzo said.

"I'll call Mara; just to keep her in the loop." Jesse hung up. Now that the ship bearing a possible relationship with Mara had sailed, he debated whether he should discuss the matter in person or just call. He longed to see her, talk to her, go out on a beer run with her. He wanted things to be the way they used to be, before she'd lost trust in him.

Rain fell in a torrent outside his open window. His ankle ached, and the onset of a migraine threatened. His best bet would be to stay in and go over reports of the investigation again, in case he'd missed something from the last million times he'd pored over the photos, statements from victims' families, and...

He grabbed his jacket and headed out the door for Mara's apartment.

Already he could tell this migraine was going to be a real mother.

Chapter 27

"Mother!"

"Mara, darling, it's been too long."

Mara crossed her kitchen to embrace her mother, and wondered if the five-foot-eight wisp of a woman might be bowled over from a hug. She'd never know, because when Mara reached her, the woman put both hands on Mara's shoulders, air-kissed her, and strode into the living room, promptly putting an end to a warmer reunion. Mara wasn't sure why she'd expected a different reception, relentlessly hopeful that people might change for the better.

Her mother's brief but powerful grip on her shoulders had likely left bruises, the natural result of Katherine Zulheimer-Silvestri's being a top-seeded U.S. women's tennis champion for the better part of her life. The cold shoulder was the by-product of being the least affectionate woman Mara had ever known.

"I'm so surprised to see you, Mother. Second leg of the ITF Seniors Tour, isn't it? Didn't think it included Rome, or I would have bought tickets." Mara dumped her school bag on her bed. Kristen and Lana exchanged greetings with the renowned tennis star and went into the kitchen to fetch her some tea.

"Rome's Open is in May, dear. I just flew in from the Mallorca tournament. Ranked second right now, with 480 points, pretty good for fifty-five, eh?" Mara restrained herself from asserting her mother's true age, while Katherine tucked back a stray blond strand into her tight chignon and adjusted her silk Armani sleeveless chemise. "I'm in Rome just through tomorrow. In for a spot of Botox, then off to Austria."

Kristen and Lana carried in a pot of tea and started filling cups. "We're just going to run and see if the guys next door have any Nutella for the breadsticks," Lana said.

Mara watched her mother take in the chipped cups, broken breadsticks, and carton of cream with clear disdain, before covering her bare shoulders with a cotton sweater and stepping toward the window.

"Thought I'd let you know that a break in my tour coincides with the spring vacation dates you emailed me. I will accompany you to distribute your father's ashes, if you wish. But, I'm on a tight schedule, and I'll likely not stay long." Her mother stroked her finger along the living room credenza, making a thin trail in the dust. She wiped her finger on her skirt and headed for the door.

"Would you like to stay for dinner, Mother?" Mara said. She eyed the streak of dirt left behind on her mother's skirt. "Or, we could go out?"

"Sorry, dear, meeting Silvio at the—"

A knock at the door interrupted her, and she opened it.

"Well, hello there, pretty lady." Signore Jack leaned his body against the door jamb and addressed her mother. "You must be Mara's sister." Her boss's saucy manner with the ladies made Mara want stick a fork in his ass.

"C'mon in, Professor," Mara said. "I'd like you to meet my mother, Katherine—"

"Zulheimer-Silvestri. Yes, indeed, I've been watching your mother for years now." Jack shifted the metal toolbox he carried from one hand to another, wiped his hand on his jeans, and offered it to the tennis champion.

Katherine took a step back and then reluctantly proffered the fingers of her hand for him to shake.

Instead of shaking it, Jack kissed her hand. "This pretty lady is quite the athlete. One of the top ranking female singles players in the industry," he said to Mara while aiming a never faltering wolf-like gaze at her mother.

"Professor, is this just a visit? It's kind of a ways for you. Is there something I can help you with?" Mara said, her thoughts anything but polite at his wolfish behavior toward her mother. *Why don't they both just leave and get a room, so she could go have a cup of tea and some breadsticks, damn it? What couldn't wait until school the next day?*

"Midterms are coming up," Signore Jack said, finally breaking his gaze toward her mother and glancing at Mara as if she'd just arrived. "I thought you and Jesse and I could put our heads together to ensure our curricula are properly covered. Is he here?"

Mara frowned. *Why would he just assume that Jesse would be here?* She hoped rumors hadn't been flying around about them.

What bothered her more was that Jack had come over without even calling first and asking if it was okay.

"I just finished spackling a hole in the apartment next door. Thought I'd stop by, check if you two were in," he said.

"Spackling? Doesn't Stella Luna have a maintenance crew for that?" Mara said.

"Guy who does it broke his leg. The roommates next door complained of an infestation through a hole near the plumbing, and RU's faculty turned to me, Signore-Jack-of-all-Trades, apparently." He turned on the full wattage of his smile and shined it on her mother.

Ugh. Mara lost her appetite for breadsticks just as Kristen and Lana returned with the Nutella. Lana rushed in waving the jar in the air. "Sorry it took us so long. The boys next door weren't there, so we went upstairs and got some from Boots' Lebanese roommate, the one who always smells like garlic."

Kristen followed behind. When she brushed by the professor, she knocked his toolbox from his hand. It clattered to the floor and burst open.

Jack's face reddened. He immediately dropped to one knee and raked every tool off the floor, as if trying to beat a buzzer.

In seconds, he'd gathered his maintenance belt, toolbox and tools, shook her mother's hand, and darted out the door. "Bring Jesse by tomorrow, and we'll put together an exam," she barely heard him say as he bolted out the lobby exit.

Her mother rolled her eyes and folded her coat over her arm. "Text me the details of your plans to spread your father's ashes next week, and I'll confirm," Katherine said as she stepped into the lobby.

"Thanks for…the visit, Mother. It's always so nice…seeing you," Mara said.

"Mmmhmm, and so nice to meet Mr. Sugardale, too. What strange friends you keep, dear," was the last thing she said before slamming the door in Mara's face.

Her typically aloof mother had actually hit the nail on the head. Signore Jack was indeed strange: Visiting out of the blue. Checking to see if Jesse was in there with her. And, racing like a demon to gather up his tools like a schoolboy who'd dropped his marbles.

Stranger still was what she'd spied him scrambling back into his toolbox with ferocious determination.

A hammer. Spattered with bits of dried plaster.

And a gob of blood-streaked, black hair.

Chapter 28

"A saw, a chisel, and a pair of cuticle scissors, complete with your fingerprints. All were found at the crime scene. Come clean, Volker, and we'll reduce your sentence from first degree to manslaughter." Many long hours after arresting him, Enzo continued the interrogation, slamming Volker for a confession.

"That's enough for today," the suspect's Calabrian attorney said. He stood and walked behind Volker, placed his hand on his shoulder. "My dinner is getting cold, and my client has nothing to say."

"The evidence of plaster body parts in his bedroom—"

"Proves nothing, Inspector," the attorney said. "I'm meeting with the judge in the morning to have the charges against my client dismissed, based on illegal—"

"You'll lose. The fact that your client refuses to cooperate demonstrates a death wish." Enzo walked out and headed back upstairs to his office. He found Jesse sitting in the same chair he always took. Ordinarily a sight for sore eyes, Jesse looked like he had something to say that Enzo was not in the mood to hear at the moment.

Enzo's phone rang. Saved by the bell. "Pronto?" Enzo listened, and when he hung up, he put his head back against the chair and exhaled deeply.

"Can't be good," Jesse said.

"I just spent hours brow-beating a man whom I believe mutilated and murdered seven young women," Enzo said. He folded his hands on the desk and met Jesse's gaze. "But now someone else just came forward and told us that they're the Sculptor."

Jesse blinked rapidly; whether in anger, confusion, or relief, Enzo didn't know. He supposed it was all three. "Who confessed?"

"A boyfriend of one of the victims. Fritz Arella."

Chapter 29

By 2:00 am, Mara still couldn't sleep. She flipped back the covers and pulled the shutter to close off the bedroom, trying hard not to wake Kristen who snored loudly in the next bed. She scrunched her feet into fluffy slippers and put on coffee, then draped her pink camouflage Snuggie over her shoulders and settled onto the sofa to organize her thoughts.

After her mother had left, she'd asked Kristen and Lana if they'd seen Jack's gore-covered hammer, but neither of them had. When she'd explained that Jack had just come from "fixing a hole" in their neighbor's apartment, all three women had stormed next door. Kristen and Lana pounded the entry, while Mara phoned. No answer.

Next, the three women had pounced on Oslo, the reception manager, demanding that he allow them entrance to Apartment 4. He'd refused, and explained that he'd seen the two roommates' exit early that morning, just after he had finished his evening shift. He'd catch hell if the uptight International Law student and his beefy partner were to return and find him and the three women trespassing inside their apartment. The women had relented, and went back to Mara's apartment to await their neighbors' return.

At eleven, Lana had left for her place, and Kristen had retired to bed.

Lying in her own bed, staring at the clock a few minutes after midnight, Mara had heard a boot thud against the thin wall behind her head. The drunken voices of the guys next door, Lance and Jason, laughing and tossing expletives at one another, had finally untangled all of the knots in her stomach. She'd groaned with exhausted relief that neither of them had been butchered and left for dead in their apartment by Jack Sugardale.

But now, at 2:30 am, her mind still refused to shut down for the night. She sipped her Kona blend and jotted notes to herself, sifting through the events of the past few weeks.

Foremost in her mind was the fresh red blood and mottled hair stuck to the end of Signore Jack's hammer, a tool he'd hastened to conceal from her and the other three women before rushing out the door. Regardless of Jesse's incessant warnings (Jesse the man or Jesse the cop?) to avoid meeting Signore Jack alone, the full-time Casanova professor and part-time Mr. Fix-It carpenter had always seemed harmless to her, until now.

Aside from the bloody hammer and frantic departure, she also considered the fact that he'd traveled all the way to Venice for their IntBiz presentations, only to return to Rome the same evening. Or, so he'd said. Perhaps Jack was the skier with the zebra-striped gloves who had thrown her from the cliff. After all, he'd also been a professor when her sister had attended RU. Had he stuck a chisel through her sister's brain six years ago? With the Swiss government paying the Italian secret police to keep the entire matter quiet, Jack would have had the opportunity to return to teaching, and, in due course, murder more students. But the same was also true for Professor Ryan Volker, who was now detained in jail but refusing to shed any light on the subject.

Then again, neither Utica nor Kiever had joined the school trip to Venice or the Alps. Utica had begged out of the trip, boasting of his spectacular motorcycle rendezvous weekend, spent with a woman whom no one had actually met. Not much of an alibi. Utica certainly had been capable of accosting Mara on the mountain. Similarly, Kiever had foregone the trip for a swim meet, but Lana gossiped that they'd hung out for most of the weekend. Had Kiever lied about competing, only to thrust Mara from a cliff in the Alps, and then return to Rome in time to hook up with Lana? Of course, it seemed far-fetched, but it was also something that was easily verified. She jotted herself a note to confirm his attendance at the meet, and pinpoint exactly when Lana had met with Kiever.

Mara sat back and reflected upon what she did know. Both Utica and Kiever had been freshman undergrads at RU during her sister's senior year. Their presence at the university at the same time as her sister meant that they were capable of murdering her, as well as every one of the six other victims. The same held true for Sugardale and Volker. As well as the two other art professors, Forte and Truri, as well as Fritz Arella.

She considered it uncanny how the handsome boyfriend of the murdered Chick Fritz had just happened to befriend many of the other murdered students over the past years. Being the son of the RU dean apparently opened up a lot of doors for the popular Arella.

Every one of these men had the opportunity and the means to mutilate these movie-star-gorgeous, highly educated women. But which one of them was the Sculptor?

At five in the morning, the ring tone on her cell phone played U2's "Two Hearts Beat as One," and Mara dashed to the kitchen table to answer it before Kristen woke.

"You up?" It was Jesse.

Her stomach knotted again. She still felt hurt by his betrayal, and she hated needing him in so many ways. "Yes, couldn't sleep," she said. "I have things to share with you about the case."

"Me too. Can we meet?"

"Where?" She prayed that he wouldn't say his apartment; too many memories of what might have been.

"Sugardale's office? He never comes in early; probably won't show until our 10:00 am class."

"Perfect," she said.

***

Once there, Mara let herself into Signore Jack's office with the key that had been assigned to her as a teacher's assistant. Jesse showed up fifteen minutes later.

"Before we start, can you clear up some technical questions for me first?" she said.

"Shoot."

"Should we make the assumption that the killer has always been on friendly terms with his victims?" she said.

"I would say so, especially when you look at every case. These women trusted this man to allow him into her bed. There has never been a forced entry. It's always consensual sex," he said.

"Okay, then, they let him in, only to find out he is a killer who desires…what? Was the killer's motive to diminish the worth of his victim, by lopping off her appendages, whether systematically or in a rage?" she said. "Or was it to put them on a pedestal of worship, by solidifying their parts in plaster, in a way memorializing them, for whatever insane reason?"

"Interesting thoughts," Jesse said.

"Just spewing theories, hoping something might apply. If we can understand why he's doing this, maybe we can get a couple steps ahead of him," she said.

"I agree with your second theory. I believe he almost idolizes his victims in a sense, maybe not for who they are, but perhaps for what they represent to him. You mentioned rage, but I can't ascribe to that. He's thorough and careful, systematic, like you said. He's never left behind a single piece of his own DNA."

"What about Volker's fingerprints on the tools?" she asked.

"I don't feel confident that this precise, detail-oriented killer would be so careless. I believe he absconded with Volker's weapons to frame him," Jesse said.

"So, you don't think it's Volker?" she questioned.

"It might yet be. But, my gut tells me otherwise."

Mara knew that such an admission of honest feelings probably rattled Jesse to the core.

"Memorializing them, as in turning them into statues, sounds more like it," Jesse said. "You're right; he plasters parts of them, but for what reason? Sometimes he takes limbs, or, as in the last crime scene, the bastard made away with her head. There's a whole lot of need-driven baggage that someone carries around to carry out a dismemberment procedure. It's tough to do, and time-consuming. And, it's rare, too. It takes an odd duck to go to such lengths." He shook his head, as if coming to grips with the idea. "But occasionally there's evidence that this killer has plastered an attached part of her body, and he likely leaves the scene with the molded casting of it. What the hell does he do with...all the cast replicas...of body parts?"

A thought crossed her mind and she was loath to suggest it, but she put it out there anyway, "A museum?"

Jesse turned to her; his eyes squinted like Kiever's after a long cigarette drag.

"I know it sounds morbid, but maybe he's creating some sort of menagerie of bits and pieces—"

"As an ode to the victim?" he said.

"Or, to someone else? Think about it, perhaps he's grieving over the loss of someone in his life. And, he's trying to recreate the essence of that person, to live on forever, or—"

"Like taxidermy?" Jesse said.

"Hey, people stuff their dogs, keep them by the hearth," she said. "Why not create an everlasting statue as a stand-in for a deceased lover?"

"Or for a woman he's been pining for, but that he could never have?" Jesse stared at her with clear pain in his eyes. She wondered whether he was still talking about the serial killer, or had he asserted a clear implication of remorse for ruining their once burgeoning relationship?

She decided to bar the path leading to a discussion of their damaged personal affair; she'd already decided not to go there. "I appreciate you playing along with my conjecture," she shrugged. "Just some random sleep-deprived thoughts. Anyway, you said that you had news for me," she said.

He shook his head as if to settle rolling marbles. "Let's see…Volker's still not talking."

"It's been over forty hours. Aren't you required to formally arraign him?"

"Italian law enforcement works a little differently than in the States. We can detain him for weeks without a fuss. We figure that it helps when trying to coerce a confession."

"How convenient," she said, rolling her eyes. "Sounds like that case with the Florentine serial killer, 'the Monster of Florence,' wasn't that what they called him back in the day?

Didn't they keep arresting people without cause, detaining them for weeks, trying them on flimsy evidence and false testimony, and even jailing them? And then they found out that the real killer was out murdering someone else, right?"

"I'm not proud of it. I just do my job, and try to get the real criminals off the streets," Jesse said.

Mara nodded. "Anyway, Volker isn't talking, but they're keeping him until he breaks. Is that all you've got for me?" Her stomach growled. She hadn't eaten since her Nutella-covered breadsticks yesterday afternoon.

"Sounds like you could eat. How about a fresh, hot *cornetto* run, just you and me?" Jesse said.

She shook her head, brushing him off. "Maybe later. Keep talking, what else you got?"

"How about the fact that Truri and Forte are no longer suspected by the police, does that quench your palate?"

She envisioned the two art professors as they were fished out of the Grand Canal, after being tossed in by the actress/supermodel in Venice. "I thought the police found sculpting tools belonging to one of them at the crime scene?"

"They've established solid alibis. And it was Volker's fingerprints, none of theirs, that covered the weapons," Jesse said.

She nodded. "Anything else, Inspector?"

"Not really." He shrugged and tried to hide a smirk from curving the corners of his mouth. "Just the fact that Volker isn't the only one we're holding right now."

She edged forward in her seat. "Who else?"

"Wait for it…" he smiled.

"Ugh, out with it, cop!"

"Fritz Arella turned himself in last night."

"He confessed? Why did you let me go on rambling for the past hour?"

"Because you're hot when you're bothered," Jesse said. "And because I don't think Arella did it either."

"On what basis?"

"Arella was tight with every one of these women. But, I think Fritz would rather dish gossip and talk hairstyles, than sleep with any of them."

"Are you suggesting he's gay?" she said. "That doesn't mean he didn't kill them. You said he never left behind DNA. Do the police have proof that he actually had sexual intercourse with any of them, or did he set it up to look like he did?"

"It's possible," Jesse said. "But, why go to such great lengths to hide his tracks for so many years, only to confess now?"

Just then, the door burst open. Expecting an uncharacteristically early Signore Jack, Mara whipped her head around to greet her boss. Instead, their fellow IntBiz student and friend, Mimi, short for Massimo, stood in the door.

"Hey, I thought I might find you two here," Mimi said, "glued to your office hours like good little TAs should."

Jesse laughed, and slid the Sculptor file out of sight. Mara opened the door wider. "Come on in. Kate with you?"

Kate and Mimi had started dating their freshman year at RU, and the word on the street was that the Calabrian native planned to propose to the Milanese beauty any day.

"We had a little tiff, and she went to her mother's. I need to chat with you two about the professor's homework on the EU debt crisis, but I can't now. Just wanted to let you know Kate's got her first gig Sunday after spring break, at Teatro dell'Opera, which is why she's been pretty tightly wound lately. It would actually ease her nerves if all her friends were there. You guys in?"

"I'm in." Jesse gave him a thumbs-up.

"I'd love to come. Thanks, Mimi," Mara said.

Her stomach growled again as Mimi ducked out the door.

She turned back to face Jesse. "Okay, let's definitely grab a bite before class," she said. "But, first, we have about an hour before Jack usually arrives. Let's search this office before he does." She explained the incident about the hammer, and together they turned the room upside down, to no avail.

Minutes later, the two had just finished putting the room back together and seating themselves when their boss burst through the door.

Out of breath and red in the face from the frantic search before his arrival, she and Jesse ogled up at him from the IntBiz exam prep they'd spread as a ruse across his desktop. Mara's stomach turned. She was sure he suspected them of something when a wry little smile crept across his face after shutting the door.

"You two mind screwing around somewhere else, other than my office? Those chairs are fine-grained leather, and they stain easily," Jack said.

Speechless, Mara's cheeks burned with embarrassment.

"It's not like that at all, Professor," Jesse said.

"Not foolin' around, then?" Signore Jack said. "Well, in that case, you must be here rummaging for my bloody hammer."

***

"I set to spackling a hole that one of those drunks kicked in with his boot, y'all know how the guys in the apartment next door can be a bit wild now and again," Signore Jack said. "The size of the rat that scurried out of that hole was the size of a God-dang hyena. I nearly shat myself when I saw it, pardon the expression."

Mara stared wide-eyed. Nodded. Her stomach growled again.

"Jumped outta the wall, onto my chest. I knocked it clear across the room, and the damn thing came after me again, with those long fangs. So, I grabbed my hammer outta my tool belt and beat the life out of that ornery sonofabitch." The professor pulled open his desk drawer and extracted a flask, pouring some of its contents into his coffee. "Looked like a nice enough piece of steak, but you just never know if salmonella's coming to dinner or maybe you're served up a belly full of rat poison, ya know?"

Mara opened her mouth to respond, but just couldn't find the words.

"Thanks for clearing that up, Professor," Jesse said.

"What do you say we put together that IntBiz midterm?" Jack suggested. "Then, maybe a quick dash to an *osteria* for some steak and eggs?"

Mara doubted she'd ever eat meat again.

Chapter 30

The rest of the week flew by as Mara busily crammed for midterms, but the following week dragged. Mara made final adjustments to her Ferrari term paper, and then emailed it to the CEO with her fingers crossed for the future. On Friday, the time had finally come for a much-needed break from school.

She'd anticipated the spreading of her father's ashes for a very long time, yet now she was filled with dread at the prospect of finally saying goodbye. The idea that her mother was meeting her in Cortona to attend the small ceremony did nothing to comfort her. Her train for Camucia-Cortona was not due to leave until later that Saturday evening, so she slept in that morning. She awoke to Kristen packing for her trip to Pompeii.

"A bunch of us are hopping on the late train after the big Roma Sud soccer game. Sure you can't come?" Kristen plucked three pairs of cuticle scissors from the blue-green sanitizing solution in the jar beside her bed and threw them into her toiletry bag, and stuck one into her purse.

When they'd first settled into their apartment weeks earlier, Mara had straddled on the cusp of asking Kristen where in Rome she'd found the Barbicide hospital-grade disinfectant to clean her supply of tress-snippers. Then she backed off. Kristen had so much to offer as a friend, as a person, that spotlighting her foibles seemed petty. And in light of Mara's own idiosyncrasies, who was she to judge?

"Thanks, but I'm meeting my mom for a few days in Tuscany. We're spreading my dad's ashes on Easter Sunday." Mara retrieved the wooden box that had become a regular fixture in their living room. She noticed green algae had overtaken their aquarium and made a mental note to clean it before leaving.

Mara wedged the box of ashes inside the plaid valise that she'd packed to cross the ocean. Her baggage seemed heavier now, and Mara suddenly felt the weight of the circumstances— saying goodbye to her father for the last time.

"I'll miss your dad hanging around here. He brought us luck for midterms. I think everyone in Stella Luna came by to rub the box at one time or another," Kristen said.

"Thanks, I find that very comforting." Mara hugged her friend. "I'll miss you over break. Since we arrived, we really haven't been apart for more than a few days at a time."

"Me too. You should really come to the soccer game at Stadio Olimpico this afternoon. A lot of us are going. It'll be good for you to be with friends, considering the circumstances…"

Mara wasn't sure if the circumstances included her father's burial, midterms, or the looming threat of the Sculptor. Probably all of the above. She had to admit that the idea of spending the afternoon at a ball game with friends sounded perfect.

She promised to meet Kristen and Lana at the South Gate to get tickets about a half hour before the 1:00 start. But first, she needed to tie up a few loose ends.

***

Mara had decided to stop by Enzo's office to let him know she'd be away. She closed the door and shared with the Chief Inspector the concerns she'd raised with Jesse about the various suspects, and her theories on what the Sculptor's motive might entail. She hoped that Enzo might have more to offer. He did not.

He reiterated that the two art professors had been scratched from their list of prime suspects, but added that Volker and Arella had moved to the top.

"Volker continues to remain silent," Enzo said. "Although his fingerprints covered the circumstantial tools left behind, the prosecutors are upholding the opinion that Arella's guilty admission trumps the evidence. So, even though my department captain wants to detain both men, it looks like Volker will soon go free."

"I'm sorry, Enzo," she said. "You and Jesse are fine policemen, but I just don't agree with the Italian legal system. Look at the 'Monster of Florence' case from decades ago, about the serial killer who murdered over twenty people in the Tuscan hills. They prosecuted erroneous, innocent people, while the killer walked free."

Enzo blushed slightly and looked out the window. "I investigated that case."

"What?" Mara said, feeling sheepish. "I had no idea."

"I was...what do Americans call it, yes, a rookie, and not officially assigned. Still, I put my heart and soul into that case, and any ideas I had or evidence that I found went unheeded. It was all politics. The prosecutors wanted to play it a certain way, no matter what the guys in the field dug up. It remains my only major, unsolved case, unofficially speaking." Enzo sighed heavily. "I'm not proud of our system, but I believe in justice, so I still show up every day, hoping to get the bad guys off the street."

"That's exactly what Jesse said, about stopping the bad guys." Mara smiled. She liked Enzo Tranchille, both for his integrity as well as his kind nature. She knew Enzo had rubbed off on Jesse, but she continued to fight her feelings for Jesse simply because she was afraid of getting hurt again. She wanted to live life with the "pain" taken out of the "pleasure-pain" principle.

As if reading her mind, Enzo said, "Jesse and some of his school friends are going to the Roma Sud game today. Might be something you two would enjoy doing together?" He shuffled papers on his desk, acting as if this suggestion had been an afterthought. Mara couldn't help but smile; these two men were definitely related.

"As a matter of fact, I do have plans to go to the game, so I should head over." She stood and walked to the door. "Thanks for the chat, Inspector."

"Mara, if you do happen to run into Jesse at the game, perhaps take some time to get to know him better. Jesse the man, not Jesse the cop. Jesse the man might pleasantly surprise you."

***

Mara arrived at the South Gate ticket office at half past noon. At the same time thousands of Roma Sud and Milano fans were also arriving, all pushing and shoving to get to the ticket window. There was no rhyme or reason for reaching the teller who stood behind glass only 500 feet in front of her, and hoards of drunken, swearing, singing, hopeful spectators blocked her path.

She elbowed her way to one of the waist-high steel barriers, originally intended to organize the queue, but now used as a method for the strongest to catapult over the weakest to the head of the line. She clung to it for support against the wave of motley barbarians swaying her forward into the thick of the throng.

"Mara!" Kristen and Lana called to her from the mouth of a subway tunnel they'd exited. She waved them over. The three locked arms and elbowed their way forward, only to be shoved backward again. Forward, then back again, undulating with the rhythm of the crowd. Kristen went down, and screamed. Mara and Lana tugged her back onto her feet. "I'm not so sure I want to go anymore," Kristen said.

Too late. The three were enveloped in a buzzing swarm that dragged them forward in a swell. Mara pulled away from a beer-guzzling, six-foot teenager that wouldn't stop groping her backside. She wriggled her arm free and socked him in the eye. Two older men cheered her, and a whooping rendition of "O...lé! Olé! Olé! Olé! O...lé! Olé! Olé! Olé!" broke out, signaling the crowd to action. The two men hoisted the teen into the air, where he was carried by raised arms above the crowd's heads toward the back of the line.

Lana shouted to Mara and Kristen, "Let's get to the perimeter, wait until the crowd floods the stadium before we try the ticket booth."

Mara nodded, but then heard someone speak right into her ear. "Should we show this crowd how it's done?"

Jesse had finagled his way beside her. He grinned slyly.

She smirked and nodded, yes.

Jesse hoisted himself onto the metal barrier, and pulled her up by the hand with him. Together, they ducked and jumped and rode the wave forward, until landing at one of the ticket windows on the far side.

He thrust his school ID and a stash of Euros at the teller who handed him tickets. With the full force of the harried spectators at their backs, Jesse smuggled the tickets into Mara's hand. "Take these; they'll think I have them."

She smiled, and shoved the tickets into her bra. She gripped his hand, and using the side rail, they hoisted themselves up, returning atop the crowd's shoulders. She could feel the men in the crowd trying to yank Jesse down and abscond with tickets they assumed he held. He withstood their muscle, and together they jumped and shimmied back to where they'd left the girls. Mara grabbed Kristen's hand, and Jesse took Lana's, and the four raced to the stadium entrance.

Inside, Kristen and Lana dashed off to reward their efforts with beers. Bruised, battered, and laughing like kids, Mara and Jesse plunked into their seats to catch their breath. The crowd roared and the game began, and Mara realized she was still holding tight to Jesse's hand. She released it, and brushed back strands of hair plastered to her face. "That was crazy fun! I cannot believe we crowd-surfed to get tickets to a game—what the hell is that!"

"You were amazing!" Jesse said, his eyes sparkling blue and sexy. He let out a deep breath. "You never let go. Thanks for trusting me."

She shrugged. "No matter how much of a pain in the ass you are, you always come through."

"It'll be tough having you out of reach over break. Watch your back, okay?" Jesse said.

"I doubt if the serial killer will be lurking over my shoulder while I spread my dad's ashes, but I promise to be vigilant. How about you—headed to Pompeii with the rest of the student body?" Mara said.

"Spending Easter with my parents, in Montepulciano." Jesse jumped to his feet and shouted at the linesman.

Mara and Jesse spent the next half hour cheering Roma Sud's team or jibing Milano's players. Jesse would inform her of a penalty seconds before the official made the call. He suggested strategy that the coaches and players failed to use until many plays later. "You really know your soccer, or rather, I should say, football."

"I played a little," Jesse said. "Want some popcorn? There's the guy."

"No popcorn, thanks." She'd never sat on his left side before, always his right. So, she'd never noticed just how indented the dimple on his left cheek was. She wanted to grab his face with both hands and maul him with kisses. "Tell me about when you played. Were you any good?"

"Okay, I guess. Drove Beckham nuts," he said. "Maybe I could get us some ice cream?" He stood to look for a vendor, and she noticed how nicely his jeans fit him, front and back.

She yanked him back into his seat. "You played with David Beckham?"

"Against him, actually. Cocky sonofabitch, but a good guy; went out drinking after a game once. Tried to convince me to tattoo my ass."

"Did you?" Mara's eyes went wide.

"Wouldn't you like to know?" Jesse said, with that dimple again.

"I'd love to know what your ass looks like," she blurted, before putting her hand over her mouth. She did *not* just say that out loud.

He stared at her. She did just say that out loud.

"Tell me why you stopped playing," she said. She realized that she'd left the harmless comfort of communicating with Jesse the cop, and was trespassing into Jesse the man terrain. Where the hell were Kristen and Lana with those beers?

"I had a good thing going, and then at seventeen, I busted my ankle, and the good thing stopped. I made some bad choices, and my parents sent me to live with my cop uncle. Straightened me out, turned me into a damn good detective. So, no regrets; just a little sore sometimes."

Mentally or physically, she wondered.

"Now, the only time I make bad choices is when it comes to my personal life," Jesse said. "I always hoped that what Enzo had with my *Zia* Matilda would have rubbed off, but a relationship that strong is tough to duplicate."

"Maybe you shouldn't try so hard," she said.

"What do you mean?" Jesse said. The wave coursed through the crowd, and the two of them stood with their section, raised their hands above their heads, and then sat back down.

"I mean maybe love isn't all it's cracked up to be. Too much uncertainty. Too much loss. Too much pain." She thought of how Enzo had lost the love of his life way too early. It hurt her heart to think how she'd lost her father as well. She thought of the pain of knowing how her sister had come to die alone. Love was too much trouble. Better to push it away, and save yourself the heartache.

"Take us for example," she said. "We had…something. But it didn't work. I think we make a better pair of friends." Mara quieted for a moment and looked at Jesse, considering her next words. She came to an internal decision, and continued. "And, it just so happens, that I wouldn't mind having really hot sex with you on occasion. So, why not try it?"

His mouth had fallen open. He closed it. "Try what?"

"Friends with benefits. Works for Lana and Kiever. Good buddies, good sex, no strings attached. Want to?" she said.

A flash of hot, animal lust passed over his face.

Then it was gone. Replaced by a sad, painful look of loneliness. His broad shoulders drooped. The sparkle that had animated his eyes fizzled out.

The wave coursed through the crowd once more. Neither of them moved. She realized that her words had done the opposite of what she had originally hoped to inspire. Instead of reeling him in, she had pushed him away.

"Say something," she finally pled. She wanted to put her arms around him, kiss him, and somehow assuage his hurt feelings. But, she'd already resigned herself to pushing love away. There was no going back now. Right?

Jesse sat up a little straighter in his seat, and he seemed to have edged a couple inches further away. "Thanks for the offer. But, with you, I just can't do friends with benefits. Friends…absolutely. Always. But, that's it." He crossed his leg and rubbed his ankle.

"I know I'm no saint," Jesse explained. "But, at this point in my life, after having met you, I can't pretend that I don't care. I know you're afraid of being vulnerable, that's just how you are. As much as I would give anything to jump in bed with you, I'll only do it for love. That's how I am. I like strings attached. Take it, or leave it."

"I don't want to lose your friendship, Jesse. I'm sorry if you feel offended. I just—"

"No offense taken. Always friends, I promise." The coldness in his voice chilled her. He stood up. "I'm going to go hunt down some ice cream."

Mara had never meant to hurt him. She hadn't realized how much she'd meant to Jesse. Before she had a chance to think about it more, Professor Jack slid into Jesse's seat.

"Where the hell did that boy fly off to, little lady?" Jack said.

"Ice cream run."

"Without you? I thought you two always bust out of my class looking for drinks and grub together?" Jack pulled out a cigar and lighter. "Mind if I light up?"

She shook her head and decided to skip past any explanations of her and Jesse's tumultuous relationship. "I'm also here with Kristen and Lana. Have you seen them yet? They were supposed to be back with beers a while ago."

He lit the Cuban with a shiny Zippo, flexed his cheeks like a puffer fish. His jagged fingernails were long, and caked with crusty, white paste.

Jack pocketed the lighter, and squinted through the smoke to watch the field. "I appreciate the work that both of you put into the midterm." He bit his thumbnail, and spit it toward the aisle.

"Also, Ferrari's so pleased with your paper on the American market that they're publishing it on their website." He gnawed at his pinky finger, and spat that nail too.

"Pardon my bad habit. Spent the morning putting up drywall, and the gypsum's a real irritant." Jack rubbed his thumb over the rest of his fingertips until the pasty remainder crumbled clean.

"Excellent digging to get the facts straight for your paper. I'm proud of you." The professor blew smoke toward the aisle. A speck of the white gypsum paste had collected in the corner of his mouth from his grooming.

"That means a lot." She wanted to flick the paste from his lip but restrained herself.

Signore Jack stood to leave. "Left my date with a full beer, and she'll be likely needing another. Please pass along my kudos to your partner in crime. You two make a great team. And, you, little lady, have a bright future."

Professor Jack Sugardale was certainly an unlikely mentor, but she respected his tutelage just the same. He was also an unlikely serial killer, but she still felt leery of him. Were Dr. Hannibal Lecter's patients ever worried that he would eat their brains after shrinking them?

Fifteen minutes after Sugardale left, Jesse still hadn't returned. Clearly disappointed by the parameters of her offer, he'd probably left.

She decided to ditch the rest of the game just as Kristen and Lana returned, arms laden with four 16 oz. cups of beer foam.

"Sorry we were gone so long. We ran into Stanky, and we smoked a couple joints," Kristen said. "Where's Jesse? We brought him back a beer."

"Went to get ice cream." Mara sipped the weak, warm brew and relaxed a little.

The first half ended, and Lana turned to Mara. "Saw you chatting with Signore Jack. You guys are tight, right?" Lana moved in closer, as if to share some secret, and Kristen edged in as well.

"Not that tight," Mara said. "He may rub himself against other students between classes, but he's...not my type. Why do you ask?"

"Well, bingo! We just heard he's banging at least eight other women. Mostly students, plus the English Lit Professor at Trinity," Lana said. "Every year since he started, he gathers himself a regular little harem of, get this, a girl from every country."

"A little group of foreign nookie dolls...a little 'international business,' you know what I mean, baby!" Kristen and Lana high-fived.

Mara looked around to ensure her boss was nowhere within earshot. "I know he's extra friendly with a couple girls, but a harem? Where'd you hear those rumors?"

"Not rumors. Truth," Lana said. "Stanky's dad verified it."

Mara shook her head. "Hold on. Why is Kiever's dad, a Senator from Arkansas, in a position to verify Professor Sugardale's conquests?"

"Brothers dish, right?" Lana said.

Mara paused a moment to connect the dots. Slowly, she nodded. "I should have made the connection before—Professor Jack Sugardale and Senator Sugardale, but why doesn't the Senator's son, Stan Kiever, have the same last name as Sugardale?"

"Stanky's mother fell from scaffolding while shooting a movie in his late teens. In her honor, he legally changed his name to Kiever," Kristen said.

"Kiever's mother is…Tish Kiever?" Mara said. "My mother loved her musicals."

Kristen nodded. "After the fall she never performed again. Too bad. She was stunning. She also won tons of Oscars."

"Funny comedienne, too," Lana said.

Kristen smiled. "Famous for her great imitations."

Mara halted their chatter to clarify something that suddenly gnawed her brain. "So, that makes Stan Kiever, Jack Sugardale's nephew," Mara said.

Lana nodded. "The deal is that years back, Signore Jack was a straight up guy, an Army Ranger. He was stationed in Naples, and when he visited Rome, he got engaged to some museum curator. He retired and moved to Rome, where he became a contractor, and traveled around as some trade show guru."

"Knew about the career; that's how he ended up teaching IntBiz," Mara said. "Heard he was engaged, but that it didn't work out somehow. And I guess later she died." Mara pulled her parka closer around her and yanked up the hood. The temperature had easily dropped twenty degrees since they'd arrived.

Lana nodded. "The story is even sadder than that. They did get engaged, and then a year after proposing, his fiancée died," Lana said. "Jack gets all depressed, threatens to kill himself, but Senator Sugardale steps in, gets his brother the RU gig. Ever since, it's like he's running a James Bond marathon—pussy galore, all day and night!"

The wind picked up. Kristen put on her hat. Even so, it didn't stop her from snipping at the ends of her curls with the pair of cuticle scissors that she pulled out of her jacket pocket.

Mara rummaged through the information that she'd just gathered and compared it to what she already knew. Then, she asked, "Jack's been an RU prof for almost a decade. He taught here while my sister attended. Did either of you pick up anything on that?"

Lana blushed, turned away, and looked through the crowd. "I think I'll try to make my way to the bathroom."

Mara held her elbow. "Hold on, fess up."

Lana slumped back into her seat. She sighed and faced Mara. "Stanky told me that Signore Jack was...close with your sister. But, at the time, he was only dating maybe six or seven other students...that term," Lana said.

"Ugh, so my fifty-something, sleazy professor screwed my twenty-something sister. There's a lot I don't know about her, but that just creeps me out." It was also a lot to digest about her so-called mentor.

The soccer game began again after the brief reprieve, and the stadium roared with renewed vigor.

"Hey, isn't that Professor Volker over there in the stands?" Kristen pointed toward the next section, a few rows closer to the field. Ryan Volker sat by himself, with empty seats on both sides of him. "I thought he was arrested?" Kristen said.

"He was. But Volker was released when Fritz Arella confessed," Lana said. "Do you believe Arella's the goddamn Sculptor?"

"If Arella's the serial killer, what the hell is he doing here?" Kristen gestured toward Volker again. Fritz Arella was now sidled in closely next to Volker, laughing and sharing his popcorn.

"Police must have released him, too," Mara said. "But, why is the man who confessed to seven murders roaming free?" Bewildered, she looked back over to where Arella and Volker sat.

That's when she understood.

Something had been clawing at her subconscious since her strategy session with Jesse. She'd asked Jesse why Arella had confessed when Volker's fingerprints clearly indicated that he was the killer, but she and Jesse were interrupted before she'd latched on to the answer. Now, it finally clicked.

Arella and Volker were a couple.

Arella may have been very close with every one of the victims, but he'd never been a boyfriend to any of them.

"They're lovers," Mara told Kristen and Lana, as she came to the realization herself.

"Well, that explains a lot," Lana said. "I tried to get Arella to ask me out, but he wasn't interested. Thought he was just fucked in the head."

"They would've had to keep it well hidden," Mara said. "The dean's son is carrying on a relationship with one of the school's professors—not good for the university's image."

Arella rested his head on Volker's shoulder, and Volker stroked his hair.

"Their relationship is obviously out in the open now." Mara ruminated for a minute. "They were probably each other's alibi. Volker must've decided that Arella's freedom was more important than his job. Now, they're both free."

"Free, in so many ways." Lana gestured to the couple, now open-mouth kissing while the game pressed on.

Jack Sugardale yelled to Mara, Kristen, and Lana from the aisle. He and his female drinking buddy were heading down the stairs to leave. Mara and the two women waved goodbye.

Jack smiled, and waved both hands gaily back at them before disappearing through the exit tunnel.

It was then Mara realized it. Signore Jack Sugardale had been wearing blue and black zebra-striped gloves.

***

With nearly the entire student body leaving for Pompeii that weekend, the Sculptor knew that now was the time to regroup after a most unpleasant debacle—the head of his latest sculpture had simply not fit the body he'd arranged.

A tub of liquid lye had sufficiently dissolved any trace of the unfortunate episode. Still, he felt disgruntled by the inefficient use of his time.

Time to sit back and reevaluate. Prepare to pounce on that perfect specimen when it presented itself.

Who was he kidding? He'd always known whom it was he needed. It had been easy to identify the subject that would complete the collection.

But he'd been procrastinating, afraid that once he completed the gallery, it would be necessary to move on. Like always.

And he'd been having so much fun this time.

Chapter 31

That evening, Mara caught the six o'clock train for Cortona with only minutes to spare.

It had taken her longer to return to the apartment after the soccer game than she'd anticipated, what with the street riot following Milano's win. She'd grabbed the suitcase that she'd left by the door, hugged Kristen and Lana goodbye, and caught a taxi to the train station.

Finally aboard the train, she wheeled her single plaid suitcase packed with clothing, toiletries, and her father's urn through the hoard of fellow Easter holiday travelers. She'd just reached her aisle seat in the second-class compartment when the train lurched forward and her phone rang. Her cell showed an incoming call from Ferrari's Vice President of Marketing, the same person to whom she'd presented in Venice and who'd been evaluating her term paper.

Minutes later, she hung up. She wiped her clammy hands on her jeans and massaged her forehead. She looked out the window, exhaled, and smiled.

Ferrari had offered her a job, a highly coveted spot overseeing the research division of the marketing department for all of Italy. After she finished wrapping up her semester internship with the company, they wanted her to commence a full-time position in late summer, and Ferrari would pay her to finish her MBA part-time for the next couple of years, with the chance to oversee the European research division upon completion.

It's what she'd always wanted. Wasn't it?

She dialed Jesse. He'd left her at the game in the capable hands of Lana and Kristen, departing early to meet with Enzo, he'd said. Mara figured it also had something to do with the deflated ego she'd served him after their "relationship conversation." So, if she was so averse to letting him into her personal life, then why was she overcome by the need to share her good news with him?

As she waited for Jesse to answer, her finger sought to end the call. But too late, he picked up. He said, "I've been trying to reach you—"

"My phone died earlier; it's charging now," Mara said. "Hey, I just got good news from Ferrari." After she described the conversation, he gave her every accolade she needed to hear. She had no idea if she was elated for the Ferrari call, or for the fact that Jesse was expressing such pride in her achievement. Either way, she could definitely get used to it.

After a couple more minutes she grew embarrassed by the praise and changed the subject. "I'm really sorry if I offended you at the game. What I'd said, about the friends-with-benefits thing, I had no idea that it would make you bolt, and I—"

"No worries. I had to get down to the station anyway; there have been some developments," Jesse said.

"I'm on top of some of it—saw Volker and Arella, together, at the game," she said.

"Yes, Enzo told me Volker came storming into the station this morning, demanding the release of his life partner. Arella's close friendship with one of the victims was just that, and her murder had been a heinous act by another's hands, not Arella's. Volker established their mutually solid alibi, and proved that he and Arella had been otherwise engaged for every one of the slayings."

"It certainly makes our shortlist even shorter," Mara said. "Unless we're missing someone, we're down to three: Signore Jack, Utica, and Kiever." She relayed her shocked finding of Signore Jack's zebra-colored ski gloves. Jesse digested her intel, but gently reminded her that he too possessed the same style of striped outerwear. "But, I like where your head's at, and your shortlist brings me to the other reason Enzo wanted me at the station," Jesse said.

"What is it?" Mara asked.

"They've arrested Utica," Jesse said. "The motorcycle rider he'd spent last weekend with—she was the murdered Norwegian."

Chapter 32

Mara and Jesse ended their call with well wishes for the Easter holiday, after Jesse had insisted that she take the GPS coordinates to his family's home, just in case, and upon Mara's sincere promise to watch her ass while she was away.

She stared out the window of the train, absorbing the news that another on their rapidly diminishing shortlist of suspects was in custody—Michael Utica. She was glad for it, hopeful that before long, the Sculptor would be prevented from killing again. But she was also wary. The recent shoal of catch-and-release suspects had produced viable alibis, and no new leads. What if all this time the police had been reeling in sunnies and scup, while the big kahuna was still out their preying on his next victim? She shuddered. Stay on course, she told herself, and pray that no one else gets hurt.

Just after dark, the conductor announced her stop, and the backlit, blue station-sign that read Camucia-Cortona came into view outside her window.

She disembarked and wheeled her suitcase down the platform, through the small station, and outside to the lot. A stocky, middle-aged chauffeur with an oval jaw and pointy ears held a placard with her name on it. She greeted him, and he nodded. She wondered if he was ex-military by the build, or Vulcan by the Spock-like ears.

He limped toward a jet-black Alfa Romeo sedan, and Mara followed his bobbing strawberry blonde crew cut. He deposited her bag in the trunk, and they sped off through the tiny town of Camucia, up into the steep winding hills that led to Cortona, a few miles away.

They arrived at a rambling stone villa tucked into the mountain. Once there, the driver turned on the lights in the entry, deposited Mara and her bag in the foyer, and explained that her mother required his services at a function that evening. Before she could thank him, G.I. Spock abruptly smiled, shook her hand, and darted back to his sedan, leaving her just inside the house that her mother had rented for the week. She locked the door behind him.

Mara wheeled her bag through the living room, and then down a short, ceramic-tiled hallway leading to two bedrooms with adjoining baths, switching on lights in the cold, stark abode as she went. She noticed that a single lamp had been lit, in a room at the end of the hall. She dropped her suitcase on the double feather bed that graced that room.

She grabbed a ripe banana from the fruit bowl on the mirrored dresser and threw open the shutters of one window. The bright moon lit a small yard in which hammocks swung from pear trees that were just beginning to sprout blossoms. The view reminded her of the one from Jesse's bedroom that overlooked the garden courtyard back in Rome.

Though she longed to feel Jesse's hands on her right now, she realized that his refusal of her sex-with-no-strings idea had been wise. She was glad for his friendship, and anything more, even if it was just physical, would have opened the door for something she'd worked hard to avoid most of her life. Though she'd had a number of lovers to satisfy her cravings during her college years, she'd firmly shot down every one of their offers to cohabit. Too many complications would derail her career goals, and that was unacceptable.

Her parents' lives had demonstrated this point clearly. Her mother had enjoyed an extremely successful tennis career, and her loving father had long suffered second place in his wife's heart. Still, her father had doted on his family, and his photography.

She was grateful for the comfort his craft provided for him, and for her as well. His work always spoke to her, as if he used it to teach her life's lessons. Aside from her appreciation of the beauty and the ravages in the world, the lessons were also personal. Through the lens of the camera, she could read straight into her father's soul, and this clarity was what bonded them. This bond was what drove her to fulfill his life expectations for her, that is, to make her name in the business world, regardless of the personal consequences. Still, she noted that, even after receiving her much-sought-after offer at Ferrari earlier that night, she nonetheless had felt empty and alone.

That is, until she'd shared the news with Jesse. If only her father had had someone, besides two busy daughters and an indifferent wife, with whom he could have shared his achievements. Perhaps this diehard reticence to share her own life achievements was actually her downfall. Maybe her life, up to now, had been devoid of a balanced blend of both personal and professional fulfillment, simply out of fear that, if she put herself out there to someone she loved, and that person departed her life for whatever reason, the pain of loss would far outweigh the joy of companionship.

Coming to that realization, Mara wondered if she had just extracted another of her dad's life lessons from the grave. Or had she accepted this truth all along and simply been too fearful to take the plunge? Her epiphany was frightening, and way out of her comfort zone, but perhaps Jesse the man was the one who could unfurl a journey that would open her eyes to this foreign concept of contentment. Could she dare to brave these waters with him?

A dripping faucet echoed from the bathroom of the next room, and she went in to turn it off. She figured that this room must be her mother's room, as the bed was turned down. The light from the open shutters shone into an armoire, which stood ajar. Evening gowns, tennis outfits, and lingerie hung neatly inside. The smell of White Shoulders perfume cloyed at her nostrils. She tightened the bathroom faucet, and on her way out, spotted a photo album on a desk in the corner. There were assorted pictures strewn about the surface of the desk around the album.

By the light of the full moon, she flipped through a few pages, and what she saw shocked her.

Her cold, distant, indifferent mother had assembled an album. It was of Mara's father. The fact that her mother had cared enough to keep these mementos, let alone scrapbook them, rattled her. She did not know whether her father's impending memorial had instigated this small token, or if her mother had always treasured the keepsake, but Mara nonetheless felt moved by her mother's sentiment. Chalk one up for enduring spousal love, regardless of how dysfunctional it seemed.

Mara smiled at the few from her childhood. There was one of her father sitting with her as a toddler in her blowup pool where they'd vacationed in his hometown of Cortona; another of him toting her on his shoulders through the streets of Venice during *Carnevale*; and one where she'd fallen asleep in his lap at one of her mother's tennis matches somewhere in the world.

There were some from Mara's teen years too: her father's handing over his keys to his pickup truck when she'd gotten her driver's license; teaching his daughters ballroom dancing (his passion, Mara's downfall); and one of her and her sister on the day when Mara had graduated high school, and Abby had been leaving for another year of studies at RU. Abby would die later that year. She wished she'd known her sister better.

Mara still hadn't revealed to her mother that Abby's death had likely been the result of a treacherous serial killer, not a tragic ski accident. So far, she couldn't figure out how to even broach the subject. Plus, she wondered if it was wise to stoke memories of a daughter's death at the same time her mother was parting with her husband's remains? There'd be time for setting the record straight when the killer was brought to justice.

She shuffled through the pictures further and found a few of her parents' wedding ceremony; some of her father's award-winning *National Geographic* photos; and one in which he appeared by himself, brushing clean a lens while standing in the atrium of what looked like the Borghese Gallery in Rome. He wore a sly grin in that one. She felt a sudden longing to wrap her arms around her dad and hear his laughter just one more time.

A cloud covered the moonlight, and her mother's room plunged into darkness. Mara turned from the desk to leave the room. She felt her way along the bed, out into the hall, and back toward her room. As she entered she flipped on a light and decided to draw a bath. She reached for the fruit basket, made a selection, and bit into an apple. The clouds uncovered the moon again, and she looked out at the lights dotting the endless, rolling hills of the Tuscan countryside. She wondered which one of the mountains bore the town of Montepulciano, where Jesse had gone to spend Easter weekend with his family. She'd have to check the GPS coordinates he'd given her.

Mara sighed and touched the window, once again feeling a powerful sense of longing. Jesse was out there, under the same moon, atop one of these hills—was he thinking about her too?

She suddenly needed to be naked, in a hot bath, for a good, solid hour at least. While she nibbled down to the apple core, she unzipped her bag halfway with her other hand, and reached inside to rummage for her robe.

Wooden box with the ashes. Silk blouse and skirt. Fuzzy slippers—ooh, she'd need those too. She pulled them from the mess inside, and when she did, she snagged her palm against something jagged and sharp, and she yanked her hand back in pain. A gash almost four inches long dripped blood on the cotton coverlet.

She dropped the apple core on the bed, wrapped a clean cotton sock around her hand, and unzipped the suitcase completely. There, resting atop her unmentionables, was a tool. A sharp, double-edged, long rapier, like the one that she saw in the display case at the Borghese Gallery.

A sculpting tool, caked in plaster. And, now, mottled with her blood.

***

Officer Lontano, a female cop with a slight build but huge hands that startled Mara every time she glanced at them, sat across from her at the villa's dining room table. Mara had refused medical attention, having cleaned and bandaged her hand in the minutes before Lontano's arrival. But now it throbbed.

Officer Lontano had just asked her to pinpoint the time when her suitcase had been out of her control since packing it, but Mara was having trouble focusing, and she couldn't stop shaking. She knew she was in shock, from the injury and from fear.

Mara turned and scooped a wool throw from the back of an upholstered chair, wrapped it around her shoulders. She took a sip of water and forced herself to think clearly. "I'd never left it unattended on the train; it'd been stowed directly above my head in the luggage bin. Then, I watched the limo driver put it in the trunk when he picked me up, and then when he removed it and handed it to me in the house."

The police officer jotted notes, and Mara backtracked further. "Someone must have tampered with it back in Rome. I'd packed it in the morning and left it by the door before a soccer game. So, someone must have gained entry into my apartment while my roommate and I attended the soccer match, and planted the tool." But for what purpose? A message? A warning?

She mentioned the Sculptor case to Officer Lontano. Of course, Lontano was well aware of it, who wasn't?

A short while later, Mara paced while the Cortonese cop examined her windows and doors, inside and out. No signs of forced entry, no evidence of foul play, just the presence of the sculpting tool caked with plaster residue and speckled with Mara's blood. Lontano had bagged it for prints, taken Mara's official statement on her iPad, and left, with promises that either one would call with any further developments. Mara shut and locked the door, and then slid the dining room credenza in front of it.

Though she hadn't mentioned any theories to Lontano, Mara now considered again her and Jesse's shortlist of suspects: Utica, Kiever, and Signore Jack. Kiever and Signore Jack had been at the game, but either one of them could have gained access to her apartment before or after, when she'd run her errands. Then again, Utica might just as easily have planted it before being taken into custody. Whoever the perpetrator was, the Sculptor had broken into her empty apartment, and had let her know that she was an idiot for thinking she was at all secure. And this wasn't the first time a possible "message" had been sent her way via sculpting chisel.

She scurried through the one-floor villa, again checking the locks on windows and doors. She looked outside, and true to her word, Officer Lontano had taken up the first watch of her promised protective custody for the duration of Mara's stay in Cortona.

Still, Mara felt like she couldn't breathe. In the kitchen, she looked around for something that could be used as a weapon. If the Sculptor had gone to these lengths, perhaps he'd followed her to Cortona, and would spontaneously appear while she was showering or sleeping. She'd need to defend herself. She haphazardly grabbed items around the kitchen. On the dining table, she threw down her assembled arsenal: a pair of poultry scissors, knitting needles, a few serrated steak knives, a wooden rolling pin, a cowbell, and a hefty terracotta urn. Shit, she was bone-tired. Of all of this Sculptor business.

Scanning her options, she wondered why the hell she hadn't demanded that Jesse give her a gun? Probably because he could tell by looking at her that the only firearm she'd ever handled in her life had been a water gun. She jotted a mental note: Back in Rome, she'd drag Jesse to a shooting range and get him to show her how to handle a gun. She could not rely on her Jet Li karate moves all her life.

Right now, though, she refused to call him. He was celebrating Easter holiday with his family, and there was no way she was going to bother him. After all, she hadn't been attacked nor had she witnessed a brutality. She'd simply found a sculpting tool where it shouldn't be. Again. She'd called the Cortonese cops, and there was nothing more that they could do aside from manned protection. No need to call Jesse and worry him at what must be close to midnight; she could handle this. There'd be time to share this new development with Jesse and Enzo in the morning.

The bleeding on her hand had ceased, and the throbbing had subsided, but she felt woozy from fatigue and worry. Mara gathered her arsenal and dumped it on her bed alongside a box of Pop Tarts and the rest of the fruit basket. She locked the bedroom door, dangled the cowbell from the handle, and set her can of Mace on the bedside table.

As she tore into the first package of pastry, she reasoned that the serial killer had likely not followed her for two reasons.

First, she'd been vague about her destination and about the timing of her plans to everyone, barely even making the train that evening herself. Second, believing that he had not followed her would be the only way she'd ever fall asleep.

After wolfing down one more pack of frosted blueberry, she rested her head on the pillow for just a minute...

***

The next morning, the bright sun streaming in through the unshuttered window woke her. Sprawled across the bed, Mara found that she'd knocked most of her weaponry to the floor in the night, and ants had found what was left of her Pop Tarts.

She was glad she hadn't overreacted and contacted Jesse the night before. Someone had planted evidence in her bag at her apartment simply to startle her. It had worked, but she felt certain that she was in no immediate danger, especially with a parked cop car outside her door. In fact, she determined not to tell her mother when they met later, as it would prove a solemn day anyway with her dad's memorial. The sculpting tool would keep. She showered and donned a long-sleeve, black knit, cowl-neck dress, and then checked her mother's room. Still vacant. It was Easter Sunday, the day that they'd set aside to remember her departed father, and her mother was as yet AWOL.

She grabbed her father by his two side handles, pocketed a couple green apples, and went out to swing with her dad on one of the hammocks in the small yard.

Crossing the driveway, she tapped on the window of the police car in the driveway. Officer DiMare, her morning protection detail, provided credentials proving his identity as such. She thanked him, gave him an apple, and walked away to the sideyard.

While she swung back and forth in the warm sun, a glimmer of metal shone from inside the property's shed. She opened the unlocked garage door. Inside was a slick gray-green, 1960-ish convertible Aston Martin. Keys hung from the ignition—gold-plated tennis rackets. Must be her mother's rental car. A scrawled note on the dash confirmed it. Only Kat Silvestri would choose a vintage rental. The hands on Mara's watch showed 10:30 am—a half hour before their scheduled meeting for the memorial, at St. Teresa's in town, the church where her parents had married.

Mara started up the Aston Martin, carefully backed out of the shed.

She pulled up aside Officer DiMare and explained about her father's ceremony. He assented to follow, promising discretion.

She wound her way through the tight curves leading up the rest of the mountain, until passing through one of the walled gates surrounding Cortona. She found a parking spot beneath a large tree and hoofed it to the church.

She walked in, adjusted her eyes, and spotted her mother's lean, tall athletic build from across the nave, kneeling in the front pew. Kat Zulheimer-Silvestri wore a short, black suit and black veil on her head. All she needed was a rosary, and she'd be the epitome of mourning.

"Mother." Mara said, and her mother nodded.

A priest approached them. "Shall we begin?" he asked.

***

An hour later, after a service of prayer and music, attended only by the two of them, mother and daughter left the church through a back entrance.

"This was the entryway for altar boys. Your father was one, you know," her mother said. Outside, her mother pointed to a small plot of land dotted with crumbling headstones. "Your father once told me that the priests used to catch him smoking before every mass, and they'd chase him around the little graveyard trying to cuff him. The bells would toll, and they'd all run inside just in time for mass. Your father was quite mischievous." Mara felt touched by her mother's nostalgia.

Over the course of the day, she and her mother walked throughout the town, recounting memories and pointing out places where he'd spent his childhood. Arturo Silvestri's parents had moved him to America in his teens, and he'd met the up-and-coming Kat Zulheimer when he'd photographed one of her matches. He was eighteen, she was twenty-one.

They had gotten pregnant, married, and lost the child within a six-month period. After, the two traveled the globe, she playing tennis, and he shooting pictures for *Sports Illustrated*, and later *National Geographic*. Years passed, and two daughters bound them together until one died, and the couple drifted apart. Then, Arturo himself met tragedy on a photo shoot, a swamp boat accident in the Everglades. Today, the commemoration of his death brought together what remained of their family to remember him.

For the first time in her life, Mara watched her mother shed tears. She embraced her for a few moments, and then her mother freed herself. "Thank you, Mara, but I'm quite alright. Let's take your father for some gelato." Mara nodded. It wasn't much in the way of family bonding, but she'd take what she could get.

They slid into their seats in the Aston Martin, and Mara put the top down. "Do you ever plan on telling me why we have a police escort?" Her mother gestured to the rear of the car.

"I didn't want to worry you today, and I thought maybe you wouldn't notice," Mara said.

"When will you ever realize, dear…I notice everything. I just don't always let on that I know."

Mara spent the next few minutes explaining her involvement with the Sculptor case, and how the discovery of the sculpting tool in her baggage yesterday compelled the need for protective custody in Cortona.

Her mother, as always, reserved emotion over the matter, and patted Mara's knee. "Sound judgment. Shall we proceed to the gelato?"

Mara smiled. She needed ice cream now more than ever. She glanced in the side mirror and thought she saw her father's same mischievous grin staring back at her.

She revved the engine once and gunned the convertible down the mountain of Cortona even before the cop had been able to start his car. Her mother opened the wooden box of ashes and freed what remained of Arturo Silvestri into his Tuscan hills at top speed, the cop behind them shaking his fist in the air at their recklessness. It was a truly fine way of commemorating her father's life, just the way he would've wanted it. The warmth of the sun on the back of her head felt like a tender caress, and she knew that her dad was finally home.

***

Mara had apologized to Officer DiMare for her little escapade down the mountain, and she'd given him a bottle of wine the next morning before thanking him and ending the protection detail.

Mara and her mother spent the next few days traveling to San Gimignano, Montalcino, and Siena, visiting all of the places that had meant something to Arturo. They dined Wednesday evening at the villa with the finest wines from those cities.

"I'm leaving tomorrow, Mara," her mother said. "I have an Austrian tournament. My driver will pick me up in the morning. Feel free to stay out the week at the villa; just return the rental at the station."

The next morning, Mara's mother nudged her awake. Bejeweled, coifed, and dressed in an Armani silk dress, she stood over Mara, with lips pursed and a wrinkle between her brows. She offered Mara the keepsake photo album, which neither had discussed until that moment. "I've had this for years," her mother said. "I'm finished with it now; time to move on. You should keep it."

Mara sat up and brushed her long curls from her face, rubbed her eyes. "But, there are so many memories—of you and Daddy, me and Abby. It's our history, of your husband and your children."

Her mother shook her head and turned briskly away. Mara sprang from the bed, almost tripped over her packed plaid suitcase by the door, and bounded down the hall to the living room.

"Mother, it's like you're giving up on your past. I appreciate the token, but please don't give away your cherished photos. Someday you might really need to see them."

"There are things you don't understand, Mara," her mother said. A horn honked outside, and Mara glimpsed the Alfa Romeo sedan, and its same driver from her first night. G.I. Spock, the pointy-eared driver with the carrot top stood by the open passenger door on the gravel drive.

Mara held the book out to her. "Just because your husband and Abby are gone, doesn't mean they should be forgotten."

Her mother set down her handbag and gripped the album. She thrust it onto the table and shuffled through the first few pages, pointing out certain photos as she did. "See these? Your father's miserable. Why? We were never happy; we just went through the motions."

Her mother flipped ahead. "Here, pictures of your sister, and later those from when you are born, and there's light in his eyes."

A few more pages ahead. "Here, your father's light was extinguished, and he never recovered."

Mara could not understand. These were shot before her sister's tragic death. Her sister was still alive, and yet, her father appeared sickly, distraught, defeated, and alone.

She looked at her mother's face, contorted in sadness and anger. Kat pointed a blood red nail to a photo of her father, dressed in a black suit, sitting on the Spanish Steps in Rome, his arm curled protectively around her adolescent sister. "The love of your father's life died that day. Your sister's real mother."

Mara felt the blood drain from her face. Her knees wobbled, and she gripped the kitchen chair to keep from crumbling to the floor. "What are you saying?"

"Your father met a woman, actually more of a girl just out of high school, on an Italian photo shoot. She lived in Rome, studied art as an apprentice, and Arturo continued to see her whenever he was assigned there, or whenever I toured Europe for various tournaments. The girl eventually became pregnant. She was Abby's birth mother."

Mara slumped into a chair. "But why...why the charade, why not..."

"The young woman's widowed father disowned her, and as an artist's apprentice, she didn't have the resources or wherewithal to raise a child. When Abby was born, she begged your father to take your sister, and raise her in the States, to provide her with better advantages. I agreed, on the condition that Arturo break all contact with the trollop. Life went on.

"After about five years, yes, it was the year I won Wimbledon, your father secretly visited Rome. He introduced Abigail to the now gorgeous, educated, and established trollop, who requested that he and Abigail move to Rome and begin a new life with her. Ah, but, the same day that your father confronted me with this, was the day that I told him I was pregnant, with you, Mara. You're father refused the Italian hussy, and he stayed with me to raise both daughters. The charade, as you called it, continued…"

Mara gripped her head in her hands. All that she'd ever known of her family had been a lie. She'd worshipped her father's strength, his character, his integrity, and the values that he'd instilled in her. They were the same values she'd spent most of her life struggling to uphold, even in his death. Now, the pedestal upon which she'd placed her beloved father had just collapsed.

Jesse's face appeared in her mind, along with the faces of the handful of men that she'd ever considered worthy of her love. She'd spent her entire life pushing them away, pushing love away. It had all been just to appease her father and his memory, believing all this time that if he could live his life supported only by the passion for his work, then she should as well.

The chauffeur honked twice outside.

Her mother continued. "Make no mistake, your father and I loved you, Mara. So, we raised two daughters the best we knew how, and we kept his secret from you and your sister to protect you from the heartache you feel now. Your sister's birth mother died when Abby was in her teens, and the secret went with her. There was never a need to burden you or your sister with the truth.

"You've grown into an accomplished woman, Mara, and I'm sorry if this conversation has caused you anguish. But the time that we've shared over the past few days has shown me that you can handle it. It's my fervent hope that you will make wiser choices in life, wiser than those that your father and I made."

Her mother came around the table to face her, high heels clicking against the marble tile as she did. Then, awkwardly, her mother extended her arms toward her.

Mara gave the woman a break, and hugged her back. Never in a million years would she have imagined curling up inside her mother's embrace. But Mara realized that it must have taken a tremendous amount of might and courage for her mom to admit her father's fallacy, and to extend this olive branch to her remaining daughter. For a moment, Mara relaxed and relished her mother's comfort. "Thank you, Mom. I know this must have been hard for you...all of it."

Her mother pulled away, stared at her. "Promise me you'll make the most of your life. Follow your heart and intuition; only then will you find your joy."

After minding her father's life lessons all her life, she couldn't believe that the one golden nugget that mattered most was coming from her mother. "Go after what *you* want. Don't settle. And, don't be afraid to have it all."

Her mother released her. She whisked out the door without even a backward glance, and seconds later, the limo outside barreled out of the gravel driveway.

The album remained on the table.

Tears slipped down her cheeks, and she opened the leather-bound portfolio. She looked through the pages with new eyes, and noticed photos that she hadn't seen her first night at the villa.

The book told an entirely different story now that she knew the truth. She still loved her father; that was certain. But, after everything she'd ever believed was called into question, his betrayal left her feeling raw and unnerved.

She compared herself with photos of her sister, and now noticed their dissimilarities. Mara still loved Abby, appreciated what little she'd known of her. After all, none of this was her sister's doing. She pitied her, as once again, Abby had fallen victim to others' wrongdoing.

There were no pictures of her father's lover, but when Mara sought out those originating in Rome, she discerned an inordinate number of shots revolving around the Borghese Gallery. She remembered traveling there with her father and sister in her pre-teen years, and meeting with the beautiful curator of the gallery a number of times. It had never occurred to her to call into question her father's friendly relationship with the woman; she simply thought he appreciated the artwork there.

She slammed the book shut and whipped it across the room, into the empty hearth. She'd endowed her father with every bit of trust she'd ever had, and he'd betrayed her. What an ass. What a silly little girl she'd been, so naïve and gullible.

Mara wanted to escape. She ran to her room where she dressed quickly. Leaving the villa, she locked the house and threw her suitcase into the trunk of the Aston Martin. She creaked open the mail slot on the absent landlord's front door, and shoved the key through it. But the key lingered in her grasp. She couldn't let it go, not yet.

Damn it! Quickly reconsidering, she reopened the villa door and ran back to retrieve the photo album from where she had thrown it, along with the few scattered photos that had slipped from the pages. Shuffling the mess together, she left the villa again, dropped the key in the slot, and got into the car, throwing all of it under the seat. She peeled from the driveway and onto the narrow lane, spitting gravel from her wheels. She needed to get the hell away from Cortona and from the memories she'd spent the entire week rehashing. She needed to grab hold of the pain in her heart, and tear it from her chest, run it down, back up and run it over again.

Mara turned the car around corners quickly, almost plowing into a three-wheeled vehicle hauling pottery uphill on the other side, and tore down the mountain with her foot flush against the floor. She pushed the automatic faster, and then came to a screeching halt when she encountered a herd of shorn black sheep crossing the road on the other side of a bend.

Forced to wait, she caught her breath, and put her head against the back of the leather seat. Dark clouds gathered overhead, and she was glad the top was up on the convertible. She plucked her GPS from her purse, and recalled the coordinates that she'd plugged in days earlier on the train. They belonged to the location for Jesse's family home, evidently only thirty minutes away.

She could be with Jesse Autunno in twenty minutes if those sheep would haul ass.

Chapter 33

Twenty-five minutes later, the GPS confirmed that Mara was approaching her destination. As she neared the hilltop town of Montepulciano, the automated GPS voice told her to bear right. She wound away from the small, bustling community of tour buses and traffic and veered toward a lane that drifted slightly southeast. After zipping the Aston Martin a few hundred yards past a vineyard and an olive orchard, she turned off onto the edge of a steep mountain drive and the voice told her she'd arrived. She parked, turned the wheels in, and yanked up the parking brake.

Mara looked through the windshield of the car and took a moment to drink in the view of the sprawling farmhouse and adjacent land. The pristine property was breathtaking, warm, and inviting. She never would have thought that a pair of prestigious vineyard owners would be the ones responsible for raising a sexy soccer player/homicide cop with an earring and a horrible denim jacket, but she supposed stranger things could happen.

Two gigantic, white, fluffy dogs stood sentry at the entrance to the driveway that was lined on either side by tall, narrow cypress trees. When she approached, the expert guard dogs rolled onto their backs and exposed their tummies for a rub. As she patted and scratched them, Mara realized that Jesse had never actually extended her an invitation to his family's home. But when the thick, black clouds overhead began spattering raindrops on her head, she figured she'd better get herself an invite or else run the risk of drowning.

She dialed her cell phone and plugged her other ear to block the noise of a passing cargo truck overflowing with olives on the main road adjacent to the driveway. She glimpsed the driver. He waved and smiled, and blew her a kiss.

Jesse.

He abruptly stopped the truck behind her car, yanked out his keys, and ran across the deserted road, right toward her. She leaned against a fence post to drink him in.

The clouds rumbled and broke, and in seconds, Jesse's face glistened with rain. His drenched hair fell over his long eyelashes, and his sweatshirt stuck to his thick, muscular chest. He'd never appeared so delicious.

"You're here!" he shouted through the rain.

Shit and a half, she should've called sooner. Damn, he wasn't expecting her, and he probably had other plans. What if he really didn't want her here?

"I am so glad you came." Jesse wrapped his thick arms around her, engulfing her in his warmth. She looked up into his blue grotto eyes, and it finally hit her.

Time to let go.

Mara gripped his waist, pulled him close, and pressed her lips against his, tasting the rain on them. She forced open his mouth with her tongue and melted into the warmth inside. He returned her kiss just as passionately, exploring her lips and her mouth with the tip of his own tongue, teasing her, caressing her, tasting her. All the while, he pressed his body so close to hers, she wondered what it would take to ever pry them apart.

Lightning flashed across the dark Tuscan sky, alighting the lush green countryside. Thunder boomed, echoed, and rolled. The rain fell harder, pelting them, and then it turned to hail. That's what it took to pry them apart.

Jesse grabbed her hand and led her into the cab of the pickup truck. A cacophony of light and sound played outside the windows like a concert, and the water teemed down onto the mountain. Inside, he held her on his lap and pushed back strands of wet hair from her face. He cupped her chin in both of his hands and kissed her, this time with a tenderness she would never have expected from one with such heavy hands.

"Tell me how this happened, Mara." He nibbled her lower lip, kissed her nose and nuzzled her neck. "Is this just a dream? Tell me you're real, and that I'm—"

Before he could finish, the two of them were slammed against the dashboard with such force, Mara was sure she'd snapped her spine.

Gripping the seat, Jesse looked her up and down. "Are you alright?"

"I'm okay. But Jesse, a car must have...hit us so hard, and...oh man, we're moving." Panic stuttered her speech. Indeed, their parked pickup had begun sliding forward, downhill. She slid quickly off of Jesse's lap and onto the passenger seat of the truck. Jesse slammed both feet against the brake pedal, no help.

He glanced in his side mirror. "Goddamn garbage truck rammed us." He fished for his keys in his pocket, but couldn't pull them from his tight, wet jeans.

Jesse's truck barreled forward even faster now, pushed on by the massive truck behind them. They were headed straight for the Aston Martin.

The garbage truck revved its massive engine and pushed harder and faster. The rancid smell of the tires burning rubber on the road permeated the windows.

Jesse reached for his door; it was jammed. He reached for the window; it wouldn't budge. "What the hell? Someone must have messed with it while we were—"

They crashed into the Aston Martin in front of them, parked on the shoulder of the curved road. Mara pumped the hand brake of the truck again, nothing happened. Together with the crumpled Aston Martin, their pickup truck shimmied down the slick, curved shoulder, running out of pavement.

Jesse pulled his sweatshirt over his head and wrapped his fist with it. "Cover your head and face," he said. She did, and he smashed his fist through the driver-side window, and cleared the glass. He lifted her and pushed her halfway through the open window.

Rain pelted her, and she tried to glimpse her surroundings through the deluge. The Aston Martin had just shot over the edge of their curved road and plummeted down the hillside, likely crashing into the Tuscan valley below. Jesse's pickup truck was headed for the same fate.

She gripped the side of the window, catapulted from the cab, and plunged into the rain-filled ravine beside the road.

Then she turned back to watch in horror as Jesse's pickup truck tumbled over the side of the cliff and down the mountainside. Mara screamed. Jesse was still inside.

She sprinted toward the cliff side. The garbage truck that had rammed them abruptly angled right and continued down the highway until it traveled out of sight.

She reached the edge and watched in horror as Jesse's pickup truck careened out of control down the steep and rocky hillside. On an impulse she tore after it on foot, not even thinking about what her next move could possibly be.

Nearly a hundred feet in front of her, the pickup plowed into a tree. Its rear wheels lifted with the impact, before crashing back down on the belly of the chassis.

Still tearing a path toward Jesse, she shouted to him. She watched him scramble through the window and fall to the ground in one piece. "Jesse!" she said again. Her heart was pounding hard. She wiped away tears she hadn't known had fallen.

He gained his footing and spotted her. He rushed forward to grab hold of her hand, and then tugged her through the trees away from the truck.

Seconds later, the gas tank exploded, and echoed loudly through the hillside. Wet olives rained down upon them a safe distance away. They stopped running and caught their breath. That's when she noticed Jesse's bloodied face.

"You're hurt," she cried. She wiped the blood from his eyes with her sleeve.

"Just a gash on my head, from slamming the steering wheel. Looks worse than it is. You're okay, though?" he said.

"I'm okay, but I'm pissed. Through the rain, I couldn't see a license plate, or any distinctive markings."

"There wouldn't be any. Guy's a pro. He managed to rig my truck in the few minutes we were inside it. Not sure if he was gunning for me, or for both of us, and not sure why. But someone wanted us dead."

The rain had eased somewhat, and they trudged back up the hill toward Jesse's family property. She stopped to examine the wreckage of the vintage rental and retrieved the photo album from the front seat. She didn't bother trying to unhinge the crumpled trunk door to retrieve the few clothes stowed there. For some reason, she just felt better leaving the plaid suitcase behind.

Neither of them spoke for a bit, and she wondered whether the man beside her was now in the mode of Jesse the cop, ruminating over whether the driver who tried to kill them was the Sculptor or not. Her heart hoped that he was Jesse the man, who might be savoring the passion they'd just shared in the pickup.

Her soul knew that the man beside her was the one she'd fallen in love with, the perfect combination of both.

***

Once inside the sprawling, two-story farmhouse, Jesse introduced her to his mother and father. His warm, affectionate mother doted on them as they told her what had just occurred out on the road in front of the house, and she plied them with food, blankets, and bandages. His father, the Chief Inspector of Montepulciano, poured them both some Brunello and questioned them.

They both refused to go to the hospital, so Jesse's mother insisted on keeping her for the night, and she lent Mara warm, dry clothing.

After a nap, Mara showered and returned to find a sequined, off-the-shoulder, low-cut gown with matching four-inch heels laid out on her bed. A pair of sweats and t-shirt would have been adequate, and just a tad more practical. But since Mara felt like celebrating life tonight, she laughed and put it on, striding into the dining room just as Jesse and his mom were laying out dinner.

Jesse's jaw dropped. Words escaped him.

"I knew that one would fit you, love," his mother said, heading into the kitchen. "Just another souvenir from my ballroom days—three time Latin champion, you know," she yelled over her shoulder.

For just a moment, Mara was stung by the memory of her father pushing her two tiny left feet around a dance floor as a child, encouraging her and her sister, well half-sister, to learn the tango. She squeezed Abby's sapphire necklace around her neck, pushed the thought away, and concentrated on the wolf-like drool seeping from the side of Jesse's mouth.

"You are stunning, just...stunning," Jesse said. "I can't...you're just—"

She slinked into the chair that Jesse had pulled out for her. He settled in alongside her at the table and clasped her hand, clearly entranced.

Jesse's father reached for the plate of crostini topped with olive caponata and passed it to her. "Mara, you'd better make up your mind quickly about this lug, because my son has apparently fallen head over bootstraps for you, my dear."

She smiled, knowing full well she already had.

***

After dinner, Jesse's mother put on Louis Prima. "I really think the two of you should put that dress to some good use." She grasped her husband's hand. "C'mon, Franco, let's show them how it's done."

Jesse's phone rang. He spoke a few moments, then frowned. He glanced at the face of the phone and snapped it shut, even before his parents had had a chance to spin back to them across the floor. "*Zio* Enzo called with more developments, and as much as I'd love to dance with you, Mara, I have to get back to Rome tonight on the eight o'clock train." He grabbed his jacket and kissed his parents on both cheeks. "Mara, please, stay as long as you like. My home is yours."

Thinking quickly and not wanting to be separated from Jesse, Mara explained to Jesse's parents that it was necessary for her to return to Rome as well, due to her friend's opera performance the next afternoon. Mara changed into a pair of his mother's jeans and a blouse for the trip back, but Jesse's mother insisted that she keep the dress and shoes, in case an occasion to dance arose. She packed them food and made them promise to return soon.

An hour later, Mara and Jesse boarded the near-empty Thursday evening train bound for Rome and found a vacant compartment.

"Did Enzo give you any indication of what's transpired? Tell me it's not another murder," she said. She curled up her legs and settled in beside him.

"He started getting into it, but my battery died."

Mara nodded. She rubbed her eyes and yawned. "Promise to keep me posted?"

"I was hoping you'd come with me for the briefing, partner," Jesse said.

She smiled and rested her head on his shoulder, knowing that she'd go with him anywhere.

In what seemed like only a few minutes, the train jostled, and she heard the announcement for Rome's Termini station, approaching in three stops. She must have fallen asleep.

She peeked through half-shut eyes and found herself stretched across three seats, her cheek resting on Jesse's thigh, probably the most comfortable pillow known to mankind.

Her body ached from the earlier car crash. Might as well snag a few more winks before they had to disembark. Her heavy lids eased shut.

Half-dozing, she felt his hand, stroking her back, rubbing her hair. His soft humming and the vibrations from the wheels of the train soothed her.

She heard him sniff. Then, he sniffed again. She realized what he was doing. She stifled a giggle and held still while regulating her breathing, so as not to embarrass him. Jesse was sniffing her hair. Did he like the vanilla shampoo she'd found in his mother's shower? She knew he did when she felt him bend his torso slightly and lift a tuft of her hair to his nose. He inhaled deeply.

His hand continued to caress her, and she lost herself in the feel of his fingertips on her spine. She felt herself slipping back and forth between awake and sleep. She didn't want to leave the feel of his touch, and she hoped she'd dream about it.

It was on the cusp of finally surrendering to slumber that she heard him whisper to her, right above her ear, making the hairs on her neck tingle.

"I'm in love with you," he said.

Chapter 34

Back in Rome, as the sun rose high in the red morning sky, Jesse sipped his hot espresso and gazed at the sleeping woman on his bed. How was it that even with her freaked out bed-head, spittle leaking from the corner of her mouth, and covers all tangled up around one leg while the other hung limply over the side, this woman looked so damn sexy?

The way Mara had clung to him as he carried her sleeping body from the taxi and up the few flights of stairs last night had made him ache for her from the cold, hard living room futon where he'd slept. But, she'd groaned in her sleep as he'd set her down, obviously still aching from the collision earlier that day. Better to let her recover in peace.

He'd finally caught up with Enzo by his landline phone while she slept. Enzo had updated Jesse on some details regarding some of the returned forensics reports. Also, the urgency that had prompted Jesse's return from Tuscany had been a matter of staff coverage. Enzo had planned a couple meetings with bureaucratic higher-ups that would detain him for a day or two, and Enzo wanted to ensure that they had enough boots on the ground handling the Sculptor case in his absence.

Mara rolled and murmured in her sleep, and the sight of her bare thigh forced Jesse to bolt for an ice cold shower.

Twenty minutes later, Jesse stepped out of the bathroom to find her standing in his kitchen, dousing a pan of scrambled eggs with a bottle of hot sauce. Her hair was tied back, and his Clapton t-shirt hugged her breasts just right. "Hungry?" she called to him.

"You have no idea," he said.

She looked up at him, her eyes still dreamy from sleep. She swept her glance down to the towel around his waist, lingered for a moment, and flicked them back up to his face. Her rosy cheeks turned crimson.

He chuckled before heading to his room to dress. He'd never been hungrier in his whole life.

***

When they finally sat down to eat, he could tell that she had something to say, but didn't quite know how to broach the subject. Guilt swathed her face like a Venetian mask. "Out with it," he said.

She cleared her throat in between bites. "Remember that sculpting tool that I found under my pillow a couple weeks back?" she said.

He stopped chewing.

"I found another one," she said.

He put down his fork.

"Inside my suitcase, last weekend," she mumbled.

"Last weekend? And, you're telling me this now?" he said.

Mara spent the next few minutes telling him about the tool she'd found upon her arrival at the Cortonese villa.

Jesse grabbed her hand and ran his finger along the long, jagged, scabbed laceration on her palm. He took a few deep breaths before looking up at her. She was the most thickheaded, self-reliant, pain-in-the-ass he'd ever met.

When he locked eyes with her, he saw that her guilt had vanished, and she stared back at him with arms crossed and her jaw firm like an obstinate child, defiant to the end.

"Go ahead," she said, "lecture me about safety; get on with it, so that I can shower, will you?"

"Do you have any idea how much I worried about you going up to Cortona alone? You swore you'd watch your ass," he said.

"Nothing happened, Jesse. It was just another stupid prank, like the first one. I don't think—"

He cut her off. "I know you don't think; this is the problem. There's a killer out there, and you're walking around like you don't care. Sooner or later, he's going to—"

Her eyes flew wide and she jumped from her chair. "Don't care? Must I remind you that the bastard likely murdered my sister in the Alps."

"You know what I mean, damn it," he said. "You don't pay attention to your own well-being. From now on, you're not going anywhere without protection, understand? You won't brush your teeth without my hovering over you, got it?"

A look of satisfaction spread over her face. "You just want to spend more time with me, admit it."

"Goddamn right I do." He pushed back his chair and slammed both hands on the table. "But, I don't want to spend it looking down at you on a coroner's table!"

She rolled her eyes at him.

He breathed, calmed himself. He reached out his hand and led her to the sofa. "This is not the first time that a weapon has surfaced in a location meant specifically for you—under your pillow, in your suitcase. These are not pranks; this is evidence of a crime. Someone is stalking you, and leading you along in a game like a pawn. He's setting you up, and it's not for fun, it's to crush you in the end."

"Not to send you into another overprotective rage," she said, "but why would the Sculptor be stalking me when he's had ample opportunity to kill me by now? He's murdered others well before my arrival in Rome, and during the time that I've been here, so why would he toy with me, instead of just butchering and plastering me like everyone else?"

She had a point.

But suddenly something clicked in his mind, and he realized that there was more to it than that. "The GPS."

"What?" she said.

"The guy in the garbage truck who tried to kill us—that was no fluke. Someone deliberately tried to kill you." He stood up and paced, gathered his thoughts.

"The GPS. You told me that you punched in our vineyard's coordinates, drove there, and the garbage truck arrived shortly after. He could have hacked your GPS whenever he planted the riffler in your bag and ascertained your destination coordinates. All this time, he was probably staking out the vineyard, and waiting for you to trigger the route."

His pace quickened. "When you arrived at my house, you immediately phoned me. Do you remember, you called?"

Mara nodded yes.

"That's when the stalker became wise to your arrival. The garbage truck, which he could've stowed at any of the nearby hillside farms, became his weapon of your destruction."

"It makes sense. All this time, he's been hacking my Blackberry, my GPS, my computer? He might have been watching my every move since I got to Rome." Mara rubbed her hands along her neck and scalp, as if wiping away imaginary critters. "I feel so violated, so…naïve."

She stood and walked to the bathroom, and shut the door.

He wanted to go to her, but he knew she hated feeling like a victim and instead gave her a few minutes of space.

He checked his messages. One from Enzo, confirming that he and Captain Sciug would be unreachable, away for the day, maybe more, at a conference, and also that Enzo had left a number of reports on Jesse's desk to review about the Sculptor case.

A half hour later, Mara exited the bathroom, freshly showered, and wearing a too-short blue towel. She padded over to him across the floor in bare feet.

"I'm sorry that I've been taking my security for granted, and that I withheld evidence from you," she said. "I've become…a little anxious to avenge my sister's death, and I didn't want you to overreact and keep things from me about the investigation. Forgive me."

"I appreciate how much you want to get this guy," he said. "But what I said about police protection is serious. You're not going anywhere without me."

The towel slipped down then, revealing the swells of her cleavage. "Does that mean that you're my official date for Kate's opera performance today?" She gestured to the sequined ballroom dress, draped over the living room chair beside her family's photo album. "I hope you like Puccini."

An evening spent watching that dress caress her breasts and long legs in time to Puccini? He'd have to muddle through. "I'd like to get over to your apartment and sweep it for evidence first," Jesse said.

"Can't do it; there won't be enough time to make the two o'clock performance," she said. "Unless you go to Stella Luna by yourself? I'm sure that I'll be safe here."

The woman was mad. Two of his roommates were still on their shortlist of suspects, and he'd just read her the riot act on watching her ass.

As if on cue, the door to the apartment opened, and in walked the man whom Enzo had just interrogated and released a day ago without explanation. Michael Utica, one of three still on Jesse's shortlist.

Utica waved a greeting and walked into his bedroom, slamming the door behind him.

Jesse shook his head. "I'll call one of the clerks at the station to deliver my reports here. We'll check your apartment later. Go get dressed before I change my mind."

***

When Mara disappeared back into his bedroom with the dress and shoes to primp for the opera, Jesse phoned his father, Chief of Police in Montepulciano. He asked him to have one of his officers retrieve the now pertinent suitcase that was still in the back of the Aston Martin. The car had been towed from the accident site and was now at the impound lot. Jesse asked that the suitcase, along with the sculpting tool bagged by Officer Lontano in Cortona, be sent by courier to Rome. After Mara's admission about the second weapon, the suitcase had become evidence, and an examination by the Rome forensics lab for prints was a key priority. Though the first weapon discovered beneath her pillow had been clean, one could only hope for a little luck this time.

A plainclothesman from headquarters showed up at his door and delivered the reports that Enzo had left for him. Jesse thanked him and plunked down with a beer to review what little they had to go on.

No ballistics reports to comb through, the sick bastard had always reverted to other means besides firearms to commit murder: asphyxiation by plaster; poisoning by bleach injection; decapitation by saw. Traces of sodium hypochlorite, calcium sulfate dihydrate, and nicotine residue had been found at every CS.

He flipped through the crime scene photographs of the seven cases. In most of them, the killer had ensured that the head and torso would remain intact. Even when the head or a limb was removed, as was the case with the recent Norwegian decapitation, great care was taken to minimize skin and other organ damage, a most arduous thing to do, as if preservation of the whole or a part of the artwork was of utmost importance.

In every case, the killer had ingratiated himself to his victim; consensual sex had always preceded the murder, never rape. Neither hate, nor anger appeared to motivate the killer. It seemed more a matter of reverence, as even the remains had been washed and maneuvered with diligent care.

He glanced at photos which had been provided by the families of the women. The beauty of each victim was key—each one was ravishing in life, bearing movie star quality features. This reverence or worship of goddess-like aesthetics, followed by its maintenance and preservation, reminded Jesse of a caretaker's practices, as in a church or museum.

The psychology expert's report coincided with Jesse's theory. The killer's obvious need to sculpt and plaster with painstaking attention to detail; the beauty of the victims; and the need to preserve rather than injure upheld Jesse's belief that the killer had to be a congenial, handsome, vital heterosexual momma's-boy. The man was not out for public notoriety, but for the achievement of some personal goal, such as validation from a mother who'd never loved him enough.

Experts had agreed that the angle of the incisions on the bodies, made with scalpels, rapiers, and saws, signified the precision of a right-handed person.

The matter of the purplish silk thread intrigued Jesse. Always planted somewhere on the victim's torso, the string was likely a decoration, a sort of gold star for a job well done. Or, perhaps it was a way of marking his territory against anyone else laying claim. Like an artist signing his work.

None of the reports confirmed whether or not the killer worked alone. None of the torsos had been dragged, which would have indicated a single perpetrator. Instead, they'd been propped, to achieve pronounced display, like positioning a museum sculpture. Either a single individual or multiple individuals may have been responsible for such an exposition. Though, the likelihood that every victim had courted multiple, simultaneous lovers was a slim possibility, thereby leaning toward the single perp theory.

The bottom line was that whoever killed these women was a strong, brazen yet precise, goal-oriented individual, or perhaps a duo, with a determination to please a familial audience after satisfying the ardor of a close acquaintance. The fact that the killer signed his works for clarity and pride, and that he hoarded trophies for likely manipulation and display elsewhere, further enhanced Jesse's theory that this was the work of a single man, but there was nothing conclusive.

The Sculptor had concentrated his violence on the female students of Rome's three major universities for years. Now, the Sculptor appeared to have selected Mara, stalking her, perhaps in order to kill her in such a manner to serve as his ultimate prize, or else to use her murder to achieve his much sought-after validation. Either way, Jesse's new mission in life was to hunt down and kill the bastard before he could touch Mara.

Jesse threw down the crime scene photos and finished his beer. From the coffee table he snatched the photo album Mara had rescued from the front seat of the totaled Aston Martin. He flipped through the opening pages of the album and skimmed through scenes of Mara in her youth. The pictures confirmed what he'd gleaned over the past month and a half about Mara Silvestri—she was gorgeous and precocious, smart and confident, goofy and self-deprecating. The fact that she adored her father was evident, and so was her need to achieve all of her goals—in sports, education, and her career.

Just then, Mara sauntered out of the bedroom in the low-cut gown she'd somehow shortened, making it practically illegal by decency standards, and he saw the gleam in her eye—the one that tried to convey her edgy strong side, but was betrayed by her vulnerable, soft side. He knew then, just as he did when he'd first laid eyes on her, that someday he would marry this girl.

She slinked in beside him on the couch, smiled, but said nothing. The smell of her perfumed body next to him made him grateful for the album covering his lap.

He reached for her and gently held her face; he put his fingers in her thick, dark hair. He trailed the fingers of one hand along her jaw, her collarbone, down to the pendant that dangled between the tops of her breasts. He couldn't believe this new bond that now existed between them. Something had changed in her over Easter weekend. Whether it was her final goodbye to her father, the time spent with her mother, or her scare involving the Sculptor's weapon, he didn't know, and moreover, he didn't care.

Ever since she'd first appeared on the road outside his family's vineyard the day before, he could just tell in her eyes, and in the ferocity of her passion, that she'd allowed herself to trust in him, maybe even fall in love with him. Now, as the sun streamed on her face through the apartment window, he leaned forward, and parted his lips to kiss her.

That's when Utica bounded out of the bedroom. "Hey you two, Kate's performing in forty-five minutes. We gotta leave in five or Mimi's gonna turn his Calabrian uncles on us. Tuna, get your ass together, man!" Utica slammed the door of the bathroom, effectively slamming the door on any action Jesse had hoped for.

Mara smiled. "He's right. You'll be swimming with the fishes. Get moving." She kissed his lips for just a second, and went into the kitchen.

Jesse sighed, and placed the photo album on the coffee table. The book was opened to a picture of Mara in pigtails, she had to be around ten years old. She sat with her teenage sister and her dad, alongside a fountain outside the Borghese Gallery. He wondered if she still wore pigtails, and hoped she did.

Near the bottom of the facing page, he found a couple photos stuck behind a larger one. He tugged them free and looked them over. These photos were a couple more ragged shots, of a beautiful older woman, not Mara's tennis-star mom, probably an aunt or cousin, sitting between Mara's sister, very young in the photo, and a man in a military uniform on a farmhouse porch. The woman wore a brooch around her neck. The same one that Mara wore now with her opera dress.

Jesse's watch beeped the top of the hour, and he tore himself away to grab a sport jacket and tie. As he buttoned his shirt, the thought struck him that the young soldier in the photograph seemed familiar to him somehow. Jesse splashed on some Drakkar and headed back to the album.

A long, slow whistle from the kitchen halted him in his tracks.

"You clean up nice, Jesse," Mara said. She offered him a glass of Santa Margherita Pinot Grigio. Utica joined them and together they toasted, to whatever magic their night would bring.

***

An hour later, Jesse and Mara sat side-by-side inside Rome's renowned Teatro dell'Opera with many of their friends from RU, Trinity, and Libby College for an interschool performance of *Tosca*. Jesse held Mara's hand through the entire first act, enjoying her closeness.

Yet, his mind was preoccupied with the decades-old photo from Mara's album, the one of the soldier, the brooch-laden woman, and Mara's school-age sister all settled on a farmhouse porch. There was some vital piece of information, some sort of connection, that Jesse knew was just out of his reach.

Halfway through Kate's second aria, the answer hit him like a ton of bricks. He realized whom the man was in the picture.

The young, dapper, former Army Ranger was Signore Jack Sugardale.

Chapter 35

During the intermission following the first act, Mara and Jesse left their balcony seats to meet with friends and acquaintances from the two other colleges in the main atrium. Jesse appeared anxious, and Mara felt as if Jesse had something important to share, but instead he excused himself to check his phone messages and headed outside.

Mara approached Kate's boyfriend, Mimi, and slipped her arm around his broad shoulder. "You must be so proud of Kate. She's amazing. I had no idea she could sing so beautifully."

Mimi hugged her, clearly reveling in Kate's achievement. He leaned in toward her. "Can you keep a secret?"

She nodded.

"Tonight's our sixth anniversary," Mimi said. "After the show, I'm proposing."

She hugged him again in congratulations.

Mimi continued, "We're dining at La Scala tonight, with friends and family, and I'd love for you and Jesse to come." She agreed, and Mimi gave her directions to the trattoria, and then left to circulate around the room and secretly invite others.

She smiled at the idea that Mimi had thought to invite her and Jesse as a couple. Was it that obvious? Had the two of them always exuded sexual tension, or were they clearly broadcasting their romantic entanglement at the opera this afternoon? Nothing she could do about it now. Something new had awakened in her, and if the whole world knew she was in love with Jesse Autunno, so be it.

Lana scooted in close to Mara and led her to the wine table. "Hey girl, how was Pompeii weekend? Did you get laid?" Lana poked a couple of cheese cubes on a stick and popped them in her mouth.

"No, Lana, I met my mom this weekend, to spread my dad's ashes. Remember, you and Kristen saw me off? Speaking of which, did Kristen meet up with Bergamo tonight?" Mara said.

Bells chimed in the atrium, signaling for the audience to return to their seats. Lana panicked and ran for the bathroom before reentry, leaving Mara standing alone by the wine bar.

At that moment, Signore Jack approached with Dean Arella. She found it awkward addressing the dean, in light of his son's arrest and the attendant student-professor relationship between Fritz and Professor Volker, but Jack broke the ice with a compliment. "You look positively lovely this evening, darlin'."

Arella solemnly nodded his agreement. Jack reached toward Mara, and boldly scooped up the brooch that hung around her neck. He dangled the sapphire between his fingers. "Such a beautiful piece, Mara."

"Thank you, Signore. It once belonged to my sister," she said.

"Such an odd-shaped stone; exquisite, really. I've never seen its equal," Jack said. Arella nodded his agreement. "I can't imagine you're here all by yourself, darlin'. Roommates? Friends? A date, perhaps?"

"I'm here...to support a good friend of Lana's who's performing, actually." Mara thought it prudent to withhold from Dean Arella the fact that she was on a date with a fellow TA. "Lana's freshening up. Kristen couldn't make it. She had plans to visit her boyfriend in Florence this weekend," Mara said.

The lights flickered, subtly ushering the crowd into the auditorium. The three turned to head back inside. The dean and Signore Jack headed left, and while Mara approached the ladies' room, Lana exited and the two headed right. As they cut through the crowd toward their brocade-draped balcony, she pondered Jack's zealous appreciation of her necklace.

Lana elbowed her and they glanced at Jesse, edging toward their balcony section from the opposing stairway.

"He's looking pretty swank. Can't believe you two haven't hooked up yet," Lana said.

Mara shook her head. "Not for lack of want." His blue eyes locked with hers, and she mumbled to Lana, "Believe me, I want."

Kiever snuck up behind them and grabbed Lana's hand. He smelled of tobacco smoke, but it was probably the first time Mara had ever seen him without a cigarette pursed between his lips. "Hey girls," he said. "Where's the third Musketeer?"

Mara smiled. "If you mean Kristen, I haven't seen her. Haven't been back to my apartment since before break. But, I hear she's in Florence with Bergamo until Monday."

"Oh, honey, poor Kristen got her monthly visit, so she skipped it," Lana said. "She's home sleeping it off."

Mara wrinkled her nose. "That's too bad." She stopped before entering her row. "You two interested in dinner tonight? Bunch of us are going for a sort of cast party at La Scala."

"Can't honey, sorry," Lana said and gestured to Kiever. "My hunky man here has a swim meet tonight. Stanky and I are ducking out in about an hour. But, thanks for the invite."

The three said their goodbyes just as the lights dimmed, and Mara skirted down the row to her seat beside Jesse.

He leaned in close to her ear and kissed her cheek, and shivers ran down her neck and back. "You look stunning in that dress," he said. "Out of thousands of concert-goers, how is that you're the most beautiful woman—"

The tall, bird-like woman behind him shushed him loudly, and the man in front of him shot him a death stare. Jesse apologized and turned back to watch the second act in silence.

Mara squeezed his hand and winked at him.

An hour later, Mara wiped tears from her eyes. Another of Kate's heart-wrenching arias really had gotten to her. When the lights went up for the second intermission at five o'clock, she found that Jesse had fallen asleep on her shoulder. She nudged him awake.

"Hi handsome," she said. "Want to skip the third act and get out of here?"

His eyes grew wide. "Beer run?"

"Tortellini run. I'm famished," she said.

"Time to go." He grasped her hand and together they ducked through the crowd like they were avoiding the plague. They walked outside into the twilight of the mild spring evening and headed down Via Ozieri.

"Ran into Mimi in the restroom, told me about the party later tonight. You up for it?" Jesse asked.

"Sounds like a good excuse to use your mom's hot party dress, don't ya think?"

"Babe, it's you that makes that dress hot." Jesse halted their progress in front of an automobile tunnel. He leaned close and brushed back her hair. He was going to kiss her, she knew it, just like he did in his pickup truck, and oh, she wanted it so badly.

Rome traffic buzzed past them. Vespas whizzed perilously close to their narrow sidewalk. Car exhaust threatened to asphyxiate them. He wasn't looking at her, instead he was darting his eyes up and down the tunnel that seemed to lead directly out of the city. Jesse wasn't stopping to kiss her. He was lost.

They walked about twenty feet. The light at both ends of the tunnel disappeared, and tiny, brick-size yellow lights did next to nothing to alight their path. Mara stopped them. "Are you sure we're going the right way?"

"Mimi told me to go this way," Jesse said.

"To La Scala?" she said. "I thought it was in Trastevere. We're nowhere near there." Mara wished the serial killer hadn't hacked her GPS. They really needed pedestrian mode right now.

"Sure we're close to it," Jesse said. "The Fountain of Trevi is that way, and the Spanish Steps are over that direction, so we must be…I think…well, Mimi told me to go this way."

"You have no idea where you are right now, do you?" Mara asked.

"Of course. I…Mimi…"

"How did they let you on the police force without a sense of direction?"

He blushed.

Mara kissed him. Then, she grabbed his hand and led him back out of the tunnel, where she flagged a taxi that took them to La Scala, twenty-five minutes away, on the other side of town.

***

The two had just finished sharing a dish of tortellini when RU students began filtering into the cellar dining area of the stone-walled trattoria. Candlelight lit the room, and the lustful faces of those who'd hooked up over spring break still glowed with passion.

The room filled quickly, and more and more tables were joined together to host a magnificent celebratory feast for Kate and Mimi, featuring all of their closest friends. More plates of pasta, meats, and desserts passed among the revelers. It was all more than Mara had ever seen at a banquet.

Fritz Arella and Professor Volker arrived together, garnering cheers from the crowd, all supportive of their open relationship at long last. Faculty and students from all three colleges filtered in, and only Signore Jack was noticeably missing.

Utica arrived and made his way to Jesse's side, and the two men shook hands. "Big package arrived by courier from Montepulciano today. I signed for it and threw it on your bed," Utica said.

Jesse thanked him, and Mara knew it must be the plaid suitcase that Jesse asked his dad to retrieve from her impounded Aston Martin.

"Do you think the two of us could talk privately a few minutes?" Utica said to Jesse, gesturing to a side room.

But, before they could slip away, the guests of honor arrived. Kate and Mimi were resplendent in their newly engaged bliss, and members of their families, as well as their professors and closest friends, offered up a string of toasts.

Soon, the music grew louder, the lights dimmed, and the champagne flowed. Tables cleared to surround a makeshift dance floor, and everyone joined in. By ten o'clock, the music slowed and so did the dancing. Stragglers headed for the bar, and only couples dotted the floor.

Utica tried to cut in between Jesse and Mara, jokingly tugging Jesse away from her. But, Jesse shoved him aside and grabbed Mara close to him. Utica saluted him and headed to the men's room.

"He's really chomping at the bit to talk to you. Sure you don't want to see what he wants?" Mara whispered into his ear.

"It'll keep," Jesse said, nuzzling her neck.

She smiled, but the thought still tugged at her conscience that something about Utica was amiss.

Jesse stroked her hair. He still wore his sport coat, and she rested her cheek against the rough fibers of the wool blazer. She inhaled his Drakkar aftershave through his open collar, and this thrust Utica's pressing concerns into the furthest recess of her mind.

She ran her fingers along the back of Jesse's head. His hair was wet with perspiration. The stubble on his chin had returned. She'd never wanted him more. He pulled back to look at her, and that's when the music's tempo changed again.

This time, Argentine tango filled the air. The floor cleared, leaving only Jesse and Mara, standing in the middle of the dance floor.

"Well, gorgeous, shall we dance?" Jesse said, offering her his hand. She grasped it, and he pulled her to him, in the traditional chest-to-chest, cheek-to-cheek embrace characteristic of the dance. They hooked ankles, broke, hooked them again, and then walked the floor, in a world of their own making. They cut, broke, crossed, and figure-eighted. Tangoing as if they'd practiced together for years, they invoked a fusion of lust and yearning that could only be expressed with an ideal partner.

They reached the end, and he dipped her. As she lay back looking up into his face, she knew that she wanted nothing more than to continue their dance.

"We can walk to my apartment in eight minutes," he said.

"Six if I ditch my spikes," she said.

He ran his eyes over the front of her dress, from her low-cut bodice to the high-cut hem, and then down to her four-inch heels. "Keep them on; they're so worth it." He flashed a mischievous grin, and she wanted to lick it off him.

She yanked him up the cellar stairs of La Scala, past Utica who called to them from the now crowded dance floor, and out into the clear, starry evening.

The air chilled her instantly. She kissed him, rubbed against him, teased him, enticed him. She felt him respond, and he kissed her mouth hard.

He grabbed her hand and cut through a side alley, behind some late-night bars. She suddenly felt uneasy, as if someone was following them. She checked in every direction but saw no one.

Jesse pushed her against a doorway and kissed her again, this time thrusting his tongue inside her mouth. She grabbed hold of his firm ass and squeezed it tightly, kneading it, caressing it.

Until the door beside them burst open, and four burly patrons stumbled out of the bar.

The muscle-bound men wore wife-beater t-shirts, spandex bike shorts, and shaved heads. Their rippling musculature must have been steroid-induced, as one of them sounded like Mike Tyson. "Hey, bitch, c'mon and let me have some of that," he said to her in high-pitched, German-accented English.

Tyson pawed her, and she swung to punch him in the face, but Jesse thrust her behind him and stared down the thug. "Walk away, or I'll destroy you," Jesse said.

The four burst out laughing in soprano-range giggles. Two of them pulled out knives. Mara ditched her stilettos.

Jesse lunged at one of them and punched the knife from the other's hands. He knocked the first man to the ground. Another tried to jump Jesse, but Jesse flipped him over his head, and smacked him to the cobblestone.

Mara kicked the first one's knife into a sewer grate, but another brute ran straight for her. She managed to karate kick him in the mouth. He spat a couple teeth into a banana crate, and then he flicked his knife at her. She dropped to the ground to avoid it, and found it wedged in the tree trunk next to her head.

Jesse caught her gaze, saw that she was okay, and then he went wild. He round-housed and jabbed them, until finally all four went down. Then, he pummeled them some more.

From out of the same bar door, three more men exited. Also with shaved heads, spandex, and wife beaters. Escapees of a neo-Nazi health club? She would have laughed, but noticed that these three skinheads sported guns.

"Get down," Jesse shouted. He lunged on top of Mara, pinning his body over hers. He grabbed the knife from the tree trunk and flung it, lodging it in one of the shooter's calves. The man squealed and went down like a ton of bricks. He dropped his gun and whimpered in pain.

Still atop her, Jesse snatched the pistol and began shooting at the other two.

She loved Jesse for fighting back, but the skinheads had gained the upper-hand and she knew that it was just a matter of time before she and Jesse were killed.

Sure enough, Jesse's pistol clicked twice, empty.

One of the thugs, whistling the German national anthem, sauntered over to them. He smacked Jesse on the back of the head with the butt of his gun, and spoke to them in his high-pitched accent. "In a few minutes, a nice round goose-egg is going form on your head. That's where I plan to plant my first bullet. The second one belongs to your bitch."

A shudder ran though her, and Jesse's hold on her tightened. He gazed into her face and smiled. "Think you could grab my ass?"

What the hell?

"Trust me," he said.

She slid her hands up his legs, curved them up and around his buttocks beneath his jacket, and then ran her fingers under his shirt along his back. Just above his waistband, she felt the bulge of another pistol and a magazine of extra bullets beside it.

Pretending to fuss about in panic, she discreetly maneuvered the magazine into his grasp, and gripped the pistol in her own. Jesse told her, "When I say so, you just roll, and keep rolling, got it?"

She nodded.

He inserted the fresh magazine into his gun and winked at her. "Go!" Jesse said. He dodged in one direction, and she the other, and she just kept rolling.

The thug shot and missed, and Jesse returned fire from a crouched knee behind the tree. Jesse shot the gun out of one their hands, but the same skinhead brandished a backup knife and took cover behind his friend, who continued to fire at Jesse, until they both closed in and cornered him.

Jesse fired back, until his ammo again ran dry. Jesse was a sitting duck.

Mara shouted to him. At any moment, they would shoot him dead.

She remembered her own pistol, and she fired at them, but missed, until she too ran out of bullets.

They closed in on Jesse. She was going to lose him. The man she loved was going to die. Right in front of her.

Suddenly, someone fired shots from out of the darkened alley.

Jesse turned and faced the new shooter, and out of habit, he trained his now empty gun at the gunman's head.

"FBI!" a familiar male voice shouted into the melee. "Lower your weapons!"

The man stepped into the glare of the floodlight. He had his back to Mara, but Jesse could see him clearly from his vantage. Even as she watched a mix of recognition and disbelief etch the contours of Jesse's face, Jesse's gun remained fixed on him.

The agent wielded what she recognized from cop shows as a Browning 9mm High Power pistol, and he aimed it at the skinhead, whose body shook and whose eyes darted between both men, but who now stood poised to shoot Jesse point blank in the head.

Seconds ticked by, and no one moved.

"Lower your weapon, Tuna. I don't want to shoot my best friend too," the FBI agent said, and it was then that Mara recognized the voice.

It was Utica.

He pointed to the FBI badge that he sported on his upper sleeve. Jesse lowered his gun, but did not release it.

Utica turned to the neo-Nazis. "I'm gonna give the rest of you until the count of three." But on "one" Utica turned and shot the man that held the gun on Jesse in the hand. Blood spewed and the gun went flying.

Jesse hitched up his pant leg and pulled out a backup pistol.

One of the men sprinted down the alley. And the other, still with the knife in his calf, raked a gun from the ground, rolled onto his back, and aimed at Utica.

Jesse shot the man in the leg, and Utica shot the gun from his hand.

And the melee ended, with a win for the good guys.

Mara stood. Speechless, she wrapped her arms around Jesse's neck and buried her head in his shoulder.

None of them spoke. The only sounds in the night were the grunts of the injured thugs still writhing on the ground and the encroaching wail of police cars.

Nestled in Jesse's embrace, Mara reached her hand toward Utica and squeezed his arm in gratitude.

A siren blared closer, and a patrol car screeched to a halt. Mara stepped back, and Utica and Jesse both held up badges to the two patrolmen.

"Hey, Jesse, what's this mess?" one of them said, gesturing to the downed knife-fighters that still lay beaten to a pulp.

"We just broke up a bar brawl is all. You guys okay to clean this up while I get the young lady back home safely?" Jesse said.

"Sure, boss, whatever you say," one of them said.

Utica flashed Jesse a grin, and Jesse patted his back.

Jesse took Mara's hand, and the three turned their backs on the scene and headed for Jesse and Utica's apartment, in anticipation of sharing old scotch and addressing Utica's surprising persona.

***

Just after midnight, Utica poured the three of them some single-malt in mismatched glasses. "I've got to get back to headquarters. Need to file a report on the incident before it bites me in the ass. But I'm all wired up, and I know you both have questions, so shoot," Utica said.

Mara sipped her drink, but it failed to warm her. She shivered violently, her teeth chattered. Jesse went into his room and grabbed the blankets from the bed. She glimpsed a package on his bed that resembled the size and shape of her plaid suitcase.

Jesse wrapped thick woolen blankets over her and rubbed her arms. "You're probably in shock over the shooting, babe. We should get you to the hospital."

She waved her ice cold hand at him. "Please, I've been through worse." In the past few weeks, she'd been rammed by a garbage truck on a Tuscan hillside, thrown from an Alpine cliff into a ravine and left for dead, and then shot at and nearly run over by the secret police. She could handle a few neo-Nazis on steroids with guns. "Think I just need to warm up a little is all. And get a few answers."

She turned to Utica. "All this time, you're FBI? What the hell?"

"Why didn't you tell me?" Jesse said to him.

"Sorry, buddy, need to know basis. But, you of all people should understand that, Inspector," Utica said.

Jesse smirked, and blushed.

"When did you learn that Jesse was undercover?" Mara said.

"Jesse is one of the brightest people I know, and he's a damn good undercover cop. Initially, I suspected, but when I confirmed it with the Bureau, I didn't want to blow his cover or fuck up our friendship, so I let it go. I figured when the shit hit the fan, the truth would ultimately unfold."

Jesse nodded in understanding. "I'm grateful."

Utica continued, "You may recall that I was arrested the other night as a suspected serial killer. That's when I came clean, and so did Enzo. The upper-ups at the Rome PD met with my bosses today to hash out how they want to handle mutual cooperation from here on."

"That's why Enzo's been incommunicado all day," Jesse said. He sipped his scotch, and finally removed his jacket. "You've been here six years. How did you end up on the Sculptor case if no Americans have been involved?"

"I was posted to cover Kiever when he started RU," Utica said, "to ascertain whether he and his father, the Senator, were tied up in an international embezzlement ring. I'm due to wrap this case at the end of the semester, because Kiever's clean. Wish I could say that about his dad, but the senior Kiever wasn't my assignment."

Mara sipped her drink. It finally warmed her, everywhere. "What about the Norwegian victim, the motorcycle rider?"

Utica nodded. "She was a great girl; it's a tragedy she died. I'd spent an evening with her, just shooting the bull over beers after a motorcycle ride out to Tivoli Gardens." He ran his hands through his hair and shook his head. "You know Kiever's girl, Pen? The Norwegian was her roommate and best friend, and it was necessary to investigate her for any intel on Kiever junior and senior, but it turned up nothing." Utica sipped his scotch.

"The Sculptor killed her the next day. Wish there was some way I could have known, some way to stop it. She was a good kid. It's too bad."

While the three sat silently for a minute considering the loss of another victim, Mara looked around their apartment and considered it in a new light. She was once suspicious of its occupants, and now it housed two officers of the law.

She tipped back the scotch, liking the burn it left on her throat. She spied a box in the corner of the kitchen, overflowing with winter hats and gloves. She spotted at least four pairs of blue and black zebra-striped gloves, and she chuckled. Apparently, zebra-striped gloves were all the rage with RU students and professors this season.

Mara hiccupped, then yawned and stretched. She was soused, in a giddy, horny sort of way, and she eyed Jesse like a piece of meat.

Utica lowered his glass and smiled sheepishly. He grabbed his wallet and jacket. "Kiever had a swim meet tonight; probably knockin' boots by now at Lana's. Arella and Volker left the opera house for the train station to get away for the weekend. As for me, I'm off like a prom dress till late tomorrow. You two...have some fun."

On his way out, he flipped the switch on the stereo, and Barry White began to croon.

***

Seconds after the door slammed shut, Mara found herself slow-dancing with Jesse again, this time on the living room floor. Jesse rubbed his hands up and down the sides of her dress. He lowered his head to nuzzle her neck. He ran his tongue in the valley between her breasts, and then raised his head and looked into her eyes, her sapphire necklace between his teeth. He winked at her.

She closed her eyes as they swayed to the music, her heart pounding in her chest, knowing she was teetering on the brink of no return. She lingered for a moment in dizzy rapture, drunk with desire, and felt empowered by her belief that she could indeed have it all.

She glanced toward his bedroom, at the mattress on the floor, surrounded by the plaster statues that once frightened her, and that now thrilled her in their exotic nude poses. She moved toward the room, anxious to finally shed every one of her inhibitions.

They stepped onto his mattress. Jesse unzipped the back of her dress with one hand, and cupped her ass with the other. This man, whom she'd once considered a dangerous serial killer, was actually more dangerous than she'd thought. He was the only one ever able to overcome her best defenses against a broken heart. She was grateful for his victory, and she rewarded him.

"I love you," she whispered.

He grasped her face in his hands, letting her dress tumble to the mattress, and kissed her lips. His tender smile belied his lusty gaze.

"I love you," he answered. "I love you so much."

At his words, her breathing grew fast and heavy and she tugged at his belt. He pulled off his shirt, revealing his broad chest. She reached down and bit his nipple, hard. He moaned and tugged her down to her knees. He knelt beside her, kissing her again, and fumbled with the clasp of her black lace bra.

His phone signaled a text message.

"Ignore it," she panted.

The phone chimed the tone that Jesse saved for Enzo's calls. Mara sighed.

"Damn it," Jesse said in frustration. He reached for the phone in his discarded pants and read the text. "It's something big. Enzo wants me to meet him at Stella Luna."

Mara resigned herself to the interruption and smiled sadly. She kissed him. "No problem. I promise you, this'll keep," she said. When he reluctantly handed her back her dress, she said, "Can I tamper with evidence and pull a pair of jeans out of my suitcase?" She gestured to her wrapped suitcase.

"Have at it; your prints were on everything anyway. Take what you need, and leave the rest for forensics."

While she threw on a sweater, the phone in her purse buzzed with a text as well. "It's Enzo. Looks like I'm invited to this party, too. Maybe new evidence on my sister's murder? Or a possible arrest?"

Before Jesse had had a chance to respond, she heard Utica burst through the entrance of the apartment and bang on Jesse's bedroom door. "Enzo wants to meet us at Stella Luna," he shouted to them.

Jesse opened the door, and he and Utica met face-to-face.

Utica said, "There's been another murder. At Stella Luna apartments."

***

Mara, Jesse, and Utica sped across Roma Centro crammed into the backseat of a taxi, spouting theories about who the next victim might be, and who they now considered prime suspects.

"Up until now, I thought you might have been the Sculptor," Mara said to Utica. "It's still tough to accept you're one of the good guys." She patted his knee when he pretended to be crestfallen. His six-foot-two body slammed into hers as the driver rounded a tight curve around Castel Sant'Angelo.

"You're an excellent agent, Utica. You had us both fooled," Jesse said. "The way you appeared so tight with Kiever, traveling and partying—"

"You traveled some of the same roads with us, Inspector," Utica said. "Believe me, it was tough to keep up with that guy and not become a drug addict-pimp. Wondered if he was the Sculptor for a while, but the guy never stops partying long enough to off anybody. The guy lives in a daze." The car slammed on its brakes to avoid a homeless woman pushing a cart across Via Veneto. Their taxi swerved around her and bolted forward again.

"Who do you think is the killer?" Mara asked Utica. Her stomach churned violently, from the ride and from the anxiety of not knowing who'd been murdered. With no other details to go on, none of them knew which student, or more to the point, which one of their friends had just been murdered. Her stomach rolled with apprehension. She stuffed her hands in her pockets to stop their shaking.

"From a professional standpoint, the net is wide," Utica said. "Could be any number of profs or students, from any of the three schools, really. But, I've had my suspicions about Volker and Arella."

"They've both been cleared as each other's alibis...unless, you think they're in cahoots?" Mara said. The possibility that the two men had acted in tandem would explain a lot in terms of logistics and even their own behavior.

"Those two are still a possibility," Jesse said. "What about Signore Jack?"

The taxi sped just outside Rome's walls and down a hill past the Coop Lazio supermarket, only a half mile from Stella Luna.

"Signore Jack? He's a good ole' boy; not much to him, other than the fact that he'll screw any student that bats her eyes at him," Utica said.

Mara cringed. Her sister had been one of those students. Was Jack the type to murder any of these students once he was finished with them?

"Speaking of Jack," Jesse said, "I was looking at your family album before the performance, and I noticed a photo of a young Signore Jack tucked inside it." He described the substance of the picture.

"It's my mother's album. She put it together for me at the memorial. I've never been through the whole thing, and must have missed that one," she said in confusion. "I'd never met the man before this semester. Lana told me that my sister dated him when she attended RU, but I was hoping that maybe they'd just been long-time friends."

"The picture of Jack showed him as a young Army Ranger, and your sister was a kid. But, the woman with them didn't look like your mom, at least from the tennis footage I've seen. Do you know who the woman might be?"

Mara sighed. "It's possible the woman is my father's mistress, and my sister's birth mom. I just learned about that whole fiasco, right after we memorialized my father. Still, that doesn't explain how Signore Jack and the woman know each other."

Mara thought a minute, then crinkled her nose. "The picture you describe also suggests that my sister knew her professor, as a child, before she dated him later at school. That's creepy. I'll be sure to ask him all about it." Her family had a very complex past, she realized. Their individual lives had spun around her just like a cocoon wraps around a caterpillar, buffering her from the painful unknown outside of it. Looked like as good a time as any for her to finally break free of the past.

She stared out the window as the taxi headed up into a more thickly settled suburban area, around the corner from her apartment building. The butterflies in her stomach had shape-shifted into torpedoes ravaging her insides.

What if the Sculptor had murdered Oslo, the sweet reception attendant who'd paired her with Jesse at the beginning of her stay? Or, what if the killer, staying true to his MO, had set his sights on gorgeous Lana, or Kristen, or any one of her friends?

The thought that she easily could have been his most recent victim was barely flitting through her mind, when their taxi nearly careened head-on with a rescue vehicle turning the corner. The ambulance flew by, lights flashing and siren raging, until it headed past them in the opposite direction.

"I know from speaking with Enzo, after his meetings with my bosses, that the Rome police have very few leads, and the FBI isn't much more of a help," Utica said. "Earlier today, Enzo informed me, on the down low, that your sister might have been another serial victim, years ago, when the tragedy had been deemed an accident. I'd been assigned to Kiever's dad's embezzlement case the same year your sister died, and the Swiss and Italian police both confirmed it an accidental death, so no other agents were assigned to pursue an investigation."

She shook her head in disgust over the incompetence.

"But, after Enzo told me what transpired the night the three of us were shot at," Utica said, "I now believe her death is tied to the rest of the Sculptor murders. That's probably why I'm involved in Enzo's meeting tonight."

The taxi arrived a block down from where Mara's apartment was located. They were barred from progressing further by flashing police cars, police tape, and curious onlookers.

Jesse grabbed Mara's hand, and together with Utica, the three produced enough ID to break through the barrier and locate Enzo in the atrium. Entering the building, Mara felt a shiver of apprehension.

When Enzo spotted them, his face fell, and Mara felt certain that whatever news he had for them would be a game changer in the Sculptor case.

Corralling the three of them away from the chaos, to the area beneath the atrium steps, Enzo grasped Mara's hand in his.

"Mara, dear one, I'm sorry. It's your roommate. Kristen's been murdered."

Chapter 36

Inside the atrium of Stella Luna, Jesse held Mara in his arms while she cried. Her roommate, and her friend, had been killed in their shared apartment.

She should have been there for Kristen. Somehow, they might have taken down the bastard who killed her together. She felt guilty that she and Jesse had been entwined in passion, while Kristen had been fearfully clinging to her final moments of life.

"There's nothing you could have done," Jesse said, stroking her back. Grateful for his sympathy, she knew he felt relieved that she had not been the one slain, and this compounded her guilt. And, her anger.

She clenched her fists and swiped at her tears. "Another notch on his belt isn't she?" she asked Jesse. Then she turned to Enzo. "She's just another one of the Sculptor's growing list of victims, isn't that right, Inspector?"

Enzo nodded. "We're in the preliminary stages of the crime scene, but it appears to be another serial murder, dear, I'm so sorry." Enzo turned to Utica. "I just phoned your boss, the one I met with earlier today. As Kristen was an American, *la Questura* will fully cooperate with the FBI. Based on your extensive background at RU, you've been assigned to the investigation."

Utica nodded. "I just received confirmation, sir. I look forward to working together. And I hope our pooled resources can stop this sonofabitch." He shook Enzo's hand, and then Jesse's. "Shall we go in then?" Utica and Enzo donned plastic shoe covers and gloves in preparation for entering the apartment.

"Are you going to be alright out here?" Jesse asked her.

Mara shook her head. "No, I'm going with you."

***

She'd braced herself for the worst. But this was beyond what she had expected or prepped herself for.

What had once been an adorable apartment, a place of comfort and refuge, had become a house of horrors.

In the bedroom, the cozy space behind the full-length shutters where they'd slept, blood was splashed and smeared everywhere. On the beds, the nightstands, the walls, the floor, and the ceiling.

Kristen's rumpled bed lay empty.

Mara flicked her eyes to her own mattress. On it was a mangled, butchered corpse, now entirely unrecognizable. Mara's stomach lurched.

Her knees wobbled, and Jesse steadied her. He opened his mouth to persuade her to leave she was sure, but she quieted his objections with her steely gaze. She looked back to Kristen's remains, she owed her that much.

The killer had stripped the torso bare, but nothing about the cadaver revealed its gender. Kristen's breasts had been slashed off, and her vaginal space carved open. Nothing was left of what once had been Kristen's gentle face. Her features had been rearranged by something serrated.

Mara's head swam, and she felt certain she'd lose the contents of her stomach. She looked to Kristen's nightstand to regain some composure. Used tissues dotted the surface. An empty pitcher lay on the floor beside her bed. On Mara's nightstand was a box of tissues, a glass of water, a container of Vicks, and a cup of tea, half full. Kristen must have come down with a cold.

Mara's dolphin paperweight also lay toppled on its side near the edge of the table, beside the body. Mara's eyes skimmed over Kristen's polished fingers that stretched toward the dolphin, past the butterfly tattoo on her wrist, along her bare forearm, and up to the elbow, where her arm had been lopped off.

Mara put her hand to her mouth and stifled an anguished moan.

The crook of Kristen's other arm cradled the top of her head. A glint of metal shone from her clenched fist. A pair of bloody cuticle scissors.

Mara ran for the bathroom.

***

Mara's body convulsed as she hugged the toilet. What was she doing here? She didn't belong at a crime scene. She was just some detective-wannabe searching for clues. She was making a vain attempt to hunt down a man who might have killed her sister. Post-mortem reports were one thing. Bloody cadavers were another. She retched again into the toilet. Her stomach had nothing left.

She propped her head against the cold tiles of the bathroom wall. Something dripped water into the tub from above her— Kristen's fishnet stockings. They had been recently washed in anticipation of a weekend getaway with her boyfriend Bergamo. Once so full of life, Kristen would never experience love or joy again.

Mara finally stood and splashed cold water on her cheeks. She washed her mouth and then moved on to scrubbing her hands and cleaning brusquely under her nails. She decided she would keep scrubbing, until the filth washed away.

She leaned against the vanity and looked up into the mirror, wishing she could see her sister, Abby, staring back at her, encouraging her to buck up and get back out there.

She looked back over at Kristen's stockings on the shower rod and remembered their first weekend shopping spree on the night of the Stella Luna orientation party and their fits of laughter when Kristen had first tried them on.

Kristen's horrific mutilation and death would not go unanswered. Nor would her sister's. Mara would do whatever it took find the Sculptor, to avenge the two women, as well as the others who she had not known, that had been so young and vital.

She exited the bathroom, and the smell of decay in the apartment reeked like a meat market dumpster. A cold breeze wafted through the open living room window, but it did nothing to abate the stench. She clenched her teeth and focused on Jesse, standing with Utica and Enzo at the dining table. They spoke to a plastic-wrapped technician, evidently a fellow member of the crime scene unit.

"Mara, this is Federico, head of Rome's CSU," Jesse explained.

He nodded to Mara, without stopping his dissertation. "This CS is an atypical representation of the Sculptor's MO. He typically takes great pains to bleach his victims and surrounding area. Here, there's a plethora of fingerprints, semen, and saliva.

"Also, in his past seven crimes, the Sculptor has never defaced any of his other victims. He's never raped them, or injured them, while they were alive, but here the victim has been sodomized and the body clearly mutilated," Federico said.

"So, this isn't the work of our serial killer, but rather someone else?" Enzo asked.

"Not necessarily." Federico gestured to the bedroom. "The gypsum flakes on the floor and on the bed, along with the curing plaster we found stuffed into the victim's throat, suffocating her around the time he sodomized her, is indicative of the plaster we found on the most recent victim, the Norwegian."

Jesse spoke up. "It's possible the Sculptor's MO has changed because he's reached some sort of mental breaking point. Becoming more frantic, making mistakes, leaving behind evidence, and corrupting his victims as an act of desperation."

"On the brink of revealing himself, perhaps," Utica murmured.

"Exactly," Jesse said.

"Is there any evidence to indicate a single or multiple perps?" Enzo said.

Federico nodded. "Two men, no more, working in tandem, with varying styles, is a possibility..." he mused aloud. "It's possible the other victim we found in the living room—"

"Other victim, wait, what?" Mara said. "I must have missed something while I was in the restroom. What other victim?"

Jesse pointed to the floor behind the table. A brown bloodstain soiled the carpet in front of the television cabinet where the fish tank hummed and gurgled, and where her father's box of ashes had once resided.

"Where is she?" Mara asked. "Where is the other woman's body?"

Jesse shook his head. "The other victim," he said, "is a man."

Chapter 37

"The second victim is a white male, six feet tall, fit build, no ID, age anywhere between twenty-five and forty-five, stabbed in the face and abdomen with a sculpting rapier, left embedded in the victim's thigh," the CSU chief said. "He was rushed by ambulance to Saint Sebastiano's. Doesn't look good."

She remembered the ambulance that their cab had nearly sideswiped minutes before arriving at Stella Luna. Inside of it was someone who'd seen what had happened to Kristen. Who was this unlucky witness?

Was it another perp overpowered by the first and left for dead?

Maybe it was Kristen's Florentine boy-toy, Frankie Bergamo? Had Bergamo always been The Sculptor's accomplice?

Arella or Volker?

Signore Jack?

Kiever?

Kiever! In the apartment one floor directly above them. With Lana.

Chapter 38

"What's all the hubbub, bub?" Lana draped her scantily clad body against the doorframe.

"Lana, where's Kiever?" Utica asked in an abrupt, professional tone that Mara had never heard him use before.

Mara nudged in behind him. Michael Bublé crooned in the background. The odor of burning garlic broke the haze of cheap Sambuca that swirled around Lana's mussed blond hair.

"Lana, is Kiever in there with you?" Utica said. "We need to speak with him right now."

"Been waitin' for him to get back from swimming, 'gainst Trinity," Lana slurred. "Cookin' him dinner, then gonna tie him up with some pretty scarves, and I'm gonna suck—"

"Lana, honey, can we come in?" Mara said.

Lana opened the door wide. "C'mon in, kids. Anyone wanna drinkie?"

Utica, Jesse, and Enzo entered the room and dispersed. Thirty seconds later, Jesse signaled to Mara that the place was secure, and she steered Lana into the kitchen and draped a blanket around her shoulders.

Mara poured a triple espresso and coaxed Lana to guzzle it down.

"Why are those guys sniffing in my panty drawer, Mars?" Lana said. "And, damn, why does my head feel like it's gonna explode. I want my buzz back." Lana pouted and reached for the Sambuca.

Mara set down the bottle and sat beside her. "I have some bad news, honey, about Kristen."

***

Shortly after Mara conveyed the news of Kristen's murder, she'd rendered Lana into the capable hands of a female police officer who'd originally responded to the call an hour earlier. Then, she, Jesse, and Enzo headed for San Sebastiano Hospital.

While Utica stayed at Lana's to interrogate Kiever upon his return, Jesse sped Mara and Enzo to the hospital in Enzo's Audi, zipping through traffic at top speed.

Like a pro running back, Mara ran options past the two men. "What about Kristen's boyfriend? He's been coming for conjugal visits every couple of weeks. Maybe this time he flipped and killed her?"

"Francesco Bergamo, the Florence grad student?" Enzo said from the backseat.

Mara nodded.

"*Il Questura* tracked him down while you were speaking to Lana. HQ said that after Bergamo and your friend visited Pompeii, they'd planned to spend Easter with his family in Florence. Once there, your friend changed her plans and returned to Rome. His parents can prove that Bergamo was in Florence the entire time," Enzo said.

"You two discussed with the CSU tech the concept that this crime scene didn't sync with the Sculptor's usual style. But, aren't there varying methods of attack?" Mara said.

Jesse nodded. "There are distinguishing factors in each case, like whether the Sculptor used a bread knife to slash or antifreeze to poison, but the perp's overall style in victim selection, courtship, method of disposal, and what not, seem to follow a pattern. But, in this case, his entire methodology was off."

"Multiple attackers, maybe?" Mara said.

"Maybe," Jesse nodded. "But, I feel like there's something more to it. In some cases, the perp is more meticulous than in others. But, tonight—" Jesse raised his eyebrows.

"Tonight, the scene was gruesome, messy. I can't attest to the others, but what I saw was far from meticulous," Mara said. "It was…" Kristen's bloody, sodomized, plastered body flashed through her mind. Mara's throat constricted, and she clutched her churning stomach. She shook off tears that threatened to spill over.

Jesse squeezed her hand, and she nodded to let him know she was okay.

"Spatter, irreverence to the corpse, general disorder at the scene...that's not typical," Jesse said.

Enzo leaned forward from the backseat. "Tonight, perhaps we have someone new committing a crime for another purpose, mimicking the prior acts to cover his tracks."

"Plausible." Jesse thought a minute, and then shook his head. "I also wonder if our guy has just unraveled, and, for whatever reason, tonight he lost it. On the other hand, I keep coming back to what you said, Mara, about a...dastardly duo, of sorts."

"What's the story on the two guys who live next door?" Mara asked. "I think they were the only ones without travel plans residing in Stella Luna this weekend, besides Lana, who's been with Kiever. Everyone else was still on break. Have the police checked out their story? Maybe they're your duo?"

"Both men had spent the evening out, at a laundry bar. The owner vouched for them," Jesse said.

"Upon their return, they heard men scuffling, and then a woman, not Kristen, scream for help on the other side of your bedroom wall," Enzo said. "One of the roommates had phoned in the emergency, and the other broke down the door to help.

"By then, they'd found Kristen, likely dead for hours, and a man dying in the living room. This man probably encountered the killer. The two fought, and the perp fled through the open living room window. Both roommates performed CPR on the dying man in the living room until the police arrived."

Mara visualized again what her two neighbors had encountered. The visceral scene had scarred her memory forever. Aside from the marked number of disparities between this and the other crime scenes noted by Federico, Mara knew in her bones that this too was somehow the Sculptor's work. Jesse squeezed Mara's hand.

Jesse glanced in the rearview mirror at his uncle. "You said the roommates had heard a commotion, but CSU determined that the victim had been deceased for a while upon discovery. According to the report, two men fought, and a woman screamed. Who was this other woman?"

Mara caught Jesse's glance. She felt as baffled as he looked. Who was this woman that had encountered the melee between Kristen's murderer and the other man? This woman and the dying man were critical to the investigation, but were they residents? Staff? RU faculty?

Enzo shook his head, jotted a few notes. He dialed his phone and briefly relayed Jesse's question and other pertinent details to Captain Sciug. Enzo then radioed police units to suspects' residences.

First, Rome police were ordered to detain Kiever after his swim meet, and Utica maintained his post at their apartment.

Second, a team headed to the dean's house, to notify him of the RU student's death, and to question Fritz Arella, who still lived in his dad's basement.

Then, two more cops headed to Jesse's apartment to question Volker.

Finally, Enzo dispatched another squad car to Signore Jack's off-campus apartment on Via Marche to ascertain his whereabouts that evening.

Meanwhile, Jesse dialed his cell and spent a couple minutes convincing the San Sebastiano ICU nurse to allow them in to question her dying patient. Mara felt convinced that the man in the hospital bed held all the answers.

Jesse drove Enzo's car into the hospital's fire lane, and left it. The three jumped out of the car and dashed inside the sliding doors of the ICU wing.

Just outside the witness's room, one thing still nagged at her conscience. Why had Kristen's body been found in Mara's bed?

The cup of tea and other cold remedies on Mara's bedside table were clear evidence that she'd intended to convalesce in Mara's bed, not her own. Mara recalled the empty pitcher on the floor beside Kristen's bed. An accidental spill of an entire pitcher of cold water on her own bed would have sent Kristen to seek comfort in Mara's dry bed.

That would mean that the perpetrator had discovered Kristen sleeping in Mara's bed, and then murdered her there.

Had the murderer expected Mara to be sleeping in her own bed? Was she the killer's intended victim?

***

Mara, Jesse, and Enzo entered the room of the man whom the killer had left behind. With only two minutes provided them by the night nurse who was unimpressed by the show of badges and

Jesse's earlier call, the three of them moved in and hovered over their only witness.

Heavily sedated, the man's swollen and bruised eyes remained shut. A stitched gash ran along the border of his forehead and scalp. His nose was set and taped, and tubes ran into his nostrils. Gauze protected what was left of the bottom lip that had been mostly torn off.

Jesse silently directed Enzo and Mara's gaze to the patient's left arm. His bicep, tattooed with an Army Ranger insignia, rested in a cast upon his bandaged torso. "Army Ranger," Jesse said. "Wonder if he knows Signore Jack?"

It was an odd coincidence that the two men had served in the same branch of service. But, Mara also experienced an odd sense of familiarity with this patient.

The set of his jaw. His unusual strawberry blonde hair color. His pointy ears.

She looked at John Doe's chart. His approximate age, his build, and his features all matched. Through the gauze and tape, and the black and blue, the man vaguely resembled someone she knew.

G.I. Spock…her mother's chauffeur.

Suddenly, the man's eyes fluttered open. He gazed blankly at the faces before him, until he fixed his stare on Mara. Breath passed his open mouth, as if to form words. Just a wheeze.

He closed his eyes. Opened them again, fixated on her. He tried to form words, but he winced in obvious anguish over his missing lip. A tear ran down his face.

The man had something to divulge to her, and she needed to hear what her mother's driver had to say about the murder of her roommate.

Mara removed a pen and notepad from her purse and nestled it between the witness's fingers. He scribbled a few moments, and then stopped.

Mara read the note:

Killer a soldier.
Knew UR mom.
Called her little lady.
Took UR mom.

She gasped, and handed it to Jesse.

Jesse's alarmed expression confirmed her worst fear.

The only man that Mara knew who had ever referred to her mom, and every other female, as "little lady," and who happened to be a former soldier, was Signore Jack.

Professor Jackson Sugardale was a cold-blooded serial killer.

Signore Jack is the Sculptor.

Now, the Sculptor had her mom.

PART III:

MOLDING & CASTING

**"The sculptor's hand can only break the spell
to free the figurines slumbering in the stone."**

—Michelangelo,
an Italian sculptor, painter, architect, and poet

Chapter 39

Mara Silvestri had never felt so helpless, or angry, in all her life. The Sculptor, who she now knew to be Jackson Sugardale, had her mother, and she didn't know where she was, or if she was still alive. All she did know was that she'd do anything to find her.

She and Jesse separated from Enzo in the fire lane of San Sebastiano Hospital. Enzo tore the parking ticket from the Audi's windshield, and sped toward Signore Jack's apartment, eight blocks away, on Via Marche. The officer that Enzo had assigned there earlier had reported back while they'd interviewed the chauffeur, saying that the professor was absent the premises. But, Enzo headed there now to meet up with a search warrant that might uncover any possible leads.

She and Jesse bolted on foot in the opposite direction, to the professor's faculty office at Rome University. There had to be some sort of evidence to lead them in the right direction.

They ran, side by side, past the ancient cherry trees that lined the long, winding boulevard along Borghese Gardens, from the hospital to the school. Mara was suddenly grateful she'd changed into her trainers. Through the fog of her panting breaths, she glanced at her watch; it was nearly two in the morning. Too pumped full of adrenaline to care about the late hour, she noticed the date instead—March 20. It had been her sister's birthday; she would have been thirty-one today. It was also the six-year anniversary of the day when Abby had been killed.

Did her mother grieve for the daughter of her husband's mistress? Mara knew that she must, and she longed to console her. It provided all the more reason to find her, before it was too late.

It took them eight minutes to arrive outside the wooden double entrance of the school. No lights shone from the windows. Members of the SWAT team that Enzo had dispatched from the hospital room stood sentry.

"No one's come or gone since we arrived fifteen minutes ago," one of the team members said. "We have six men scouring the inside. So far, every classroom and office is deserted. We've secured the perp's office; no sign of him there." The officer handed Jesse a fresh Browning 9mm, the same weapon that her father would pack on his photo expeditions into the bush or onto the mean streets of East L.A.

The members of the SWAT team entered and fanned out.

Jesse removed his second pistol from the inside of his jacket, the same one from the earlier gunfight with the skinheads, and inserted it into his ankle holster. He tucked the new Browning into the rear waistband of his khakis, smiled at her and chucked her chin. "Stick close to me."

She nodded.

"We'll find your mom," Jesse said. "I promise."

Together, they trudged to Sugardale's office, where she and Jesse had held office hours as the professor's teaching assistants for the past two months. She had always been leery but yet never able to prove that the brilliant, laid back, smooth talking ladies' man, Signore Jack, was actually the Sculptor. Now she knew for sure.

Jesse turned on the lights in the office. Neither spoke as they roamed the room, inspecting the desk, the shelves, the file cabinets, and the bookcases for any clue to the professor's whereabouts.

Jesse's cell phone buzzed. He picked up the call, sat down behind Jack's desk, and straightened the cardboard blotter while he listened. In his agitated state, he rearranged the pencils, straightened the blotter a little further to the left, rolled a pink eraser back and forth between his palms, and bumped the blotter's corner a little further to the right with his knuckles.

Mara turned away from Jesse's tense machinations; they only worsened her own desperation. She looked out the window, down into the vacant alleyway below. On a crate, two cats clawed a rat carcass, fought over its entrails like vultures.

Jesse hung up. "Enzo and a few men are inside Sugardale's apartment. Jack's AWOL, and they're tossing the place. Utica's back at headquarters, helping coordinate the FBI's end of it."

She looked back at him. "What if Jack decides to run? Hops a train anywhere, and then kills my mom? Or worse—"

"Police and Special Agents are posted at every train station, airport, and bus terminal in Rome," Jesse said. His hands continued prodding the objects on the desk even as he spoke. "We have an APB out for your mom's Alfa Romeo sedan. It would have been helpful if we could track your mom's or Jack's cell phones, but Enzo told me that neither of them are in service anymore. It's possible that, hey, what the hell is this?"

Mara turned back to face him. In one hand, Jesse held up the once askew blotter that had seemed to threaten his sanity a minute ago. In the other, he held a photo. She dashed behind the desk to get a better look.

"It's a duplicate of that picture I found in your mom's album," he said. She recalled Jesse mentioning the picture earlier, and Mara examined it now with fresh eyes.

The photograph showed a good-looking soldier in full uniform sitting with a young girl on the front porch of a stucco ranch overlooking a yard full of lawn ornaments. They sat beside a woman that looked just like the little girl, most likely the child's mother. The officer looked a lot like a younger Signore Jack, as Jesse had suggested earlier. The young girl most certainly resembled Abigail.

Why was her sister sitting on Army Ranger Jack Sugardale's lap? And why were they both in the company of a woman who could only be Abby's biological mother, and therefore her father's mistress?

"The little girl is my sister, I'm sure of it," Mara said. "And, that's definitely Sugardale."

Jesse nodded.

She pointed to the tall, dark woman in the blue satin dress and bright red lipstick. She gasped when she noticed that the woman wore the same sapphire brooch that Mara wore now. Mara clasped the piece in her hand.

"I'm certain that woman is my father's mistress, who's also Abby's birth mother. But why was there a copy in my family's album? I'm sure my father must have loved the photo of mother and child and kept it as a memento, but what's Jack's significance here? If my dad snapped the photo on a visit, then he must have been acquainted with Jack. This other copy of the same photograph on Signore Jack's desk clearly shows a connection between my family and the people in this photo." Mara flipped it over. Scrawled on the bottom was the date of Abby's seventh birthday. And then the words, "Rome, Italy" beneath it.

She studied the picture closer. Those weren't lawn ornaments. They were plaster statues of famous artwork. She recognized Daphne, Cupid, Venus di Milo, and others that speckled the lawn of the stucco farmhouse. That's when Mara struck on it—the woman in the photo must be Jack's deceased lover, the museum curator.

"She's the woman that Jack told us about when we went drinking at Trilussa," she said.

Jesse nodded. "He said he'd been in love once, and then she died." He pointed to the grinning Army Ranger. "There's no mistaking that sappy look. That woman is the one he was in love with. And he looks fond of the little girl, too."

"That's quite a love triangle, or trapezoid, or something," Mara said, "Both Jack and my dad loved this woman, but it's quite clear from this picture that Jack had felt as strong a bond with Abby as my dad, my mom, and the curator had felt. And when the woman died, my mom said that my dad was devastated, but what happened to Jack after that?" She chewed her thumbnail. "What happened to Jack in the time between when his curator died, and when his brother, Kiever's dad, got him a professorship at RU?"

Jesse pounded the desk with his fist. "The love of Jack's life had just died, so he went into mourning, maybe took a nosedive. With the curator out of the picture, your dad no longer had any reason to visit Rome with Abby, the one thing left in the world belonging to Jack's true love. Jack must have developed some sort of kinship with the curator's daughter, and...Jesus, unless, maybe Abby was never your father's daughter to begin with? Does anyone really know your sister's parentage? Perhaps Abby was actually Jack's biological daughter?" Jesse stared up at her.

Mara's head spun. She felt dizzy and nauseous. She leaned heavily against the desk for support. Had both her father and Jack had a relationship with the curator all those years ago?

When the trollop had gotten knocked up and disowned, did she simply choose the best path for her child--a wealthy, stable two-parent household versus an Army Ranger with no roots? Was this picture actually a family portrait? Of Jack's shattered family? And, once shattered, had he developed a lifelong grudge against Mara's family for picking up the pieces?

If all of this was true, then it was more important than ever to find her mother, before Jack was able to exact his revenge against her. Her mother had raised Jack's child, with her father, the man who'd been lovers with Jack's true love behind his back.

"The statues," Jesse said.

"In the yard?" Mara said.

He nodded. "I've seen them. I've been there."

He plucked the photo from her fingers and studied it. "Years ago, Enzo and I drove there, to pick up the pergola that he hired Jack to build for Enzo and Matilda's backyard."

"And?" Mara prompted his memory.

"Jack owns the place now. Doesn't live there. But, he keeps power tools—" Jesse locked eyes with Mara. "Jack's carpentry shed is behind the curator's house. That's where he took your mom."

Chapter 40

Jesse phoned Enzo and conveyed their theory that Jack was holding Mara's mother captive on the curator's property. Enzo made Jesse promise not to go there until backup arrived. Jesse never made promises he couldn't keep, so he hung up on him.

Besides, Jesse figured that by the time they made it to the farmhouse, only minutes away from RU, and pinpointed Mara's mother's exact location on the premises, the cavalry would have arrived, and they could take down Rome's most notorious killer together.

Jesse and Mara cut straight through Borghese Gardens and exited onto Via Nazionale on the other side. Normally a bustling avenue, it was deserted at three o'clock in the morning. The two clambered through a small piazza behind some houses, until the trees thickened, and the pavement gave way to a grassy area.

A few minutes later, he spotted it, the stucco farmhouse. Tucked back away from the rest of civilization, hidden among the trees, the property sprawled out beneath the moonlit sky. The layout and structure of the farmhouse was just as he remembered it, only now it stood in marked disrepair. The stucco crumbled from the frame, and the wrought iron gate around the porch was covered in ivy that had run rampant.

The yard smelled of fig trees and rotted wood. The frontage by the porch was dotted with the same white statues as the photograph. Deep-set cracks in the plaster spewed forth a bounty of moss and leaves, leaving the faces of the figures nearly unrecognizable.

No lights illuminated the interior of the main dwelling. Jack was likely in his work shed, around the back. Together, he and Mara crept closer. Jesse pulled the Browning from his belt and held it in front of him, keeping Mara behind him. He had to get Mara's mother away from Jack before it was too late. There was no way he would let Mara down.

The wooden shed, barn-like in its structure, looked condemned. It had caved in on one side and its paint was peeling, its chimney was crumbling, and the few steps leading to the huge, front entrance were broken and splintered.

Smoke curled out of the chimney. The inside appeared lit, but the few windows were painted over, so that one could not look out, or in.

A couple tomcats screeched near one of the garbage cans beside the shed. Mara gripped Jesse's arm tightly. Still, they moved forward, circling around to the back of the shed. The grove of rotted fruit trees provided them cover.

Nearly ten feet away from the back of barn now, Jesse could hear Jack's voice inside. He was singing Sinatra's "I've Got the World on a String."

Jesse settled Mara behind a clump of tangled branches. He checked his Browning; it was loaded and ready. He pocketed his ankle pistol in his jacket for easy access, and turned his phone to vibrate mode. "We can't afford to wait for Enzo's team, Mara. Every minute that goes by puts your mother in further jeopardy. You stay here until backup arrives. I'm going in."

"Wait!" she said. "Can you hear it? My God, it's my mother's voice."

Jesse heard a woman inside the barn bargaining for her life.

"Goddamn it, Jack," the woman said, "just let me go. You need serious help. I can get you that help…"

"She's still alive," Mara said. Tears filled her eyes, and she swiped them away. "Give me one of your guns. Let me go with you. I need to go with you," she said.

Mara's mother continued to beseech her captor. "I can give you anything," she said. "Name your price, and I'll see to it that you get away clean. Please, Jack, my wrists, the rope is burning, please."

Inside Jack apparently ignored her pleas, continuing to sing, otherwise engaged.

Jesse did not want to know what occupied Jack's time. Whatever it was would not be good. There was no time to lose. But, he would not risk Mara's safety.

He turned to face her. "Your mother witnessed the murder of a young woman tonight, and then her driver was butchered. She was abducted and tied up, awaiting her own fate. If you bust in there now, your mother will be forced to endure the murder of another daughter. I don't think you want that."

Mara's beautiful, sexy, resolute glare disappeared. Her shoulders drooped and her nose crinkled in annoyance. "Fine," she said. She walked back behind the clump of brush and stooped down, shaking her head at him.

He appreciated his small victory. Didn't matter how pissed she was at him; there was no way he was putting Mara's life in danger.

The moment abruptly ended, when from inside the shed came the buzzing clamor of a circular saw. Followed by the piercing scream of Katherine Silvestri.

Mara shot out from behind the bushes and headed straight for the barn door.

Chapter 41

Mara reached for the wrought iron door handle.

But Jesse tackled her before she could swing the door wide.

She looked up at him from the hard earth, wanting to scream at him to let her go, but his heavy hand covered her mouth.

The sounds of the buzzing saw and her mother's screams had both stopped. After a few seconds, she heard her mother's whimpers, proof that she was frightened but alive.

"You go busting in there, and he'll kill you and your mom faster than you can say you're a goddamn thickhead," Jesse said.

Mara nodded, and he uncovered her mouth.

"You're a goddamn thickhead," she muttered to him.

He shook his head in obvious frustration. "There's an open window around back. I was just about to sneak in, but then you went ape shit. You need to remain calm if you want to save her."

She nodded again.

Then, Jesse did something that impressed her. He thrust his small handgun into her hand. "Point and shoot, like a camera. Make sure you aim first."

"Thank you." She kissed him, tucked the gun in her jacket pocket, and then rounded the corner of the shed.

Relieved to hear the resumption of her mother's mundane, persistent pleas, rather than cries of agony, Mara calmly followed Jesse as he crept up to the rear window and peeked inside.

She spotted her mom inside, bound hand and foot, and tied to a wooden chair in a corner of the room, her back to Mara and Jesse. She looked tired and scared, and a bit out of place dressed in one of her tennis outfits, but otherwise she appeared unharmed.

Strangely, her mom's bound feet were soaking in a small footbath of…milk?

Mara's eyes flicked up into the twelve-foot, bare rafters. The shed itself was about the size of an American two-car garage, with a single barn-like hinged door in the front. A deep, cavernous fireplace with a long brick hearth, akin to a Venetian glass house kiln, crackled in the center.

A workbench ran along the back wall, stopped at the window, and then continued. The bench bore every sort of carpentry tool, or actually, what Mara perceived were more likely sculpting tools: hammers, chisels, saws of every size and shape, small hand tools like rapiers and carving knives, and hooks and apertures.

The thought of what Jack had done to all of his victims with those tools made her tremble. She also spotted bags of gypsum, cement, and road salt in another corner. Piled high beside those were various lengths of drywall and wooden studs.

No visible signs of statues, severed heads, or body parts. Maybe Jack kept all of his trophies in the cellar of the main house. Or, maybe in that chest freezer beside the workbench. She shuddered.

Jack stood in the center of all of his toys, wearing a carpenter's tool belt, jeans, a wife beater, and a red bandana over his ponytailed hair. He stopped to take a long swig from a container of boxed wine, and then he hosed down the table saw with water. Steam rose from the circular blade.

He plunked down the boxed wine and went back to work, cutting a plank of wood into a long, curved shape. Finished, he dragged it to a long wooden crate in the corner, and joined them; nailing hinges to the plank, hammering together something that looked like…a coffin.

Time to get her mother.

Jack turned the blaring saw back on. Mara pushed up the window and heaved herself in, undetected by Jack and her mom. Jesse slipped in behind her, and they crouched hidden beneath the window and behind some boxes.

"Stay here," Jesse said. "I'm going after Jack. When he's contained, then you can untie your mom. Got it?"

She nodded.

He kissed her. Then, he readied his stance as if to spring.

That's when Jack shut down the circular saw and spoke words aloud that chilled Mara to her core. "I'm so glad my teaching assistants could join us for a little lesson in torture."

***

Mara and Jesse halted immediately.

"Mara!" her mother yelled.

Jack swung around, flashed one of his charming, toothy grins, and reached for the boxed wine.

Jesse crouched down on one knee, gun drawn, and shouted, "Police, drop your weapon."

The idea that Jesse had just commanded Jack to drop his White Zinfandel seemed comical to her. That is, until Jack whipped the Craftsman 987 Turbo-Charge Nail Gun from behind the Franzia White Zin, and began spraying her and Jesse with six-inch long, quarter-inch wide, drywall nails.

One of them pierced her left arm. She'd never known worse pain.

Until another stabbed her upper thigh.

Mara screamed louder.

She heard her mother screaming for her. Mother apparently responsible for her set of lungs.

Jesse tackled Mara for the second time that night, and knocked them both down beside the chest freezer. He lifted the lid for added cover and gasped at the contents.

Mara gripped the head of the nail in her thigh and yanked it out. She screamed louder this time, and it helped alleviate the pain somewhat.

From behind the cooler, Jesse shot back at Jack with his Browning.

Mara reached for the second nail in her shoulder. The nail protruded at an odd angle, evidently lodged in the bone. She closed her eyes and yanked it. Still stuck. She tugged again, until it finally came free.

Her arm and leg seared with pain. Shielded by its lid, she felt around inside the freezer for some ice. She couldn't believe what was inside.

It had to be a lifetime supply of boxed wine.

Jesse reeled back against the wall, his neck grazed by a projectile nail. He cupped his hand over the bleeding wound and kept shooting.

From the side of the cooler, Mara spotted her mother standing now, her feet still in the footbath, apparently intent on making a break for it amid the gunfire.

Her mother tried to step forward, but at the last second, she lost her balance, as her feet were firmly lodged in the overturned basin. She toppled headfirst into the newly furbished wooden coffin, and landed with a thud and a groan. Her legs protruded from the full-length crate. The once pasty white liquid had hardened into a chalky plaster cast around both of her mother's feet, binding them together and preventing her escape from the coffin.

Jesse's gunfire ceased. Mara looked over, and saw Jesse with both hands up.

"Throw it down, Jesse," Jack said. He now hovered over the coffin with the nail gun. "Or the mother gets one in each temple."

***

Jesse dropped his gun. It clacked onto the cement floor, and it sounded like the Grim Reaper rapping against the front door with his bloody scythe.

"Mom, are you alright?" Mara peered around the freezer at her crumpled mother lying on her side in her custom-made death box.

"I'm humiliated," was all she said. Mara was grateful that her mother's strong will was still intact.

"C'mon little lady," Jack said to her mom, "you have nothing to be ashamed of. You're right where you're supposed to be." Still holding the power tool, Jack gestured for Jesse and Mara to come out from behind the cooler into the open. "Unlike me, who was never really sure where I fit in," Jack said. He tipped the wine box to his lips, tapped the last few drops out of the empty carton and tossed it aside.

"But, now that the remaining members of the family are reunited, we can all rehash a few memories, and then rejoin our dear departed loved ones. Anything for family." He retrieved another box from the cooler, opened it and gulped it down like a gallon of milk.

He ambled close to Mara, offered her some wine. She turned away. Jack shrugged, tipped back the box, and drank.

Jesse leapt toward him, landed on him, and began pummeling his face with his fists.

The ex-Army Ranger took the beating in stride, waited, baited, and then, when Jesse's right arm fell just slightly below his face, Jack reached up and gripped Jesse by the larynx, his bicep bulging like an anaconda that had swallowed a full-grown pig.

Jesse continued to swing at Jack's mid-section. Jesse delivered hard, solid hits, like Rocky Balboa smashing slaughtered beef, all the while coughing, gagging, and gasping for breath in Jack's viselike chokehold.

"My God, Jack, please let him go," Mara yelled.

Soon, Jesse's swings, and his breathing slowed. Jesse's face turned purple. Then blue. His eyes rolled back in his head.

"You're killing him!" Mara screamed. She rushed forward to beat at Jack's sweaty back, to no avail.

Jack turned and gazed at Mara. "This is how I killed your father, you know." A devilish grin ate up most of Jack's face. He resembled a troll.

"What did you say?" she and her mother said in unison.

Jack released Jesse, and let him drop to the ground.

Mara crouched down and scooped Jesse's head in her arms. His face regained natural color again, but he continued to gasp for air. She pressed the front of her shirt to his wounded neck, and she wondered if she should give him mouth-to-mouth. But, he squeezed her ass, and she knew he'd be alright. Then, he slipped his hand up her good thigh, and into her jacket. Jesse would be okay.

"Not so close to pretty boy, little lady." Jack waved her away from Jesse with the nail gun, and she inched off on all fours.

Mara's mother asked again, "What did you just say about my husband?"

"I killed him. In the Everglades. Coordinated a fake photo shoot. Met him in the swamp. Killed him, cut him up, and fed him to the 'gators." Jack strutted over to the coffin and hovered over her mother like a peacock. "My daddy used to wrestle 'gators you know," Jack said. "Now, *that* guy would do anything for family," he muttered.

Jack rolled a cart over to Jesse. Jesse reached up and cracked him in the knee with his fists.

Jack's leg buckled and he howled. Then, he took another swig of the boxed wine, and kicked Jesse in the face.

Jesse's head clunked against the brick hearth. He fell away to the side, and blacked out on the floor. Sparks crackled and popped from the hissing fire inside the oblong fireplace, as if trying to rouse him. Didn't work. Jesse was out cold.

Jack clamped Jesse's left ankle into a metal vise on the rolling cart and left it hanging there.

"Why did you kill Arturo?" Mara's mother said. "What had he ever done to you?"

"Mother-fucker fucked her mother, that's what!" Jack said, slurring his words. He walked to the workbench, his hands shaking, and shot the nail gun a few times into the air. "Your husband was fucking my woman," Jack said. "Now, I was alright with that. All's fair in love and war, and all that shit. I still loved my precious little lady, you know. And as long as she was okay with only occasional visits with Abigail whenever Artie would bring her by, then I went along with that too. She swore it was the best course of action for her little girl. But when the love of my life got sick and passed away, I wasn't quite right for a while, and they sent me away."

Jack turned toward Mara and her mother, his face flushed and his breathing fierce. "For years, I lived in an institution, while your goddamn family continued to raise that little girl. I fail to see how that is right!"

Kat Silvestri shook her head slowly. "But, she was Arturo's daughter."

"The hell she was," Jack spat at her mom. "I knew my woman was fucking around, so I had a blood test when Abby was born. She was 100 percent my own. I would do anything for family."

Mara looked over at her mother, who was stunned silent. Abby was definitively Signore Jack's daughter, not her father's lovechild. With this confirmation, Mara's world as she'd once known it had shifted again.

Jack settled down on a wooden bench beside her mother's coffin. "That's why when I found out you all were sending my grown-up baby Abigail to school in Rome, I made my brother, the Senator, arrange to get me a job there. And, after all those years of being apart, my baby girl and I finally got close. I guess you could say, we bonded. No thanks to any of you."

"That's what this is all about? You're pissed at my family?" Mara said. "So then, you must be the one who threw me from the cliff in the Alps a couple months ago?"

"That was me, little lady," Jack said.

"And, you tried to bulldoze me and Jesse off Montepulciano's hillside in the garbage truck?" Mara said.

He put up a finger. "Guilty."

Her mother spoke up. "And I walked in to find you mutilating that young girl in her bed tonight. That was you trying to kill my daughter, you sonofabitch."

With a pompous lilt to his drawl, he again held up his index finger. "Ah, yes, that too was yours truly." He grinned at both women.

"I've spent years honing my technique," Jack said. "And now that I have both of you here, my task is complete." He looked at Mara. "I suffered Abby's untimely demise for six long years, and now I plan to make you suffer for it."

"Untimely demise, but you—"

His eyes suddenly brightened, and then narrowed as he focused on Mara's neck. "What the hell is that shiny bauble, little lady?" He reached for her throat, and she tried to pull away, but he shot her in the other thigh with the nail gun.

Her leg was on fire! She scrambled to reach for it, to wrench the foreign object piercing her thigh. Her nerve endings screamed in agony.

Jack yanked back her hair with one hand, swiped at her throat with the other. All the while, she scraped and scratched at his face, her leg twitching and writhing in pain.

He pulled away from her, and as she tugged the nail loose from her convulsing muscle, she noticed he'd torn her sapphire pendant from around her neck. It swung back and forth in Jack's hand.

"I gave this to my love when I asked for her hand. She died before she could give it to me," Jack said. "I gave the pendant to my daughter at her mother's funeral. It was the last time I ever saw the pendant again, until tonight. What the fuck are *you* doing with it? It's only for family!"

Mara did not answer.

Jack put it around his own neck and tucked it inside his wife-beater tank. Then, he lunged at her. He threw down the nail gun, and grasped her head with both hands. "You had no right! None of you! You had no right!"

She grabbed his hands, but his grip was fierce, and she wasn't strong enough to pry his fingers from his hold on her head. She tried to pull away, but he kept her planted there, forced to stare into the madness of his contorted face.

"You had no right!" Jack shook her as he ranted, and he squeezed her head like a grape. She needed Jesse, but he'd been knocked out and cuffed to Jack's vise grip. She wished she could just twist her head to look at him one last time before Jack crushed her, but the death grip was too damn strong.

Mara's mother was screaming. She heard scraping and rolling and wondered if her mother had managed to drag her plastered feet out of the coffin to help her. She'd never needed her mom as badly as she did at that moment.

More scraping and rolling.

More violent head-banging, squeezing, and crushing. It felt like her head might explode. Her eyes lost focus, and she closed them. She lost her strength to stand, and Jack pushed her down to the floor, his hands still encasing her throbbing head.

She smelled something rank and sour. She opened her eyes, but she still couldn't focus. It smelled like—a basin of liquid plaster. Through the shaking of her brain, her eyes glimpsed the milky white of the plaster mix. Her face was hovering right over it.

Scrape and roll.

"Mother!" she screamed. Mara knew she couldn't resist much longer. If her mother didn't haul ass, Jack would plunge Mara's face deep into the plaster mix. It would seep into her eyes, her nose, her mouth, her ears. Her mother's feet had taken minutes to harden and dry. Mara would likely become asphyxiated in mere seconds, her nose and throat clogged with curing paste.

"Help me!" Mara screamed.

Two shots rang out. One more. Jack's shaking stopped, and the grip released.

She jerked her body to the side, hoping to avoid ingesting or inhaling the paste.

One more shot, then the empty clicking of a spent barrel. Had the police finally arrived? She sat up and tried desperately to focus through her concussive haze.

Jack slumped to the ground beside her. He was shot full of holes, but still grinning.

She spotted Jesse through her cloud of diffused light and snowy dots. He sat ramrod straight just feet away, his leg still gripped by the vise, and his gun clutched in his outstretched arm. He tossed aside the now empty pistol, the same one he'd slipped from her jacket when he'd grabbed her ass earlier.

Jesse scraped and rolled the cart close to Jack, and grabbed hold of the front of Jack's wife-beater shirt. Then, he punched the shit-eating grin clear off Jack's face, leaving him to die a death that could not come soon enough.

Jesse loosened the vise grip, and wrenched free his ankle. He pulled an Ace bandage from his jacket pocket. "Ex-soccer players always carry a spare," he said.

Mara thought he was the funniest man she'd ever met. And, the smartest. And, the bravest. And, the hair—he had a great head of hair. She crawled to him, reached for him, and they kissed until her mother interrupted, demanding they exhume her from her coffin.

Only then did Enzo and Utica bust through the front door with five other men who immediately posted the perimeter. Seconds later, Enzo sent the SWAT team away, and radioed for a crime scene unit. He nudged at Jack's body. Still breathing. He sighed, and then radioed an ambulance.

Mara ran to her mother, still entrenched in the coffin with cement shoes, and embraced her. For the second time since she could remember, her mother hugged her back.

She extracted her mother's upper torso out of the coffin and onto a wooden bench, and she cradled her mom while they waited for the ambulance that would help release her from the plaster cast. Her mother dozed in her embrace, and Mara listened to the murmured conversation between Jesse, Enzo, and Utica.

"I still don't understand why the monster killed his own daughter in the Alps years back," Enzo said.

"Abby and Jack apparently had a rumored 'special relationship,' incestuous at best it seems, though I was never sure whether or not *she* knew she was related. Delicate stuff; not something I felt was necessary to investigate further," Utica explained. "Anyway, it went on while I was investigating Kiever, possibly even before I arrived. When she and Kiever had become fuck buddies, Jack put on blinders, and chose to believe that I was the one screwing her in our apartment, not his nephew."

"Which wasn't entirely untrue," Jesse said. "She'd come over a lot your first month, and hung out behind closed doors."

Utica shook his head. "Wasn't like that. She was a great girl. Just had a lot of baggage, most of it stemming from messed up relationships: Jack, her father figure and professor, and

Kiever, likely her first cousin. Again, not entirely sure she even knew that she was blood-related to Jack."

Mara cringed. Sounds like her sister had had enough baggage for a trip around the world. Mara sighed. She regretted that they'd never been close enough sisters to share such intimate information. Looking back, she'd barely known her older sister at all.

Jesse nodded. "'Anything for family' explains a lot with this guy."

Mara heard the ambulance sirens drawing near. Her mother cried out softly in her sleep, and Mara stroked her mother's hair.

The three men huddled closer together.

"Makes for a saucy Thanksgiving, you know?" Utica wisecracked. "Anyway, Jack went off on Abby one day in class. I overheard him say that he'd found out about her fucking around on him. He transferred her out every one of his classes, and broke contact with her. Shortly after, she died in the Alps.

"FBI investigated, but the Swiss and Italian police showed no foul play." Utica shook his head. "Even after the case was closed, I always wondered whether maybe the sick freak killed his own daughter. Guess now, I wouldn't put it past him."

With a loud groan, Jack Sugardale rose from the cement floor like a shot. The ex-Army Ranger ignored the four bullets imbedded in his torso and limbs, and he thrust his massive frame toward the wooden coffin. Right for Mara and her mother.

Signore Jack wielded a sculpting tool. The same kind she'd found on her pillow. The same type she'd uncovered in her suitcase. A long, sharp, jagged rapier.

Mara thrust her mother's upper body across her lap on the bench, and then conjured a human blanket. She heaved her body forward, covering her mother's with her own. Mara waited for the stabbing pain of the Sculptor's jagged tool through her flesh.

None came.

Instead, she heard Jesse grunt as he yanked Jack's body away from the coffin. She looked up to see Jesse hurl the man across the room.

Wielding the rapier in a fist above his head, the drunken, bloodied sadist stumbled, then awkwardly lunged toward Jesse. Jesse sidestepped him, and deftly spun around, as only a pro soccer player could. Pushing Jack from behind, Jesse charged forward, and rammed Jack, full force, into the blazing fire of the deep, cavernous fire pit.

Jack's head and chest alighted in flames. Utica gripped Jack legs that still protruded onto the brick hearth, and together, Jesse and Utica thrust the serial killer's body deep into the fiery depths of hell.

Chapter 42

Mara had spent the early morning delivering her police statement to Enzo at the hospital while the ER stitched her nail wounds. She then copped a couple hours of shut-eye in a plastic chair while doctors freed her sedated mother from her plaster shackles. She awoke around nine in the morning to find her mom sound asleep.

The female police officer charged with Lana's security at Stella Luna had driven Lana to the hospital for observation the previous evening, as she had proved inconsolable over Kristen's murder. Today, Mara visited Lana's room, but found her resting in tranquilized slumber as well. She wondered if Kiever knew that Lana was here, or if he cared.

Mara returned home in the back of a squad car. Enzo had cleared her to return to the scene of Kristen's murder to retrieve a few personal items before moving to a vacant Stella Luna apartment a few doors down. She'd promised to confine herself to locations in the apartment not restricted with police tape, in the hope of gathering a few clothes and her school books. She wasn't quite sure yet how she planned to emotionally handle what remained of the crime scene.

Jesse had kissed her goodbye inside Jack's work shed the night before, and then he'd sped off with Utica to the station to tie up loose ends, file reports, and notify victims' families that the most renowned Italian serial killer since the so-called Monster of Florence was no longer a threat. That morning, she'd asked Enzo if Jack might have been the Monster, but Jack had had an alibi during the '80s, serving in the U.S. Army in Asia over the course of those crimes.

Dozens of investigators and cadaver dogs had continued to comb the curator's premises long after Mara had left the scene, digging and searching for additional victims that the Sculptor might have left behind. Enzo had told her that so far, no human remains encased in plaster or otherwise, had been recovered.

The police escort neared the university, and Jesse called to tell her that he'd be in meetings for most of the day with the FBI and police.

"Federico and the rest of Stella Luna's crime scene unit have been temporarily relocated to Jack's farmhouse," Jesse said, "but I wouldn't blame you for not wanting to go back to your apartment. Feel free to hunker down at my place until we're able to send in a cleaning crew to yours. Mine's vacant. Apparently Volker moved out, Utica's with me, and Kiever never came home last night, so feel free to recuperate in my bed.

I'd love to find you in it when I'm finished here. Though, looking at this mountain of paperwork, it may be awhile."

"Thanks," Mara said. "You're sweet to offer, but my computer is at home, and I need to play catch up on the next term paper. I promise to take a rain check. Also, I know I thanked you last night, but I hope you understand how grateful I am for...everything."

"Mara, I'm sorry, gotta run. Captain Sciug just called a meeting. We'll catch up later." Jesse the cop hung up on her.

***

Minutes from Stella Luna now, Mara rubbed her eyes. The wind outside picked up, and the squad car swayed while it was stopped at an intersection. Flashes of the previous night inundated her brain like the ocean crashing to the shore during a hurricane. Just as waves leave behind debris, her memories left behind unanswered questions.

For one thing, she'd expected Jack's lair to be filled with plastered trophies, a sort of "museum of horrors," where Jack displayed the body parts he'd removed from his victims. She supposed the gallery would turn up in due time, either at the farmhouse property or elsewhere.

Also, Jack's "anything for family" mantra continued to resound in her ears. If he was so steadfast about this proclamation, then why would Jack murder his own daughter in the Alps, after spending years trying to reestablish contact.

She pushed these and other swirling thoughts from her mind, set her head back on the seat, and dreamed of boxed wine.

***

The patrolman woke her and dropped her outside Stella Luna. The wind whipped her car door shut, and he took off.

The atrium was empty, and the complex appeared vacant. The rest of the student body was probably reveling in its last few days of spring break, but she knew all hell would break loose upon their return, when they learned of Kristen's murder.

Once inside her apartment, Mara stripped down, and headed directly to the shower, redirected to the fridge for a six-pack of Kronenbourg and then went back to the bathroom, all the while diverting her eyes from the police-taped, shuttered bedroom.

She tested the water with her fingers, willing it to heat up faster. She smelled chlorine on her fingers, probably from the sacks of powder in Jack's shed. Her hair smelled like smoke, too, likely from the fire burning in the kiln. She jumped in and scrubbed until her fingerprints practically rubbed from her tips.

In the shower, she always did her best thinking. But, today, she just wanted to turn it off and relax. Not to be.

Mara drank four beers, one after the other, and spent almost an hour washing away the filth and rehashing events. Or, maybe she was just trying to avoid the taped off bloodstains outside the bathroom door. She should have taken up Jesse on his offer and waited for him in his bed. Was that the beer talking, or her freshly scrubbed nether regions?

She dried, and wondered whether her amorous thoughts were too morbid in light of Kristen's murder. Though she hadn't known her dear friend long, she did know that Kristen would have wanted her to grasp at whatever sense of normalcy she could, to sort of spit in the face of such monstrous brutality by seeking human connection.

Maybe it wasn't too late. She reached for her cell to call Jesse and perhaps arrange that meeting at his apartment, but then she remembered he'd rushed off to a meeting. Jesse the cop, no longer Jesse the man.

Someone knocked on her front door, and she answered it in her too-short robe. Perhaps Jesse had decided to whisk her away and replace all remnants of the Sculptor's wrath with something much more beautiful and alive.

But, when she opened the door, she found Stan Kiever leaning against the door jamb. He wore a Yankees cap and a plaid shirt, and he had his backpack slung casually over one shoulder. He was sucking a butt as usual.

"Hey beautiful. Heard about Kristen, too bad. Lana's not home right now. Maybe you want to come upstairs, relax in her fresh digs? Take a load off? Maybe you need a little...comfort?" He breathed out smoke through his pursed lips, and tried to pry the towel from her wet body with his eyes. "Stanky's here to provide that comfort, babe."

Speechless, she stared at him. Ran her eyes up and down him. She didn't know if it was the beer, or her exhaustion, but suddenly something deep inside her clicked. And, in that moment, everything changed.

"I'll meet you up there in a minute," she said. "Let me just grab some beer, and I'll be right up." She left him hanging on her stoop and ran across the room into her walk-in closet, slammed the door. She put on a tight tank top, and even tighter jeans.

She reached for the doorknob, but she did not grasp it. What was she doing with Stanky? She pulled her phone from her backpack hanging on the back of the door. She dialed Jesse, got his voicemail. She phoned the station directly, told them who it was, and asked to interrupt Captain Sciug's conference. She was connected directly to Jesse. After a few minutes of heated discussion, she hung up. She now knew that the few beers she'd had in the hot shower had just altered the rest of her life.

Kiever was likely waiting for her upstairs with a grin on his face, and not much else. She took a deep breath and decided to go for it. She swung open the bedroom door to her closet, scooted past her police-taped, shuttered bedroom, and headed for the beers in the fridge.

But, Stan Kiever wasn't upstairs. Instead, he was lounged across her living room couch like a panther. In the middle of a crime scene.

Nope, the beers weren't the reason for her change of heart. But, the guy on her couch would surely prove to be.

Chapter 43

"Nice of you to come over. I'd wondered what took you so long," Mara said to Kiever from the kitchen.

"You mean with Lana temporarily out of the picture?" he said.

The mention of her friend stabbed with her guilt, but it only lasted a second.

"No, I mean since I first arrived in Rome. What took you so long to…pay me a visit?" She stood at the counter mixing each of them a scotch and ginger ale. She heard him looking through her CDs. One could tell a lot from a man from the CD he chose to set the mood.

"Not sure why I waited so long to come see you, babe. Trust me; it's not for lack of want." She heard him take a long drag from his cigarette and insert music into the player. Then he said with a butt between his teeth, "I just always thought you were with Jesse. Didn't want piss in another man's pool. But, I knew you'd be a little down about Kristen, so I thought I'd just...ya know..."

"Take advantage of the situation?" She sauntered into the living room and handed him his drink. She knocked his backpack from the couch, and sat cross-legged on the middle cushion, facing him.

"Exactly," he said, slinking in beside her on the same cushion. He pulled the cigarette from between his full lips and stamped it out on the heel of his Doc Marten.

Sara McLaughlin's voice peppered the air with melancholy and dark yearning, and Mara suddenly felt a little light-headed.

She stood and opened a window, not the one the CSU had wiped for prints, the one behind the Cichlid tank. She wanted no part of that CSU bullshit right now. Instead, she wanted to live in the moment, and drag it out for all it was worth.

She sat back down again, beside Stanky on the couch. It had been awhile since she'd gotten laid, and she wanted to take things slow.

Too late. Kiever leaned in close. He nuzzled her neck, and the scent of his Turkish tobacco wafted up from his hair. He nibbled her neck, bit it lightly, and moved higher to suck her ear lobe, bit it, sucked it.

She nudged him backward, wanting to slow him up a little, but he pushed back, harder, almost holding her down. The wind shrieked through the window, and the yellow caution tape that stretched through parts of the room fluttered in the cold breeze.

He kissed her mouth, ran his slick tongue along her bottom lip, and nibbled it. Her breaths came short and fast, and she wasn't sure she could endure any more foreplay. She moaned and leaned her head against the seatback. He ran his tongue along her clavicle, and she moaned once more.

The room suddenly darkened, and noontime shadows from the cloud-covered sun crept along the floor and up the walls. He pressed his pursed lips hard against hers, forcing her mouth to take in his tongue. Just as a gust howled through the window, she gasped deeply, almost losing her breath.

He gripped her shoulders with both hands and pressed her against the pillows.

She thought of Jesse. Pushed the thought away.

She thought of the Sculptor. Pushed the thought away.

Kiever grabbed her breasts. She pulled him closer.

Gazed at him. Closed her eyes.

"You're so beautiful, Mara," he breathed into her ear. Tongued her ear, slobbered it, bit it. Found her mouth again. Reached down, grabbed her ass and squeezed so hard, tears sprang to her eyes.

"Oh, baby, do you know how much I want you? Can you feel it, huh?" Stanky grinded his hard package against her at the same time that he wiped away the few tears that had leaked from the corners of her eyes.

"You want me as much as I want you? Tell me, baby, tell me how much you want it." He unbuttoned the shirt she wore over her tank top, and then pinched her nipples through the ribbed fabric.

She moaned louder. "Ooh, yes...I want you...so bad. But, I feel a little guilty."

"About Jesse? Lana?" he murmured. "Forget them, babe. It's just us now."

"No, I mean about Jack," she said. "I'm sorry the police had to end your uncle's life. You okay?"

"Jack and I weren't tight. No worries, babe." He tugged her hair back and kissed her throat. "Feel so good right now."

The wind shrieked, and rain splattered inside the window onto the credenza. Kiever reached both hands beneath her ass, and picked her up. He swiped aside a cardboard evidence bin and crashed her down beside it on the credenza. He slid his hands through the droplets of spattered rain and ran the wet along her face.

She squealed and wrapped her legs around his waist even tighter.

"Ooh, you like it wet, don't you, you nasty bitch." He pulled his sweater over his head, and pressed his bare chest against the sheer material that separated them. He groped at her top, tried to tug it out of her waistband, kissed her.

She eased his hands off her shirt and back to her ass. "Mmmm, can we do this for a little while? I love the feel of the cold rain on my back, and the warmth of your body against mine."

He wound one of her damp curls around his finger. "You have hair just like my mother. It's crazy how much you look like Mom. Except," he kissed her, "you're so much more...vital." He ran his tongue down her throat. "Come to think of it, you look a lot like your older sister, too."

"I heard you two were...close?" Mara said.

"She was goddamn sexy, but nothin' more than a math tutor to keep me on the swim team." He reached for his drink, jiggled the ice, sipped it. "Tried to fuck her, but she had a thing for Jack and wouldn't let me touch her. Too bad, really, how that movie star face ended up smashed into a tree. Would have liked to keep her around."

"Me too," Mara said, dropping her chin down to hide her tears.

He picked her chin back up with his finger and kissed her lips. "I think I'd like to keep you forever, babe."

She giggled. "It's not sexy, but it'll do." She kissed him back.

"No, I mean it. I wish I'd come a lot sooner than this. I always knew I wanted you. Just never knew how much."

In just his jeans, he walked over to his backpack and set it on the credenza. He rustled around inside it.

She raised her eyebrows to him quizzically.

"Protection. Always carry it with me. Just can't seem to find it," he said.

She reached out her hand to him, beckoned him with her eyes. "I've got it covered. Condoms are in the bathroom medicine chest."

"Not that kind, beautiful." He smiled that sly grin he always wore, as if he carried a secret.

He pulled a small box from his rucksack, the size of a pack of Pop Tarts. He tore the strip off the top and poured the contents into her fish tank. White powder filtered into the liquid, dispersed.

She eased off the credenza, took a couple steps away from Stan Kiever.

"I always carry protection," he said. "Well, no, I suppose, it's more like..." He pulled a long, stainless steel chisel from his bag and stirred the rapidly thickening paste.

"More like...preservation."

***

Mara plucked her button-down from the floor and pulled it on. "I had no idea the Sculptor would reveal himself so...quickly. Usually, you wait until you've made love before you slaughter your victims. I thought...we'd have more time."

"You are so smart, and beautiful," he said. "I plan to keep you in my collection. Mom would be pleased."

Mara backed away. Tried to make her feet run, but they wouldn't respond. She reached into her pocket for her phone and speed-dialed Jesse.

He reached forward and slapped it out of her hand, onto the floor. "I think I could love you, Mara. Don't you want that?" Kiever said.

Mara scrambled to close her shirt buttons, but her hands trembled so badly, she could not make them work. "I know I don't want what you have to offer."

"Just like your sister. Such an uptight bitch. Abby slapped me when I tried to cop a feel on the chairlift in Switzerland. Screamed for Daddy when I stabbed her and chased her down the slope. If it wasn't for that tree, that lovely face could have lived on...right next to yours," he said, gazing at Mara's face, as if she were a specimen. Or a piece of artwork.

Kiever pulled the chisel through the thickening muck with greater effort now.

"You're right. I never told any of my lovelies my plans in advance. They loved fucking me, but the poor souls had no idea that I planned to keep them forever. They were already dead. You're the first, Mara. You're special. One of a kind. My *piece de resistance*," he hissed. "And, now that you know, it's time to die." Kiever pulled an eight-inch, two-sided, serrated rapier from inside his pack.

He lashed at her, flicking the blade toward her neck.

She sidestepped him, and karate chopped the rapier from his hand and into the thick plaster muck.

For a moment, they both looked down at the tank in amazement. Then, she roundhouse kicked him in the back of the legs, knocking him to his knees.

Like a viper, Kiever struck out and smacked her thigh with his fist, smashing her stitched nail gun wound. Blood seeped through her denim in seconds.

She kneed him in the face, and his head whipped sideways.

He looked back, his nose spewing blood. He struck out quickly and smacked her wounded knee again before she could dart out of the way. She went down sideways and hit the back of her head against the dining table.

The world spun out of focus. She felt a cold breeze on her cheeks and tried desperately to get up, but he was on her in seconds, pinning her against the floor like a wrestler.

It wasn't supposed to be like this. She needed more time. She needed Jesse. Jesse should have been here.

Kiever reached for his pack, surely intent on pulling out another lethal weapon.

She heard the wind rattle the window against its hinges. Rain drizzled onto her face; it helped her regain a bit of focus.

There was no way she'd let the Sculptor kill her. No way she'd end up like all the rest of his victims.

She focused on him rustling through his pack, and she pulled up her leg and kneed his testicles into his abdomen.

He doubled over, cupped his balls with both hands, and she rolled out from under him.

Through his anguish, he managed to snag her leg and pull her back toward him. "Let's not make this such a chore, babe," Kiever said with a grimace.

He grabbed the hair at the back of her head, and yanked her to her feet, dragged her to the fish tank. With his other hand, he gripped the rapier and pulled it out of the plaster stew with a sucking sound.

He tugged her head way back, until her hair dangled on the credenza, and he exposed her neck.

She flailed and kicked, tried to knock the rapier from his fist, but only toppled a chair. She beat his arms and back. She clenched and unclenched her fists, clawed at his naked chest, scrambled to grasp any sort of weapon in which to defend herself.

She clenched the hand that held the rapier only inches from her jugular, pushed it away, but her strength began to wane.

The wind rattled the window. Or was it the door?

She spied the dolphin paperweight left in the evidence bin beside her on the credenza.

He spied it first.

When he reached for it, she pulled her head forward and lashed her teeth at him, sinking them into his shoulder.

He howled.

She grabbed the paperweight from the crate with one hand and raised it, pausing briefly to maximize her grip.

In her moment of hesitation, Kiever swung the rapier high to slash her throat.

Before he could, the door to the apartment flew open.

"Police, drop your weapon!"

"FBI! Drop it!"

Caught off guard, Kiever lowered the rapier for a split second.

Long enough for Mara to ram her knee deep into his solar plexus, and smash the side of his head with Kristen's glass dolphin.

Kiever collapsed forward, and rolled to the floor, clutching his bruised head.

Jesse rushed him, picked up Kiever, and plowed him against the dining table. He tore the rapier from his mitt, and cuffed him. Jesse looked over at Mara, with a mix of anxiety and relief plastered across his face.

"What took you so long?" Mara said. She collapsed into the cushions of the couch, and the paperweight rolled from her hand to the floor.

Utica seized Kiever by the waistband of his jeans and thrust him toward the door, high-fiving Mara on the way.

"My dad's a U.S. Senator," Kiever wailed. "I'll be back on the street tomorrow morning, babe. We can pick up where we left off."

Jesse put up his hand to halt Utica's progress. Utica nodded, stopped.

Jesse punched Kiever in the face.

Kiever cowered. "Not the face, man," he whined. "Chicks dig this face."

Jesse smashed Kiever a few more times in the face for good measure. Jesse held up his cell phone. "Mara placed the call.

Your entire conversation's been recorded. Not even Daddy can get you out of this one, you sick fuck."

Jesse hauled back, punched him in the gut this time. Jesse nodded to Utica who resumed marching Kiever to the exit.

For the second time in twenty-four hours, cops and agents spread out through Mara's apartment. She was done with Stella Luna.

Jesse wrapped his arms around her, pulled her to him, and held her there while shock tremors coursed through her.

"I never should have agreed to this," Jesse said. "We got held up on the way. I could hear the things that freak was telling you. The Sculptor could've—"

"But, he didn't. And, he won't, anymore," she said.

Enzo placed his hand on her shoulder, kissed her forehead. "I understand now, what Jesse means, when he calls you...what's the word?" He turned to Jesse.

"Thickhead. She's a thickhead." Jesse reached for her face to kiss her, but Kiever interrupted, calling to her from the threshold to the atrium.

"Mara, just tell me, babe, how'd you know? How'd you pull this off?" Kiever said. "I was so close to having you. How'd you get the gumption to fuck me over?"

Mara smiled. "Call it...self-preservation."

EPILOGUE:

CARVING & CHISELING

"Imitation is the sincerest form of flattery."

—Charles Caleb Colton,
an English cleric, writer and collector

I

Two hours after finishing her final exam, Mara sat on a hand-carved wood bench in Enzo's backyard curled on Jesse's lap. A Moretti was in one hand, and a soccer ball in the other. A bonfire sent sparks into the twilight sky, as Utica, Mimi, Volker, and Fritz Arella tossed two-by-fours and carved posts of a broken pergola into the blaze.

"What do you think about getting a student Eurail pass and traveling around with me over the summer?" Jesse asked her. "I've got some time coming to me since wrapping up the Sculptor case, and I think we could both use some R&R."

She nuzzled his cheek. "Especially after the semester I had, picking up your slack when you ditched your TA post."

"Baby, when are you going to learn that I was not really a statistics major? I just play one on TV," he said. "I'm a cop, and proud of it."

"My brave detective…" she said.

They kissed, until Lana came over and tugged at Jesse. "Will you two unlock your lips long enough for Jesse to cut his cake?"

Mara and Jesse reluctantly parted their lips. Jesse tucked the soccer ball under one arm and walked to the table hand in hand with Mara, where Enzo had just set his homemade, three-tiered cannoli cake, beside the RU students' end of semester celebratory tiramisu.

"Why do I get a separate cake?" Jesse dipped his finger into the ricotta and placed it to Mara's lips.

Jesse's mother spoke up. "It's not everyday my baby gets promoted." She kissed his cheek. "Now, when do I get to see you two cutting your wedding cake?"

Mara gasped. Jesse turned scarlet. "Uh, we're not...we haven't..."

"I'm not really sure...we haven't..." Mara sputtered.

"Okay, my wife's had enough to drink for one night," Jesse's father said. "Besides, I promised to take her salsa dancing. Have fun, kids."

Jesse's parents hugged Enzo, Jesse, and Mara, and then waved goodbye to the group crowded into Enzo's backyard before leaving.

Jesse hugged her and whispered in her ear. "You know I love you?"

"Always?" Mara whispered back.

"Always and forever." He kissed her, and then she plucked the soccer ball from his grasp. "C'mon kid, let's show these guys what made Beckham shake in his cleats." She threw it down on the grass and tried to keep it from him, but Jesse deftly recovered the ball.

Until Utica intercepted it. "More like shat in his shorts." He ran to the grassy area on the other side of the fenced-in property, and others soon followed.

Jesse laughed and took her by the hand to give chase, but Enzo winked at her, and she broke from Jesse's grasp. "You go. I'll catch up in a minute." Mara pulled Jesse close. "And, in answer to your question, I'd love to roam around the continent with you. As long, as we can start in Pompeii? Have a little well-deserved hedonism of our own?" she said.

"Boo-yah!!!" Jesse beat his chest and barreled toward Utica, where he snatched a pass intended for Mimi, and dribbled it down the yard with lightning feet before scoring between two cypress trees.

Enzo offered slices of both cakes to Mara.

"In a minute. I've been dying to do this all night." She strolled over to the remains of Signore Jack's pergola, axed earlier by Jesse and Utica until all that was left was a heap of scraps and nails. She picked up some broken posts and tossed them into the fire, watched them smolder and burn.

Enzo strolled over and tossed one in. "I must apologize. Your family pendant is still in the evidence locker. I've been meaning to return it."

"Thank you, Enzo. Pawn it, and donate the proceeds, just as long as it's not to any art museums. They give me the creeps."

He chuckled. "I'm sorry your lovely mother couldn't make the party."

"I'm sorry too. She and her chauffeur send their regards from New Zealand," Mara said. "They'd apparently had a thing for years, and he proposed from his hospital bed. They're postponing the wedding until after the senior circuit season finishes. She seems very happy."

"I'm so glad," Enzo said.

She smiled. "I appreciate all that you've done for me and my family, Enzo."

"And, I appreciate what you've done for my nephew." He gestured to Jesse. "I've never seen him happier."

She hugged him.

"As for you, dear," Enzo said, "Have you ever considered joining the police force after school? We could use your brainpower. And, some of that thickheaded gumption I've heard about."

Mara smiled and shook her head. "Thanks, but both Ferrari and Vespa have offered me jobs after I graduate. It's what I've always hoped for." She tossed in another piece of wood. "But, I'll let you in on a secret. When I signed up for next term's courses, I threw in a couple criminal justice classes, just for fun." She shrugged. "You never know."

Enzo beamed. "You never know." He took a bite of his cannoli cake, and seemed to savor it before he tossed his shoulders in a shrug. "Not as good as Matilda's, but still good."

"Your cake is amazing. Enjoy the fruit of your labor, Enzo; you deserve it." She kissed his cheek. "Will you excuse me?" Mara wiped the soot and grime off her hands, "I plan to dazzle Jesse with a few moves."

II

Months later, Chief Inspector Enzo Tranchille tacked the postcard that Jesse and Mara had sent him from Amalfi on the bulletin board behind his desk at Rome's *Questura*.

He sifted through the rest of his mail and tore open a complaint filed by the former Senator Kiever against the Rome police department for improper police procedure and false imprisonment of his son. It had been dated before Stanky Kiever, a.k.a. the Sculptor, committed suicide in the maximum-security mental facility two weeks ago, in early August.

Enzo opened his cabinet of closed cases. He pulled out the triple rubber banded, accordion folder that was the Sculptor file, but before he could slip the complaint inside it, a number of photographs fluttered to the floor. Pictures of some of the victims, before and after Kiever had butchered them.

Enzo reached down for another that had wedged beneath the desk leg. It showed Kiever's post-mortem photo: a bloody torso, devoid of its penis. He'd apparently carved that specific part of the male anatomy out of his own body, and flushed it down the toilet bowl of his holding cell. The last body part he'd ever severed from living flesh had been his own. And as part of some inexplicable grand gesture before slitting his throat, he'd ushered his most prized possession to the world.

The police inspector snapped the three thick rubber bands back around the flimsy cardboard file, but just as he was about to thrust the folder back into the cabinet, one of the file's seams busted open, spilling everything into his chair. A stray Ziploc evidence bag flittered to his desk.

Inside it was a bloody string.

It had been presumed, of course, that Kiever's penis had been flushed, in that it had never been recovered. But, the fuchsia silk string that he'd likely wrapped around it before plopping it in the metal latrine had somehow resisted the flush. CSI had retrieved the string, and later had thrown it into the file.

Enzo shook his head. Apparently, the Sculptor was not only a sadist, but a masochist, in life, and in death.

He slammed the file cabinet shut, and grabbed his jacket. Enzo planned to register the bag downstairs in the evidence locker, and then head to Borghese Gardens to feed the pigeons. Then, on to some target shooting. Never hurts to stay limber. One never knows.

Enzo stopped at the restroom first, and relieved himself, baggie still in hand.

Murderers had ceased to mystify him years ago. As a rookie, when he'd unofficially sniffed around the Monster of

Florence, and the victims had begun piling up, he had just figured some men were born and bred to commit evil acts. But, on oneself? How could any man cut off his own penis?

He placed the baggie on the sink and washed his hands. All this time, he'd been certain that the Sculptor had, in fact, been the Monster of Florence, reinvented into a fresh, new persona for the benefit of what? Not getting caught? Relieving boredom? A change of scenery? But, Stan Kiever hadn't even been born at the time of the original slayings, so it was not possible that he'd been the original monster.

Enzo felt elated over the closed Sculptor case, nonetheless he knew that the one case he could never solve, the Monster file, would stay with him until the day he died.

He picked up the bag and headed to the stairwell. He flicked it between his fingers, trying to bite down on something that nagged his thoughts.

Original slayings. The serial killer's calling card. The silk string left behind. Originality. Emulation. Reinvention. Fresh, new persona.

Enzo's heart beat faster. His hands curled into tight fists. Enzo's thoughts shifted once more, then finally pieced together into something cogent. And then he knew.

Perhaps…the original Sculptor had left his calling card, the fuchsia silk string, with his latest victim, Stan "Stanky" Kiever, who was, in actuality, a mere copycat serial killer. Which meant…

The original Sculptor was still out there.

III

The Sculptor deposited the key to his Museum of Horrors in the curator's inbox at Rome's Borghese Gallery. He wouldn't need it anymore. He had officially completed his work in Rome. Time to move on. Satisfy a new whim.

He regretted leaving his mother's decrepit plaster casting behind, but he'd hauled it around the continent long enough. Time to sever the apron strings. Besides, if he truly began to miss her again, he'd fashion himself a new statue.

He'd grown weary of sculpting. Time for a new calling, a reinvention of sorts. He'd been "dead" so many times, and in so many cities, it was more like…a resurrection.

Besides, he'd completed his masterpiece, his *piece de resistance*. There would be no standard of comparison, no other mark of excellence aside from this, his final work.

Once the curator eventually reported the key, the Rome police would ultimately locate his gallery, and become

GINA FAVA

impressed, he was sure, with his attention to detail in his greatest work to date.

He'd left his last piece beneath the cupola, upon a pedestal, so the sunlight would illuminate its essence. The final piece, an exact replica of his copycat, Stanky Kiever, brought the Sculptor great pride.

A rare and magnificent work, it was the only one out of hundreds that he'd ever signed—"The Sculptor." Of course, they'd never find him, so he'd never be able to formally accept the accolades of his genius. No matter, the true genius was in the creation.

True genius was not based on the superb workmanship of perfectly preserving the penis he'd severed from the writhing man's scrotum to seamlessly incorporate it into the plaster statue. Rather, it was the essence of the piece that extolled genius.

Wherein the original master creates an imitation of the imitator-apprentice, the imitation becomes the true original.

And, imitation is the sincerest form of flattery.

THE END

Gina Fava's *The Sculptor* Playlist

I love a great movie soundtrack that really resonates, during the experience and long after. Here's a playlist that coincides with *The Sculptor*, songs that traipsed through my mind or throbbed loudly enough to shake the walls while writing it. Whether a tune shaped a character's voice, or created the mood for a scene, or just inspired some creative madness, each of them became a part of the story for me. Maybe they'll haunt you too.

➢ The Smiths, "How Soon is Now?"
➢ Alanis Morissette, "Uninvited"
➢ Lady Gaga, "Bad Romance"
➢ Muse, "Madness"
➢ Elton John, "Your Song"
➢ REM, "Losing My Religion"
➢ U2, "Two Hearts Beat as One"
➢ OneRepublic, "Secrets"
➢ INXS, "One Thing"
➢ Sarah McLaughlin, "Possession"
➢ The Cure, "Why Can't I Be You"
➢ Frank Sinatra, "I've Got the World on a String"

ACKNOWLEDGEMENTS

Special thanks, as always, to my readers. I hope that you spent sleepless nights with *The Sculptor*; that was my goal. If you enjoyed it, please leave a review at Amazon or Goodreads; it would mean the world to me. I love meeting fans of *The Sculptor* and *The Race* at signings, and I appreciate your book reviews, letters, emails, posts, and tweets. Please continue to spread the word about my books to your friends, family, book club, co-workers, neighbors, workout buddies, the guy sitting next to you on the plane, etc. Learn more about my next novel at www.GinaFava.com. Many thanks!

I bow humbly to Stephen King, Dean Koontz, Thomas Harris, Lisa Gardner, Harlan Coben, and Douglas Preston. Thank you to Mystery Writers of America, Sisters in Crime, International Thriller Writers, and the many authors who have shown me the way.

To the students and faculty in Rome with whom I studied, traveled, and snagged beer runs back in the day. "Any resemblance is purely coincidental," or "imitation is the sincerest form of flattery," you choose. To the journalists, *carabinieri*, and residents of Italy who helped shape my crime scenes; any mistakes are mine. To Officer Puletz, NYPD's finest, for your informative insights, and for allowing me a moment to patrol Times Square as part of Mounted Division.

To Ed Latawiec for sharing your photographic art with me and the world. To Bruce Skinner, my cover designer, for never hesitating to add more blood to the shot. To my editor Amanda Clark at Grammar Chic, and my proofreader Wendy Janes for your brilliant eagle eyes. To Cheryl Perez for putting it all together.

Finally, sincerest gratitude to all of my family and friends who've supported me throughout my life. I value the lessons you've taught me, and the laughter we've shared. To my brothers and sisters, you always have my back, and I'll always have yours. To Sabrina and Mario, Mommy loves her babies. To Mom and Dad, thank you for sending me to study abroad. "When in Rome, Mickey...when in Rome." And to Jamie, always and forever, for inspiring these pages, wherein art imitates life.

ALSO BY STEEPO PRESS

THE RACE

*The first thrilling novel in the HELL Ranger
series by Gina Fava*

Turn the page for
an excerpt from
THE RACE…

Sample Excerpt of Chapter 3 of *The Race*

Devlin and Lupo arrived atop the square on Via Marche hill, in full view of the sprawling railway station. They paused to let a group of nuns cross the street. Bells tolled from a nearby church.

Sitting atop his idling scooter, Devlin glanced toward a statue of the Caesar warrior, Marcus Agrippa, which guarded the square. A dark, bearded man leaned beside it, chomping on a candy bar, clutching the immense marble statue around its waist. He, too, gazed down at the train station at the base of the rise. The man turned and peered back at Devlin.

Devlin gasped. The man had a long scar that trickled down his face, from his eye down into his beard. *I feel like he's looking right through me. Almost like a gypsy...*

The man continued to stare at him.

Why does he seem so... familiar?

The nuns passed, cleared Devlin's path, and he dismissed the scarred man from his thoughts. He and Lupo raced their Vespas toward the station that loomed 500 feet down the hill. After driving nearly thirty feet, his eyes widened in astonishment. *Why does the building look like it's... expanding?*

He forgot about the gypsy. And everything else.

The world as Devlin Lucchesi knew it changed forever, right before his eyes.

***

It happened in mere seconds...

A slab of concrete the size of a swimming pool jettisoned skyward from the center of Termini Station, but Devlin never saw it land, because, the sheer force of the blast had finally reached him, hundreds of feet from the epicenter. Devlin's six-foot frame, still clutching his Vespa, hurtled backward, end-over-end, through the air.

In the upswing, he flew from his motorbike and slammed onto his back, bounced once, and then landed, with his arms and legs splayed out like a pinwheel from his body. He recalled the time he'd smashed his racecar into a cement wall at 150 mph. This was worse.

The skull-splitting sound of the blast had left his head ringing. He threw his hands over his ears. He clamped his eyes, shutting out any light that might intensify the reverberation behind his temples. *Oh, God, make it stop. Just let me die.*

After a few minutes, the ringing subsided into a dull hum. Nausea wrenched his abdomen. *I must be dead already. And now, I'm in Hell.*

Minutes later, the pain in his head dissipated enough to open his eyes. He turned his head to shield them from the midday sun and found that he'd come to rest on a grassy patch near the roadway. He yelled out Lupo's name, but didn't hear the sound of his own voice issue from his lips.

A soft breeze wafted an empty candy bar wrapper through the springtime air. He batted it down from his face and crunched the dark brown paper in his hand.

Devlin turned his head in the other direction. A looming pillar blocked the sun. He'd landed himself at the base of the

Agrippa statue he'd passed earlier. *Jesus, I must have flown fifty feet.* He propped himself up on one elbow and groaned. He shouted again to Lupo, and wondered if his friend was still alive.

A figure sat slumped on the other side of the warrior statue. "Lupo?" He shouted again. *He probably can't hear me, if I can't hear myself.*

The figure turned toward him, but it wasn't Lupo. It was the gypsy.

The scarred, bearded man clung to the marble statue for support, gazing down at the horrific scene below.

Devlin closed his eyes. He shook his head for clarity. *There is no way after that horrific explosion that I am seeing what I think.* He opened his eyes, and they confirmed what his mind had refused to grasp.

The bearded gypsy was smiling. Beaming, with a wide-open, toothy, shit-eating grin.

Whether for the odd sense of familiarity or his disdain for the gypsy's gleeful reaction, Devlin felt compelled to know the bearded man's identity. He stumbled forward. *"Chi é Lei?* Who are you?" he said.

The man broke free of his mirth-like trance and faced Devlin. That's when the stranger's delighted grin disappeared. His features contorted from one reaction to the next: recognition, surprise, and, finally, rage. It was as if the man knew him.

Tires screeched, and a black Mercedes pulled up beside the stranger, breaking their eerie connection.

Devlin looked down at his left hand. It clenched the candy bar wrapper that had belonged to the gypsy.

The gypsy man opened the car door and Devlin stared at the wording printed on the brown wrapper. They were written in Arabic letters.

The scarred, bearded man turned to Devlin, and uttered in perfect English, "What goes around, comes around." Then, the man slipped inside the car and was ushered away.

Devlin put his hands to his throat; it was so hard to swallow. His mind flashed images one after another.

The Empire State Building...helicopters...a cargo ship...his mother...and a man, whose face he would scar.

B.I. Scotti...stealth fighters...race cars...Lupo...and a man with a scar.

Ella and her swollen belly...Marcello playing toy trains...and a man with a scar.

Termini exploding...his city in ruin...a man standing beside a marble statue...the man with the scar.

Lupo scrambled beside him. Shook him. "Why won't you answer me?"

Devlin focused on Lupo's gaze. With his hands still clutched to this throat, Devlin murmured, "I remember...*everything*."

"I kept calling your name over and over," Lupo said. "You wouldn't answer."

Devlin shook his head. "That's because...you were using the wrong name."

STEEPO PRESS PROUDLY PRESENTS

The next thrilling novel in the HELL Ranger series by Gina Fava

RAGING WATERS

Turn the page for a preview of Devlin "Lucky" Luccesi and his HELL Rangers' latest mission in *RAGING WATERS*…

CHAPTER 1

Devlin "Lucky" Luccesi gunned his 2.4-liter, V8 engine toward the tight La Rascasse corner of the Formula One Monaco Grand Prix at 120 mph in fourth gear. In seconds, he downshifted into first gear and decelerated to 40 mph, then pulled his vehicle around the wicked hairpin turn, into full steering lock and out again with lightning dexterity. Gaining speed, Devlin yearned to tear off to the Noghes turn in pursuit of the leader, Ferrari's Giancarlo Diavolo, but both his wits and his crew chief had already convinced him to pit.

Devlin wrenched his race car from the narrow streets of the Monte Carlo track, and hastened between the glittering steel guardrails of the pit lane. Approaching the Luccesi garage, he passed Scuderia Ferrari in its apron, the team already raising its racer's chassis. Devlin glimpsed Ferrari's driver glaring at him, and Devlin stabbed back at his longtime rival with a menacing sneer.

Giancarlo Diavolo was one of the most competitive drivers on the circuit—smart, adept, and daring. But Devlin thought the guy was an ass. So did most everyone else. Diavolo was hated by racing fans for his brash arrogance, by the press for his standoffishness, and by colleagues for bad sportsmanship. Ferrari's squad likely kept Giancarlo Diavolo around for just one reason—he knew how to win.

Devlin maneuvered behind his painted stop-marks. A throng of twenty-two mechanics descended on his vehicle like the undead on a victim. Every one of Luccesi's crew was a brilliant pit technician, as well as an undercover special op HELL Ranger. Devlin trusted them with his life, in the racing pit, and on HELL Ranger missions, like the one in Sochi, Russia, in which their covert force had been responsible for discreetly averting a terror attack during the Olympics' Opening Ceremony.

The head of Devlin's crew, B.I. Scotti, held the "Brakes On" lollipop in Devlin's line of sight and barked orders. The jack men worked in tandem to lift the 1300-pound chassis inches from the pavement. The wheel gun crew unbolted all four tires. The first wheel team rolled off the blistered Pirelli tires. The fuel team locked in the fuel hose and began pumping in high-octane petrol.

Two seconds had elapsed since pitting.

Fitti modified the rear wing. Trips checked the car's air intakes.

Two and a half seconds…

One of the pit monitors displayed four competitors speeding past, parallel to his location, making up time on their laps while he sat idling in neutral. Adrenaline surged through every muscle in Devlin's body. He needed out of this pit right now.

Three seconds…

The second tire team hefted on four warm Pirellis with deep grooves, and the wheel gun crew swooped in to tighten the bolts. The pit monitor showed Ferrari's crew chief already signaling first gear, nearly two hundred feet behind Devlin. Any moment, Diavolo would be blasting into the pit's fast lane. *Damn. Damn.*

Devlin respected Giancarlo's hardcore performance in every race, but his ungentlemanly nature, on and off track, made Devlin's skin crawl. Diavolo drove dirty, and he always blamed his crew for a loss or bad prelim. He refused autographs and interviews as beneath him. And he courted new sponsors almost as often as he bedded prostitutes, to the dismay of his fiancée, Runa, the daughter of Diavolo's primary sponsor, FONTUS Co. The guy was an ass.

Four seconds elapsed…

The jack men dropped his racing machine back to the ground, and Devlin's crew dispersed from the car. Devlin gripped the wheel and threw his thunderous 900 horsepower engine into first gear, his right foot above the accelerator, ready to launch.

But something in Devlin's peripheral vision halted his forward momentum, and he flicked his eyes to a side mirror. Rampaging down the pit's common lane, Ferrari's driver had cut left, and was steering his machine right toward Devlin's garage, aiming straight for Devlin's men.

"Incoming!" Devlin warned his crew through his helmet mic. His pit boss frantically waved the brake sign up and down, and most of Devlin's crew dove for cover.

In the split second before imminent disaster, the Ferrari driver veered his car to the right, barely avoiding the slaughter of Devlin's men by mere inches.

Still, Diavolo's rear airfoil clipped the metal brake sign and ripped it from Scotti's grip. Like a javelin, it catapulted through the air, nearly impaling Devlin's fuel man, before slamming into Red Bull Racing's garage.

Giancarlo Diavolo grinned at the Luccesi team, and shot them the bird, before the sweaty, bucktoothed bastard rocketed his vehicle past them. Ferrari's car motored out of the pit lane and back onto the street course.

"Scotti, talk to me, are you guys alright?" Devlin asked, unsure whether to assist his crew or rejoin the race. "Is anyone hurt?"

The pit monitor revealed to Devlin that most of his men, along with fifteen or so members of Red Bull Racing, had stormed Scuderia Ferrari's pit—obscenities and fists were flying. Scotti stood rooted to his original mark on their pit apron, uninjured and clearly stunned, yet wholly in control. The crew chief looked Devlin in the eye, pointed toward the track, and said, "Get him!"

Devlin slammed his foot into the accelerator.

Devlin steered his way around the nearly 90-degree right-hand turn of the Sainte Devote corner. Out of the bend, he blasted his car from 35 to 160 mph in 1.8 seconds and roared up the steep, bumpy hill leading to the Massenet. He gnashed his teeth and mumbled curses at Diavolo, wanting to tear him apart for endangering his men.

Devlin wound out of the Massenet's long left-hander with a 3.5 G-force, zipped past the casino to the tight Mirabeau corner, and then shot down to another ridiculous hairpin, where Devlin maneuvered his car with perfect precision. He blasted out of the second bend at Portier. There, Devlin spied the demon Ferrari, heading into the tunnel.

Bile rose in Devlin's throat, and he gritted his teeth. Entering the ninth turn in his 54th of 78 laps, Devlin clenched the steering wheel tighter, determined to take his vile opponent down.

Countless times Devlin had overtaken the best drivers in the world...and the baddest. Today, Devlin planned to chase down Ferrari, chew 'em up and spit 'em out.

Luck was gonna dance with the devil...and win.

***

Soon, only three and a half laps remained in the Monaco Grand Prix, and Devlin trailed in second place behind Ferrari.

Devlin accelerated up the hill toward Hotel de Paris, and then he passed the casino. By then, he'd closed the distance between himself and the leader to mere tenths of a second.

Devlin cut left, trying to pass Ferrari. Together they plunged down the hill toward Hotel Mirabeau.

Two more laps…

If he could just increase his speed by ten mph on the chicane…

He did it. He reached 150 mph in sixth gear. He rocketed past the swimming pool complex and the harbor. Then, he eyed the right-hand Rascasse turn ahead. And, he pushed like mad.

Cornering the curve, Devlin's legs felt like dead weights, his tires were shot to hell, and the road beneath his low-rider felt a foot thick in marbles.

As he sped out of the Noghes turn, he shifted into third gear—his 3000th gear change of the race. A quarter of a second later, Devlin shifted into fourth. Then, fifth.

Final lap.

The marshal waved the white flag as if he were welcoming a fleet of UFOs.

The rivals charged up the steep, bumpy hill toward Casino Square. Flying down the hill toward Mirabeau, Devlin glimpsed his chance to trip up Ferrari. Devlin skulked forward, but Ferrari refused to relent.

Devlin glimpsed the checkered flag hovering over the track in the distance. Though his body shook with fatigue and dehydration, Devlin leaned his body forward, determined to outrun the demon. His blistered hands clenched and unclenched, and he fought like a bastard for the win. Side by side, Luccesi's and Ferrari's machines jetted across the finish line in a blur.

***

The crowd, driven mad by the close finish, cheered like banshees for the announcement of the winner. The Jumbotron replayed the photo finish again and again, and every fan and mechanic waited for the official ruling to come from the judges.

Devlin slowed his car to a halt near the foot of the Royal Box where the crowned rulers of the principality awaited the customary award ceremony. He unbuckled his harnesses, popped off the steering wheel, and jumped out of the steaming chassis. He stripped off his gear and whipped it into the monocoque, and then strode toward the Ferrari parked two dozen feet away.

Giancarlo Diavolo wiped sweat from his face, and cannon-balled shots of grappa right from his sponsor's bottle, thrust into his hand moments earlier by a busty race steward who'd tongued her congratulations.

Devlin marched directly to Ferrari's driver and knocked the bottle from his lips. It fell and smashed on the pavement. Devlin head-locked Giancarlo Diavolo "playfully" for the cameras, laughing and waving as he did. But beneath his dimpled grin, Devlin vocalized his displeasure, "You almost killed my crew in the pit lane, you sonofabitch." Devlin squeezed his neck hard, smiling all the while for the cameras, yet continuously jabbing Diavolo in the face as he did.

Diavolo whimpered from inside the crook of Devlin's arm. The Italian gurgled and gasped in broken English, his trachea constricted beneath Devlin's death-grip. "It is...part of...the game. I never meant to—"

"You *ever* do something like that again, I won't be quite as charming." Devlin wrenched Giancarlo's neck one last time and then released him. Ferrari's driver leaned heavily against his red car. He rubbed his neck, but waved and smiled at the photographers to keep up appearances.

All twenty-two of Devlin's pit crew had gathered on the finish line. He ran to them, and threw himself headlong into their group hug. At this, the crowd erupted into song, "*O, laaay, Olay, Olay, Olaaay, O...*" Women of all ages screamed, "Luckeeee!" Win or lose, Devlin appreciated his crew and his fans for their enduring support.

Suddenly the crowd hushed. Had the results been posted on the Jumbotron? Devlin looked to the screen, and was shocked by the visual.

It showed Ferrari's driver, doubled over, gripping his abdomen with both hands as if kicked by the stallion that graced Ferrari's emblem. He retched, and reared back his head to reveal anguish in his contorted features. He coughed up blood, and spewed foaming saliva from his mouth. His fingers clenched into talons. His eyes rolled up into his head...

The crowd's earlier screams of adulation turned to terror.

Heedless of their past animosities, Devlin darted toward his colleague to assist him. A crowd surrounded Giancarlo, but Devlin pulled and tugged his way to the driver, now on his back, writhing in violent convulsions on the ground.

Ferrari's team doctor tore open the top of Diavolo's jumpsuit and delivered compressions while shouting for the track ambulance.

Devlin inquired in Italian what he could do to help, but he was shoved aside by a Ferrari squad member. Devlin explained to Ferrari's crew chief that he had medical training, but the man gestured what Devlin could go do to himself.

Devlin shook his head and took a step back, stepped on the broken glass from the FONTUS grappa bottle. He spied the discarded cork with the sponsor's logo amid the shards, and a voice in his head convinced Devlin to pocket it.

As Devlin turned to rejoin his own crew, he overheard the Ferrari physician tell the paramedic that Diavolo had no known allergies, no pre-existing medical conditions, and had been the picture of health as of that morning's pre-race physical.

It was then that Diavolo's fiancée busted through the throng of fans and press reporters, crying and shouting his name, begging Giancarlo to be alright. The Jumbotron flashed the scene, and showed Diavolo's bloody, disheveled face as the paramedics loaded his gurney into the emergency vehicle. When the doctor stepped aboard the ambulance, Ferrari's pit boss held the door open, allowing access to the grief-stricken woman, whereupon she slapped Diavolo's face and spat on him, and then disappeared into the crowd.

Devlin flicked his eyes from the live footage on the screen back to the area where Ferrari's pit crew had gathered. Devlin noticed their pit boss surreptitiously edge closer to the busty steward who'd awarded Diavolo the grappa. He held up a document and pen as if requesting her signature. She grabbed it from him, gesticulated wildly toward the departing ambulance that bore Diavolo, tore the paper to shreds, and thrust it down the front of his pants before marching away.

Between ambivalent racing fans, a jilted press corps, warring sponsors, an enigmatic crew chief, and a forsaken fiancée, it appeared Giancarlo Diavolo had more enemies than he could shake a stick at.

It was then that Devlin knew…his instincts on pocketing the grappa cork were probably right on. Forensics just might reveal that Ferrari's driver, Diavolo, fighting for his life against a potentially lethal and mysterious ailment, and clearly fraught with an abundance of enemies, was poisoned. The devil may have finally met his match.

Made in the USA
Middletown, DE
13 June 2021